"This is story-telling at its best."
Award-winning author Maggie Osborne

He was searching for his wife in name only . . .

Drew stared at the woman who stood across the ballroom, barely moving, looking only at him.

"Do I know you sir?" she asked. "You seem familiar, yet I cannot think where we might have met."

"I have been away," he said, puzzled. "I have not seen her in many years."

The woman tilted her head. "But you appear lost. Perhaps if you tell us for whom you search, we might direct you."

"I search for my wife. If you will excuse me?" Before she could reply, Drew turned away. The woman disquieted him, distracted him, intrigued him. Who was she?

A frisson of awareness danced up his spine. The music faded until it seemed to be a part of the air itself.

He knew the woman had followed him, that he would not find it so easy to escape her again. "You have not located your wife?" she asked, an odd note of emotion in her voice.

And suddenly he realized the truth . . .

Other **AVON ROMANCES**

EVE BYRON

My Lord Stranger

AVON BOOKS ◆ NEW YORK

This is a work of fiction. Names, characters, places, and incidents either are the product of the author's imagination or are used fictitiously. Any resemblance to actual events, locales, organizations, or persons, living or dead, is entirely coincidental and beyond the intent of either the author or the publisher.

AVON BOOKS, INC.
1350 Avenue of the Americas
New York, New York 10019

Copyright © 1999 by Connie Rinehold
Published by arrangement with the author
Library of Congress Catalog Card Number: 98-93543
ISBN: 0-380-80364-X
www.avonbooks.com/romance

First Avon Books Printing: March 1999

AVON TRADEMARK REG. U.S. PAT. OFF. AND IN OTHER COUNTRIES, MARCA REGISTRADA, HECHO EN U.S.A.

Printed in the U.S.A.

WCD   10 9 8 7 6 5 4 3 2 1

With love to Sam—the best hero of them all

And to Lucia Macro—editor extraordinaire

With heartfelt thanks to
Gini Rifkin, who asks too many questions—
thank God.
Audra Harders, Lelsie Sartor-Mallo,
Dianna Benson, and Joyce Farrell,
who won't let me get away with a thing.
Mary Francis Stark, for seeing spots
that should have been there.
Loopy Sisters, one and all, for the joy of community.
And the Avonladies of whom
I am so proud to be a part.

Prologue

Natura vacuum abhorret
(Nature abhors a vacuum) . . .

FRANÇOIS RABELAIS (1494–C.1553),
AN ARTICLE OF ANCIENT WISDOM

Saxon Hill
England, 1813

Where was she—his knobby plank of a girl with straight hair and spots on her face? His sweet, disarming friend who had brought sunshine and smiles into his life?

Harriet, Countess Saxon—his wife in name only.

Her name.

Drew stood among people he'd known throughout his childhood, yet not one of them was familiar to him now. Even if he did recognize someone, he would have precious few recollections of a moment they might have shared. He'd become proficient at keeping his emotions to himself, tamed and properly caged where they could neither rule nor overwhelm him. It had seemed necessary in his childhood. Then it had become habit.

Only rarely in the past had he been rendered

vulnerable to his own emotions—usually to find amusement in something his wife had said or done, or to be disturbed when she was unhappy, or to feel regret and guilt when he'd left her. Or like now when he felt a keen sense of anticipation to see her again. Yet Drew tried to push all sentiment aside in favor of his usual detachment as he reentered the society he had escaped from twelve years ago.

All about him were activity and color and the texture of personalities, of people going about their lives and participating in the world—enjoying it, or merely surviving it as best they could. He muttered a curse as the cream of society milled around him. He felt constricted in the layers of clothing dictated by fashion. But he knew he would have been tossed out on his ear should he have worn buckskins to his wife's ball. That he hadn't known she was giving a ball was of no consequence. The only planning he'd done before riding for Saxon Hill was to acquire suitable clothing, not wanting to barge in on his wife looking like the trappers he'd traveled with.

Harriet, Countess Saxon, was one of the few women in England who held a title in her own right. His Twinkle—a name he'd thought far more suitable to her from the moment he'd first seen her as a frolicking four-year-old, pampered and demanding without being obnoxious about it. Still, he'd wanted to prove to her that she could not twine him about her little finger as she had her father, his foster father, and the entire household staff, for that matter. To prove his point, he'd taken to calling her Harry, a name she'd hated.

He'd been far too susceptible to her. Far too fond. He hadn't wanted attachments. Not when he hadn't known who he really was or why he'd been handed over to strangers like castoff clothing. Not when he'd had nothing to offer her—not even the name he'd been born with.

"Where is Lady Harriet?" one lady asked another as they passed him.

"No doubt with Brummell. They are quite the pair. . . ."

He inhaled sharply, startled that he felt as if he'd just taken a knife in the heart. And it infuriated him, as he had been infuriated to feel his energy slipping away not so long ago, not with thoughts of losing his life but with the knowledge that he would never see Harry again.

Brummell. Drew had never met him, yet he'd heard of him. Who hadn't? Brummell, Prinny's Pet and trendsetter, well liked by some, resented by others. The man was too old for Harry, too jaded.

Drew wondered why he was here, why he'd opened himself to suffering the lapses in control only Harry could bring about. He pivoted toward the grand staircase leading down to the entrance hall two floors below. Better to take a room at an inn and formally announce himself tomorrow.

He halted and stared blindly at the staircase, at the way out. He'd done enough walking away. Enough removing himself because he didn't belong. He'd wandered the world and could only think of home. He'd lay dying, fighting it, refusing to surrender to release, and had been able to think only of Harry. For so many years, home had become closer with each thought, each task accomplished, each goal met. He'd become trapped by his own aspirations for so long, feeling as if he were in a runaway carriage, unable to jump, refusing to lose what he had gained. His choice. He would not willingly make the same mistake again. He would not escape again.

He turned and halted abruptly at the sight of a woman weaving through the crush, too stunned to do anything but blink and absently step to the side.

She was a vision, arresting, unique, enchanting. Her hair was an odd shade of light brown yet with a smoky quality that gave it richness and depth, seeming ever changing in the light and shadow of the candlelit room. Her figure was narrow, yet nicely rounded. Her entire bearing spoke of regal presence and warmth and pride.

He well understood pride. For him it was a curse. On her it looked like breeding and control and strength.

Who was she? he wondered, as the bracelet he always wore on his upper arm seemed to warm and vibrate. He'd felt the sensation before when he'd thought of Harry or read the letters she'd sent him over the years. He'd accepted it as he'd accepted the immediate attraction he'd felt for the piece that seemed to have been made for him alone though it had been years—perhaps centuries—in the ground.

He continued to stare at the woman who stood across the room, barely moving, looking only at him, as if a thread connected them.

Who was she? he wondered, feeling as if he

were drowning in her silver-blue eyes. Magic . . .
she was magic. Compelled to study her every feature, he couldn't look away. As he'd always felt
when Harry was near. Yet she could not be Harry.
Nothing about her was familiar. She was too
poised, too elegant, too sedate. Harry was the exact opposite—artless, more gamine than woman,
twinkling with energy. It was what he loved most
about her.

Rejecting the spell cast by her presence, he
turned away and searched the crowd for Harry.

"Don't tell me you have found another hapless
bachelor for your matchmaking," a cultured male
voice drawled from behind him.

"I do not make a habit of matchmaking and you
well know it," a soft, surprisingly husky feminine
voice replied.

Somehow Drew knew it belonged to the woman
whose image seemed permanently burned into his
mind. He turned slowly and focused on a point
over her shoulder, reluctant to look at her at such
close range, to fall under her spell more deeply.

"Do I know you, sir?" she asked. "You seem
familiar, yet I cannot think where we might have
met."

"I have been away," he said, puzzled at his dis-
inclination to offer more information.

The woman tilted her head, studied him. "You
appear lost."

Lost. Harry had said that to him just before he'd
left her.

"Perhaps if you told us for whom you search,
we might direct you," she offered.

"I search for my wife. If you will excuse me?"

Before they could reply, Drew turned away, not caring if it was rude. The woman disquieted him, distracted him, intrigued him.

Damnit, where was Harry?

He wandered through the crowd, his heart lurching in his chest each time he saw a thin girl, then contracting each time he realized it was not Harry. More than once, he inadvertently caught sight of the woman and met her gaze, held it, feeling her fascination as keenly as he felt his own, recalling the genuine warmth and concern in her voice, delivered with the same note he remembered from a thousand times with Harry. A warmth and concern he'd missed ten times a thousand since leaving here. It was that he'd responded to, nothing more.

Who was she? The question hovered in his thoughts like a shadow.

"Who is he?" someone asked, as Drew strolled out to the balcony. Leaning his forearms on the rail, he stared out at the fairy lights sprinkled in the trees. Harry loved fairy lights—

A frisson of awareness danced up his spine. Warmth and energy and the scent of carnations surrounded him as the music faded until it seemed to be a part of the air itself.

He straightened, knowing the woman had followed him outside, that he would not find it so easy to escape her again.

"You have not located your wife?" she asked, an odd note of emotion in her voice. She placed her hands on the rail, yet stood stiffly, warily, beside him.

Something drew his gaze to her upper arm, to

the outline revealed by the clinging silk of her long sleeve. His heart thumped harder and faster with every second that passed as he stared at the shape of a band, a bracelet that he instinctively knew matched the one he wore. Impressions and thoughts tumbled over one another in his mind— the dimple centered in her chin, a slightly squared chin easily set by stubbornness below a mouth that had always spilled laughter enchanting enough to make angry gods smile.

Only one woman could possess such traits. Only with one woman had physical desire ruled him as it did now. Only one woman had eyes that twinkled like the stars above them—except he remembered her as a homely, engaging girl.

"The bracelet," he said hoarsely, too stunned for coherence, and unable to merge his memories with the reality standing before him. "Where did you get it?"

She caught her breath. "It came from my husband," she said simply, her eyes wide as she stared at him, as if she were afraid.

He grasped her arms and felt the outline of the band on her arm. "It is gold," he said, "wide strands interwoven in Celtic design with herons facing one another, ages old, yet showing no signs of time and wear."

Anyone could have purchased the bracelet, he told himself. This could not be Harry. Yet why else had he been drawn to this woman and only her? Why else would the world have receded except for her? Harry had always had the power to dispel the nightmares and emptiness that had dominated his life. He took another step back, but could not release her, dared not release her for fear she would disappear.

Her lips parted and her breath snagged with an audible catch. Her hand trembled in his. She stumbled and wrapped her hands around his upper arms to steady herself . . . and froze, too late to arrest her small whimper. Her face was pale as her fingers traced the outline of his bracelet beneath the sleeve of his coat.

"It can't be," she whispered. Her hands lifted to his face, trembling and frantic as they traced every feature beneath his closely cropped beard, then his eyes, his forehead, then his mouth again. "Oh dear God, it is you." She wrapped her arms around his neck, holding him so closely, so tightly.

He felt moisture on his neck and knew she wept. Squeezing his eyes shut, he held her just as tightly, knowing that this was why he'd pursued his goals so relentlessly in spite of his weariness, in spite of the loneliness that ate at his soul until he wondered if anything was left. This was why he had needed to come home. Harry . . . only Harry.

"They said you were dead but I didn't believe them. I knew you weren't dead. I could still feel you—" Her breath shuddered in and out as she stilled for a moment, then pushed away from him, glared up at him. "I'd given up on your return . . . accepted that you would never return . . . that you didn't want to return."

He winced at the accusation in her eyes, the anger building in her voice as she struggled to wrest away from his hold.

"I waited for you," she said, her chest heaving. "No matter what you said in your letters, no matter how many times you told me to secure my freedom from you. I believed you'd be back because you promised you would. And then your shipments continued to arrive even after your letters stopped. And then the letter saying you were dead and everyone thinking I was mad to believe otherwise." Her struggles ceased suddenly; her eyes flashed with fury. "What if I had believed it, Drew? You were supposed to return home two years ago. What if I had believed you dead for all that time?" Her eyes narrowed and her expression smoothed out, showing nothing. "What if I had gone on and married again?"

The idea of it ignited his temper. Harry going on without him after she had convinced him that she would wait for him. Yet she said it as if it were nothing unusual, nothing significant. One husband dead and quickly replaced. It was irrational for him to feel such fury and pain under the circumstances. It stunned him to know he *could* feel such fury and pain. "I made it a point *not* to die, madam," he said stiffly, "because I had promised to return."

For the barest moment, she seemed to waver, to lean into him. And then she straightened even more, her chest heaving and her hands clenched tightly, as if she were containing the urge to strike him. "You seek your wife, sir? She no longer exists," she said, with a calm that chilled him.

His thumb caressed the bracelet beneath her silk sleeve. "If she did not exist, she would not be wearing this—"

"And she will not wear it again." She jerked her arm from his hold. "It obviously belongs to you and will be returned in the morning." She turned her head and summoned the footmen flanking the doors so unobtrusively that Drew hadn't noticed them until now. "Please show Mr. Sinclair to a guest room."

"Mr. Sinclair-Saxon," he corrected, needing to remind her of their rather odd arrangement, that he had married her and taken her name because he'd had none of his own, because he'd acceded to the wishes of his foster father and the pleas of her father. Because he had never once deceived her regarding his intentions and she had accepted his terms.

Drew arched his brows as the men took positions on either side of him, close enough, it seemed, to hold him if necessary. They stepped back as he met each gaze in turn. Satisfied, he again focused on Harriet. "A guest room, Harry?" he asked, deliberately baiting her. Some habits never died. "If I am not mistaken, I already have a chamber in the master suite."

She smiled, the artless, engaging smile he remembered so well through years of wandering and searching and then being lost in a winter wilderness that froze all but a drop of life from him. "The second chamber in my suite is for the use of another."

He felt it then, the cold creeping up from his feet and hands, freezing him again, waiting to claim him completely. He bowed formally and straightened. "Then I shall take a guest room . . . for now. I suggest that you make certain my bedchamber is vacated and the linens burned and re-placed before I take possession tomorrow." He swept his gaze over her from head to foot and back again, then turned and strode across the ter-race, toward the stone steps leading to the lower floor. He shot a narrow-eyed glance at the foot-men on either side of him. "I know where the guest chambers are. You will remain with my lady," he said, the words as stiff and cold as he felt.

The footmen withdrew as Drew continued on without looking back.

Harriet stared at his broad back and powerful strides, at his dark hair pulled sleekly into a long queue at his nape and wrapped with a leather thong, feeling as if she would fall to her knees. Why hadn't she realized that Drew would broaden and mature and grow whiskers? She grasped the arm of the nearest footman, dimly aware that she dug her nails into his coat, yet needing his support far more than she cared about propriety.

Abruptly, she released him and all but stag-gered to the balcony wall, trusting her own strength more than she could trust her footmen. For the first time in her life, the servants had not put her first. They had obeyed Drew.

Drew . . . it could not be. After all this time, after struggling to force herself to go on without him, she wasn't certain she wanted it to be true. She was afraid to believe that this tall man who moved with such control and confidence was her hus-band. Afraid that the danger she'd sensed in him was real. This was not the thin and beardless seventeen-year-old boy she'd married. Not the boy whose eyes expressed both determination and fear the night he'd left her. Not the boy whom she'd loved and to whom she'd been faithful all these years.

"Milady?" a footman said gently.

Inhaling sharply, she reminded herself of the anger toward Drew that she'd nurtured for the past few years. She caught a last glimpse of Drew's form as he rounded the corner, of the strength and power he exuded in every movement. There had been a flicker of pain in his expression quickly followed by anger when she'd deliberately given him the wrong impression about who occupied the other bedchamber in her suite. One would almost think he was jealous, or possessive—both traits that were not a part of the Drew she remembered.

Dear heaven but he was an intriguing man. And still so full of pride. Enough pride to take him away from her again because her words had outrun her mind. Why had she implied that the bedchamber meant for him was occupied by another man? Why had she lied?

Wonderful—all it took was his presence to render her a silly twit of a girl once more.

She blinked furiously against the sudden burning in her eyes and tried to swallow the lump growing in her throat. He had returned a man whose eyes were bleak and cold and wary, as if more phantoms had gathered to haunt him. A man who had the strength and confidence to fight them.

She sagged against the carved marble ringing the terrace and bit back a cry of sorrow. Her Drew had been able to bend a little. He had smiled at her and laughed at her and goaded her with devilment in his eyes. This man smiled with winter in his eyes.

The second footman cleared his throat. "Shall we follow him, my lady?"

She sighed in resignation. "Yes, by all means follow him at a discreet distance to make certain he does not enter an occupied room." Wrapping her arms about herself, she shivered, feeling inexplicably bereft . . . completely abandoned as she had not felt when Drew left her twelve years before. . . .

Her fault. She'd all but sent him on his quest with her efforts to help him. She'd fed the questions in his mind rather than answered them. Yet she hadn't worried; she'd been so convinced that he would soon return to her. He'd told her he might be gone for years, yet she hadn't had the sense to believe him.

And now she feared that he would leave her again before she could search for the man she had loved. Before she could discover if she loved him still.

Her arms unfolded from her waist and stiffened at her sides, her fists clenched. Not again. Never again would he leave her to wait and to wonder, to stare into a blank future that seemed too much like a vacuum in her life—at least, not until she had some answers.

The bracelet seemed to heat and thrum against her skin as if it were molding around her arm, seeming to become a part of her she would never be able to remove.

As she feared Drew might always be a part of her life, impossible to forget.

Pure twaddle. She straightened and locked her knees to keep upright as she met the footman's gaze with a steely one of her own. "Once he has gone inside his room, lock the door and stand guard, and before you consider following his orders again, please remember that Saxon Hill belongs to me and you are employed by me—not my husband."

Whitson's face flamed as he glanced down, then he nodded to his companion and hastened after Drew.

She pressed her hands to her cheeks, ashamed that she had spoken so to a loyal servant and horrified that she had issued such an order. She whirled around and leaned forward over the rail, staring out at her garden, at the place where she and Drew had spent so many hours over so many years during their childhood.

Every memory she had of Drew flashed through her mind in a blur of images and emotions, reminding her of every silly assumption she'd made so long ago. How certain she'd been that Drew had been dropped into her life because he was meant to be hers.

PART I
The Search
1800–1812

He that communicates his secret to another
makes himself that other's slave.

BALTASAR GRACIÁN, *THE ART OF WORLDLY WISDOM*

He that is neither one thing
nor the other has no friends.

AESOP, *THE BAT, THE BIRDS, AND THE BEASTS*

Chapter 1

Saxon Hill
England, 1800

Harriet sighed happily as she ran through the garden, giving in to the exuberance of knowing her life was and always would be perfect.

Drew would be hers. She'd known him most of her life, loved him most of her life. And now he would be with her for the rest of her life. It was meant to be.

They had both been four when he'd arrived twelve years earlier at Singletrees, the neighboring estate, to live with Lord Sinclair as his adopted son. They'd spent many days in the company of one another at either Saxon Hill or Singletrees as their fathers engaged in the companionship of a lifelong friendship. In spite of their similar ages, Drew had always seemed so much older to her, always too serious and too restless to be thought of as a child.

Drew didn't know where he came from or who he was. All he recalled from his first four years was a nightmare.

At the age of twelve, she'd plowed into him while chasing a rainbow in the gardens of Saxon Hill. The more she'd wailed that the rainbow was fading, no longer hers to capture, the broader he'd smiled. Such a foolish thing really, yet she hadn't minded that he'd thought her silly. He'd *smiled*, and nothing else seemed to matter.

His smile had become her rainbow and she'd been chasing it ever since.

Drew hadn't seemed to care that she was all spindly arms and legs, or that her straight hair of dark, nondescript blond was ruthlessly pulled into tight braids coiled over each ear, or that her face had developed spots in a distressing condition that Papa said was common to adolescents.

Instead, Drew had called her Twinkle, because he'd said that she was like a bright butterfly flitting everywhere and alighting nowhere.

He'd sought her out often over the years, sometimes just to watch her and chuckle as she screwed up her face with the effort to produce a passable watercolor, or to tease her about her sudden eagerness to cultivate the qualities of a lady. She'd told him that she did it for him and he'd smile then, too, as if he thought she were teasing him back. Of course she hadn't been teasing and told him so just last year.

Since then, he'd called her Harry, which she hated.

She caught herself as she rounded a bend in the garden path and nearly toppled forward. Drew was there, pulling spent blooms from flower stems as he paced about.

She stared at his thick hair the color of chocolate, and his long lashes that framed deep, dark eyes browed with sweeping arches in a face that any sculptor would love. But there was softness in his features, too, and he'd yet to grow whiskers. Her abigail had told the parlor maid that he was like a sculpture without the finishing touches of character and experience. Cook had told the butler that Drew needed some meat on his thin bones.

She liked him just as he was, because he liked her just as she was, even if he did rebuke her occasionally for being pampered and spoiled and far too flighty. She wasn't so flighty that she couldn't spend forever making him happy. She could do that; she just knew it.

She was sixteen now—no longer a child. She would give him what he needed and continue to make him smile. He would love her for that . . . as much as she already loved him.

He glanced up and smiled and sat on the bench, leaving room for her.

She approached him, her hands clasped behind her back—a trick she'd learned to make her arms seem less long and spindly, and to emphasize the bumps on her flat chest that had finally appeared and would someday surely grow into proper breasts.

She sat as close to him as she dared and groped for the right words. "I have a secret to tell you." Nonchalantly, she smoothed her skirts. "But, you must promise never to tell where you heard it or I shall be sent to the nursery in punishment for eavesdropping on Papa and Lord Sinclair."

"And if you don't tell me, then the question will not arise and you'll be safe."

"But I must tell you, Drew. It is what you've wanted to know ever so long . . . about where you came from."

He stiffened and paled and stared straight ahead, saying nothing.

"Oh really, Drew, you are too proud by half," she said in exasperation. "Just once I would like to hear you actually ask for something." Sighing at his stubbornness, she continued, knowing she would lose her nerve if she waited too long. "I heard your father talk about how he'd found you when you were four, living with a farmer and his wife, and how it had broken his heart to see you in such poverty."

Drew seemed to tremble but he sat so straight and still, she couldn't be certain. "Where?" he finally asked, his voice strained.

"Ireland," she said with inexplicable dread. "Not terribly far from Cassidy Tower."

"Cassidy Tower . . . where Father's half-brother came from and where his wife was killed," Drew said and shuddered. "It's a place to start."

"To start?" she asked, the dread smothering her.

"I will go there first."

"Go? But you can't," she cried. "It's all been arranged."

"What has been arranged?" he asked, obviously preoccupied.

"You cannot inherit the Sinclair title because you are adopted," she said quickly, realizing too late why she was suddenly afraid. How many times had Drew spoken of searching for his origins, for the answers his own lost memories would not provide? And she had just given him a place to begin his search. "But now it doesn't matter a whit. I will inherit Papa's title, you see, and become a countess. Papa says that it is a fortunate thing that his title is not entailed as most are, so you are to marry me when we are seventeen and then you will have my name and my money, too. I have pots of it, you know."

He stiffened even more, then forced a smile as he tweaked her nose. "You could not have heard the whole of it."

She stared at him, at the smile that was too strained to give her pleasure. "I heard every bit of it. They worked it out so that you will be Drew Sinclair-Saxon, and I saw them sign the contracts, and toast them with Papa's best French brandy."

"Impossible. Uncle Edward wouldn't do that to me." Abruptly he shut his mouth and pressed his lips together in a flat line.

Harriet stared at him in horror as she heard his words and the anger behind them. "Do what to you?" she asked, as she lurched to her feet and glared at him. "They want to give you everything a man could wish . . . and since you have no line of your own—well, not really—then why should you object to taking my name to continue the Saxon line?"

He, too, rose and his gaze seemed foreign to her as it swept over her from head to hem. "Uncle Edward would not marry me to a child, who requires more maintenance than two estates put together—" Again he snapped his mouth shut.

Harriet curled into herself, hunching her shoulders and jerking her arms into a fold at her waist as she glanced down at her slippers sticking out beneath her flounced hem, the view unimpeded by womanly curves. Suddenly she felt like the stick she was, brittle and about to snap in two. Every blemish on her face, real or imagined, seemed to burn and throb as if they were all red and ugly and huge, as if her face was one enormous spot. And what did he mean by requiring maintenance as if she were a cotter's hovel in constant need of repair?

"I am a woman," she said in the "countess" voice she'd been practicing. "I assure you that I—" She caught herself before she blurted that her body functioned like that of a woman even if it wasn't shaped like one. "I can give you an heir the very moment we are wed."

He snorted and averted his gaze. "An heir to what, Harry? To *your* title and *your* fortune? I certainly have nothing to pass on to a child."

The bleakness in his voice, in his expression, pulled her into the pit into which he seemed to stare so often, freezing her to the spot as he turned and strode toward the house.

"I'm sorry, Drew, but it is all arranged. Harriet will have her Season in the Spring and then you will be married," Edward, Viscount Sinclair, said as he sank heavily into a chair. "I cannot give you back your past, but I can see to your future."

Drew folded his arms across his chest and shot a wary glance at Harriet listening from the open

French doors. "You knew I had plans that did not include marriage," he said tightly, barely able to contain his rage as he glared at his foster father. "You said you understood."

"I do understand, Drew, but that does not mean I agree," his father said. "Your future is far more important than your past."

"It isn't just my past and you know it. I want to make my own way and plan to use my trust to build an independence, and that will take years; you said so yourself." He lowered his arms to his sides, his fists clenched. "Marriage is unthinkable until I establish myself. And I am not about to take my wife's name or her fortune."

"It's perfectly acceptable, Drew," father said with a deep sigh.

"It is not acceptable to me. She will be a countess one day and should be able to choose any man she wants for husband. What have I to offer . . . ?"

Voices faded and all eyes fixed on Harry as she stepped forward.

What was she up to now?

"I wish to marry you. We get on so well together, Drew. We are friends. And if you feel you must go, I'll go with you," she said firmly. "It will be a grand adventure."

Horror spread across Lord Saxon's face. Drew's father's brows snapped together and his mouth hung suspended between heated words.

Drew scowled at her, frustrated by her lack of understanding. "I'll not be taking any baggage with me, Harry, human or otherwise."

Her expression crumpled as she took a step back. He'd hurt her feelings again and it wasn't

what he'd intended. Harry had given him a place
to begin the search he'd been preparing for since
he was old enough to understand his lack of family or heritage. It wasn't her fault that he felt compelled to make his own way, or that their fathers
had arranged their marriage, or that he had too
much pride to accept whatever she and her father
would choose to dole out to him, whether a name
or an allowance.

Drew plowed his hand through his hair. "It will
not be a grand adventure, Harry," he said gently.
"It will be constant travel to countries that are not
always friendly to us. I don't know how long it
will take. And we are too young. There is plenty
of time for decisions such as marriage."

No one spoke, as if they were all leaving the
matter to her, infuriating him further. Panic beat
furious wings in his chest as the silence spun out.
Surely they weren't considering her cork-brained
suggestion. She should be sent to her room, allowing the adults to settle such weighty matters.

She clasped her hands behind her back and
lifted her chin. "Very well. Drew can marry me
and then go off on his . . . crusade. I will wait for
him."

Wait for him? Had she taken leave of her
senses? Why didn't their fathers do something?
He watched her from the corner of his eye, his
panic doubling as she squared her shoulders, preparing to say something else he was sure he
wouldn't like.

"Drew, it is the wish of our fathers and the least
we can do for them," she said firmly, though he
saw the slightest tremble in her dimpled chin as

she pressed her hands to her chest in an impressive pose of entreaty. "We are all they have, you know."

He ground his teeth together. Clever girl, to administer guilt at this precise moment. He might very well be haunted by a past he couldn't remember, but he loved his foster father and would do almost anything for him. And she knew it, damn her.

"Drew," she said softly, "surely we can indulge them as they have always indulged us."

Earl Saxon stifled a snort and schooled his features into forced gravity. "Yes, Drew, surely you can indulge us—"

"As we have indulged you," his father finished.

"This is a blatant manipulation," Drew said, as he shot an angry glare at Harry. He might adore her and be disposed to indulge her whims, but just then he was more disposed toward indulging his urge to throttle her.

"It is," his father agreed. "I have never asked anything of you until now, Drew. If you are not willing to grant my request, then I shall order it. The contracts are signed. If you continue to fight me on this, I will not release your funds to you."

Drew bit back a bitter retort. He needed his trust in order to pursue what he considered a necessary ambition. That his father would use it to blackmail him after years of seeming to understand Drew's need to achieve independence felt like betrayal. Yet love for the man who had raised him kept him from making such an accusation.

"Why now?" Drew asked instead, as he faced Harry's father. "Harry is barely out of the schoolroom. And Harry will be a countess. Any number of titled men would—"

"—Marry her, use her money and title to further their own ends, and ignore her in the bargain," the earl cut in. "Drew, I wish to see my daughter protected by marriage, but not enslaved by it as so many women are. I wish her to have full benefit of her inheritance without being bound by the demands of a careless or thoughtless husband. Naturally, I would also like to see the Saxon line continued, but that is not my primary concern. Harriet's security is. Whether you are here or away, I know you would never mistreat or disrespect her."

Drew turned to again stare out the window, wishing he could brush aside the most compelling argument yet. Remembering the young aristocrats with whom he'd attended school, he knew why Harry's father was concerned. Harry was a free spirit—a quality he had always envied and would hate to see crushed.

His mouth twisted at the irony of it. He, who felt he'd never had choices, possessed the power to ensure that Harry always would. He, who felt shackled by a past he could not remember, could give freedom to another . . . to Harry. In some queer way, the idea appealed to him. And obviously it would make his father happy.

He'd known all along that it would be the height of selfishness to leave the only father he could remember, yet children left the nest every day. He also knew that the one time he had mentioned searching for his origins his foster father had paled in obvious fear that spilled over onto Drew. He had to know why.

And it appeared he had to marry Harry. She and their fathers had done a good job of convincing him he had no choice but to walk into the trap they set for him. Still, he would be able to leave afterward with no further arguments against it, and apparently Harry wanted this. Or she thought she did.

He leveled a narrow-eyed stare on her, fighting sympathy for her suddenly lost expression. She had to be certain of this or nothing would be accomplished by their marriage other than locking Harry in the same trap he'd occupied for all his life.

Drew fixed his foster father with the same narrow-eyed stare. "There will be no further arguments against my leaving?" he asked.

"Actually, I think it might be beneficial in some ways," the earl said thoughtfully. "That you and Harriet have always seemed to share an uncommon bond of friendship encourages me to hope that one day after you have become more settled and matured—" He smiled apologetically at Harry as she gasped in outrage. "—that you both may discover how well you suit. And I must applaud your refusal to accept the ease of living off of my daughter's money. You are both very young and impulsive. There will be time enough to build your marriage after your . . . ah . . . other issues are settled. Perhaps then, you will both realize the merits of what we do here today."

His father nodded.

Harry met his gaze. "I said I will wait for you, Drew," she said earnestly.

Drew breathed deeply, trying to control his frustration. They left him with no way out of this insane marriage—giving with both hands far more than he wished to have and making it clear he would take all or nothing. "Very well, I will do as you wish if Harriet has not found a more suitable candidate during her Season . . . and then I *will* leave." Without another word, he strode from the room.

Sighing, Drew headed for the stables, suddenly besieged by visions of Harry being courted by an assortment of Corinthians—all with names of their own, each wanting what Harry could give them rather than Harry herself.

Ruthlessly banishing the images and the disturbance they visited upon him, he mounted his horse and spurred him across the park land, his mind a knot of confusion as he tried to convince himself that once Harry was exposed to London Society, she'd lose interest in him. She'd set the *ton* on its ear. Who could not adore her? Who would not find her as enchanting as he did?

Saxon Hill, 1801

He'd been wrong.

Drew watched Harry make her bow at court and enter Almack's for the first time. He watched her shrink a little more every day as Society snickered at her and left her standing among the potted palms while they danced. They did the same to him—a nobody in their eyes—but he didn't give a hang if they accepted him or not.

He did give a hang about Harry's hurt. He watched the life drain from her and the twinkle dull in her eyes as she realized she did not fit in with the pretty girls and was not desired by the eligible bachelors.

She was as much an outcast as he.

He danced with her and lavished attention on her—out of pity, he told himself. He couldn't bear to see her humiliated and rejected by Society. He couldn't bear to witness the slow dawning of cynicism in her eyes as she began to avoid him with one excuse or another.

She insisted upon returning home after only a fortnight in London, her smiles subdued, her spirit crushed. She'd been a failure.

"...A dismal failure," she said flatly, when he'd finally cornered her in the garden at Saxon Hill. "I'm nothing like the other girls my age, you know. They have charms I do not possess. They are quite round and pretty, and I daresay some of them are not spoiled."

"And many of them are so spoiled that their behavior curdles milk," he said softly, hating her lack of sparkle, willing to do anything to bring it back. "You *are* spoiled, Harry, but in a sweet way. You may not look like them, but your pleasure in life shines brightly in your eyes and in your smile. The others do not twinkle as you do."

She shook her head vehemently. "No, Drew, I am sadly lacking. Only a few desperately impoverished young nobles of the *ton* paid me any attention at all and then it was halfhearted at best. I don't blame you for not wishing to marry me." She averted her gaze and scrubbed at her eyes in a childish gesture that broke his heart.

"Do you still wish to marry me?" he said with no clear idea of what he was doing—only that he must do something to bring his Twinkle back.

"No. I shan't marry anyone."

"I see," he said though he didn't see at all, particularly not the thrust of disappointment in his chest. "Well, you're right, of course. I'm not good enough for you. No one is. You'll be far better off without a husband."

She turned back to him and clutched his arm, as if she feared he would walk away from her. The fear hurt him, panicked him. Harry had always been so intrepid, embracing every part of her world, good or bad—

"Don't you ever say that," she said fiercely. "You are perfect, Drew. I didn't come home because none of the men wanted me, but because I realized that you deserve a pretty wife who needn't force you to marry her."

"I wasn't aware that you had forced me to do anything, Harry," he said, wincing at what was uncomfortably close to a lie. "It rather puffed me up to think you would want me, even if it was out of pity." That, at least, was the truth. It had felt good to know she wanted him in spite of his lack of prospects. And it had become a constant struggle to withstand her charm and her smiles, needing to keep his anger alive, frustrated that it was so difficult.

"Why should I pity you?" she asked, genuinely confused.

Drew groaned inwardly, feeling as if she were nailing boards, one by one, over a trap of his own design. Feeling as if he were supplying the nails and hammer. Of course Harry was confused. While she was quite good at manipulation, her efforts were always spurred by her belief that she was doing what was good for her victim. She had no idea of how to use people to her own ends, and wouldn't even if she did.

"Marrying anyone out of pity would be quite stupid, don't you think?" she asked, watching him as if his answer were very important to her.

"Incredibly stupid," he blurted, suspecting he had nailed in a board himself.

"So if we were to go ahead and marry, neither of us would be doing it for any reason other than that it is the right thing to do," she ventured.

He shot to his feet and paced. "Blast it, Harry. What should I say to that? I don't mind marrying you at all. But you will mind greatly when I leave shortly after."

She swallowed and took a deep breath. "Will you be gone forever?"

"Of course not."

"Well then, we will both have what we want, so I won't mind at all," she said with a firm nod. "Besides, how long could it take to make your fortune? A few years?"

Damn her for being the sweet innocent she was.

"Harry," he said, carefully controlling his voice, "Do you have any conception of how long it takes just to get from one place to another? I will first go to Ireland, then on across the Channel, where I will find goods that can be sold here, and then to America where I hope to invest in lumber and other commodities that are becoming scarce in England."

"I didn't realize you had it all planned out."

He rolled his eyes but managed to keep her from seeing it. "I have been studying the markets for years, Harry, planning what to invest in that promises a significant return. Did you think I would go off willy-nilly and let fate do the rest?"

She shook her head. "I can't imagine . . . business . . . trade . . . it is not acceptable in our class, you know."

"Harry, I am not really part of any class. And it is not acceptable to me to depend on your inheritance to keep me in neck cloths and boots. I will not return until I know I can take care of myself as well as my family. Father has more wealth in tradition and title than he does in pounds and pence and will need my help to make necessary improvements to his properties."

She lowered her head and traced the yellow floral print on her muslin frock. "I suppose it is better than having a husband who gambles everything away, or one who is never home because he is with his mistress." She sighed. "Still, Drew, your pride is misdirected. After we are married, my money shall be our money." She bit the corner of her lip and lifted her gaze. "But Papa says I cannot fight your pride, nor your ambitions, so I will agree. You must do what you must, I suppose."

He returned the nod with a jerk. "Fine. Then we shall be married as soon as the banns have been posted and read." As soon as the words marched out of his mouth, he wanted to call them back and begin the conversation again, with him fully in control. But it was too late. Her beam of happiness pounded the final nail home and he could not summon a single argument to secure his release.

Damn him for being a cowardly fool.

Driven by a growing sense of impotence, he bowed stiffly and walked away, repeating to himself all the reasons why marrying her only to leave her would not be cruel. He was giving her the protection of marriage. The other men, one of whom he had hoped would show her that a better bargain was hers for the asking, had proved his earlier belief true. They were not worthy of her. Not one of them would appreciate her. At least marriage to him would give her the freedom to remain in her family home and conduct her life as she wished.

Freedom was all he had to give her.

Chapter 2

" . . . **T**o have and to hold . . ." Drew repeated his vows stiffly, looking neither right nor left.

Harriet stood beside him, her arm looped through his, holding onto him as the vicar read the marriage ceremony. She'd drifted in a haze of happiness since the day he'd confessed to his belief that she wanted to marry him out of pity. Now that he knew better, everything would be all right.

Silence fell inside the small chapel. It was her turn, but she hadn't been listening and couldn't recall the exact words. *I will do whatever I must to keep you,* she wanted to say. Instead she grasped at scattered words she remembered the vicar saying but could not string them together properly. What did it matter? God would know what she meant.

"I, Harriet Dianna Gwyneth, most certainly do take him as my husband and all else that you said, sir."

Papa coughed. Lord Sinclair made a strangled sound. Her bosom bow, Lorelei, sighed in exasperation beside her. Drew did not move but remained without expression in his body, his face, his voice, as the vicar continued the ceremony.

"You may now kiss the bride," the vicar said quickly.

She waited, then tipped her glance up to Drew, taller than last year, yet still thin and beardless, his face still a bit soft and seeming younger than he behaved. But then she was still thin and breastless and despaired of ever rounding out properly.

Drew said nothing, did nothing.

Harriet wanted her kiss. She'd been waiting forever for it. Standing on tiptoes, she dropped her nosegay and grasped Drew's cheeks and pressed her mouth against his, darting her tongue out to playfully trace his lips, meaning to make him smile.

He jerked away from her, scowling as he clamped her elbow in his hand and all but dragged her out of the chapel. "You will not do that again," he ordered from the side of his mouth.

She had the awful thought then that he had run out of smiles. That it was her fault.

Harriet stood in the sitting room, her eyes wide and unblinking as she stared at the valise, then up at Drew. "You *are* going, then," she said in disbelief. He couldn't leave her; he just couldn't. Not when she'd already planned the entire rest of her life around him. "I thought—" She pressed her lips together, not knowing what to say. Her husband was leaving her on their wedding day and she had given her permission for him to do so, never believing he would take her seriously, never believing he would actually go.

"I fear there is nothing we can do to keep him here," Lord Sinclair said with a despairing shake of his head. "As we have said our farewells, I will leave you now to explain yourself to your wife." His head bowed, Lord Sinclair left the room, then glanced back with a look of sadness so deep it hit her like a blow. It occurred to her that perhaps he had come for one last look at the man he loved as a son.

"How can you do this to him, to me, and to yourself?" she cried, as she turned back to her husband.

Drew met her gaze slowly, as if he were in a trance, with a frightened expression that wrung a shiver of fear from her. He looked like a lost child, afraid he would not be found before darkness fell.

But he'd never been a child in her eyes. He had always been strong and calm and clever, making her feel safe when he was near, making her feel as if he could solve any problem, or at least meet it with courage. He had nightmares every night yet did not cower or talk about them. When she had nightmares, she always ran trembling to her father or to the housekeeper and spilled out every grisly detail, seeking comfort until the sun came up.

Besides, only a grown man could choose to leave his home . . . his wife.

She stared at Drew, morbidly fascinated by the anguish she saw in that flicker of a moment. A strangling panic accompanied her disquieting thought that he was asking for help or counsel or comfort. She could soothe a hurt or cast a positive light on disappointment, but this was beyond her experience. She had never before been confronted with anguish.

Perhaps he didn't want to leave. Perhaps that dreadful look in his eyes was a plea for her to stop him from doing what he thought he must even if he didn't want to.

"You will be an earl, or near enough," she said softly. "You can assume Papa's seat in the House of Lords. You have my fortune." *And me—you have me,* she wanted to say, but feared to say it. She raised her head to meet his gaze, to endure his expression that had become distant and forbidding. "How can you leave all this?" she asked, with a sweep of her hand to indicate the newly refurbished master suite at Saxon Hill.

"I leave it all in your hands," he said, as if it were all tawdry bric a brac. "You will have everything your heart desires and the freedom to use it as you wish. I've had papers prepared to that effect. Your friend Lorelei has agreed to stay with you for a while, and you have both our fathers in your pocket. Your life will continue to be quite pleasant."

"What do you know about what will make my life pleasant?" she asked. "I want my husband and I want children—" She shut her mouth, horrified by the plaintive quality in her voice. Never had she begged . . . ever.

"And I told you that I am not certain I want to father a child in a world that discards them as easily as yesterday's leavings." Kicking his valise out of the way, he advanced on her, his expression twisted as if he suffered terrible pain. "I do not know who I am. I do not know where I came from. I know nothing except that somewhere out in the world I have an existence that was not given to me out of a sense of honor and obligation and pity. I aim to find the man I was intended to be. . . . and I aim to make my own place in the world."

"Drew, you were four years old when you came here. How much of a past can you expect to find?" she challenged desperately. At his hard glare, she backed away, barely aware that tears burned behind her eyes, unable to fall for the sheer force of her will. What could she say against his conviction? "I want so badly to understand," she said in a choked whisper.

"How could you understand?" he said, still angry, still impatient with her. "You have never wanted for the love of your parents. *Your* parents, Harry. Not someone who took you in because your own family found it easy to part with you."

"But I am your family now, Drew. I want to be your family. Why—"

He seemed to waver on his feet just then and sadness dulled his eyes. "How horridly, unbearably sad and lonely and . . . lost . . . you seem," she said, as she raised her hand to his jaw.

"Exactly," he replied. "I have always been lost, don't you see? I feel as if I was dropped into the world without a proper introduction even to myself."

"But you have thrived," she said more to herself than to him as painful awareness forced its way into her mind. How little she knew of the world beyond Saxon Hill or the people in it. How little she'd cared simply because there had been no need to care. *Others took care of her*, not the other way around.

For the first time in her life, she experienced shame.

"You are very young, Harry," he said wearily. "You've had no concern for anything beyond trapping me, and you did that very neatly." He gave her the barest hint of a smile. "So now your father and my father are happy. You are happy. The least you can do is try to understand that I am not happy and that I need to discover why."

Harriet turned away from him and stared down at the new Persian carpet. His misery was more than she could bear. "I believed I could make you happy, but I see that I cannot."

"Twinkle," he said softly, "I'm sorry."

"I've waited a long time for you to call me Twinkle again," she whispered.

"And I've waited a very long time to search—"

"For who you are," she finished for him. "I do not understand, Drew. You have but to look in the mirror to find yourself. You are . . . *you*."

He did smile then. He even chuckled in an old-wise way that made her feel very young and very silly. A strange voice inside her urged her to let Drew go with the memory of the twinkle he seemed to admire. Her own voice joined in, suggesting that he might miss the twinkle and regret leaving her behind, that he might—he surely would!—wish to return to her one day soon.

"You have always been certain of your place in

the world. You *own* your place in the world without a single doubt to contest your certainty," he said patiently, as he always did when she was being obtuse and needed an explanation.

"I am quite certain that you should not go away," she retorted smartly. "In spite of your grand plans, you haven't a clue as to where to go and so you shall ride around in circles."

"And you think I should remain here and revolve around you instead, a piece of shapeless rock circling a bright, twinkling star?"

She snapped her eyes open, certain he had just delivered an insult. At least it had sounded like one. It also sounded final, like a farewell message.

With a sigh, he picked up his valise.

Impulsively, she stood on tiptoes, wound her arms around his neck and kissed him. He stood stiffly for a moment neither rejecting nor accepting, then made an odd sound in his throat and wrapped his arms around her waist, holding her tightly, returning her kiss and holding her tighter still.

Something lurched and spun inside her, spreading warmth and excitement and an odd floating sensation, as if she were leaving the world far below her. She parted her lips on a gasp and clung tighter. His hand slid up her side and his thumb brushed her woefully flat breast. She whimpered and thought her knees might give way at the shock and pleasure of it—

"Damn you, Harry," he muttered, as his valise bumped against her back, a heavy thing that dragged her back to earth. He hadn't released it.

No matter what she said or what she did, he would leave her.

She jerked out of his embrace and backed away, her throat convulsing with misery at his curse. "Good-bye, Drew," she choked out, her gaze clinging to him. "I *will* wait for you." Unable to maintain any semblance of dignity, she brushed past him to run into her bedchamber, pushed the door shut, and firmly turned the key. She pressed her back against the door and gulped back a sob, telling herself over and over that he would be back. He could call her spoiled all he wished but he'd had the same advantages as she. He'd been just as pampered as she. No inn in any country could match what he was leaving behind.

He was loved here and he knew it . . . didn't he?

She cried out and whirled toward the door, fumbling with the key and the latch. Beyond, the sitting room door opened and closed. She called his name and dropped the key, picked it up and couldn't seem to get it back in the lock properly.

"Drew! Wait!" she called more loudly and finally wrenched open the door. The sound of horse's hooves clattered outside, fading by the moment. She ran to the window and lifted the sash. "Drew! I love you!" she shouted out the window, but he rode on. "I love you," she said over and over, her voice fading like the sound of hooves clattering on the cobbles. The tears escaped restraint, pouring down her face and strangling each breath as she sank to the floor and hugged her knees to her chest.

He was gone. And she had been too thoughtless to tell him that she loved him with all her being.

She curled around herself more tightly, her body shaking with dry, wracking sobs long after her tears had been spent. Drew had turned her upside down and inside out and made her see things that she didn't want to see.

Drew thought his real family had discarded him. He didn't know that she loved him enough for a whole world of family. And loving without being loved in return was lonely—frighteningly, wretchedly lonely, as if one wasn't quite whole. Until now she had never known what it was to be lonely, and Drew had felt it every day of the life he remembered.

He had to know that she wasn't so spoiled that she couldn't understand at least that much. She had to believe that since the world was round he would wander about in a circle and eventually end up here, where he had begun his search. Here, with her.

Drew spurred his horse into a hard gallop, Harriet's cries of love nearly bringing him to ground as they surrounded him, like walls closing in on him. He'd known that her feelings for him had gone beyond mere fondness. How could he not, with her cow-eyed looks and stumbles contrived to hurl her into his arms at every opportunity?

And her kiss. God, her kiss. He hadn't known she'd taste so sweet.

He spurred his horse harder. It was adolescent infatuation. She would outgrow it as she outgrew other things on a weekly basis. One day she adored pink and the next yellow. Another time she swore she would expire if she did not have a pony cart. She'd driven about Saxon Hill for a full month before flitting on to a new passion—a mongrel given to her by her friend Lorelei. She'd ordered the pony cart ripped apart and a dwelling for the beast fashioned from the wood. He preferred not to recall that she'd loved and cosseted that damn silly lapdog for five years until it had died. She would turn him into her pet if he allowed it.

He was a man, not a beast to be cosseted and forced to eat out of a woman's hand.

But at the moment, he felt like a boy, horribly young and inept, a pretender to age and wisdom. His reaction to Harry's kiss proved it. How could he have nearly given in to the temptation to stay with her after years of being so certain of where he had to go and what he had to do?

How could he have even thought of using Harry in such a way when only that morning in the chapel he'd realized that he was not ready for marriage? He'd repeated his vows because he hadn't known what else to do. How could he have and hold anything when he couldn't even remember who he was or where he'd come from? How could he take care of Harry for richer or poorer when he had nothing of his own? How could he honor and cherish her when he had been barely able to keep from taking her on the sitting room floor?

Realizing he was pushing his horse unnecessarily hard, he reined in slowly and murmured apologies to the animal. The pace slowed into a rhythmic trot, soothing Drew as he rode toward London. Sanity and calm crept back into him as the distance lengthened between him and Saxon Hill. He had kept his word to his foster father and to Harry. Now he had to keep his word to himself. He hadn't lied to Harry when he'd promised not to be gone forever. He would return certain of who he was and what place he wanted to occupy in the world.

Chapter 3

Ireland, 1802

Vanished . . . without a trace. Nothing remained of the once imposing keep but shadows looming against the night—of crumbled
towers and charred wood, a stone skeleton left behind after fire had consumed the heart and soul
of the place.

Yet he had seen it before, in dreams that
haunted him—of a knot of people surrounding
him, forcing a bitter liquid down his throat as a
strange horseman waited to carry him away.

Be a good boy . . . remember none of this . . . an old
woman had whispered over and over as he sank
into a drugged stupor. She'd faded into the group
standing beside her, hunched over with the others
until they appeared to be a many-headed monster
wailing in the wind. . . .

He knew that this was where the nightmare had
begun . . . where he'd begun.

He'd explored the ruins. He'd dressed like the

natives of the area, sat in a corner of the pub, and asked a single question about the tower keep, stunned that the Irish lilt he'd affected had spilled from his mouth so naturally that all were convinced he was a fellow countryman. He'd known without doubt in that moment that he had come from here, that somewhere in the depths of his mind, memories lurked and peeked out at him without warning.

"The Tower were home to the Baron Cassidy," an old man intoned, as if he had told the story a thousand times before. "His half-brother were the Viscount Sinclair, a Sassenach, come to visit with his wife. Full of airs she were."

"Naught else is known for sure," a barmaid said.

The proprietor snorted. "Naught but that Cassidy took up with Mary Margaret Collins and her being a slut who took off her clothes so a redcoat officer could paint her picture."

"And him having his friends come in to talk and watch," another added.

"She were a patriot," the barmaid said hotly. "She did it to get information for the rebels. A sacrifice it was. She slept with none but the Baron Cassidy."

"Aye, and the Sinclair woman not liking her brother-in-law taking up with a common girl instead of marrying high and proper," a farmer added. "It was Lady Sinclair who turned Mary Margaret in for treason to the Crown."

"Got 'em all killed that night, she did. All but Lord Sinclair, and him not knowing that Mary

Margaret birthed his half-brother a son four years before.''

Drew's stomach twisted as he listened to the story unfold, as the pieces of the puzzle fell, one by one, filling in the emptiness of his past.

"Near went mad, Lord Sinclair did, when his wife and brother died in the tower fire. Had to hold him back, the soldiers did, to keep him from running inside. And then Mary Margaret trying to get away and being shot for it. Held her, Sinclair did, as she told him of her son and begged him to take the boy away with the money she'd saved.''

"Thirty thousand pounds it were,'' the old man slurred. "Sassenach coin paid for her body and the secrets she sold them. She were a slut.'' His fist hit the table with a thump.

Cold numbed Drew, held him in his chair, his hands clenched around his tankard of ale, his knuckles white and aching. Thirty thousand pounds—the exact amount of the trust he'd received upon his marriage to Harry—

"She did not spy against her own kind. She told the redcoats what the rebels wanted them to know, is all.'' The barmaid crossed herself. "God save Mary Margaret's soul for all she endured— letting those filthy soldiers gape at her self whilst loving a man she couldn't have.''

"A good thing it were,'' the old man said, "that Mary Margaret told Cassidy's brother about the boy afore she died. Sinclair weren't a bad man at all—cried when he saw the child—held him tight and promised he'd watch over the boy good. That boy did good for himself without knowing a thing. More likely he was got from a redcoat, or a rebel, than from Baron Cassidy."

The cold hand of truth tightened around Drew's throat, suffocating him, as he rose to his feet and lurched from the pub, the facts dogging his heels as he'd stumbled through the night toward the ruin known as Cassidy Tower. A woman who removed her clothing for any man who wanted to watch, a woman who sold secrets, was his mother. His parents had not died, leaving him with grandparents unable to feed him, as he'd imagined.

He was a bastard, perhaps the son of Edward Sinclair's half-brother, or of a redcoat officer, or of an Irish rebel. Definitely the son of a whore and a spy. Long before she'd died, she'd sent him away from her, away from a father who might have wanted him. Out of revenge?

Betrayal burned in his stomach, his heart, his soul. The nightmare made sense now, though he still could not remember anything that went before. Nothing but the voices and the otherworldly croon of a woman that drifted through his dream, more mist than substance as the others handed him up to the horseman, none seeming to hear or see her.

He'd never told his foster father the details of the dream. He hadn't wanted to share that one small scrap of his identity with anyone, even the man who had adopted him.

How many times had he wondered who he was. A son? A brother? Loved? Despised?

Instead, he was the bastard son of a woman who sold her body as well as secrets.

His foot caught on a stone, dislodging it. Moonlight washed over the ground beneath his feet, spilling iridescence over an object jutting from the earth. He bent over and closed his fingers around metal, cold and smooth and shiny, and seeming to leap from its nest in the soil as he straightened. Two open circles twined together, clinging together as they warmed in his hand. He pulled them apart and stared at them, a pair of bracelets fashioned in gold bands braided in a Celtic design, each too large to be worn on the wrist. The moon glow seemed to follow the bracelets, caress them, enchant them. They appeared newly made, though the insides were worn nearly smooth, obscuring the inscriptions that had been added— names and dates, perhaps?

He stared up at the jagged edges of destruction, at the shell that remained of his past, blinking as his vision blurred and his throat constricted around a breath. Edward Sinclair's wife and half-brother had died here. Drew's mother had died here. His memories had died here. No one survived to know or to claim him. Nothing was remembered but gossip and speculation. Nothing remained but the nightmare.

His legs folded, dropping him to his knees as he continued to stare at the shadows. And then he fell forward and pounded the earth with his fists, his chest heaving with rage, his body shaking with it.

"No." It began as a single word repeated over and over again until his howl of anguish struck the crumbling stone and shattered into a thousand echoes of grief.

My dear son,

John, Earl Saxon passed away this afternoon. Harriet told me that she had known he was dying, but had promised him she would not tell anyone. What a burden she had to bear. Naturally, she did so with uncommon courage and is bearing up better than I. . . .

Drew,

Your father told me that he informed you of Papa's passing. If your first thought is to return home to comfort me, please do not unless you mean to remain. It would not be a kindness to me at this time. If you return for anything less than forever, I will refuse to see you rather than face having to say good-bye to you again. Papa is gone. You can do nothing about that. In any case, I am certain Papa is in a far better place and quite happy to be reunited with my mother. I have had some bad moments thinking that she has been looking down on me all these years and has by now told Papa all my secrets. Every time thunder booms, I imagine it is Papa scolding me for past mischief.

Harriet

Harry,

I have no words to express my grief at the loss of your father. He was the best of men and as close to family as I can remember having next to my foster father. How much more difficult it is for you, I cannot imagine. I had begun arrangements for my immediate departure to England, but then realized you were right. By the time I received Father's letter and the one he included from you, over six months had gone . . .

Father,

I leave for Greece tomorrow with William Whitmore, a historian and entrepreneur who has invited me to join him in his quest to unearth remains of ancient civilizations as well as engage in trade to establish his own income and thence my own. His family owns a plantation in the West Indies, but he has no desire to live there and so seeks his independence. That we share the same goals is an irony that is not lost on me, though William seeks the means to spend his life digging up the past for study, while mine is to overcome my lack of a past by establishing my proper place in the present.

Which brings me to the admission that the longer I am out in the world, the more aware I become of my inexperience and the arrogance that led me to believe I could accomplish everything on my own. This discovery prompts me to dash my pride and ask a favor of you. I took advantage of the Treaty of Amiens to travel throughout France, where I have purchased a large supply of laces, silks, scents, soaps, and the latest fashion dolls, which should appeal greatly to English ladies. I need someone in England to oversee the placement and sale of any merchandise I acquire, and ask that you direct my shipments to a reliable agent. You have my gratitude in advance. Please convey my regards to Harry. I remain your devoted son

Drew

My dear Husband,

You send your regards to me through your father? I beg your pardon? I have accepted a great deal from you, most notably your absence, but will not accept your "regards" from anyone but you. To ensure this, I have engaged a courier to carry letters back and forth, for I cannot trust the post in foreign countries. Mr. Briggs is a tenant who has displayed a dismaying lack of ability in farming, or carpentry, or in the stables, and faced losing his lease. I do expect you to cooperate in providing Mr. Briggs with a living by corresponding regularly with me.

I am thoroughly piqued that you didn't think to ask me to act as your agent. I need to feel married in one way or another. This will do for now. Though a perfectly good fortune is already at your disposal here in England, I comprehend the demands your pride places upon you. Really, Drew, pride is such a detriment to reason and logical behavior. Still, I am most happy to aid you, believing that your success will oblige you to come home that much sooner. I remain your enterprising wife

Harriet

Drew,

I find it disquieting that Harriet not only insisted upon undertaking the task of placing your goods, but that I indulged her. She insists that since the death of her father, she must have something to do or go mad—a contradiction, since she has been running with Brummell and Baroness Winters and setting trends that keep Society gasping. Her growing reputation for being the best hostess in the ton sits well on her, and standing in as her host ensures that I will not fall into ennui. I do prefer to see Harriet bouncing about rather than mourning as she has for the past few years, first because you had gone and then for her father. I feared that she *would conduct her entire life in a continual state of melodrama. . . .*

Mr. Briggs settled beneath a cypress tree far enough away to afford Drew privacy, yet close enough to keep him in sight. Harriet's courier would continue to dog his heels until Drew gave him answering letters to carry back to England.

Torn between amusement and annoyance at having a watchdog set upon him, Drew sat beneath the old ruins of a Greek temple, dangling a pair of gold bracelets from one hand and the letters from the other. His annoyance increased as amusement gave way to alarm.

Scowling, he reread one letter then the other, berating himself for neglecting to ask his father not to mention his need for an agent to Harry. But the door was opened and would be difficult to shut now that Harry had slipped inside and taken it upon herself to manage the sale of his goods. Women didn't conduct business. What was his father thinking to allow it?

He was indulging her, of course, just as he and Lord Saxon had indulged her manipulations to so neatly trap him into marriage. Even that was unconventional. Drew Sinclair-Saxon indeed. He had no idea what legalities were involved in pulling that off. From the first time he'd seen his name written thus he'd felt like a damned consort rather than a husband.

And now she was handling his business. He didn't like the idea of her pottering about his merchandise and haggling with merchants, much less that she would have any sort of hand in his affairs, especially when he'd finally made the decision to do what he should have done immediately after leaving Ireland.

Now seemed the ideal time. She had apparently begun to build a life of her own, finding and pursuing her own interests. She was going on without him—a circumstance he'd hoped for. A circumstance that visited a sadness on him he'd not anticipated. Harry—gone on without him. Harry—no longer a part of his life. Harry—no longer loving him.

Yet it was what he'd wanted. She'd not understood what she was choosing when they married. He'd not understood the scope of his selfishness in going along with it. It was past time to make it right.

Rising, he stared down at the bracelets he'd been carrying since he'd found them at Cassidy Tower, loath to part with them for some unfathomable reason. They meant nothing to him and should bring a good price. Yet they always brought images of Harry to mind, seeming far clearer and more vital than mere memories—

Impatient with his misplaced sentimentality, he wrapped each in a separate cloth bag and added them to a crate being prepared for shipment to England. The gold alone was worth a year's income. A year closer to success. He could not cling to these last remnants of his past any more than he could cling to Harry.

As he walked away from the men nailing crates shut, a single cloth bag fell onto the ground and a single band of gold gleamed in the Mediterranean sun as it rolled toward him.

Harry,

You try my patience, madam. I forbid your involvement in my business and have written to our solicitors with instructions and authorizations to oversee my affairs. I much prefer thinking of you rigged out for a ball than breaking the rules of proper behavior for a lady of your station. Obviously you are bored and dissatisfied with your lot in life to even think of such a thing. I must insist that you obtain an annulment and seek a more normal way of life with a husband who will be everything to you that I am not. I should have fought our marriage with more conviction. We were quite young and given to delusions when we married, but surely you have matured sufficiently to see that we have no marriage. It only remains that you make it official by honoring my wishes regarding an annulment. The world can be yours, Harry, if you will but reach for it. Please do so now for your sake as well as for mine.

Drew

Drew,

You forget, sir, that I know you too well to be fooled by your nonsense. Really, Drew, you can be such a twit with your misplaced nobility. Now you are approaching useless martyrdom as well. I rather adore a twit but cannot abide martyrs unless they are holy ones. Insist all you wish, but do not expect me to fall in with your absurd notions. Please recall that our marriage began as one of convenience—my security for your freedom. I believe that is how Papa put it. Well, it is convenient for me to continue the bargain. When you return, we will decide what is to be done. Until then I shall feel quite secure in my determination since you are not here to enforce your wishes.

                        Harriet

Caribbean,
January, 1808

Drew,

Parliament has issued Orders in Council, which states that all shipments of a foreign source are subject to duty. The Americans threaten an embargo in retaliation and I fear another war will ultimately follow. In this eventuality I would advise you against exporting goods from America. In any case, I see no need for you to continue such mercenary activities for much longer. Play in your ruins if you must but please avoid becoming entangled in this row between nations. I remain your loyal wife, though it severely strains my imagination to understand it.

                        Harriet

Drew folded the letter and tucked it into his pocket as he stared out at the landscape of tropical waters, volcanic rock, and lush vegetation. It had taken Mr. Briggs well over a year to trail him from Greece to Persia to Egypt, and finally to this Caribbean plantation owned by the family of his friend, William Whitmore.

He and William would soon leave for America, where they planned to purchase timber to replenish the shrinking supplies in England, and then journey to the West to meet with trappers and in-

vest in the new markets opening in the export of
beaver pelts so prized by European haberdashers.
In England, his trust would have quickly dwin-
dled to nothing, but with this last journey, he
should succeed in parlaying his thirty thousand
pounds into enough to finance a lifetime.

Without Harry's aid, thank heaven. He'd anticipated that she would argue with him about her
involvement and had been relieved that she had
not. Relieved and a bit uneasy. Harry was usually
stubborn to a fault when she set her mind to
something, yet she'd not said a word in her letters
about it. But then what could she say? It was his
business and he'd taken the precaution of turning
matters over to his solicitors. Instead, Harry had
defied him on the annulment, which he hadn't expected.

That she would choose to fight for a marriage
that barely existed was another source of unease.
By now she should have been so put out with him
that she would be happy to quit their "bargain"
with a minimum of fuss. Surely she'd long since
outgrown her illusions.

Oddly enough, her defiance did not irritate
him—a circumstance he'd refused to think about
at any length, instead making his own choice to
pursue his goal with reinforced determination.

The sooner he returned to England, the sooner
they could settle the matter. They couldn't possibly have anything in common after so many years
of being apart from one another. That his anticipation to see Harry again grew with every passing
day was another circumstance he chose not to explore.

"All is well, I trust?" William said, as he joined Drew on the verandah of the plantation house.

"Yes, all is well," Drew replied. "But from your expression I gather *you* have a problem."

William grimaced. "Priscilla is badgering me to take her with us to Boston."

Drew groaned at mention of William's sister—a girl of eleven who in some ways reminded him of Harry. But Miss Priss, as they called her, displayed a selfish thoughtlessness that was not in Harry's nature.

"Mother has suggested that we leave tonight after Priss is asleep," William said, with the familiar gleam of anticipation in his eye. "She sent word to the docks that we sail on the tide."

"Coward."

"Indeed, I am." The gleam faded as William's expression sobered. "Mother placed a condition to her cooperation with our escape."

William's tone alerted Drew that Mrs. Whitmore's conditions involved him. "Do I want to hear this?"

"Probably not," William muttered. "Mother wants Priss to go to England when we return," William said heavily. "I must say I agree with that. M'sister is too headstrong by half. She requires the refinements taught at the schools for young ladies back home." He met Drew's gaze. "Trouble is we have nowhere to send her since we have no family left in England, and Mother has too much to do here to go herself. The plantation, not to mention Father, would fall apart without her."

Drew arched a brow as he regarded his friend. "Well, I have no one capable of handling Priss—

if that is the bush you are circling. Father can barely keep up with my wife . . ." His voice trailed off as he realized where William was going. "William, there is little I would not do for you, but Harry has no such loyalty to you."

"It would require only that she enroll Priss in the appropriate boarding school and dole out the funds sent for Priss's needs." William spoke quickly, with desperation. "There is nothing for her here; surely you see that. She hates the island as much as I do, and I want her to have a secure future away from this place. Once she's finished school I will go to England and remain until she marries." He lowered his gaze to his hands. "Actually, I plan to remain in England for good. God knows there are enough libraries and ruins in the kingdom to keep me happy for the rest of m'life. Why, Hadrian's Wall alone—" He sighed and cleared his throat. "I might even marry me a blue-stocking heiress."

Drew sorted through the pertinent elements of his friend's dialogue, then opened his mouth to argue but found no suitable reason to deny William's request. After all, Father had said that Harry wanted to keep busy. . . . "All right, William. I will write to Harry about it when the time comes, but if she's not willing, then we'll just have to find some other way."

"Well," William slapped his hands on his knees and grinned, "don't fret, old boy. Priss is only eleven and we don't want to send her off until she is fourteen or so. You'll be back home well before then, I daresay. We have plenty of time . . . plenty of time indeed."

American wilderness, 1811

Dearest Twinkle,

If you are reading this then it must be supposed that I am dead, frozen or starved while waiting out a winter in a dugout beneath a mountain of snow in the American wilderness. I will not belabor the cause of our current predicament except to say that I have been unavoidably detained by nature as well as a series of mishaps. Since I have difficulty believing fate could be so inventive, I cannot expect you to believe it. In any event, I find it poetically just for you to remember me as an irresponsible fool who embarked on a search for myself and lacked the sense to look in my mirror as you once advised . . .

Ominous shadows hovered on the walls of the dugout as the candles burned down at an alarming rate. A few hours earlier, he and William and the two trappers they'd been traveling with had abruptly descended into silence as they reached an unspoken agreement to take advantage of their last few candles by reading, melting snow, and putting their affairs in order.

Drew bent over his paper and squinted to bring the words into focus, determined to finish. He had to know that he had set the words down in case their bodies were found after the spring thaw. He wanted Harry to know how he felt about her, how he'd always felt about her.

Quickly, he filled the last page, even writing in the margins, wryly acknowledging that he had taken to writing in circles as well as traveling in them. He added his signature, then sagged back against the rough wall and rubbed his arm, felt the reassuring presence of the gold bracelet inches above his elbow. He rolled up his sleeve to remove it, to study it as he did whenever his mind needed soothing. He turned the band over in his hands, compelled by gold capturing the dim candle glow, reflecting it outward in bright glimmering stars of light.

And as it always did, the bracelet immediately inspired thoughts of another kind of beauty—of Harriet and her twinkling laughter and flighty nature. Harry never hurt anyone, never accepted what others could not afford to give in emotion or in material objects. She had taken from him only what he had been willing to offer her and then she'd said good-bye with tears and a sweet unschooled kiss that had rocked him to his soul.

He had wanted so badly to return to her, to make things right with her, even if it meant letting her go. Seeing her again had become such a small hope for a man who had always been afraid to hope.

He held the bracelet and traced the braided design as bright and finely detailed as if it had been fashioned a day ago rather than years, or centuries.

Whimsical . . . twinkling . . . like Harry.

The last candle guttered and winked out, immersing him and his companions in darkness. William cursed in impatience. One trapper sighed. Another began to weep. Drew stared into the black well of his life, recognizing the darkness for the enemy it was.

By touch, he carefully folded the letter in oilskin

and tucked it into his saddlebag, praying that someone would find them and send the letter on to Harry. It was his last remaining hope in a life riddled with futility. He did not want to go the way of his past, lost without a single echo of his existence. . . .

Vanished . . . without a trace.

Chapter 4

Saxon Hill
Late August 1812

Where was Drew? Harriet wondered, as she tried to attend the conversation her friend, George "Beau" Brummel, insisted upon having. She had no intention of redecorating Saxon Hill as he suggested. She liked the continuity its well-worn and familiar furnishings represented. In each piece of wood or porcelain or picture, she found a happy memory—the old chair where her Papa had held her on his lap while telling her stories of dreams come true, the threadbare draperies that Simmons the butler pulled aside to keep an eye on her when she was outside, the chipped porcelain elf Drew had given her for her fourteenth birthday.

Drew . . . she had so little of him. She would not willingly put any of it in a trash heap.

The wedding of her dearest friend the day before had brought too many thoughts to the surface—of love and hope, of anticipation and disappointment, of regret and too many what ifs. After Lorelei and her new husband had left in a flurry, loneliness had coiled around Harriet like a cocoon, separating her from everyone around her and shrouding her in silence. Drew should be here, to share the opera with her, to stand by her side as they welcomed guests, to dance with her beneath a crystal chandelier.

Where was Drew? She hadn't heard a word from him since receiving the letter he'd sent from Boston over two years before implying he would return to her the following spring. What dreams she had spun from those few cherished words. Yet he had not returned, nor had he written. She could only conclude that he had changed his mind and undertaken yet another profitable enterprise. Or that he had discovered that she had ignored his edict and browbeaten the solicitors until they had happily given over management of Drew's business to her and was too angry to write to her. A pity she had fallen in love with a man of ambition and pride rather than one who would be content to be one of the idle rich.

"My lady," Fellowes, her secretary interrupted. "A . . . uh . . . shipment has arrived."

This was the third shipment since his last letter, all sent through an agent in Boston.

She rubbed the bracelet she had purloined from one of Drew's shipments and always wore on her upper arm. It felt cold and hard against her flesh when it usually was warm and caressing. "Please see to it, Mr. Fellowes. I will go over it with you later." She turned to Beau, determined to concentrate on life as it was rather than as she wished it to be.

"Begging your pardon, ma'am, but I think you must see to this one yourself." Her usually cheerful and often irreverently humorous secretary looked disturbingly tense.

She rose and swept out of the salon, wishing she was hard enough and cold enough to let the blasted merchandise rot in the drive.

"Heaven forbid the beaver pelts have molded." Beau said as he accompanied her to the front of the house. "I was looking forward to taking my pick for a new hat."

Harriet left the house and strode out onto the broad portico supported by columns Papa had commissioned in an attempt to divert her from her grief over Drew's departure—dear heaven had it been eleven years ago? Confused, she surveyed the circular drive but only a coach and four stood before her—no wagons loaded with goods to be stored in a portion of the stables she'd had converted for that purpose.

A voluptuous young woman descended from the coach followed by an older woman looking bedraggled and frantic.

"What is this, Mr. Fellowes?" she asked, with an inexplicable sense of dread.

"Miss Priscilla Whitmore, my lady, sister of your husband's friend. She claims Mr. Sinclair-Saxon sent her to you to be educated in the refinements of a lady before her Season in two years."

"He did what?" she said in a low, controlled tone.

"Mind your manners, countess," Beau whispered, as he brushed past her and bowed elegantly before the young lady. "Miss Whitmore? I am George Brummell, at your service."

The girl curtsied prettily, though her gaze remained fixed on Harriet. Her hand tucked into Beau's arm; she walked beside Beau and curtsied to Harriet with a sweep to the ground more appropriate for royalty. "My mother asked me to give this to you the moment we arrived," she said, as she held out a letter. "I believe it contains news of Drew and my brother."

Harriet stared at the letter, not wanting to take it, afraid to learn for certain that Drew had decided not to return home.

"Ma'am?" the girl said. "Are you quite all right?"

Mind your manners, Harriet silently reminded herself. It would not do to kill the messenger. She summoned a perfunctory smile and all but crushed the letter in her hands. "I'm quite all right, thank you, Miss Whitmore. I must admit that I am at a loss regarding your presence."

"Oh! Please ma'am, don't tell me Drew didn't write you about me. He promised he would. He said you wouldn't mind a bit taking me in and helping me become a lady."

Drew? This overgrown child called Harriet's husband *Drew?* And her voice dripped sighs with every letter pronounced. "I'm afraid I knew nothing of your existence until now," she said in a smooth tone that concealed a whirlpool of dark thoughts.

"Oh! Drew is really too naughty neglecting to

notify you of his agreement. Mummy would certainly have Daddy's head on her best platter for such a thing. But then Drew said you were the soul of kindness. I shall be sure to tell him he was right. Any other woman would have tossed me into the streets straightaway." She straightened, her chin held as high as a martyr's. "I shall take a room at an inn until Nanny and I can book passage—"

The woman who must be "Nanny" groaned.

Beau cleared his throat. "As you said, Miss Whitmore, Countess Saxon is the soul of kindness. You must allow for her shock. It isn't every day a woman finds a bundle such as you on her doorstep."

Harriet jabbed her elbow in Beau's ribs as she dredged the depths of her "kindness" for another smile. "Hinton," she said to one of the footmen flanking the door, "Please have Mrs. Simmons show Miss Whitmore and—" She tilted her head at the companion, her heart going out to the poor woman who had been trapped on a ship with her charge.

The woman stumbled as she attempted a curtsy. Harriet rushed forward and caught her arm, holding her steady until she regained her balance. The poor dear was chalk white with exhaustion and anxiety.

"Everyone calls me Nanny, my lady," she said, as she looked up at Harriet in gratitude.

"I would like to call you by your name," Harriet said gently and wrapped her arm about the woman's waist, for clearly she was barely able to stand. "I am Lady Saxon."

"My name is Clara, ma'am."

Harriet nodded as Beau took Clara's other side and gallantly offered his arm. "Hinton, take these ladies up to the blue guest suite directly, then have Simmons send for Dr. Alistair." Harriet rapped out orders, anxious to get Clara settled and Miss Whitmore out of her sight before the footmen visibly drooled over her opulence. "And tell Mrs. Simmons that Clara is to have a bed-chamber for her own. I'll not have her sleeping on a cot in the dressing room."

"I don't need a physician, ma'am. I just suffer from *mal de mer*, and it has been a long trip—all of it on water. I'll be quite fit by morning."

"All right, Clara, but if you are not improved by morning I will call in the physician." Harriet patted her hand as she and Beau led the procession into the manor.

Priscilla half skipped to catch up. "Oh! Dear Nanny, I am so sorry you are not well. You should have told me. Lady Saxon is quite right. You must rest."

Giving her a sharp glance, Harriet saw sincerity and genuine concern for her companion in Priscilla's expression, albeit far too late. She bit back the comment that tossing up one's slippers for the whole of a journey might have brought Clara's distress to her attention sooner if she had bothered to look. But Priscilla was obviously the sort of person who was too preoccupied with herself to notice the distress of another unless it was pointed out to her.

"She doesn't know any better," Mr. Fellowes

commented beside her. "The girl's more coddled than the last egg in the hen house."

Beau chuckled as he herded Harriet into the salon. "Well put, Mr. Fellowes. I think you should make all haste in arranging tea and perhaps some brandy for Lady Harriet."

Harriet stood in the center of the room, barely aware of Beau and her secretary as she stared down at the letter. She didn't want to open it. Yet she must open it.

Beau stood in front of her and gently took the letter from her hands to break the seal, unfold the paper, and hand it back to her.

One paragraph leapt out at her:

I regret to tell you that your husband and my dear Willie are most certainly dead. Mr. Briggs set out to find them and sent word through a rather complicated string of contacts that the winter in the wilderness had been extremely harsh and no one had seen Drew and Willie since the previous spring. It is with great desperation that I put my grief aside to see to the welfare of my only remaining child, Priscilla. Drew indicated that you were a generous soul who would most certainly take care of my baby, though this was relayed to me through Willie before they left for America. I must presume on your generosity, for I truly don't know what else to do. Priss requires more education than we can provide here in the islands if she is to make a good match . . .

The letter fell to the floor from suddenly numb fingers. She felt frozen, incapable of any movement, any sound.

Dimly she saw Beau bend to pick up the letter. His breath whooshed out as he scanned the contents. "Oh God, Harriet—"

"He is not dead," she choked out as the bracelet warmed again and seemed to thrum softly like a living thing. "He . . . is . . . not!"

"Harriet—"

"No!" She shook off his arm and rushed to a small desk, cursing as she fumbled with paper and quill. "He is alive because I am still alive," she said fiercely, somehow knowing it was true and believing it utterly. "And to prove it I am going to write him this very instant." She plopped into the delicate chair, dipped her quill in the ink pot and wrote so furiously, she tore the paper. With barely a pause, she swept it aside and began again on a fresh sheet. "Do stop standing there looking helpless, Beau," she said without looking up. "It doesn't become you. I will take brandy as soon as it arrives. Thank you for thinking of it."

"Oh my lady, you feel it too. You know Drew isn't dead just as I know my brother can't be dead." Priscilla ran into the room and fell to her knees beside Harriet's feet.

Harriet gave her a dispassionate glance, skimming over her dramatically earnest expression, then returned to her writing. Of course Drew was alive. He wouldn't dare die before she had the opportunity to unleash the full measure of her fury on him.

Beau escorted Priscilla from the room.

Harriet raised her head, her gaze landing on the window that overlooked the garden and the bench she and Drew had shared a lifetime ago.

Heat penetrated her senses as Beau tilted her head up and poured brandy down her throat. Coughing, she gripped his arm with both hands. "Blast it, Beau, he isn't dead . . . and I am not an invalid. I can pour brandy down my throat without your trying to drown me in the stuff." She lowered her head and focused on the ink stain spreading over her skirt, then fixed Beau with a steady gaze. "I don't believe it for a second." She frowned as the bracelet seemed to curl more closely around her arm, as if in approval. It had always felt rather strange, but in a comforting sort of way. Now it seemed alive.

She shook her head and bent over her letter. Alive indeed. Next she'd be thinking that it possessed magical powers—

Mr. Fellowes rushed in without knocking, his freckled face pinched with strain. "My lady, we must go to Singletrees at once. It's Lord Sinclair. He's collapsed."

Drew,

Imagine my shock to find a young girl on my doorstep with a letter from her mother informing me that you and her son were dead. Of course you are not dead. I could not possibly be this angry with a corpse. Regardless of that, Mrs. Whitmore feared waiting any longer because of the war between England and America, and took the liberty of sending her daughter, one Priscilla Whitmore, to me for education in the art of being a lady. Imagine my confusion upon learning that you had agreed that I would take in the girl.

You agreed? May I inquire as to when I agreed? I

*do not believe that the vows I took eleven years ago
included taking in stray young women. The girl is pur-
portedly fifteen, but I am skeptical on that point. I certainly did not look like that at fifteen. The girl positively
reeks of . . . feminine charm, for want of a better word,
and the footmen are sniffing with appreciation. She has
not even the hint of a single spot. What adolescent does
not suffer at least one of the dreadful things? Nevertheless, I will see to the girl's welfare because you promised it, and pack her off to Chatsford School for Young
Ladies, though she is too old. Still, two years of "finishing" is better than none.*

*Now that I have assured you that Priscilla is safe, I
will turn my attention to you. You have gone far beyond the boundaries of acceptable presumption, sir. I
am outraged that you neglect to write even a note ap-
prising me of the reasons for your tardiness. I have
given you eleven years because I trusted you enough
to have patience. But patience is gone and trust destroyed by your thoughtlessness. It is a cruel thing to
destroy trust. I never thought you capable of it. You
always seemed so mature to me, so calm and certain of
everything—your direction, your purpose, your goals.
I nurtured my daydreams while you sought to banish
your nightmare, and I wallowed in the romance of it
all—a man of mystery leaving me to slay his dragons
while I waited patiently and lovingly to welcome you
back. Romance, I have discovered, leaves a great deal
to be desired.*

*But enough of that; there are far more important is-
sues to discuss than the state of my illusions. You at
least owe me the satisfaction of presenting you with
annulment papers and then tossing you out on your*

*ear. I remain your impatient wife for only a short while
longer.*

                                                    Harriet

Drew stifled a roar of fury as he folded the first
letter he'd found waiting for him at the Whitmore
Plantation. A second waited to be unsealed and
read, but not yet. Not until he gained control of
emotions that had been advancing on him from
all sides since Mr. Briggs and a group of trappers
had found him and William in the dugout, too
weak to do more than stare at new faces and sip
at the tea Briggs had brewed and spooned into
their mouths.

Nothing would ever taste so good as that tea.

He'd lain on a travois being dragged by Briggs's
horse, impotent against the impatience that grew
with every slow mile of their progress eastward.
Impatience roiled into anger as they were attacked
by a small band of natives. Snarling in fury, Drew
had fought them as if he were alone, firing his gun,
then swinging it like a club, barely noticing his
wounds. He'd been too weak to do more than listen
to the news that war had been declared against England by President Madison. Too ill to enforce his
demand that Briggs steal a damned ship if necessary. Briggs had ignored his curses and shouts as
he'd taken him and William to business associates
in Connecticut, stating that they would wait there
until one of the Rutland cousins returned and
agreed to take them as far as the West Indies on one
of their ships. There they would find British ships
aplenty to take them to England.

Another winter lost as he'd lain fevered and helpless beneath Briggs's ministrations, hanging onto the thread that had kept him alive through the long days that followed the guttering of their last candle in the dugout. He'd finally lost consciousness, drifting between memories of Harry and the nightmare that never faded, never changed. Another year lost while Mrs. Whitmore sent Priss to Harry with news of his death.

He leaned his head back and breathed deeply. Harry didn't believe he was dead. She hadn't accepted it.

Harry wanted an annulment.

Not bloody likely. Not when Harry had insisted upon waiting for him when he might have endured losing her. Not when he'd survived hell and cheated death to return to her.

Reason told him that he deserved it. That Harry had tolerated enough. That Priss was the final nail in the coffin of their marriage. In spite of his lack of experience with women, let alone wives, he knew that literally dumping a strange young girl on his wife's doorstep without explanation or permission was not a wise thing to do. It didn't matter that he was not guilty. Harry thought he was.

He folded the first letter and opened the second, resolving to get it over with. Who knew? Perhaps Harriet had developed a sudden fondness for Priss after realizing that her initial assessment of the child was greatly exaggerated. Or perhaps she had remembered her fondness for him and had forgiven him.

He swiped his hand down his face at such idiocy and began to read—

Drew,

In spite of my continued outrage over your actions, I cannot withhold news from you. It is not happy news, so please do sit down. Your father suffered a seizure and passed away a few days later. Though, like me, he did not believe that you were dead, the lack of word from you for so long sank him into great despair. No man could love a natural son more than he loved you. It is a pity that it was not enough for you, though I reluctantly tell you that he understood what drove you and had great respect for your determination to make your own way.

As I write, I experience shame for rebuking you at a time like this, and resent my own anger with you. I do not like anger, yet mine continues to grow. Nevertheless, I have no words to express my sorrow for your loss. I miss Lord Sinclair so greatly that I have become quite maudlin and introspective. I have never been alone, you see, and feel quite without direction or connection. Even Lorelei is gone, having fallen madly in love and married during my last house party. In fact, her husband is Adrian Rutland, Viscount Dane, and one of the owners of Rutland Shipping, which has made you so obscenely wealthy. I did solicit a hug from the cook in a weak moment, though it nearly gave the butler apoplexy. But I babble in an effort to avoid speaking of what I would rather pretend is not so.

Lord Sinclair entrusted his affairs to me and my advisors until such time as you return. His cousin's grandson will inherit the title, though Singletrees is yours.

Your father's last words were of his love for you and how much joy you brought into his life. I am feeling churlish enough to tell you that I wish I could say the

*same. I remain your wife only because it seemed wrong
somehow to seek an annulment while in mourning for
Lord Sinclair.*

Harriet

Drew stared at the letter through eyes blurred
with grief. Gone. All of his past gone now. Except
for Harriet, his "impatient wife for a short while
longer."

He remained very still in his chair facing the sea,
afraid that if he moved, he would kick the traces of
his restraint and shout his rage to the heavens. He
had not been with the only father he had known. He
should have been there. He would have been if
he had not been so driven to succeed.

Instead, he'd lost two years fighting the death
that had seemed so inevitable in the dugout. That
was the worst of it—being trapped beneath the
earth where he could not escape himself, being
held an unwilling captive when he should have
been back in England, telling his foster father a
thousand things he had always assumed he would
have time to say . . . later.

And now, Harry was alone. She didn't know
how to be alone.

Now he was returning, the prodigal with no one
left to greet him.

Except his very angry wife.

PART II
Discoveries
England, 1813

Since it is not granted to us to live long,
let us transmit to posterity some
memorial that we have at least lived.

PLINY THE YOUNGER, *LETTERS*

Chapter 5

Saxon Hill
Spring 1813

Harry—with a lover. The very idea of it had grated on his temper, Drew thought with disgust as he strode toward the guest wing.

For a man who had spent only five hours with his wife before leaving her twelve years ago, he had behaved every inch the outraged husband. For a man who had been home for only an hour or two he felt absurdly possessive of a wife he hadn't even recognized. Who could have guessed the homely, yet endearing, girl he'd left behind would change so drastically? He'd remembered her in one way and she'd had the dismaying effrontery to transform from a twig to a woman. He'd rather adored her angles and even her spots. Now her complexion was soft and clear as dawn on a cloudless day, and while still small, her frame was embellished with a most provocative arrangement of curves.

As he'd held her and stared down at her, it had been easy to believe that the second bedchamber in the master suite might be occupied.

Harry, with a lover? In hindsight he couldn't credit it. *His* Harry was too young and too naive to deal with a lover. Too innocent. Lady Harriet seemed equally incapable. In hindsight he could recall how her face had reddened and innocence still lingered in her eyes as she'd suddenly averted her gaze upon implying she was having an affair.

Harry, with a lover. In hindsight, he could believe that no more than she had believed he was dead.

Besides, she had purloined the bracelet from one of his shipments. It seemed somehow significant that she wore it even under a long sleeve, indicating it was more to her than a mere ornament that caught her fancy. Had it moved her as it had moved him? Did it warm against her flesh and seem to embrace her arm when she thought of him as his did every time he thought of her?

He paused and shook his head. He'd spent so much time pottering about ruins that he had grown moss in his brain. Bracelets did not embrace; gold did not possess mystical qualities—

Hearing a suspicious scurry behind him, he glanced over his shoulder and caught a glimpse of the red and black livery worn by footmen of Saxon Hill. He was obviously being followed. Either that or his brain was succumbing to rot.

Making a decision, he cut sharply to his left, yanked open an arched door, ducked into a private corridor that led to the family quarters, and waited, his back against the wall, listening to the same two footmen who had been on the terrace walk by on tiptoe.

"We didn't lose him, I tell you," the one said in a loud whisper.

"So what if we did?" the other replied. "I'd rather face my lady's displeasure than his. My lady is smaller than we are. He is not and looks capable of using us as cleaning rags on the banisters." Whitson frowned. "I still can't credit that he is the same person who used to go fishing with us as boys."

"Fishing or not, milady ordered us to follow him and lock him in. . . ."

Drew narrowed his eyes and watched them continue down the hall and disappear around a corner. Those were the village boys he'd fished with? Harry had ordered them to lock him in?

Scowling, he surveyed his surroundings and compared it to his memory of the manor.

The house had not changed at all—a comfort, since all the people had changed beyond recognition. The place was filled with Harry and her family—mementos and whatnots that had value only to the Saxons, portraits of generations of Saxons lovingly preserved, old frayed and worn upholstery on the settees and chairs placed here and there in the broader hallways and even a soft chair on each landing, everything kept clean and brushed and aired. He studied the paintings. Harriet's watercolors, each placed wherever she could reach it at the time she'd completed it.

He'd forgotten how warm and comfortable Saxon Hill had always been, seeming to embrace him in welcome the moment he'd crossed the threshold. He thought of the bedchamber Harry had so carefully furnished for him before their wedding. She'd likely thrown him the hint of a lover to keep him from discovering that she had preserved it for his return; it would be just like her, sentimental as she was.

Lock him into a guest room, would she? Not bloody likely.

Until he'd overheard the footmen, he hadn't decided what to do with himself, or with Harry. Then, he'd allowed habit to direct him. Habit that seemed to come naturally to him whenever Harry was nearby.

She was so incredibly easy to goad.

He halted as he caught his reflection in an ornate looking glass hung at the bend in the corridor, wavy and flaking with age.

Good Lord, he was smiling.

Harriet trembled like a tree being stripped by an autumn wind as guests flocked toward her in droves, chattering birds plucking at the remains of her composure to line their nests with fresh gossip.

"Who was that extraordinary man?" one chirped. "He looked positively savage with that long hair and fierce scowl."

"Quite beyond extraordinary," another remarked. "Is he married?"

Now, that was an intriguing question. One that Harriet was not about to answer . . . yet. Not until she knew why Drew had come . . . and if he would stay.

Did she want him to stay? She stifled a whimper

at that. Not until Miss Priss had appeared on her doorstep had she considered anything but his return to her, taking it for granted that he would do so uttering heartfelt and contrite declarations running the gamut from "I was such a fool" to "I could not live without you a moment longer." She'd embellished those visions after receiving his letter telling her he would be coming home after that one last venture. He could not bear to be apart from her, he would say. He'd never been able to forget her.

Her body may have matured, but obviously her imagination had not.

Over two years had passed after she'd read that letter. Two years of waiting and watching the drive outside the house. Two years of slow, agonizing realization that he was not coming back to make earnest declarations of devotion.

She was the fool. The cold stranger who had not recognized his own wife would never say such things. She refused to consider that she had not recognized him either. Of course she had . . . somewhere in her mind. Why else had she been so drawn to him upon first sight of his tall frame and deep, dark eyes? Why else had her body reacted so markedly? Only Drew had ever given her heart palpitations and damp palms—thank heaven she was wearing gloves—and puckered nipples that had been the only protrusions on her chest when last he'd seen her. She batted down the urge to cover said chest as she recalled how much more pronounced her reaction to him had been tonight. How much more pronounced it might have appeared through the tissue silk of her bodice. She really couldn't bear it if he had seen—

"A pity *you* are married, Lady Harriet," yet another lady meowed, successfully rendering the flock speechless. "He seemed quite taken with you."

The comment undid her completely, driving her to flee with barely a muttered excuse to the crowd avidly watching her every move. It wasn't every day that Lady Harriet slipped out into the night air with a stranger as readily as a mistress slipped out of her peignoir. Actually, Lady Harriet never slipped anywhere with anyone—except Brummel, and that was scarcely worthy of comment unless the gossip mills were empty and the *ton* was desperate for an *on-dit*—any *on-dit*, no matter how false.

Glancing in both directions down the hall, she darted into the butler's pantry and stopped short.

"May I help you, my lady?" the butler inquired, his brows raised in affront that she should invade his domain at a time when anyone might witness the impropriety.

"Yes . . . please leave," she said in a choked whisper. "Now, Simmons."

"But my lady, I must see to the replenishing of the tables. Your guests—"

"Let them starve," she snapped, then sighed. "They are not hungry for food tonight, Simmons. Trust me on this."

"As you wish, my lady." Simmons bowed out of the pantry, his mouth twitching, though he had the good grace not to chuckle out loud.

Harriet kicked out with her foot, pushing the door shut behind him and backed up until she connected with the wall, then slid down to the floor, wrapping her arms around her bent knees. She really should do something about the staff, though it had never seemed necessary as long as they behaved with all the formality and snobbery expected of proper servants when guests were present. The rest of the time they treated her more like a favorite niece than their mistress. After her mother died in childbirth, they had become threads that held hers and Papa's world together.

Papa had always said that families came in many guises and she'd applied that to the servants. Unseemly it might be, but they had sustained her with their care and fondness, filling the emptiness after her mother died, teaching her that love recognized no class. Teaching her that family was a part of the heart rather than the blood.

Drew had always seemed like family to her . . . until now.

Drew had returned—a stranger whose tanned face might have been cast in bronze—hard and cold as a statue and as unsmiling. She shivered and lowered her head.

If only he had smiled—just a bit, just for a moment—perhaps she might have behaved differently, spoken more wisely. Perhaps she would not feel as if in his search for his identity, he had truly lost himself.

"I see that he has yet again driven you into a corner," a cultured voice said from the doorway. "It was wise of me to tell your guests you had torn your hem and nothing would do but to have it repaired at once. You certainly can't return to them in this state."

"Go away, Beau," she said into her skirts. "And I am not in a corner . . . and he has never driven me into one. And I don't care a fig for my guests."

Beau Brummell stepped inside and closed the door. "Granted, you are at the center of the wall—in the butler's pantry, of all places—but you are tucked into yourself like a forgotten hankie lost in the cushions of a chair."

"How do you know it was Drew?" she asked, as she peered up at him.

"Well, I should have realized when I witnessed the heat rising in waves about you and him while you were 'discovering' one another on the balcony; it was most disconcerting to see the chaste Countess Saxon blazing with lust in the arms of a complete stranger. But I was too fascinated by the way perspiration broke out on the foreheads of everyone who observed the spectacle to reason it out. Really, old girl, lust for a stranger is far more appropriate. Who ever heard of being attracted to one's own spouse?" He examined his gloves, then smoothed an imaginary wrinkle in his coat. "By the way, your footman—Whitson, I believe—came to me greatly distressed and informed me that your husband is again lost."

Harriet moaned and again buried her face in her skirts, not knowing whether to submit to humiliation, despair or relief. She had made a spectacle of herself with Drew before she had known it was Drew and then she'd had the gall to suggest that *his* behavior was improper.

And now Drew was gone. No, the dangerous stranger bearing only a trace of Drew had left. *Her* Drew had been gone for twelve years and now she would never know what happened to him—

"I gather you ordered Whitson to follow your husband and lock him in a guest room," Beau prompted with both amusement and impatience. "I'd say 'badly done' if it had worked. Really, Harriet, I do not like what he does to you."

She snapped her head upright. "He has never done anything to me, Beau." And that was the problem, she admitted. She'd lived in a state of "if only" for a dozen years.

"I beg to contradict you. Every time you received a shipment from him, you went off into a corner, or you created one in which to brood, though you certainly showed signs of turbulent life when Miss Priss arrived." He leaned over and grasped her elbow, pulling her to her feet whether she liked it or not. "I much prefer the Lady Harriet who manages the *ton* with warm smiles and grace, or the one who displays wifely outrage over her husband's misdemeanors, than the one who weeps into her frock as if the head has toppled off her favorite doll."

"Drew is not a doll," she said, though something inside her wondered if perhaps that was what he had become to her—a means of imposing her own image of what she thought Drew to be, wanted him to be. Not that it mattered. Drew was gone, as was the man who had stirred her beyond description with his touch, with the way he'd looked at her as if no one else existed, and then devastated her with his coldness.

He wore a bracelet just like hers—a discovery that moved her beyond explanation since he hadn't known she'd kept the thing. Had he been as drawn to it as she? Did it warm against his flesh and seem to tingle when he thought of her as hers did when she thought of him?

"I think," Beau said in a soft, tender way rare to him, "that I should escort you to your chambers where you may, in privacy, wail or throw things or whatever it is you do when agitated."

"I do not wail or throw things," she said with a weak smile.

Beau sighed dramatically. "I was afraid of that. Well, come along, then. If you must insist upon reducing yourself to a bit of cloth rumpled on the floor rather than behaving with a proper display of offense and pugnacity, I have no wish to see it. Wounded and whimpering animals greatly upset my sense of order."

Harriet could not help but smile at her old friend. "You are so very good at arranging things into their proper order, Beau—even my emotions. If I promise to toss one breakable figurine across the room, will your sense of order be restored?"

"It's a beginning, as long as you clean it up forthwith," he said dryly. "Actually, I would be far happier if you hunted your errant husband down and tossed him over the balcony."

Nodding miserably, Harriet took his arm and meekly allowed him to escort her to her rooms all the while darting her gaze down corridors, searching for Drew.

Chapter 6

He sat sprawled in a chair by the fire in the sitting room of the master suite, his boots off, his stockinged feet as close to the flames as he could get them without catching fire, as if he were cold . . .

Harriet halted in the threshold, her heart hammering, her mouth suddenly dry, her gaze captured by him, enthralled by him.

And he still seemed a stranger as he stared at her with deep, dark eyes.

"Do come in," he said without rising, as if she were the intruder and this was not her apartment.

She ripped her gaze away and reached out to her side to clutch Beau's arm. What did one say to a husband one barely recognized? A dozen words sprang to mind, none of them ladylike or congenial.

Prying her fingers from his coat, Beau grasped her elbow and urged her into the room. "I take it you are the husband?" he asked as if he requested the time.

"Am I?" Drew inquired with a lazy-lidded

glance at Harriet. Still he did not rise.

All she could do was nod.

"And you are Brummel," Drew drawled. "The lover."

"Am I?" Beau asked with lifted brows and a half smile.

"Yes," she blurted, needing the shield he offered. "No!" she amended as she jerked her arm from Beau's grip and stalked to the opposite end of the room, her ire rising with every step. When had she become such a coward?

"Are you quite certain?" Beau asked gently.

Pinching the bridge of her nose between thumb and forefinger to keep from shouting, she shook her head in denial. "Yes, I'm certain, though I appreciate the offer."

"And one my wife need not consider now that I am home," Drew said in a bored tone.

Not to be outdone by Drew's aplomb, Beau strolled to Harriet, lifted her gloved hand, kissed the air above the backs of her fingers, and sketched a polite bow to Drew.

Drew nodded with kingly condescension. "Shut the door on your way out, will you?"

Beau's mouth twitched. "May I listen at the keyhole?" he asked Harriet in a stage whisper, then sauntered to the door. "I will entertain your guests in your absence. Should I offer a sudden headache in addition to the tear in your hem as an excuse?"

She waved Beau away with an absent air. Her guests. She'd forgotten them. Yet she couldn't care what interpretation they would put on her ab-

sence so soon after the mysterious stranger had
disappeared.

"Perhaps we should present ourselves to society," Drew drawled. "I daresay we can provide
them with some amusement.

Put out with both men as well as herself, she
glared at Drew and then at Beau's back as he left
the room, wishing them both to drown in the
moat—if she had a moat. How could they make
light of the situation? How could they behave like
such beasts? How could she feel like the felled
prey? This was her house and her ball. Beau was
her guest.

And Drew was her husband.

She had never been afraid of Drew. He didn't
deserve her fear now. She glanced over her shoulder at him, then turned away quickly. With her
back to him, she inhaled deeply and willed calm.
She had never fainted in her life. She would not
faint now.

She would not—

"Why?"

His voice sounded like a distant roar in her ears.
Dear heaven, he had seemed closer to her when
he'd been far away than he did now, further annoying her.

"Now that covers a multitude of subjects," she
said, surprised that she could articulate at all,
much less calmly. "Would you care to narrow it
down a bit?" Walking across the room, she concentrated on removing her gloves, very carefully,
setting them on the back of the settee, very carefully, sitting down, very carefully, then fingered a
delicate figure on the table next to her. It wasn't

valuable and could be easily replaced. She wasn't that fond of it. She eyed it and wondered how easily it would break and how much damage it might do to a man's skull.

"To begin with," Drew said with a wary eye on the small statue she held like a club. "Why did you want me to believe you had a lover?"

"What makes you think I do not?" she parried.

"Perhaps it is the pink upholstery and obviously feminine trappings on the dressing table in my bedchamber," he replied.

"Rose," she corrected. "Not pink."

"For all his affectations, Brummel does not strike me as the sort to favor 'rose' wallpaper and yellow bed hangings."

"Tea-dyed—the bed hangings are tea-dyed," she corrected again, and felt the beginnings of hysteria. Her husband had been gone for a dozen years, had appeared out of nowhere at the first social function she'd given since coming out of mourning for his father, and she was discussing the decor. There were so many things she wanted to discuss with Drew, she didn't know where to begin, or even if she cared to talk with him at all.

"Why, Harry?" he asked gently. Too gently, as if he were lulling her before moving in for the kill.

She met his gaze with a steady one of her own, hoping it was as glacial as his had been earlier. "Because I *should* have a lover, Drew. I *should* be taking advantage of the 'freedom' you gave me by enjoying all the pleasures of marriage without any of the bother." Continuing to meet his stare, she wondered who would blink first in this absurd game of wits.

"All right, why aren't you?"

"Because I don't wish to be in the power of a man ever again," she said flatly, feeling more calm by the moment.

"Then why haven't you gotten an annulment?"

"Because I could not bring myself to abandon you." Still, she held his gaze. Let him ask his questions. Hers could wait until morning when her guests would be gone and she'd have the entire day to question and vent her anger.

He flinched and leaned his head against the back of the chair. "You've grown sharp teeth, Harry."

She dropped the figure onto the table with a clatter as she studied him. How weary he looked. How defeated and vulnerable. In that moment he looked like the Drew she remembered. A young man, lost and afraid and so determined to carve out his place in the world with his bare hands.

A young man who she had loved with all the fervor of youth and naïveté. She loved him still, though she didn't know if he existed any longer, or if he had been completely replaced by this hard stranger she barely recognized. A man who seemed to have forgotten how to smile.

"I am nearing thirty years old, Drew," she said softly, almost to herself. "I have been alone for almost half that time. And for the last year everyone around me has behaved as if they were in the presence of a Bedlamite because I refused to believe that you were dead. At times I would spend a single moment wondering if you were dead or alive and did not know which would be easier to bear." She rose and walked toward her bedchamber, turning as she reached the door. "Did you think I would not grow sharp teeth?" Stepping inside, she shut the door and stiffly made her way to the dressing room. To remain with Drew would be to scream like a shrew at him, to throw every last bit of the frustration and anger and misery she'd suffered over the years at him. It would accomplish nothing. The years were gone and she'd been as much to blame as Drew for their emptiness.

Numbness crept steadily upward from her feet, claiming her, giving her relief from the pain of seeing him as he was now and wishing he were as she remembered—sweet and droll and teasing. She would rather see nightmares in his eyes than the emptiness reflecting back at her as she'd passed him, as if she'd hurt him in saying she could not abandon him.

She'd wanted to hurt him as she'd hurt a hundred—no, a thousand times—over the years. And yet she'd done it inadvertently, meaning to strike a blow at his pride rather than at his soul.

Her abigail lurched from a chair and hurried to help her undress.

"Thank you, Jane," Harriet said as soon as her gown was unfastened. "I'll manage the rest. Go to bed."

The sleeve of her gown caught on the bracelet and tore from the seams. She raised her head, saw her reflection in the cheval glass as her gown slid down her hips to pool around her feet. A wide-eyed woman stared back at her without expression. She touched her hair, so magnificently coifed with Grecian curls falling from a gold ornament at the back of her head and pinned in place above her neck. Smaller wisps framed her face . . . *her* face with fine lines at the outer corners of her eyes and sharper angles than she'd had in youth. She lowered her gaze to the full breasts rising above her corset and barely covered by her lawn chemise, to the narrow waist and hips that had widened just enough to give her shape. She'd grown up and hadn't really cared until now.

Until a stranger had held her and made her feel like a woman in such brief moments of discovery.

She raised her head as a sound reached her. She stood frozen at the reflection of a man standing behind her, staring at her, seeing what she had seen only a moment ago.

"You've grown in other places as well," Drew said in a husky voice. "None of them sharp."

No. Please go away, she wanted to say. She could not be strong just then. She could not even be angry with his voice so strained and his expression so bleak. The numbness faded as heat radiated through her veins. Yet she didn't move, couldn't move, was afraid to move with his eyes full of hunger and something else she could not name.

"Why did you have to change, Harry?" he asked as he reached out, traced his fingertip along the ridge of her spine above her chemise, spread his hand over her shoulder. . . .

"I could ask the same of you," she said, breathless at his touch, at the strength and warmth of his hand, at the quiver that flowed from belly to breasts and back again. Never had she felt this way. Never had she wanted so desperately without knowing whether she wanted him to go or to stay. To touch her everywhere or nowhere.

His gaze found her nipples, puckered beneath fragile lawn, waiting for his caress, wanting it. Suddenly she became aware of the music drifting from the ballroom, of the moon reflected in the looking glass and framed by the window behind them, of the fairy lights strung in the trees.

She turned to escape, but he caught her in his arms, holding her loosely, his hands on her waist, his thumbs just beneath her breasts. Her lips parted on a silent gasp of realization. She didn't want to escape. She couldn't escape. She'd been waiting forever for a moment like this. . . .

With Drew. Only Drew.

He lowered his head, slowly. Panic clutched her, urging her to run, but he angled his head one way, then the other, as if he didn't quite know what to do. And then he smiled—a rueful, exasperated expression, but a smile nonetheless.

In that moment he was not a stranger to her, but the man she had always loved.

Panic receded with the rest of the world as he groaned and yanked her against him, wrapping his arms tightly around her, holding her with his strength and with his kiss.

His tongue thrust into her mouth and his lips moved over hers, not gently, but roughly, desperately. His fingers opened and closed on her waist as he leaned into her, pushing her against the wall cushioned by her gowns hanging along its length. Soft silks and satins enfolded her, brushing her flesh with coolness and sensation as his mouth plundered hers, as she responded in kind, driven to madness by urgency and heat, so much heat.

She gripped his shoulders but it wasn't enough. She caressed his chest through his shirt but wasn't satisfied. She jerked it open and felt the hair on his chest, the plated muscle, and puckered male nipples. She wanted more.

She felt wild and free and primitive as he swept his hands upward to cup her breasts, pushing them up until they spilled over the low scoop of her chemise. She cried out as he found her nipples, stroked them with trembling hands, ground his hips against hers, slid her petticoat up to her hips, baring her. He groaned as she fumbled with the fastening of his breeches, not caring if they tore, caring only about finding him, guiding him . . .

He wrapped his hand around the back of her knee, urged her leg up over his hip, then the other. Leaning against the wall with fabric all around her, she instinctively wrapped her legs around his waist, sought him, found him hard and hot and demanding, cried out again as he thrust upward, filling her.

It was pain, sharp and tearing, and it was pleasure, deep and consuming, and then it was more than she thought she could bear as pressure built inside her, as he seemed to harden even more, fill her even more.

Sensation gathered and then spread through her as he thrust upward again and again, rocking her, shattering her, wringing every bit of feeling from her, making her experience his urgency, his need. She tightened around him, bathed him in her response as tiny quakes shook inside her, ever more frantic, ever more desperate.

It was magic. It was breathtaking. It was completion as she had never imagined it could be.

He thrust again and stilled, holding her tightly, convulsing inside her, as his lips gentled on hers, as he sighed his pleasure into her mouth.

Not once had they broken the kiss that had begun so swiftly, so wildly.

She panted and gasped for air. Her limbs felt like warm honey. *She* felt like warm honey, flowing around him as he sank to his knees, taking her with him to the floor, holding her as if he would remain joined with her forever.

Forever. . . .

He angled his head back as a flounced hem drooped over his face. A shoe pressed into her bare thigh. Drew's chest was slick and hot against her breasts. He felt so good, so right inside her.

He left her slowly, his eyes squeezed shut, then opening slowly as if he were regaining consciousness.

A gown fell between them. He tossed it away and stroked her cheek with his forefinger. She turned her head to kiss it, to taste him again.

"Oh my," she said on a sigh.

"Sweet Lord," he said at the same time.

Dazed, she stared at him, was rewarded with his smile . . . the smile she'd been waiting for. Waiting . . . so long.

He smoothed her petticoats down over her legs and gathered her loosened chemise to ease it over her breasts, his gaze following his hands, looking at her as if he were drinking in the sight of her.

Framing his face with her hands, she urged his head up to meet her gaze. "No," she said. "No," she repeated. "Do not leave me just yet."

Drew opened his mouth to say something, then kissed the tips of the fingers she pressed to his lips.

"Please . . . do not speak." Her hands tightened on his face. "Please . . . do . . . not . . . think."

He rose to his feet and grinned sheepishly as he swayed, steadied, then reached down for her, helping her to stand, holding her hand as they walked side by side into the bedchamber.

She complied with her own request as they halted beside the bed, saying nothing, refusing to think, wanting only to feel again what she had never dreamed possible.

Opening her hands over his shoulders she slid his shirt down his arms, hesitating on the feel of gold, then swiftly moving on, to his waist to ease his breeches down, staring in fascination at what had so recently filled her, growing as if reaching for her. . . .

She glanced up at Drew, at his bemused expression—the same as when he'd first watched her chase a rainbow.

He'd been hers then. She'd been so sure of it . . . then. Realization unfolded like pain inside her. He had never been hers. Yet now she was his and always would be no matter what happened tomorrow. The discovery frightened her at a time when she didn't want to be frightened. Not when magic lurked in the corners, beckoning to her from the darkness, promising her that for tonight, she could believe that Drew did belong to her.

She straightened and turned and held her hair up from her neck, a silent request for him to untie the laces of her corset. She trembled at the brush of his hands on her back, sighed at the release of stays, closed her eyes at the feel of night air wafting over her legs as her petticoat fell to the floor. As his hands grazed her shoulders and slipped her chemise down her arms, she felt no shyness, no trepidation.

She turned to him, faced him, saw the heat misting on his flesh. Through the still open door of the dressing room across from them, their reflections stood naked but for the gleam of gold on their arms as if she and Drew were shackled by them.

Tomorrow, she would remove her bracelet. Tomorrow, she would face life as it was. Tomorrow, she would think about what to do next. But not tonight while time stood still. Tonight was a part of forever. Drew was hers as he had never been before. Tonight she wanted him inside her, a part of her, to feel as if he were touching her soul, to feel the world slide away, to feel nothing but Drew.

Tonight, it was meant to be. . . .

Her wedding night.

My wedding night . . .

Drew heard her whisper and knew he should stop. Yet he could not leave her, could not stop himself from reaching for her, from twisting to lower her to the bed and covering her with his body, from lowering his head and opening his mouth over her breast, beginning again the magic, the need, the urgency.

She opened for him, took him inside immediately, as if she, too, welcomed the loss of control, the loss of thought, the swelling of pleasure. Need. Giving.

No one had ever given to him as she did now. As she had a few moments ago.

She arched her hips, drawing him inside so deeply he thought they would be forever joined.

He drove into her desperately, frantically, knowing that forever could not possibly last beyond tonight.

Chapter 7

Forever ended with sighs, and disappeared as a hush descended in the bedchamber. The moon slipped away and the fairy lights in the garden were snuffed one by one by silent servants. Time again held power over them.

Shaken by his complete loss of control, Drew lay on his back beside Harriet, staring up at the ceiling. Beyond his own behavior, he didn't know what to think of what happened. He'd been like an animal, felt like an animal. And Harry had taken it.

She'd given it back in full measure.

Since the moment he'd seen her, his emotions had run riot, seeming to become larger than he was. He was afraid to move, afraid that he might still be helpless against them. He didn't like feeling helpless, out of control. From the day he'd awakened from a drugged stupor at Singletrees at the age of four, he'd fought to contain fear and rage and helplessness, remembering only the words whispered to him as he'd been handed up to the horseman who'd taken him away. *Be a good boy . . . forget.* Every night he'd heard them reminding him to be good, reminding him that he had been sent away without being told the reason. He'd fought the nightmare in silence. And he'd struggled to be good, to not make trouble, to behave properly so that he would not be sent away again.

Now he'd arrived back in England resigned to letting Harry go. He'd convinced himself that though he'd always adored her as a friend, in marriage they would be like a hand and glove that didn't fit each other—she with her confidence that the world was hers to fashion in any way she wished and he with the belief that he was merely a figure to be placed wherever one was needed to fill space.

With Harry, tonight, he'd felt as if he had found the place he was meant to be. He'd grabbed for it like a child, taking possession as if he feared it would be snatched away before he could settle in. Until tonight he'd thought he'd outgrown that child and his fears. Fears that Harry had awakened with her anger and her passion.

Yet there was more to consider than simple desire. There was a great deal more to Harry than the girl he'd left behind. He knew more about her body than he knew about her soul.

She'd been untouched. She'd waited for him in a way he'd never had a right to expect.

Amazing, how vulnerable such a profound experience could render a man. He didn't like it. He might on occasion have been a fool, but he'd made sure he wasn't vulnerable to anything or anyone. Now rationality was elusive, a will-o'-the-wisp flitting in and out of his mind. Yet he couldn't just continue to lie there, searching for flaws on the ceiling and finding too many within himself.

"Harry?" he said without moving.

"What?"

"I don't know. I was rather hoping you would take it from there."

She took a deep breath and released it slowly. "If I do, I will bring up subjects best left until tomorrow."

The world he'd left behind the moment he'd barged into her dressing room caught up with him. A dozen years of living apart. A homecoming that was three years late. Priscilla. . . .

He sighed at the reminders of all they had to discuss and settle. Thank God, they weren't going to attempt it now. Amazing, how cowardly one could become with the knowledge that trouble was coming and there was no way to stop it. He groped for something to say. Of course, there were the obvious and most immediate concerns to address. "Are we still married?" he asked. "Or have I compromised you?"

She was silent, as if she were considering her answer very carefully, or perhaps didn't know what answer to give. "We are married, Drew. But I do not think that tonight proves it."

"No, tonight proves only that we are easily overcome with lust for one another," he said without inflection.

"It does prove that," she agreed. "Damn you."

His eyebrows rose, and in spite of his shock at her language, he couldn't help but grin.

"I waited a long time for this," she said softly.

"I even contemplated taking a lover in hopes that I could look forward to being with someone who was within reach. You ruined me, Drew. No man can compete with a memory . . . and then you had to change, to become a stranger . . . and I still wanted you. I'm not at all happy about it."

"Should I apologize?" he asked, refusing to mention that she, too, had changed and that he didn't like it either.

"For what?"

"For the way I—" Damn but this was bloody difficult. He'd never felt the need to apologize before. But then he'd never been so carried away before.

"I was as . . . demanding as you."

"I'm glad to hear it. Some women might consider it to be force."

"You did not force me," she said. "I was quite willing—" He heard a rustle, the sound of her head turning on the pillow. "How do you know what some women would consider? Have you so much experience?"

He flinched yet still he didn't look at her. "Some," he admitted. He'd never lied to Harry. He wouldn't start now.

"A mistress?" The mattress shifted as she rolled to her side away from him and left the bed. "A woman you love?"

He turned to look at her then, alerted by the tremble in her voice. Her face was averted from him, her cheeks tinted with a slash of color, her body wrapped in a throw she'd taken from the chair in the corner, as if she were shamed to show herself to him now.

"How lovely. I could very well be the other woman," she said, before he could reply.

"No mistress," he said flatly. "No affection. I merely visited one establishment or another when the need arose."

Her face paled, all color bleached away. "You paid someone for what . . . for what we—"

"No," he said harshly as he sat up on the side of the bed and reached for his breeches. "Nothing like what happened between us." He shoved one leg then the other into his pants and stood to pull them up. "You seemed to know the way of things between men and women, Harry, but perhaps you do not. Shall I explain?" Spying a tray with a decanter and glasses on a table by the door, he stepped toward it and poured himself a glass of water. He frowned down at it, wishing it were cheap Caribbean rum.

"No, thank you. I'm sure I will figure it out on my own." She sounded so prim, and so hurt, as stubborn and full of pride as he was. That, at least, had not changed.

"If it makes you feel any better about it, I'll tell you that I am no happier than you at the turn of events. I returned expecting an annulment, either as a thing already accomplished or a thing to be done." *And expecting nothing to have changed*, he added silently as he raked his hand through his hair and realized that at some point the leather thong had unwound. He must truly look the barbarian now. Perhaps he was one in fact. "You made it clear that we had no marriage to reclaim."

She caught an indrawn breath as she backed away and pulled the throw higher on her shoulder. "And do you now think that because we fell upon one another and enjoyed it, we do have a marriage to reclaim?"

"We bloody well acted as if we do," he said, roughly. He took a swallow of the water, concentrating on pulling himself together, on sealing any edges she had ripped open with her candor before he spilled too much of himself on the floor where it might be swept away.

"That indicates nothing but that we are not so far above animals in heat," she said fiercely. "And if you think we can have a marriage based upon our mutual lust, then it seems that any woman in the 'establishments' you visited would do as well as I."

He heard hurt in her voice, saw it in the way she winced and turned away. He'd never been able to stand seeing her hurt. He'd ultimately agreed to marry her because she'd been so wounded by her disastrous Season. "It's a beginning, Twinkle," he said in a near whisper, then raised the glass to his mouth for something to do. He felt blasted awkward and out of his depth. Even when he'd thought he was dying he hadn't begged for his life. Yet it felt as if he were begging now—or close enough. As if he had found a place to belong and was terrified out of his skin that he would be rejected.

Bull. He'd outgrown that particular fear long ago. He was no longer a child afraid that he would be tossed out into the streets, too young to fend for himself. He'd been fending for himself for a long time now. He knew how to be alone. He'd become accustomed to loneliness.

Or so he'd believed until a few hours ago.

"Do not," she said hoarsely, "*do not* for one moment believe that it is a beginning. I have no desire to be so caught up in passion that I cannot think of tomorrow or the next day, or the next. Or that I will not care about the state of our marriage as long as we share a bed every night. I know women who accept that because it is all their husbands offer them." She whirled around and glared at him defiantly, appearing every small inch a goddess with the throw draped around her like a toga and the bracelet a darker shadow on her arm. "I know the difference between mere contentment for one's lot in life and true happiness." She headed toward the dressing room. "If I am to be merely content it will be with my own company. I do not need a husband for that, as I have discovered in the last dozen years." Pausing, she tossed him a glance over her shoulder. "And unlike you, I can assuage my frustrations without arbitrarily seeking help. Really, I am disappointed that men are so unimaginative." With that, she entered her dressing room and shut the door.

Drew choked on the water he'd just tried to swallow. Had she said what he thought he'd heard? Never had he heard a woman speak of such things. He hadn't realized that they knew about such things, or that they needed to employ such measures.

It occurred to him then, as he slowly walked into the sitting room, that he was pathetically ignorant about women.

She wanted everything or nothing. Fine. That particular brand of greed had driven him for most of his life. He could have been quite content to live with her, to be her husband and her friend. But then he'd known precious little contentment and had looked forward to the experience. As for friends—he'd generally found them to be more faithful than family, as his foster father had been. As William and even Mr. Briggs had been.

As Harry had always been.

He slammed the glass down on the table, strode into the sitting room, and glanced around for his shirt, then remembered it was lying on the floor on Harry's side of the bed. He'd be damned if he'd go back in there after her little speech.

She'd been waiting a long time for what happened and since no one could compete with the memory of her adolescent fantasies, she had allowed him to indulge them. Her curiosity was satisfied. She appeared completely recovered from the experience. He, on the other hand, doubted he'd ever recover.

He entered the pink bedchamber, located his valise, and rummaged for the robe he'd purchased, along with a few basic items of clothing to keep him until the tailor completed the wardrobe he'd ordered. He would have to send someone into the city to request an earlier delivery. . . .

He'd returned to take over his own affairs. Harry could do whatever she wished with a marriage that had always been more hers than theirs. He'd accepted that a long time ago.

A long time ago, he'd been a hell of a lot more convinced than he was now.

He paused and stared at the wall as he realized that he'd made a decision without giving it any thought at all. He was staying. Out of pride, he told himself—because Harry was alone and surely needed help. Because he had to live his life rather than simply pursue ambition. Because, through no fault of his own, there were too many questions that needed answers.

Grabbing the dressing gown, he snagged a quilt from the bottom of the bed and returned to the sitting room, where he could have a fire to warm bones that seemed as if they would never thaw after his winter in the wilderness.

Harry's bedchamber had a fireplace. . . .

Dismissing that particular temptation from his mind, he added coal to the hearth, wrapped the quilt around his shoulders, and sat in the chair he'd previously occupied, absently listening for sounds of Harry moving about, finding comfort in them. After what seemed more than a lifetime of lying beneath the frozen ground in silence, he needed to hear the sounds of life to remind him that he hadn't died. That he had been given a second chance to do something besides wander through a wilderness of lost memories.

He sank deeper into the worn chair, feeling the cushions give way and conform to his body. The furnishings in here had been stiffly new when he'd left. He'd searched everywhere known to man for a place into which he would fit, and had found nothing. A world of possibilities had opened before him tonight. Possibilities he'd refused to contemplate when he was seventeen. He'd always known what he needed to do and had been driven to succeed—in finding where he'd come from, in amassing a fortune of his own.

But those were basic needs required for one to get on in the world.

Here, he'd found what he wanted.

Here was Harry—still fascinating, still a world unto herself. Harry—shooting sparks rather than merely twinkling, warming him with her brightness as nothing else ever had.

She looked a fright, Harriet thought critically as she examined her reflection in the looking glass above a small washstand in her bathing chamber. Her hair was hanging in a snarl down her back. Her mouth was swollen and red. Her eyes were too wide and haunted.

Yet she still looked like herself, felt like herself. She should at least *feel* different. She should feel shame or disgust for so recklessly disregarding the future.

With a vengeance, she scrubbed her body with a soft linen cloth and her best soap, trying desperately to scrub away Drew's scent, to overcome the sensations that still lingered beneath the skin, tantalizing her, tempting her to seek him out again, and to blazes with ideals and principles and pride. No doubt Drew had been quite smug to find her untouched after all these years. And of course she'd had to add to his conceit by admitting that the memory of him had prevented her taking any other man into her bed.

It wasn't fair that women had no way to conceal virginity while having to take a man's word for whatever claims he made. Of course, men didn't have to make such claims. Their reputations did not suffer for a few indiscretions, or many of them, for that matter.

A beginning, indeed. She'd always thought Drew had more intelligence than to assume a night of making love could also make a marriage. She'd thought many things about Drew—all of them fashioned from ideals rather than reality. He was a man, and like all of his kind, too full of arrogance to believe a woman might want more than bluster and pride and a good performance between the sheets. But Drew had never blustered; he was too honest for that. As painfully honest as his desire for her. She supposed she should feel quite smug about that, and she did, but it was an empty thing with no substance. Especially when he could just as easily summon his lust for a prostitute.

There seemed little left of the boy with whom she'd fallen in love. An ideal love, perfect as rainbows were perfect. As dreams were perfect and life was not.

They had both changed, both become adults with clearer, less rosy views of the world. Her dreams had become more practical. And while he seemed to have learned to live with his nightmare, his pride still seemed cast in iron.

But changed or not, she loved Drew. She always would. Tonight *had* been a beginning, no matter what she'd said. It had shown her how far she would go to hold onto Drew, to have whatever parts of himself he was willing to share with her. It wasn't enough. There had to be more than an old fantasy and new passion. She'd told the truth in that, at least. She could not settle for mere contentment with him. She loved him too much, too completely. . . .

God help her.

She donned a nightrail and crossed through the dressing room, avoiding the sight of the pile of gowns lying on the floor against the wall.

Against the wall . . . mindless . . . primeval . . . incredible.

It had been as extraordinary as Drew. He had changed so much in appearance and manner. What had happened to him over the years to hone his body to solid muscle and tanned flesh? What experiences had molded his face into hard, uncompromising lines, engraved cold purpose into his expression, deepened the sadness and torment in his eyes that always retreated, leaving only emptiness behind? There was so much she needed to know yet was afraid to ask. So many decisions to make with no idea at all of what she wanted.

She halted just inside her bedchamber, unaccountably disappointed to find him gone. Really, he had refined his habit of leaving her without a word to a fine art.

But she'd had the last word—several of them. And not one had encouraged him to remain. Really, her habit of defending his actions was becoming an embarrassment to her sensibilities.

Feeling a snit coming on, she paced the length and width of her bedchamber, then flopped into a chair to pout. But she'd lost the knack over the years. She glared at the door leading into the sitting room. She'd been too busy to pout. What a shame she couldn't blame Drew for her lot in life. As Papa had once pointed out to her: she had made her own bed, her own choices . . . whatever. Really, she would feel far more secure if she had someone else to blame for her predicament.

She cocked her head to listen for sound in the next room and heard nothing. She smiled at a sudden image of Drew sprawled on the bed in the second bedchamber amid rose upholstery and tea-dyed lace—

Frowning, she wondered if he expected to permanently occupy that room. For all they'd said, they had revealed precious little, as if they were wary of one another.

Drew had always kept his thoughts to himself—she didn't to this day know what his nightmares were—but she had always been a open book for him to read at will.

And he'd certainly read her earlier.

Her face burned with the memory of renewed sensation, like a dream that lingered long after awakening. She'd not only opened herself for him but turned every page of her emotions for his perusal.

A pity she hadn't bothered to have a look at his. Drew was still a mystery to her, and the only emotion she could identify was confusion. She'd made several rather shocking speeches to him, yet what had she said? If he was going to remain for any length of time, they must reach some agreement on how to go on with one another.

She had no idea how she would tell him that she'd ignored his edict and continued to oversee his business affairs in England. He wouldn't like it, though she surely ought to be able to make him understand. After all, it hadn't been difficult to convince the Messrs. Janes and Holworth that she should be the one to tend to her husband's interests. And, he must be told about the papers Lord Sinclair had left for him regarding his legacy. She knew she shouldn't have read them, but temptation had bested her. More than once during her weekly visits to Singletrees, she had reached out for the box holding the papers, then jerked her hand back besieged by conscience. One day she'd surrendered to curiosity. Surely it could do no harm, she'd told herself. Surely, as Drew's wife, she had a right to know. Surely her years of waiting for him entitled her to know.

Her hands became clammy and cold as she'd read the letter addressed to Drew. She'd sagged against Lord Sinclair's desk, her heart aching beyond bearing as tears spilled from her eyes. Oh, dear heaven, she'd never imagined—couldn't have imagined—what Lord Sinclair had lived with for so many years. And Drew—dear God, what would it do to Drew? According to Lord Sinclair's letter to Drew, he'd been told lies in Ireland. Horrible lies fostered by gossip and conjecture.

She stared blindly down at the box as she tucked the papers back inside, wishing she'd never opened it, praying she would forget what she'd learned. Such a small box to contain so many truths, so much pain and loss. Truths she had no right to hear from anyone but Drew.

Shaken, she snapped the lid shut just as Priss entered Lord Sinclair's library.

"What a lovely box," Priss had said, as she'd traced the inlaid wood. "What is inside?"

"Lord Edward's private papers," Harriet responded without thinking, and unsure why she should be so wary of the girl's motives in asking. Curiosity was a common trait shared by humans.

"About Drew?" Priss asked casually.

"Among other things . . . Priss, would you be so kind as to locate the steward and inform him we are leaving?" Harriet said crisply, reluctant to have Priss know where the box was kept. In fact, she would find a different hiding place. No one must know what was inside. No one must touch it except Drew. He had waited a lifetime to know the secrets his life represented. A childhood of wondering . . . and years after that of learning to live with what he'd heard in Ireland. No wonder he hadn't told her what he'd found.

She pulled in a shaky breath and dashed away sudden tears as she tried to forget the words Drew's father had written with so much anguish and sorrow, feeling as if she had violated the hearts and souls of both men with her curiosity.

Priss paused at the doorway and glanced back at her. "Have you read them?" she'd asked with a gleam in her eye.

"Of course not," Harriet said, as guilt and shame threatened to knock her to her knees.

Her stomach lurched as Harriet remembered her perfidy that day. And her pain for Drew. How he would take the truth, she couldn't guess and feared to find out. She'd spent more than a bucket of tears every time she remembered the letter. She'd agonized for long, lonely hours trying to put herself in Drew's place, to feel what he would feel upon reading them, to understand so that she might help him. She'd failed miserably.

But Drew was home and he would soon know. She could do nothing but wait in silence for his reaction, praying he would not guess that she had intruded where she didn't belong.

Better now to address other matters, like Priscilla Whitmore. She'd managed to forget about the girl for days at a time until now. Now, she had a bad feeling that Priss would be like the worst memories, always turning up to bedevil them. She'd tried to befriend Priss, to care about her, yet something held her back, warning her to be wary of the adoration the girl showered on her.

Perhaps it was the cow-eyes and dreamy smile Priss always had when Drew's name danced on her tongue. Perhaps it was how often Drew's name was on Priss's lips. Perhaps it was Priss's insatiable curiosity about all things pertaining to Drew . . . and to their marriage.

Chapter 8

Patience was a virtue, Mummy had always said.

Priscilla congratulated herself on having been exceedingly virtuous. She had devoted every thought and action to learning the skills and behavior of a lady, though really, Mummy had taught her so much of it that she often had to struggle to pay attention the daily lessons. But Mummy had also said that practice made perfect, so she hadn't minded overmuch having to spend the last eight months at school with a gaggle of girls younger than she.

Smiling smugly, she stared fondly at her brother as he rode away from Chatsford Hall on his way to Hadrian's Wall even though it was quite late. Willie, returned from the dead. Priscilla had known all along that Willie and Drew could not be dead, though, for the headmistress's benefit, she'd pretended shock when he'd appeared at the school.

The old dragon had been quite nice and sympathetic and had even allowed Willie to extend his visit beyond the dinner hour. She could be such a dear when one was properly meek in one's requests. If she hadn't allowed Willie to stay, Priscilla would have simply sneaked away to meet him in the gardens. There was so much she'd needed to know.

Dear Willie. He had been through so much. And Drew . . . Drew had believed he would die in that ghastly thing called a dugout. Of course, Mummy had been convinced that Willie and Drew were dead when they didn't return. She'd even written of her certainty in the letter to Lady Saxon.

She'd watched the countess read the letter, her face draining of all color, her hands shaking so hard she could scarcely hold the foolscap, her lips trembling with the need to cry. But she hadn't. She'd simply read on and then stared at her with eyes glazed by unshed tears. Priscilla had admired her fortitude—something she hadn't expected from a refined lady. Daddy had said for years that the aristocracy was going to refine itself until it had no substance upon which to stand. But the countess proved that Daddy could be wrong about some things.

Lady Saxon had displayed great strength as she'd swiped at her eyes and stated firmly that she did not believe Drew was dead. Not that she wouldn't believe, but that she *didn't*—a fine distinction that had not been lost on Priss as Lady Saxon continued to write letters to him, though she had no idea where to send them.

Priscilla hadn't disagreed with Lady Saxon. She hadn't believed that Willie and Drew were dead either. She was quite certain that if Drew and her

beloved brother had died, then she would have
shriveled into nothing at the exact moment they
expired. Lady Saxon had smiled when she'd said
that, as if she'd felt the same way. It had disturbed
Priss to think that Drew's wife might care about
him enough to shrivel up, that perhaps she was
wrong in thinking Drew would be better off free
of his marriage.

She'd liked Lady Saxon immediately, which
made things difficult enough. She was quite an
amazing woman. And quite nice. But really, anyone with a brain would know that she wasn't right
for Drew. She was too independent and strong.
Drew needed to be needed and the countess
didn't need anyone.

She'd been obviously put out upon hearing that
Drew had agreed Priscilla should go to her in England. Priscilla hadn't bothered to tell her that
Drew had simply promised to ask his wife if Priscilla could be sent to her, and that Mummy had
taken the matter entirely upon herself before Drew
could keep his promise. Lady Saxon's outrage
would be just one more reason for the countess to
get the annulment Priss had overheard her discussing with the vicar shortly after her arrival.
She'd had to ask Nanny what an annulment was
and had been ecstatic with the answer. Drew had
never shared a bed with his wife—further proof
that their marriage was doomed to failure.
Mummy and Daddy slept together every night
and sometimes, Priss heard noises other than
Daddy's snores. Interesting noises that she'd later
learned were caused by making love. She grinned

as she remembered how Daddy always smiled and whistled the next morning.

Making love. What a lovely thing to look forward to with Drew.

Priss ruthlessly stamped down her unease at the thought of taking Drew away from his wife. Lady Harriet had made her welcome and given her a lovely room and helped her choose a new wardrobe for school. She'd even talked to her as if she were an equal, though she sprinkled comments throughout her conversation about how careful a young lady must be in her deportment.

But Priscilla would do anything to have Drew, even suffer through the lessons Mummy had taught her long ago.

And Drew would be so happy to have her when he saw how grown up she was and how refined she had become.

Twirling about the empty parlor in which she'd been allowed to receive her brother, Priscilla sighed with the joy of it. Drew was back in England. And she would soon be back at Saxon Hill. He would see her and his wife together and realize the differences. Lady Saxon was pretty, but she was rather small and her hips were far too narrow. And her hair—why, the color was odd, to say the least. And the small lines around her eyes would become more pronounced with every year that passed. She was almost thirty—much too old and set in her ways to make a vigorous adventurer like Drew happy.

Obviously, he'd already concluded that, since he had left his wife immediately after their wedding. Lady Harriet was a warm and generous lady, but she would never make a proper wife. She was too immersed in matters better left to men.

No doubt she would be grateful to have Drew taken care of. He would want things from her that she was far too busy to bother with. And she could be such a stick. Priscilla couldn't imagine the countess making noises in bed, much less making Drew smile and whistle the next morning. While reading Drew's letters to Lady Saxon, she'd been ecstatic to learn that Drew had ordered his wife to obtain an annulment. Obviously, Lady Saxon and Drew did not want one another.

Still, she thought she should help matters along by letting Drew see the differences between her and his wife, even if she had to manipulate a thing here and there. He was such an honorable man that he might require convincing that love was so much more important than pride and honor.

She leaned toward the looking glass hung over a table and fluffed her golden curls. Smiling coquettishly, she examined the dimple in one cheek, pleased that it was deep and rather charming. She bit her lips and pinched her cheeks, then made a pouty moue. Turning sideways she held her shoulders back and thrust out her breasts, pleased at how they pouted when she thought of Drew. Her waist was small and her hips wide enough to bear all the children Drew could wish.

How could he not want her?

Checking the hall, Priscilla darted upstairs to her cubicle in the dormitory and pulled her portmanteau out from under her bed. It would hold

enough for now. Drew would send for the rest of
her things later.

She had to travel quickly, before Drew became
too settled at Saxon Hill. It was a comfortable
place but rather worn and shabby for her tastes.
And after all that Drew had suffered, he deserved
the luxury of Singletrees . . . and of a doting, sub-
missive wife like her.

A wife who knew exactly what to do to protect
him and his future.

Chapter 9

Out of patience with her restlessness, Harriet left her bed and shrugged into a dressing gown, thinking it an absurd affectation under the circumstances. She strode to the door, yanking it open and maintaining her momentum until she reached the center of the sitting room. She had to know if Drew remained in the master suite.

The door to the second bedchamber was ajar, affording her a view of the bed. It was unoccupied. She threw a quick glance around the room, her gaze skidding to a halt at the sight of a protrusion from the chair by the fire. A fire that was built unusually high with embers glowing red hot.

She tiptoed nearer and caught her breath. Drew was slumped at an angle in the chair, his eyes closed, his long legs stretched out toward the hearth, his arms crossed over his chest, hugging a quilt around him as if he were cold.

The room was positively sweltering.

Yet he definitely appeared to be cold. He didn't look sick, and he certainly hadn't behaved as if he were ill earlier. During their childhood days, he had always been quick to remove his jacket and neckcloth when no one was looking. He'd rarely bundled up in cold weather as others did.

He shifted slightly and stretched his legs closer to the fire.

Carefully, she slid out of her velvet dressing gown as she approached him and checked the placement of the screen in front of the fire. Any nearer to the coals and his feet would be charred.

She paused to study him as she hadn't before. Lord Sinclair had told her Drew was always a restless sleeper. She'd rarely seen him being anything but restless. Yet now, he seemed to be sleeping soundly, barely moving, and seeming to be barely breathing.

She'd really expected to find him pacing. Or for him to barge into her chamber demanding yet more answers. Drew had ever been impatient for answers.

How she'd dreamed of soothing him, of giving him peace and happiness. How she'd believed that she could, that in time, he would depend on her to fill the empty places inside himself.

She leaned closer as a pale jagged line on his temple caught her eye. A scar ran from the outer tip of his eyebrow down along his hairline, disappearing into his beard. Faded and long healed, it would be easy to miss unless he turned just so. She hadn't noticed it because she had been too busy looking for the Drew she remembered. And then she'd been too overwhelmed by the rest of him.

Her stomach clenched as she wondered how he'd gotten the scar. How he might have died if not given proper care. And then her stomach rolled into a twisted knot as she thought of all those agonizing days and nights she'd spent waiting for him to return, then watching for him to ride up the drive after his last letter had arrived.

Had a serious injury delayed him after he'd said he was coming home? Was that why there had been no word of him or from him?

She thrust such thoughts away and kneeled to move his feet from danger and gently tuck her robe around them.

"Shall I be heartened that you do not wish me to freeze to death?" he asked in a sleepy voice.

Her heart lurched in her chest and his feet escaped her hold, landing in her lap as her gaze flew to his. "Take it as a warning that I will not let you escape me again until we reach some agreement between us. If you must cook yourself to a turn, you will please wait until our business is settled."

"I didn't escape you, Harry. Nor did I abandon you. I abandoned myself."

His voice was so even, so firm, that it wrenched her already unsettled emotions. She wanted to be controlled, calm, logical. Yet nothing about their situation had ever been logical or reasonable.

"I agreed to your leaving so abandonment does not apply," she said crisply, as she lifted his feet and dropped them onto the floor a safe distance away from the fire. "I am merely informing you that I will not agree again until—"

"Matters are settled between us," he finished for her. "I wrote to you of my desire to do just that."

"Yes, you did, and then you did not come—"

Her voice cracked. She pressed her lips together and swallowed, then took another direction. "You mentioned an annulment, which led me to believe you wanted one." She sank back on her heels, afraid to move lest it disrupt the first constructive conversation they'd had. "As you know that is no longer an option."

"No one has to know, Harry"—he looked away from her, every element of his expression tight, seemingly angry—"if that is what you wish."

"We were careless, Drew. What if we were too careless? Should I hie off to the continent, then hand our child over to a farmer's wife for care . . . *so no one will know?*"

His face paled, then he grasped her wrist, pulled her up until they were almost nose to nose. "Never," he said, with cold warning in his voice and pain in his eyes.

"Have you changed your mind about wanting a child?" she asked softly.

"I've had no need to think of it one way or another," he replied flatly. "I expected the question wouldn't arise, since you expressed your desire for the marriage to end."

My desire? she thought wildly, as the size and heat of him penetrated her clothing as if it were little more than mist. He had been the one to bring it up, though she had mentioned it later. Yet she didn't want to remind him of it. Not when she'd begun to doubt her earlier conclusions that he wanted to be rid of her. Could it be that he thought she wanted to be rid of him? "The question has arisen now, Drew." Half kneeling, half standing, she struggled to maintain her balance before she tumbled over onto his lap. She ran her tongue over suddenly dry lips as her gaze skipped off said lap and what rose beneath his breeches.

He wanted her still. Heaven help her, but she wanted him too—more than ever.

He gave her a lazy, seductive smile that seemed to melt her legs. He tugged on her wrist and neatly shifted his hold to her waist to position her astride him. "In for a penny," he murmured against her mouth as his hand found her breast.

"One would almost think," she said breathlessly, as she turned her head to the side, "you were deliberately setting a trap."

"A trap." His hands paused, then released her and gripped the arms of the chair. "I believe that is your calling, Harry, not mine. Or have you forgotten how we came to be in this predicament?"

Shivering, she slid off his lap and stood, staring down at him. "I haven't forgotten. Our fathers drew up the contracts and then we each agreed." She backed up a step. "Or do you refer to our more current predicament? In that, too, we are both responsible."

He leaned his head back and closed his eyes. "Go to bed, Harry. I will meet you in your office at noon, where we might behave like the friends we once were."

He was doing it again—leaving her as surely as if he were walking away. She glared at him, refusing to be dismissed. "Not until we complete at least one conversation," she said with a calm she didn't feel. Never had she known such frustration.

"All right," he said without opening his eyes. "I came home looking for my wife—a gangly duckling of a girl with spots on her face. I wanted to find her and finish the kiss we began twelve years ago. A kiss that haunted me wherever I went. I returned home to find a swan and went a little mad. I didn't recognize you, Harry." He opened his eyes and fixed her with a gaze that was both impenetrable and penetrating. "All I knew was that I have never been so affected as by your kiss then and by your kiss now." His cheeks flared with color and his mouth twisted in a self-deprecating smile. "And if you don't get the hell out of here—now, Harry—I will again demonstrate just how affected I am."

She opened her mouth and closed it again, not knowing what to say, to think. Instead she turned and crossed the room to her door. "Drew?" she said as she paused in the threshold, "what if you had found the duckling? Would you really have still wanted to—"

"I would have been a damned sight happier than I am now," he growled, and said no more.

Wounded by his words, she was certain her heart had just turned to lead. She'd wished so hard to be pretty and shapely and she'd been so excited when her body had finally caught up to her age and the spots had finally disappeared. She'd anticipated the first time he'd see her again and daydreamed about how he would be overcome with love and admiration and desire for her. Well, he'd certainly desired her, but it was not the joy she'd thought it would be. Not when he wasn't happy about it. Somehow she managed to lift her chin as she turned the latch on her door and walked into her room, dragging the weight of a pain she was not sure she could bear. In the future she would have to remember to be careful of what she wished for.

Chapter 10

Harriet heartily wished Drew would go away. But he'd arrived at her office a full two hours before their appointment, his curved eyebrows climbing ever higher as he studied the wallpaper of violet, yellow, and green stripes, the delicate chairs covered in gold damask, the large Grecian style chaise irreverently upholstered in floral chintz. He'd strolled inside the room built into a breezeway connecting the main house to the solarium, then prowled about, picking up one thing then another to examine it, pouring a cup of coffee from the service on a table by her desk, testing one chair, then another, then lounging on the chaise to observe the proceedings without expression.

Thoroughly rattled, she forgot about the invoice she'd been studying and studied him instead. The sight of his newly clean-shaven face with his remarkable wide-set eyes, high cheekbones, and bronzed skin undid her completely.

Dear heaven, but he was an eyeful.

He must have grown an inch or two taller after

he'd left, for surely he towered over her more than
she remembered. And he certainly filled out his
clothing more than he had twelve years ago. The
memory of what he filled them out with pounced
on her unexpectedly, bringing visions of hard
muscle and controlled power, sensations of strong
hands crushing her against him, then beneath him,
of sensuously sculpted lips trailing fire over her
skin—

She sliced her gaze away from his masculine
elegance and stared blindly at the invoice, praying
that the heat she felt would not mist on her skin,
giving away her thoughts.

Mr. Fellowes, her earnest and gregarious secretary, ran in to announce the arrival of a tenant,
then left, apparently flustered over the sight of
Drew sprawled on the chaise and looking far too
much of a fixture in Harriet's domain.

With a strength of will she hadn't known she
possessed, Harriet managed to divert her attention
to each matter her secretary brought before her,
though she had to pretend interest more than
once. More tenants came and went. She checked
ledgers and made decisions on everything from
leaseholds to the day's menu. She concentrated on
paying strict attention to the business of the day
and ignored her silent husband, whose eyes narrowed too often for her comfort, as if he were ap-
proving and disapproving her actions.

At least the guests were gone on to London for
the beginning of the Season, sacrificing a good
day's sleep for the rounds of fittings and gossip.
It took little imagination for her to know who was
providing grist for the mill. She and Drew had

created a spectacle last night. She had refused to comment on it earlier that morning as she'd seen her guests off, dodging questions and curious looks until she'd wanted to throw rocks at the departing carriages. No doubt Beau would be pleased to know she'd been reduced to wanting to throw a tantrum—

"My lady?"

She glanced up at James Beale and frowned, trying to recall why he was here, perched on the very edge of one of her delicate chairs and looking completely out of place in her bright and cheery office.

"My roof?" the farmer prompted.

"Yes," she said briskly. "I cannot approve of your allowing your children to play on the roof. Not only did I replace the thatch two years ago, but one of the children might have fallen through and harmed himself." Shifting behind her desk to keep Drew out of sight, she fixed Beale with a stern look. "I will furnish half the cost of materials, Mr. Beale, but you and your oldest sons will have to do the work. Perhaps if you are all aware of the labor and cost involved, you will not be so careless."

"But my crops—"

"With six sons, you should be able to portion out the work. The days are getting longer." She shook her head to silence the argument he was obviously primed to make. "No, Mr. Beale. You are responsible for the damage. You shall repair it. And I fervently hope that you will keep a closer eye on your offspring to prevent the broken bones and bodies that are inevitable if you don't."

"But half the cost—"

"Is more than fair. Any other landlord would not pay any portion for damage you caused." She turned to her secretary. "Please arrange it, Mr. Fellowes, and do not authorize one half-penny more than half the cost of materials. Mr. Beale will be responsible for the labor."

Beale glanced at Drew. "Begging your pardon, sir, but I heard that you're my lady's husband."

Drew nodded.

Harriet glared at both men and then at Mr. Fellowes. Her secretary showed no surprise at the revelation. Swallowing a groan at the way gossip spread faster than a water spot on silk, she glared at Drew.

"Well, sir, seems to me that I should be talkin' with you rather than the lady," Mr. Beale said, with a belligerent glance at Harriet. "Shouldn't have to do what she says when you're here. Ain't proper."

Drew rose to his full height, and gave the man a forbidding frown that chilled Harriet and prompted Mr. Fellowes to hover nervously near the door. "It isn't *proper*, Mr. Beale, to ignore my lady or her decision. I suggest you inform everyone else you speak with that she holds your leases and has every right to dictate how they will be maintained."

"But she's a woman—"

"Who has," Drew interrupted, "been far more lenient than I would be. Now, I suggest you make haste in repairing your roof as my lady has ordered."

Beale rose and shuffled out the door, his hat crushed between his hands.

"Mr. Fellowes—a moment, if you please," Drew said, as he again sprawled in the chaise.

The secretary ushered Mr. Beale out and turned to Drew. "Yes my lo—" Flushing, he snapped his mouth shut and gave Harriet a helpless glance.

"Mr. Sinclair," she said, without meeting Drew's gaze.

"Mr. Sinclair-Saxon," Drew corrected.

Fellowes flushed brighter and bowed his head in Drew's direction. "Yes, Mr. Sinclair-Saxon. My apologies. It becomes rather confusing."

From the corner of her eye, Harriet saw Drew smile mockingly.

"Of course it does," Drew said with a mocking smile. "Especially since my wife has not yet come around to deciding my fate. Judging from her solution to Mr. Beale's dilemma, I am not sure I want to know."

Fellowes gave him what Harriet thought of as a "commiserating male" grin, then sobered. "She is quite fair, sir."

"A veritable Solomon," Drew agreed soberly. "Now tell me: is it always like this?" He waved his hand at the stacks of ledgers and papers that collected in her office on a daily basis and the farmer outside shuffling toward the gates. Harriet met her secretary's questioning glance without expression, then took pity on him and shrugged.

"Well, no, sir. It's calmed down a bit since—" He abruptly snapped his mouth shut at a warning glare from Harriet. All she needed was for Drew to discover her disobedience regarding his shipments before she could find the proper way to tell him herself.

"I see," Drew said, and fixed her with another narrow-eyed stare. "One wonders why estate business would require so many ledgers. What of solicitors and the steward? When do they consult with 'your lady'?"

"Oh, they don't, sir. My lady does it all, you see. The agent—a solicitor, actually—does take care of collecting funds, but. . . ." His voice trailed off as Drew scowled.

Harriet scowled back, still annoyed by Mr. Beale's behavior and quite put out that the men were discussing her as if she weren't present.

"Lady Harriet keeps all the accounts?"

"Well . . . no, sir." Fellowes said in an apologetic tone. "I am quite good at sums and enjoy keeping columns of figures, so my lady granted me the privilege."

"I'm relieved to hear it," Drew said, with the flash of a grin at Harriet. "She never did have a head for figures."

Instinctively, Harriet smiled back. Her ineptitude in mathematics had always been a great source of amusement for Drew, inspiring many jokes between them. Mr. Fellowes had begged to take the task upon himself rather than have to continually correct her work, making a mess of crosshatches in the ledgers, which drove him to distraction. Drew held her gaze, sharing memories with her in that single tender look.

She tightened her mouth to banish the smile. Really, one would think they were still children playing at being grown-up and a dozen years had not passed since the last time they had teased one another. Yet she couldn't look away, couldn't break the thread of the past that still seemed to stitch them together.

Fellowes cleared his throat and cast a frantic glance at the door. "I . . . we . . . if you will excuse me, I must see a farmer about a roof." Mr. Fellowes's gaze darted from Drew to Harriet as he backed toward the door.

Drew pulled his gaze away from hers, freeing her from the grasp of longing for what had once been. "I hope he is better at sums than he is at proper form," he said, as the door closed behind the secretary. "Does he pomade his hair into spikes, or does it grow that way?"

"You know we have always been a shamefully democratic household, Drew," Harriet said, in defense of her efficient secretary. She'd given up long ago on Mr. Fellowes's habit of plowing his hand through his carrot-red hair. "I have no patience for formality when only family is present, particularly when an employee works as hard as Mr. Fellowes in areas more important than silly rules of proper behavior."

"I remember well your democratic household," Drew said, with a note of nostalgia. "More than once, I enjoyed the banter in the kitchens while drinking hot chocolate and eating freshly made bread with you. Cook bustled about and the other servants wandered in and out for a bite or taste of whatever she conjured from mounds of flour . . . I used to enjoy kneading dough," he mused.

"*I* enjoyed kneading dough; *you* enjoyed tossing bits of it at me," she corrected, again caught in memories of her own. "You had an amazingly poor aim. Poor Cook was always picking dough from the back of her skirt." How lovely the memory was. How she wished they could again feel such ease with one another. Her eyes widened as she suddenly realized that they were doing just that.

And on the heels of realization charged a new army of misgivings and discomfort. She couldn't allow them to fall back on memories. They'd been children. Everything was different now. Surely it was.

The clock chimed twelve. Abruptly Drew set his coffee cup on the table at his elbow. "I believe it is now my turn for an audience with *my lady.*"

The moment vanished as if it had never been, replaced by awkwardness on her part and a sharp perusal of her on Drew's. She'd set the appointment to keep him at a distance. He'd foiled her by watching every move she'd made all morning, his physical presence reminding her of how little distance there had been between them the night before. So little she doubted a breath could have wedged between their bodies.

It didn't help that he lounged on the oversized chaise in breeches that fit to perfection, one booted foot resting on the opposite knee, or that he shrugged out of his coat with a sigh of relief, his wide shoulders extending well beyond the armholes of his waistcoat, or that he'd shaved off his beard, reminding her of the incredibly expressive face that had enthralled her upon first sight so many years ago. He'd once looked like an angel to her. He looked like one still, though a bit more tarnished, and a great deal more human.

"I didn't know, Harry."

Jerking her gaze from the fit of his breeches over long, muscular thighs, she found great interest in the quill she was mangling with nervous fingers. "What?" That seemed a safe enough response.

"I thought you would trust your steward and your secretary to take care of estate matters, and now you are managing Singletrees as well."

"Perhaps you thought I still worked at my watercolors and wailed over the state of my complexion, much too selfish and vain and self-absorbed to think of actually being useful."

He leaned forward in blur of abrupt motion. "I never called you selfish."

"How very comforting."

"And you never took offense at my every word before."

"Of course I didn't," she said heatedly. "You were so perfect in my eyes that I couldn't imagine that anything you said or did could possibly require any response other than the greatest admiration. I cannot believe I was such a cow-eyed paperskull." Sighing, she turned in her chair to pour coffee for something to do.

"No," he said softly, simply, as he leaned forward, his elbows on his knees, his head bowed. "We've got it all skewed, Harry. We wed as children who had a rare connection with one another. It was a beginning, yet we have had no middle and have no idea of what the end should be."

"What end do you wish?" Coffee spilled onto her saucer. She set it down quickly and ignored the rattle of china as she clamped her trembling hands together in her lap. She wanted so badly to hear him say he knew what he wanted, to hear him say that he wanted her.

God help her, but she loved him more desperately and more completely than she had twelve years ago. She had been so certain that she didn't, until she'd seen him last night. So certain that she could live without him, when she hadn't been living at all—not really.

Never, not even during her Season twelve years before, had she suffered a blow to her confidence like the one she'd suffered since he'd walked back into her life. It seemed so much worse now. It hurt so much worse now.

She'd be damned if she would let him see it.

"No story ends until it has had a proper middle," he replied.

"This is utter chaos," she said, afraid to interpret his comment as anything so foolish as hope. "We are as disordered as this room."

"And by the end of the day you will have everything in its proper place."

"How could you know that?"

He rose and strolled over to stand before the desk, towering over her. "Because you always took care of your things, Harry. When you worked at your watercolors, your easel and palette were a mess, but after you finished with them you cleaned your paints and brushes and put each item very carefully into your wooden case."

He leaned over her and tilted her face up with his hand under her chin, subjecting her to a scrutiny that made her feel like a bug in a jar.

"You look tired. I noticed it last night, but

thought it was due to preparations for your ball. Now I know better." Releasing her, he straightened. "Beginning tomorrow, I will take over here. It is time for you to—"

She shot straight up from her chair. "I beg your pardon?"

"I believe we speak the same language."

"Indeed we do not!" Her chair toppled as she kicked it back and rounded the desk. "You cannot barge in here after twelve years and 'take over,' dismissing me as if I were still a child who had completed a chore without botching it."

"You cannot continue as you are now," he said firmly.

"And why not, pray tell?"

"It is too much for a woman to handle. I cannot allow it."

She halted and planted her hands on her hips. "But you already have, Drew. You've allowed it for a dozen years. 'I will leave it all in your hands,' you said, just before you left me on our wedding day, implying that you thought me quite capable of seeing to my own affairs. My being a woman didn't appear to concern you overmuch then." Agitated beyond recall, she paced around and behind him, careful to remain just out of reach. "If you wished me to believe that I was a helpless female, you should never have left and provided me with the opportunity to discover that females are only as helpless as they wish to be."

"You had nothing else to occupy you twelve years ago, Harry," he said. "That has changed. Your place now is as a hostess and a wife. My place is to care for you and our holdings."

"Really? May I remind you that Saxon Hill is *my* holding? You refused to accept any part of the responsibility or the rewards. When we married, I might have been content to stand in receiving lines and languish in the salon while deciding which frock I should wear to the next rout. But it is too late for that. I have run Saxon Hill since before Papa died. I have managed Singletrees, keeping it in good order for you since your father died. I will not allow you to come in here and belittle that—or me—by insinuating that the ability to do anything more complex than sorting embroidery silks depends upon the number of protrusions one has on one's body."

His brows snapped together in disapproval, yet his mouth twitched in stifled amusement.

Annoyed by both expressions, she cut him off before he could issue another ridiculous edict. "I like being busy and succeeding, Drew. I like making my own decisions. If you wish to find the same sort of satisfaction"—she opened a cupboard door that was covered with latticework, pulled out a locked box, and slammed it on the table—"you may find it elsewhere." Fumbling with the keys hung on a chatelaine she'd tossed on the desk earlier, she found the right one, jammed it into the lock, and swung open the lid. She held out a key. "There is a box at Singletrees containing instructions and personal letters for you, which your father wanted you to read immediately upon your return." She paused to take a breath, sobered by the reminder of what she knew was in those letters. "I hid it in the priest's closet." She glanced at him, wondering if he recalled their games of hide-and-seek in the cranny secreted into a wall centuries ago to hide priests when roundheads happened by.

His expression softened even as his brows arched. "The priest's closet? Whyever would you hide it there? For that matter, why would you hide it at all?"

She struggled not to turn away in guilt and groped for the right explanation—any explanation other than that she had read the letters intended for Drew. "Because Lord Sinclair said they were deeply personal. I didn't want to risk a servant finding them. You really should go on to Single-trees now and read them," she said quickly, then diverted the subject back to one with which she was comfortable. "I'm certain you can find enough people to order about while you're at it."

"Not yet," he said very softly. "There are other matters of a deeply personal nature which must be seen to first. I'm certain Father would agree if he were here." His voice cracked and his expression seemed regretful, perhaps guilty.

Breath left her in a *whoosh* and energy deserted her; she was dangerously close to sputtering. Drew considered their marriage more important? She couldn't bring herself to object or insist that he read the letters after such an implication. She was too afraid the truths they revealed would divert him. "Very well then," she said, struggling not to react to the bleakness in his eyes. "How do you propose we address those matters? We have yet to discuss anything in any detail without veering into anger.

"By introducing them one at a time?" he suggested with a straight face. "And perhaps by keeping the length of a very large room between us?" he added, his eyes taking on a drowsy, seductive look.

She could only glare at him as her body responded to immediate images of the night before. "Thank you so much for mentioning that," she said with mock sweetness, "which has effectively destroyed the last of my hope that we might engage in a productive discussion now." She flushed hotly as his eyes gleamed and a smile spread slowly across his face.

Oh, dear heaven, his smile—so much more than she remembered, so eloquent of desire as his gaze seemed to caress her lovingly. The length of a large room, she feared, would not be enough distance. Not when she melted at a single look from him. "It appears neither of us has the ability at present to think or behave logically." Without giving Drew another look, she headed for the door.

Her breasts slammed into his chest as he caught her arm and pulled her back, holding her fast against him. "We still have that rare connection, Harry. Perhaps it's time to strengthen it."

"No." She shook her head. "It can't be that simple with so many more complicated elements in our lives," she blurted, too agitated and too desperate to escape his spell to care about what she said or didn't say. "Not when we have both changed so much. We're no longer children to believe we can pick up where we left off and expect fate to cooperate." She pushed away from him and stepped out of his reach. "Especially when you expect *me* to 'cooperate' with your arrogant edicts. I'll not have my life run for me, Drew. And I require more than charm and passion to convince me that we have any connection at all."

Drew's expression closed like a door slamming in her face. She wanted to call all her words back, to return to those sweet moments when they had shared recollections of the past. She opened her mouth, then shook her head. "I'm afraid to trust in anything I can't hear or see or touch, Drew. I can't subsist on stale memories." She turned away, unable to look at the coldness in his eyes, the stiffness of his body. "Ever since you arrived, we have too easily taken shelter from our misunderstandings in anger. We are too ready to *have* those misunderstandings. I'm afraid we will not be able to behave otherwise. . . ." It sounded so final, as if she were pouring out what was left of her heart for him to dispose of. "I hate that we could not remain children who believe we have an endless supply of tomorrows. But when Priscilla brought me her mother's letter stating a belief that you had died—" She shivered at the memory of her agony in that single moment of reading the words, and then of the battle she had fought to convince others that she knew—*she knew*—that he still drew breath somewhere in the world simply because she still drew breath. "I realized as I never had before that our tomorrows are limited. I have to be sure and so must you be sure. We must do it right."

"Would you care to elaborate, Harry? I've done precious little right since I was four years old."

She heard the wistful quality in his voice and thought it might be safe to face him again without being frozen by his expression, unable to touch his thoughts. "I don't know how to do it. Neither of us has had any practice at . . . *being involved*, have we? We certainly don't know how to be married." She fixed him with a stern look as he raised his brow and quirked his mouth. "No, Drew, anyone can do that, with or without marriage. But not every married couple can love one another. I must have that. I cannot live with you without it." Even as she said it, she wondered if she was wrong.

"Have you become so cynical that you altogether discount the possibility of love between us?" he asked softly, seductively. "How will you know if we do not try?"

Unsettled by his question and the resurfacing of hope, she caught a sudden sob before it escaped and struggled with the fear that she was ending something precious before it could begin. "Perhaps it would be best if we had time to think before making any decisions," she said in desperation. "You must read your father's letters and you must also decide what to do about Priscilla Whitmore. I cannot feel comfortable with her and I have a deep resentment that you sent her to me without my permission.

"I do apologize for that, Harry. It was never my intention—"

"Yes, I know. Clara—Priscilla's companion—told me that Mrs. Whitmore thought you dead and took your agreement to speak with me as my agreement to abide by your wishes," Harriet interrupted, wanting to end this, to go to her room and think. "But it doesn't help at the moment. Please, Drew, I am bombarded with confusion and seem unable to summon a single rational thought. I must be alone for a while to sort it all out."

Again he shuttered his expression, shutting her out. "Very well, Harry. I suppose what is good for the goose is good for the gander. But you should recall that it is separation—which I freely admit was my fault—that created this situation in the first place. But you chose to remain married to me and as you said last night, you were not forced to consummate our marriage." His eyes narrowed, became glacial as he stared down at her. "So I suggest you take as little time as possible to accept that we are married and will remain married. I aim to get on with it even if you insist upon kicking and screaming every step of the way." His throat convulsed as he strode past her and walked out the door, leaving her in the world she had created for herself. . . .

Alone.

Chapter 11

◠◯◯◠

"If she were my wife, I doubt I would have the fortitude to walk away from her." Beau Brummell fell into step beside Drew as he left Harry's office and headed for the stables.

"Leave off, Brummell. It's none of your bloody business," Drew snarled. He didn't need the further aggravation of a temper already out of control. He needed to have a hard, fast ride while he collected himself and figured out why he was so furious. Harry's request was not unreasonable. Her dilemma was not unfathomable.

He wished he could say the same for himself.

"Ah, but it is my business," Brummell said. "I have been here while you have not. I have watched her blossom from a stick of a girl into a vibrant, provocative woman. I have watched her watch the drive as if she expected you to ride up at any moment, even though she knew you were half a world away. I have comforted her—" He clicked his tongue and sighed in dismay. "But I should not be telling you this."

Drew shot his unwanted companion an ugly

148

look and picked up his pace, hoping the dust he stirred up would offend the high priest of fashion and manners enough to chase him off.

Brummell easily kept up with him. "Have you returned just to leave her again?" He shook his head and answered his own question. "I think not. To leave Lady Saxon would be the act of a fool, and you are not a fool . . . precisely."

Drew glanced at Brummell. "Precisely?" he asked, his mouth twitching in spite of himself. He'd been calling himself every kind of fool for years.

Brummell shrugged. "Well, you did leave her once, though she has ever been quick to point out that you were very young."

"Has she?"

"Mmm. She has refined defending you to a fine art. I'm rather surprised that she seems hostile to you now that you have returned. To hear her talk all these years, you are a paragon of nobility and pride, not to mention industry." He scowled down at the dust rapidly collecting on his boots. "Though I fail to see how industry can be a laudable trait in a gentleman."

"I never claimed to be a gentleman," Drew said, surprised to realize that it didn't bother him as it once would have. Once, he'd wanted nothing more than to fit in with society. Now he couldn't care less.

"Ah, but you are one. There are any number of ways you could have handled yourself last night, few of them civilized, given Harriet's attempt to gull you and my regrettable willingness to go along with her. You could have planted me a facer or challenged me to a duel, which I would have employed my considerable wit to avoid." Brummel shuddered. "Aside from that, I saw the way you looked at her, as if she was fire and you wanted melting, which means you are not the idiot I'd thought you. And—" he paused for effect, "—you have excellent taste in clothing, which means your sensibilities are quite noble."

"I do not want melting," Drew muttered, though he knew he was lying. It seemed as if he'd been frozen in the past, in his ambitions and in his apathy for everything but his goals. He'd been on fire with purpose when he'd first set out and had chilled so gradually, he wondered if he'd been frozen long before his winter in the wilderness, his "sensibilities" completely numb to time and the changes it had wrought within him. Until last night, he'd thought he'd never be warm again, yet with Harry, his temper and his body burned with equal intensity. "I do not look at her any differently than any other man must."

Brummel shot him a disbelieving smirk. "On the contrary, you look at her as if no other woman exists. Few men look at her with anything but admiration and respect and some with outright fear. She can be quite formidable in her subtle manipulations, and her candor can give one the kind of cut that does not bleed immediately."

Drew said nothing to contradict him. Harry had indeed drawn blood from him more than once since he'd arrived last night. And last night he'd discovered just how potent she was.

"Dash it. I've no taste for wriggling into a subject so I shall jump right into the middle of it,"

Brummell said. "What are you going to do?"

"I have no bloody idea," Drew admitted, finding it all too easy to confide in Harriet's friend. The man was not only likable, but had a knack for inspiring trust as well. That Harry obviously liked and trusted him was a testimony in itself.

"Why not? Don't you yet know what you want?"

Drew slanted a wry smile at Brummell's "yet." "It appears that I do know what I want; I just haven't had the time to adjust to it *yet*."

"Why not?" Brummell asked again.

"Because, damnit, I expected to find Harry—my friend and companion. I expected comfort and contentment and companionship—"

"And you discovered so much more," Brummell interrupted. "Knocked you for six, did she?"

"An understatement. She rendered me mindless."

"Ah," Brummel grunted in understanding. "Not a comfortable condition for a man. Makes most of us feel rather helpless against women and they render us quite helpless against ourselves." He slanted a suspiciously ingenuous glance at Drew. "Most men don't think they're men if they get all soppy over a woman. On the other hand, I always thought it took a woman to make a man. Take Prince Paris, for instance. He was perfectly happy to begin a war to have the woman he wanted and no one thought he was a milksop. And Helen of Troy's husband wasn't ridiculed for fighting to retrieve his wife. I've often wondered how many lost their lives over that one woman."

"I thought you didn't like to wriggle into a subject," Drew remarked, suddenly unsettled by the direction of the conversation.

"Don't," Brummell said on a heavy sigh. "Very well. I seem to have the unfortunate habit of being within earshot of private discussions whether I mean to or not. I also seem to have a weakness for listening when I could walk away."

At Drew's silence, he sighed again and kicked a stone with the toe of his boot, then grimaced at the scar it left on the fine leather. "You and Harriet are married. I know enough of the story to know that no one bamboozled either one of you into it. I was there when she received your letter about an annulment. She was ready to hunt you down and drag you home . . . said you were hers, had always been hers, and if you didn't know that yet, she'd enlighten you with a blunt instrument, if necessary."

Inordinately pleased at that bit of news, Drew chuckled. "Harry *is* a blunt instrument," he mused. "She manipulates you, then tells you she's doing it, and convinces you it's for your own good." His smile lingered. He couldn't seem to help himself. Harry's reaction to his bid for an annulment all those years ago had eased him, made him feel lighter . . . and it had made him happy. He held his breath as the realization caught up with him. Just before he'd left her, he'd told her he wasn't happy. It hadn't occurred to him until just now that Harry had made him happy simply by refusing to free herself from what he'd considered a bad bargain for her.

She hadn't thought it a bad bargain. She'd believed in him more than he'd believed in himself.

"But you weren't convinced that your marriage was for your own good and continued to fight it even after it was a *fait accompli*."

Pausing outside the stables, Drew frowned at the answer that sprang up so readily in his mind. Instinct dictated that he end this conversation now, before he made a fool of himself, yet he couldn't do it. He liked Brummell. He appreciated the man's loyalty to Harry. He admired the sincerity that was apparently reserved for the sole benefit of his friends. And the man was no doltish fop, as some claimed. Something in Brummell's eyes spoke of wisdom gained through hard experience.

"Harry was and is the best part of my life," Drew said baldly. "I've loved her since the day I caught her chasing rainbows."

"And you fell *in* love with her . . . when?"

Certainty seemed to stroke Drew's heart, giving it life. Still he didn't answer. Was afraid to answer. Brummell brushed the stable wall with a handkerchief taken from his sleeve and leaned against it as if he had all the time in the world.

"When I was waiting for her reply to my demand for an annulment and realized that Harry *is* the rainbow," Drew admitted softly, waiting for denial to set in and rip the discovery apart.

"Well, at least you can admit it to someone. When are you going to accept it without a fight?"

"It's doubtful that there will be any point," Drew said. "Harry is not ready to hear it, and I wonder if she will ever be."

"She has good cause for suspicion and wariness," Brummell said, so bluntly it hurt. "Until last night, she could pretend you loved her and you weren't here to prove otherwise. She could love you with all the romance and excitement and sweetness of a fantasy without a single thing to spoil it. Now you're here and she doesn't know you anymore. The fantasy requires more than her imagination, and she has no idea what." Shifting, he examined the shoulder of his coat for dirt and then leaned against the wall again. "I've never seen Harriet afraid before—not even when she received the letter telling her you were dead. Her heart has no experience to guide her. She has a right to be frugal with her acceptance of you. Surely you know that."

Drew did know it. Hell, he'd known years ago that she had a right to hate him. He'd wondered more than once during his journey home if he hadn't been afraid to return for fear he would be met with hate or indifference from Harry.

"And what, pray tell, is *your* excuse for waffling?"

Drew gazed at the long line of the building, unwilling to admit to his fear that Harry would flit out of his life and leave it without color and brightness. Frowning, he realized that the far section of the stables was new and that Brummell had steered him away from it while occupying him with conversation. He glanced from the new wing to the old. The Saxons had never kept more horses than necessary for transportation and the existing stables had been more than adequate. Why had Harry felt the need to build an addition?

Brummell cleared his throat, interrupting his train of thought. "Really, sir, interfering in the affairs of friends is a rather messy business that I prefer to avoid. The least you can do is attend my efforts."

"I believe you have strained yourself quite enough for one day," Drew said, still distracted by the addition to the stables. It looked odd, taller than the old structure, and with wider doors—

Brummell pushed away from the wall and managed to stare down his nose at Drew, even though he was several inches shorter. "I will strain a bit further by voicing my suspicion that it may well be too late for Harriet to think of an annulment . . . which certainly reduces your choices regarding the future. Choices, I might add," Brummel continued as if Drew hadn't spoken with cold warning in his voice, "that might very well be denied you by the arrival of a child nine months hence."

Drew's attention snapped back to Brummell, the stables forgotten. "You go too far, Brummell, and are coming dangerously close to that appointment on Primrose Hill."

"Therefore, I submit that you need ask yourself only one question," Brummell again continued as if Drew hadn't said a single hostile word. "Is there any reason why you should be suspicious, wary, afraid, or reluctant to love your wife as she deserves, and as you quite obviously wish to do?"

Drew opened his mouth, shut it, then opened it again, wanting to blacken both of Brummell's all too discerning eyes. But he was too preoccupied with Brummell's question and his own logic to follow through. He had never been wary, afraid, or reluctant where Harry was concerned. Suspicious, yes, when Harry manipulated him, but that hardly counted, since he'd always recognized her manipulations in plenty of time to brace himself for the onslaught. Being married at seventeen had terrified him, but that had to do with his lack of age, a name, and a fortune, with which to support her. Harry had never caused him a moment's doubt, except with regard to her ability to make such a decision without regretting it later.

Now he had her name and his own fortune and the years and experiences that had convinced him that *here* was where he wanted to be. Hadn't that been why he'd fought for life? Wasn't that why he'd have crawled across America to return to her? Wasn't that why he was sleeping in a chair rather than finding comfort at Singletrees?

Was there any reason to deny what he felt and what he wanted?

He arched his brows and met Brummell's smug expression with one of his own. "Not a single one," he said simply, as he brushed past his inquisitor and strode into the stables.

"Not a single one," he repeated under his breath, as he found the horse he'd brought back with him from America, saddled him, and leapt up onto his back.

"Not a bloody damn one," he shouted to the sky, as he galloped across the park land, feeling freer than he'd ever felt in his life.

Drew reined in his horse and stared at Singletrees in the near distance. Once, it had been his home, his haven. Now, the mellow golden stone of the old manor house seemed dingy and grim in the afternoon light, the square towers at each corner lonely and abandoned with no pennants flying, the windows empty and bleak, though he knew the staff was inside continuing with their duties as if the master was not gone. As a cloud dimmed the sun, the place looked too much as it had when he'd first arrived, a frightened boy surrounded by strangers. It looked as it did in his nightmares.

He would gladly trade it for his foster father's life. He would gladly give up all he had acquired to find that it had all been a mistake and Lord Sinclair was simply dozing in his chair in the library.

The warmth and charm were gone as his father was gone. It was no longer a home, but simply an old house echoing with memories of family and better times. Memories he was not yet ready to confront. He wasn't ready to walk inside and face the final realization that his father would never again be there to greet him.

Turning his mount, he headed back toward Saxon Hill, where life bustled—servants humming as they went about their tasks, gardens a riot of color growing on the fringes of control as Harry liked them, the interior worn and comfortable and reflecting the happiness of its inhabitants.

And Harry herself, filling every corner with her scent, her warmth, her sweetness.

He rode into the yard and dismounted, again puzzling over the new addition to the stables, appearing so odd and out of place. Nothing had been added to Saxon Hill in two generations except for the wide portico at the front—a thing for which Harry had begged for years until Drew had envisioned it existing just as she'd described it throughout their childhood.

He handed his horse over to a groom and strode toward the addition.

Chapter 12

❝**D**rew, wait!❞ Harry ran out of her office and halted, clutching her skirts apprehensively, it seemed, as she stared at him in horror. "I must speak with you," she said, as he faced her across the yard.

"Then join me and show me what you have done," he called back.

"No, please don't go in there. It ... isn't ... safe."

The anxiety in her voice alerted him as he glanced from her to the new wing. She didn't want him to go inside; that was clear enough. "In that case you shouldn't accompany me. I'll be out directly." He stared at the sturdy stone walls, then studied the high windows and the boxy shadows on the other side of the glass that looked like crates—

Suspicion narrowed his eyes as he turned back to Harry, noted the way her hand covered her mouth and how her face had paled. "What exactly *have* you done, Harry?"

Her hands fluttered in a helpless gesture.

"Please wait, Drew," she said. "We must talk first."

"I think not," he replied, as he turned and stared at the padlock and chain securing the wide double doors. Crates and locks and high windows, as if the room held valuables to be protected. Like a warehouse. "The keys, madam," he said in a low voice, suspicion growing into a bad feeling in his gut.

"Not until I can explain." Harry set her mouth in a mutinous line.

"You may explain as you unlock the door . . . now, if you please."

As if he had been summoned, Mr. Fellowes emerged from the office with Harry's chatelaine in his hand. "I'll show you around, sir," he called, with a commiserating glance at Harry.

Shaking her head, she held out her hand for the chatelaine. "Thank you, Mr. Fellowes, but I will do it." She took the keys from her secretary and stepped toward Drew, her head high, her pale face without expression. The keys tinkled and the chain rattled as she released the padlock and pushed the heavy doors open. Dust motes danced in the sunbeams filtering through the windows and splintering over crates and burlap sacks that were piled neatly in rows the length of the large room. Every sound echoed as Harry found flint and lit two lanterns, saying nothing.

Drew strolled down the aisles formed by the crates and bags, identifying each and knowing what it held.

"The lumber, tobacco, and foodstuffs are sold immediately," Harry finally said from the doorway. "I keep the artifacts and dry goods until the right price is offered. The cotton is scheduled to go to the looms next week."

"Were you going to send it out in the middle of the night so I would not know?" he asked stiffly. Anger bubbled and threatened to spill over as the full implication of what she had done hit him like a blow from behind.

"I had hoped to tell you at dinner tonight."

"The question is: why didn't you tell me this morning?"

"Because I didn't know how," she admitted quietly. "I still don't know how."

"I've never known you to be at a loss for words, Harry," he said, as he assessed how much was stored in the warehouse, using his memory of the last bill of lading he'd read and trying to curb his temper. The goods in the crates were non perishables that would better serve him by being stored until the market was right for their sale. For years, his ventures had brought him impressive profits. For years, investments made—some suggested by his agents, he'd thought—had increased his wealth.

With Harry's help.

The Messrs. Janes and Holworth were merely a smoke screen for her involvement. Every instruction he'd given over the years had been followed to the letter with embellishments that had amazed him. Harry's embellishments. Harry's management.

"I told you I needed to feel married in one way or another," she said from behind him. "I wanted to help you, to be a part of your life in some way.

I knew I could do a better job of seeing to your interests than someone hired to do it."

He said nothing as he kept his back to her. Too many old feelings were rising to the surface. Too many reminders of why he had gone away in the first place. "You changed the only name I had," he gritted out. "You manipulated me into marriage so you could *give* me everything you owned. You allowed me to believe that I was achieving independence on my own. To believe that I had fashioned my future as I would have it rather than as dictated by others. To believe that I could." He gave a mirthless laugh, the sound hurting him from the inside out. "And all the while you were manipulating every transaction, every farthing spent and gained. Every decision. You did it. I am thirty years of age and I still don't know if I could have done it or not."

"I see little difference in whether it was me or a hired agent," she said quietly. "Why is one acceptable and the other not?"

"Because, damnit, it was not my choice. It was *my* money and *my* ambition and *my* need to accomplish something on my own," he shouted, hearing the words and knowing they sounded churlish and juvenile. Lowering his voice, he held up his hands and took a step back, angry that she stared at him so defiantly, so proudly. "In that at least, madam, I should have had a choice."

"Every major decision was made by you," she said hotly. "I merely carried them out. And when the need arose, I made smaller decisions that any good agent would have made because you weren't here to respond to the situation."

"You aren't an agent, Harry. You're a wife—by your own choice. Wives do not interfere in their husbands' work."

"None of the husbands I know work at all." She crossed her arms over her chest. "But if they did, I wager their wives would most certainly aid them, particularly in areas of common sense. Of course the men would take credit for it. Heaven forbid that the world should have to recognize that women have brains rather than fluff in their heads. One wonders how Queen Elizabeth managed for so long." Angling her head, she regarded him with a cocky smile. "I mucked about in your merchandise and bargained with shopkeepers, yet still managed to be a hostess and do my bit for charity. I sorted and inventoried and watched every penny, yet still managed to gull the men of our society into thinking I was just another fragile being sitting happily on my pedestal. I enjoyed every moment and took great pleasure in aiding you," she said, as her voice lowered to a monotone. "And you needn't worry that my reputation or your position were compromised. I have been the soul of discretion in all my dealings on your behalf. It was rather gratifying to accomplish the forbidden with no one the wiser."

"I congratulate you, then," he said. "One of us should feel gratification in the amassing of a fortune."

"If you do not feel gratification, Drew, it is because you allow your dratted pride to rule your common sense. I do not believe there is a law that prohibits a wife from aiding her husband, or that she should not occupy her time while he is off building his pride to intolerable levels." She poked her finger at him with each sentence she uttered. "There is no law against a man accepting help from those who love him. Only a few hours ago, you demanded that I step aside and allow you to take over and you were quite put out that I refused. If you can logically explain the difference to me, I will gladly listen."

"Can *you* explain the difference, Harry?" He grasped her hand and enfolded it in both of his. "Recall that discussion and tell me why you were so outraged at the idea of me taking over your affairs. And then perhaps you can comprehend how I feel now."

She caught her breath as her eyes widened. "It's not the same," she said, with a tremor in her voice. "I know it isn't, though I'm not clear on why." She pried her hand away and backed away from him. "It will come to me, I'm certain."

She didn't look at all certain of anything. She looked vulnerable and fragile and confused. He didn't like it. Harry had always been clear on the right and wrong of things even if others didn't follow her path of reason. And he didn't like the way his anger was softening with the urge to hold her in his arms and tell her it would be all right. That he understood and forgave her. Unfortunately, he couldn't do that until he knew it would be the truth.

"Harry, I faced you directly with my wish to ease your burden of work and to do my share as your husband. I did not go behind your back. I did not wish to do it to serve myself."

"Well, I did interfere in your business to serve

myself, as well as to help you," she said firmly.
"You were off doing what you wished. Papa
died—quite willingly, I believe—so that he could
be where he wished, with my mother. There was
no one about to see to what I wished except myself. I wished my husband home. I wished not to
be alone. I wished to be useful in ways other than
providing the *ton* with a good party. I wished for
you to be as proud of me as I was of you. I will
not apologize for that, Drew."

"I didn't expect that you would." He turned
away and stared at the crates. "I will have Briggs
see to the disbursement of all this. Please inform
Mr. Fellowes that I would like the ledgers removed to the library for my perusal."

"Thank you, Harry," she said sarcastically.
"Thank you for helping me become a rich man."

"Thank you, Harry, for making me feel quite
useless," he said flatly, and strode down the aisle.

"That, sir, is entirely a state of mind," she retorted. "And it is one which I sought to avoid by
becoming a part of your life in the only way open
to me."

He heard the swish of her skirts and knew she'd
turned toward the entrance. As the door slammed
behind him, he flinched and hung his head, wondering when he had lost control.

The answer presented itself without fanfare. On
the day he'd married Harry and taken her name,
he'd rendered himself vulnerable to all that he'd
loved about her as a friend. The day that he'd ridden away from Saxon Hill, he'd relinquished direct control of his life here. The night he'd
returned home and taken Harry against the dress-

ing room wall, he'd become a husband again, no longer a single entity, but part of a whole who must be concerned with both halves. And the moment he'd fallen in love with his intrepid wife, he'd committed to the vows he'd made a dozen years ago. . . .

For better or worse.

Harriet stalked across the yard from the stables to her office and stormed inside, so furious that everything about her had the tint of red. "Mr. Fellowes, bring me the current ledger for my husband's business, please. I must make a final entry."

Her secretary lurched to his feet and reached for the appropriate book in the same movement. "Final, my lady?"

"Yes. And after I finish, please take all of his ledgers and papers to the library. Mr. Sinclair-Saxon will be using it as his office . . . for the time being." Spreading her skirts, she sat in the chair behind her desk and immediately opened the ledger Mr. Fellowes placed before her. She had to do this now, before she lost her nerve. Now, while she was angry enough to believe it was the right thing to do. She snatched a scrap of paper from a drawer and began calculating figures.

"Shall I do the sums for you, my lady?" Mr. Fellowes asked.

As she scratched out a number and began again, she considered the wisdom of allowing him to do the mathematics and lamented her lack of skill with numbers. It had to be correct and it had to be fair—no more, no less. And she had to do it herself. She pulled out a fresh sheet of foolscap and wrote a few brief lines, sanded it, and set it aside to dry. It would be her final act as his partner—a title to which she had attached great meaning over the years. Now, with one swipe of the quill, she would reduce herself to the status of an employee.

She double-checked her figures and transferred the sum to the ledger page, adding a sweeping flourish for good measure, inserted the foolscap inside and slammed the book shut.

Now, she would have nothing to contemplate but her status as the wife of a pigheaded, prideful man who was not so different from all the other men she knew—men who thought nothing of seeing a common woman plowing a field, but were horrified at the idea of their own wives and daughters dabbling in "men's work." Men who thought nothing of reducing impoverished sisters and aunts and cousins to the drudgery of unpaid servants for the privilege of having a roof over their heads, but berated those same women for wishing to earn a living in the shops.

Blast them all to perdition.

And blast Drew for reducing her pride in her accomplishment to guilt and shame. *Shame!* She had no business feeling such a thing for doing what she'd thought was right. He'd had no business pointing out that she had done exactly what she had rebelled against him doing only hours before.

Sighing, she sat back and glared at the ledger. Drew's point had found its mark. He'd been right. She was as guilty of pride as he was. Now she would have to collect herself sufficiently to reason out the intricacies of yet another element in their relationship . . . as if she hadn't enough confusion already.

Oh, blast.

Chapter 13

The bed linens were like a shroud around her, keeping her from moving. Harriet kicked and struggled against the covers she'd drawn tightly around her out of habit. She'd always needed the illusion of being held as she slept, as if she were not alone.

Awareness dragged her up from the depths of slumber induced by the first sleeping powder she'd ever taken in her life. A sound? Blinking, she focused on the doorway leading into the sitting room and saw nothing, heard nothing.

Since her bosom bow, Lorelei, had married and gone away, she hadn't been able to sleep with the door shut. She needed to see that there was something beyond the loneliness of being in the dark, the silence of having no one nearby, as Lorelei had so often been when she'd visited for months at a time. How desperately she needed Lorelei's no-nonsense approach to life, her attitude of this-is-what-I-am; accept-it-or-stand-aside. She needed someone to jerk her out of this ridiculous state of denial. But her friend had gone on to live her own life. Even Beau had departed shortly after Drew had discovered the warehouse, looking unaccountably pleased with himself as he told her he must leave "to afford you and Drew privacy to sort yourselves out."

She didn't know where to begin to sort herself out. Her family of friends could not help her. She needed to do it herself . . . as soon as she figured out what it was she should do.

Still hearing no sound, she closed her eyes. No doubt she'd been dreaming and her mind was too foggy to distinguish imagination from reality. That's what she got for resorting to a sleeping potion. She'd cursed Drew with every swallow of the concoction Cook had made for her, and cursed herself now for wanting to escape. Drew was the one who liked to escape. She was the one who remained behind. She'd remained behind for the last two days, seeing Drew only from a distance as he rode across the park land or crossed the yard to the warehouse. She knew he'd slept in the chair by the pile of embers she found in the hearth every morning. The servants would certainly never build the fire so generously.

Tonight, he was late getting in.

She might not be justified in resenting him for leaving her twelve years ago—not when he'd warned her of what was to come and she'd accepted it—but she could resent him for leaving her now, even if it was by simple avoidance. How could he so easily ignore the present situation and continue to conduct his life as if no one was involved in it but him? Why should he be able to leave problems behind when she had to live with them and solve them whether she liked it or not?

She caught the corner of her lip between her teeth as she stared at the dim outline of the bracelet she'd removed two days before and placed on her dressing table, loath to tuck it out of sight, or to give it back to Drew. It seemed to glow brighter, though that couldn't be possible with no light for it to catch. Her arm tingled as if the bracelet were still there, comforting in its solid presence, in the centuries it represented and the memories it held.

Her eyes snapped open at the sound of muffled footsteps in the next room. It was Drew, she was certain, though she didn't know why she should think so. She hadn't seen him at all today after he'd ridden out of the yard and spurred his rather odd looking horse toward Singletrees. She'd been agonizing over that, and more than once had turned toward the stables, wanting to ride over in case he needed comfort or someone to talk to or simply to know he was not alone.

How easily she slipped into the role of wife, as if she'd had a dozen years practice . . .

A dozen bloody, blasted, miserable years . . . and two wretchedly miserable days—

Her temper suddenly flared as she threw back the covers, sprang from her bed, shrugged into her robe, and stormed into the sitting room. *First things first*, she told herself. She would take their problems one by one from the beginning and thrust them at him from every corner until they were solved. She would start at the beginning, with the question she really didn't want to ask for fear the answer would not justify her years of waiting.

"What took you so long?" she blurted, then halted abruptly at the sight of him.

Drew glanced up from his sprawl in the same chair he'd occupied the night before, his face shadowed by midnight and the soft glow of the embers burning in the grate. She could think him a phantom come to seduce her if not for his large feet as close to the fire as possible and the blankets covering him from chin to ankles. "I went for a ride," he said simply.

"That is not what I meant and you well know it." Clenching her hands into fists at her sides, she fixed him with a challenging glare. "You wrote that you were returning home three years ago. You are two years late. Where have you been?"

"I wondered when you would ask." His mouth quirked in a wry grin. "You sound very much like a wife, Harry."

She tapped her foot and crossed her arms over her chest. "And as such I have a right to an explanation as to why you did not return when you said you would."

He sighed and sat up, the blankets settling over his lap. "Only if you sit down." He nodded toward the chair opposite him.

She sat down, stiff and straight, in a chair designed for comfortable slouching, and tapped her fingers on the arm.

"I have been in America, first Boston, then Connecticut, then the wilderness beyond the Mississippi River, and even beyond the Missouri River," he said, and then began to elaborate.

With every word he uttered in a weary monotone, Harriet gripped the chair arms more tightly,
breathed more carefully, listened with fear growing beyond bearable proportions. He'd hunted for
beaver and traded with natives. He'd learned to
skin the animals and had been attacked and
wounded by savages. He'd been lost for months
in a land too vast for her to comprehend. He'd
broken a leg and been stranded for the winter in
a horrid thing called a dugout beneath tons of
snow. He'd been found by Mr. Briggs and hauled
over hundreds and hundreds of miles in a litter
dragged by a horse. And then he'd been trapped
by war in a hostile country. He related it all so
simply, so starkly, as if it were nothing.

"You almost died," she said just as starkly, her
flesh cold and her heart racing with panic at what
he didn't say.

"I didn't," he replied with a shrug.

It was the outside of enough how he belittled it
and made it seem so ordinary. "You almost died,"
she repeated, and nearly strangled on the words.
She stared blindly at the blanket covering him and
understood why he huddled so close to the fire,
why he kept it burning so hotly, and why he used
the blanket like a cocoon. Her gaze rose to his face
as she tried not to envision his body stiff and frozen, his face covered with ice—

He smiled, that wonderful smile that had always made everything all right for her, that softened every jest he'd ever made at her expense,
every indignity she'd suffered, from a fall on the
flagstones to the prick of a thorn to the cruelty of
humans. "I had an inkling that you wished the

privilege of seeing to my demise yourself and could not disappoint you."

"Don't . . . joke . . . about . . . it," she said through clenched teeth, as she lurched to her feet and paced the room. "You didn't write to me after you returned to civilization," she accused, to beat down the fear of what had been so close to happening.

"We are at war with America," he reminded her. "What with blockades and privateering, it took us over a year to make our way back to the East, then months more to get to the West Indies. If I hadn't invested in Rutland Shipping, and they hadn't had ties here, I would likely still be cooling my heels in the Colonies."

"The Americans might have killed you," she said, shivering as reality piled upon reality. "What on earth possessed you . . ." she cried, as she rounded on him, "to go to a country where you face death every time you take a step? How could you take such risks with your life?" *And mine,* she wanted to add, but caught herself before the words escaped as she paced faster and faster in agitation. "Was it fun, Drew? Did you enjoy hunting and skinning small animals while your father and I waited and wondered and waited some more? And what did you think while you lay in that . . . that dugout, freezing to death? How proud you must have been to know that you were about to die so that the fops of London could have new hats."

"Contrary to what the pundits claim, death and pride do not coexist."

She rounded on him again, too stunned to speak.

"I thought of the waste, Harry," he said in a near whisper. "I thought that I had gathered wealth and experience and none of it was worth a damn because none of it helped me to survive. I thought of how I'd wasted your years and your dreams just to learn that much, and for a brief moment, I thought I deserved to die. And I thought of all the years I had wasted just to learn that much."

"Waste? All those years a *waste?*" She raised her hand to her mouth, stifling a sob or a shout of anger; she wasn't sure which. She stared down at him, needing to cry, wanting to cry, yet held upright and calm by an anger held paralyzed by the force of its own strength. "I waited for you. Prayed for you. Feared for you. I suffered loneliness and heartbreak, and then, the hardest to bear, disappointment in you. I wondered why you could not see in yourself what we—Papa and I and your father—saw. But Papa had taught me that a goal was worthless and became a regret if not seen through to the end. I used that lesson many times over the years to justify your absence and my tolerance of it."

She lowered her hand and walked stiffly toward him, afraid she would topple if she didn't keep her back perfectly straight. "Not once did any of us think of those years as a waste, or that you were not worth the wait and the loneliness. Yet you tell me that none of it was 'worth a damn.' That you deserved to die." She stood over him, a tear sliding down her cheek as she drew her arm back and forward, wincing at the sound of her palm connecting with his cheek. "*Damn* you,

Drew." She could say no more aloud. Could do nothing but walk back to her room and gently close the door as she silently continued to curse him.

Damn him for not lying so she could continue to be angry with him. Damn him for making her want to hold him and never let him go. Damn him for returning to her a stranger, stronger and wiser and more cynical than the boy who'd left her. A stranger whom she loved so deeply it frightened her.

She had given the boy she'd married her youth. How much more would she be willing to give the man?

Drew prowled the sitting room all night with the blanket draped over his shoulders like a cape. What had she expected? Pretty stories of social adventure in the ballrooms of New York and New Orleans and St. Louis? Would she have preferred hearing that he'd been indulging in masculine pursuits and had simply forgotten about all that waited for him back home? He'd thought long and hard over what to tell her, how much to tell her, torn between not wanting to upset her and needing her to know the truth that he had not chosen to be delayed.

He'd decided that either way, she would be upset, and the truth would at least convince her that he had been unavoidably detained. He'd wanted understanding rather than the horror he'd seen in her eyes. He hadn't expected that she would dwell on what had almost happened.

Obviously, he knew nothing about women.

Dawn came with a blaze of color on the horizon and with it realization. It wouldn't have mattered what he told her. Harry had been angry since her shock had faded at finding him an uninvited guest in her ballroom. She wanted to be angry. And as he reviewed all that she'd said to him since his arrival, he knew that Brummell was right, that she was afraid. Afraid to trust, to believe, to want.

Afraid of him.

He could understand it, since he felt the same way. The force of his reactions to Harry scared the hell out of him. He scared the hell out of himself.

Yet he'd accepted them as fears he could deal with. Fears that convinced him he wasn't frozen inside. Fears that he would make a hash out of his second chance with Harry were more tolerable than the resignation that she didn't want him at all.

He'd returned expecting either black or white—rejection or acceptance. He'd been completely immersed in gray. He'd hoped for a continuation of the friendship he and Harry had shared for so many years during childhood—a nice, safe, comfortable relationship that involved gentler, less demanding emotions of the heart, leaving the soul untouched. But then, he'd returned expecting the same Harry that he'd left behind and found a woman with a woman's needs and a woman's passions and a woman's pain.

A woman who inspired the same needs and passions in him. And there wasn't a damn thing he could do about it except deal with that, too. Somehow.

Odd, that of all the difficulties mounting between them, the only one he could not seem to work through was the matter of her invasion into his business. He'd spent the last two days thinking about it, wrestling with it, and he still couldn't accept it. It didn't matter that he was right because she had been right, too. Stalemate. He found it insupportable to allow her to continue meeting with her tenants when they would surely react as Beale had. He found it downright impossible to accept that his success was not solely his.

Somehow, he and Harry had to turn stalemate into compromise. But since Harry seemed more interested in dwelling on the past, it appeared that it was up to him to force the issue of the future.

He chuckled mirthlessly over the irony of it as he strode to the bell pull and yanked before he lost his nerve.

Chapter 14

Why on earth was she so timid? Harriet wondered, as she glared at the wash of dawn giving way to morning sunshine. If Drew was still in the sitting room, what did it matter? She couldn't remain in her bedchamber forever. Resolutely, she left her bed and shrugged into her dressing gown, then hesitated at the door and whirled back toward her dressing room. If she was going to face him, then she would do it fully dressed. . . .

But then it might indicate her unease. She never took breakfast downstairs unless she had guests, and she never dressed until she was properly refreshed by her favorite hot chocolate and toast with honey. Did Drew know that? Would he care? Perhaps he would still be sleeping and she could sneak past him—

She turned back to the door and then veered into her bathing chamber. She could at least wash her face and clean her teeth, and while she was at it, she really ought to brush her hair.

Leaning over the washstand, she examined her

reflection in the looking glass, searching for spots, never mind that they resurrected only during her time of the month. Anxiety struck with the realization that she might not have another visitation of the "scourge" for nine months.

She dropped her hairbrush into the basin and jumped at the clatter. She couldn't be with child. She just couldn't. Not when she wasn't at all certain that she had a husband who would remain long enough to be a father.

Ridiculous thought. Of course she had a husband. He'd been quite insistent on that, and she'd had little inclination to defy that particular declaration. She just didn't know what to do with him. And she'd always wanted children. If she was increasing, she'd tie Drew up somewhere to keep him from leaving her again. She'd grown up with only one parent, and though her beloved Papa had been wonderful, she'd dreadfully missed having a mother. It hadn't been quite the same, receiving a woman's comfort from Mrs. Simmons or Cook or relying on Lorelei to furnish her with the important details of becoming a woman. No one had ever tucked her in at night unless she had a bad dream and Papa carried her back to her room.

Her stomach rumbled, reminding her that the day would progress whether she liked it or not. Determined to be composed, she again headed for the sitting room, yanking on the bell pull in her bedchamber on the way. Hopefully, her breakfast would not take too long—

She stopped short in the threshold and stumbled forward as her bedchamber door smacked into her back. Pots and plates were set perfectly at opposite sides of a table set up on the small balcony. A vase of daffodils occupied the center. Drew glanced up in the act of pouring coffee into a cup. Rising, he skirted the round table and held out the unoccupied chair.

A flush heated her face at the sight of him in tight doeskins, tall boots, and a white shirt, unbuttoned to the center of his chest, inviting a caress. His long hair was pulled straight back and bound at his neck with a leather thong. She wanted to loosen the thong, to tangle her fingers in his hair as she pulled his head down for her kiss. Panic rattled her at the firm set of his jaw and the narrowing of his eyes as he studied her dove gray brocade robe that hugged her body to the waist and the froth of lace at the neck of her sleeping gown.

"Sit down," he said softly.

She half turned toward her bedchamber.

"Or we can picnic on your bed," he added.

She stood frozen, searching for escape. She couldn't face him yet. Not until they were both fully dressed.

"Sit down, Harry," he ordered. "Now."

She walked to the chair and sat down, averting her gaze from the bronzed flesh on his chest and the snug fit of his breeches.

Drew served her, pouring chocolate into her cup and placing a piece of toast on her plate.

"I'm sorry I struck you," she blurted. It had plagued her all night that she would resort to such a thing, that she could lose her composure so completely.

"I've received worse from a mosquito," he said, with a slant to his mouth. "But I would not advise another attempt. When we skirmished with the Indians, I discovered that my disposition does not react well to physical attacks."

"Did you kill any of them?" she asked with morbid fascination and a need to delay conversation of a more personal nature.

"We discussed the past twelve years last night, Harry," he said as he sat down across from her, partially shielded by the daffodils. "We will not reprise the conversation now."

"When did you become such a bully, Drew?" she asked, discomfited that he seemed to so easily prompt defensiveness in her.

"About the same time you became a coward, I should imagine," he said calmly, then clicked his tongue. "Really, Harry, picking on me when I was too tangled in blankets to defend myself. And then there was the time you knocked me into the brambles. And what of the apples you tossed at me in the orangery?"

The memories softened her mood, tempted her to smile, as he was smiling. But she would not give him the satisfaction after he had ordered her to sit and presumed to choose what she ate. That it was exactly what she ate every morning made it worse. He'd been asking the staff questions about her. Or, worse, he remembered her habits from childhood. It wasn't fair for him to remember. Not when she'd been convinced that he'd forgotten her altogether.

She rubbed the bridge of her nose with her forefinger—a feeble attempt to forestall the headache threatening to besiege her.

"All right, no pleasurable conversation," Drew said, again softly. "We shall instead discuss the decisions I have made . . . after you drink some of your chocolate and eat something. You always were peevish in the morning until you were fed."

Was there nothing he didn't remember? she wondered, on the brink of hysteria. And what decisions? About what . . . or whom? Her mind raced with possibilities. He wished an annulment after all. He was moving to Singletrees and they would conduct their marriage apart. He was leaving again.

"I have no desire to hear about your decisions, Drew. This time they are mine to make."

"Be quiet, Harry," he ordered with a pleasant smile, though she could barely see it through the flowers. Just as well. His smile did terrible things to her resolve to be cautious and methodical in all things pertaining to Drew. "If we continue to address our mutual and individual concerns, one each day, we will still be sorting ourselves out fifty years from now."

Averting her gaze, she reached for her cup and sipped, broke her toast into quarters and nibbled, dawdled over spooning honey before each bite. She didn't want to hear whatever he had to say. She would be either angry, or disappointed, or she would fall on her knees and beg—

The blazes she would. She popped the last quarter of toast in her mouth all at once, quickly washed it down with the last of her chocolate, then sat back in her chair, braced for whatever came. She'd survived twelve years of missing him. This time, she would *live* very nicely without him.

Raising her head to meet his gaze, she saw only bits of him through yellow petals and lush greenery. Good. The less she saw of him the better. He was too handsome, too seductive, too disarming. With Drew it was best to be fully armed with determination and control.

"As I said, I have made some decisions"—he sighed in impatience and slid the vase of daffodils out of the way—"regarding our future together." Holding up his hand, he forestalled anything she might have said.

If she could have said anything with her mind snagged on "our future together."

"We are married because you wished it so. I offered you freedom, which you refused by not seeking an annulment. I was prepared to offer it again, but through our actions, that is no longer an option—"

"You said we could lie," she croaked, barely able to articulate for the rush of memory and sensations from their turbulent reunion in her dressing room. "You said that no one had to know."

"We cannot lie at the moment. And by the time we know if we *can* lie, no one would believe we were not living as man and wife."

"You could live elsewhere—"

"Harry, do hush until I finish. My mind is having enough difficulty keeping a straight line with your knees rubbing mine. I don't need your interruptions as well."

She twisted in her chair, jerking her knees away from his and folding her dressing gown more closely over her lap. Odd, how she'd accepted that small contact without a single thought, as if it were the most natural thing in the world—

Drew leaned forward with his elbows propped on the table. "We are married, Harry, and we shall remain so. I did not spend twelve years shoring up my pride by gathering a fortune for nothing." He shook his head as she opened her mouth to remind him of their disagreement in the warehouse. "I had some demented notion that I should be worthy of you. I saw it through because Father had always taught me that to abandon a goal was to be a failure." Picking up a pot, he poured more chocolate into her cup. "I will not abandon our marriage without trying for the same reason."

"Trying?" She shook her head and attempted to adjust to what she had been so certain he would not say.

"Trying," he said firmly. "And succeeding. I am willing to allow you to dictate the pace at which we proceed. I will not, however, buckle to your every whim."

"I do not have whims—"

"I also will not play the fool to your queen," he continued, as if she hadn't spoken. "It appears that we have been partners for quite some time and must continue to be partners if we are to have peace between us. I expect you to abide by that." Again he held up his hand. "I will not interfere in the affairs of Saxon Hill beyond meeting with the tenants . . . for obvious reasons. You have already had a glimpse of the attitude they will have toward your authority when they know a man is available with whom to deal. If you persist in meeting with them, I will be forced to defend you and I would preserve their goodwill rather than cultivate their resentment.''

"Of course your pride has nothing to do with it,'' she snapped.

"I have pride, Harry. You knew that before we married. I will not be your pet to heel, fetch, and sit. I *will* confer with you on decisions and settlements whenever possible.''

"How kind.'' Her chair toppled over as she rose abruptly, her fists clenched. "I told you yesterday that I will not allow you to take over—''

"When did you become unreasonable, Harry?''

"When waiting did not get things done and no one else was here to do them,'' she shot back. "When I had to learn how to be alone and responsible for every man, woman, and child at Saxon Hill *and* Singletrees.''

He pulled in a long, slow breath and released it in a *whoosh*. "If you do not sit down and listen to me, I will tie you to the chair.'' His voice remained low, but with the grate of anger. "Harry, we have yet to have one conversation that follows a sensible direction to a satisfactory conclusion. We will have one now, and we will finish it, whether you like it or not. Now ... sit ... down ... please.''

He was right, blast him. And Harriet was more ashamed than she'd ever been in her life. She was the one who had diverted each of their conversations into *her* anger, *her* fear, *her* pride, and her attempts to battle them.

Very slowly, she leaned over to right her chair and then sat down.

"I do not know if I am right or wrong, Harry,''

he said on a weary sigh. "I do know that dissension between us will settle nothing. We shared a great many happy moments, and we have had a friendship I have always treasured. Is that not true for you as well?"

She pressed her lips together to keep a sob from escaping. How she wished their past could translate into a future. How badly she wanted it. How terribly afraid she was that it would not be possible when so many years and so many changes divided them.

"Harry, if you cry, I will hold you," he said, his voice husky and gentle. "If I hold you, I will undress you, and you will allow it. If I undress you, I will taste every inch of your body, and you will no doubt repay me in kind. If we are unclothed, we will end up on the floor with me inside you . . . and your abigail or Briggs will no doubt come upon us, bonded together for all time."

Suddenly, her mouth dried and heat quickened in her belly. Her breasts tingled and her skin felt every touch of air. Suddenly, scents became potent, intoxicating. Suddenly, everything else in the universe became insignificant compared to Drew being here, Drew forcing her to listen and to think of the present rather than the past . . . Drew wanting to try to build a future.

He wanted to try. He wanted a future. He wasn't leaving again.

She returned his small, whimsical smile, a rainbow she wanted to chase.

"We will try, Harry, because we have come this far, and because we must, and because we *want* to try."

It was a whisper in the silence of the room. A breath of promise. A beginning they both wanted. She battled back disappointment that he hadn't mentioned love, yet she wondered if she would have believed it, if she was ready to believe it.

"You believe I wish this?" he asked.

That, she did believe, as she stared at him, captivated by the gravity of his expression. Collecting herself and tucking away the passion he so easily aroused in her to make room for more important things, she nodded. "You may be tardy on occasion, but you do not lie, Drew."

He closed his eyes for a brief moment then forced a smile, as if he were weary to the bone. "I've already ordered changes made to the second bedchamber," he said flatly.

"Thank you. It distresses me greatly to see you sleeping in that chair."

"We will meet with the tenants according to your usual schedule."

"We?"

"I said I would conduct the meetings, Harry. I did not forbid you to attend." He slanted his mouth in self-mockery. "I am not experienced in such things, nor am I experienced with handling people. Someone must kick me under the desk when I'm about to cast myself into the briars."

"Please remember you said that," she said with a catch in her voice.

"You may kick me, Harry"—he gave her a small, gentle smile—"but not hard enough to draw blood. You've done quite enough of that already."

She returned his smile, caught by his gaze, enchanted by it, seduced by it. "I will try," she whispered. "I want to try."

Something held her still, staring at him as he stared at her, thinking of his first night home and the images he'd evoked just a few short minutes ago. Unclothed, tasting one another, making love wherever they happened to be. Her lips parted and her fingers stroked the tablecloth. He gripped his cup, snapping off the handle.

Abruptly, he rose and backed up one step, then two. "I wish you would cry, Harry, so I *would* be compelled to hold you." Shaking his head, he turned and strode into the second bedchamber, then emerged, shrugging into his coat.

Harriet sagged back in the chair, fanned herself with her napkin, and wondered how he could behave so coldly at times, yet always generate so much heat.

She sobered as the magic seemed to drift out of the room on his heels, reminding herself that she must be cautious. That she could not be the impulsive girl he remembered. Not in this. After so many years of loneliness and frustration and anger, they both deserved a chance to be happy, but not at the expense of one another.

She'd known he hadn't loved her as she'd loved him when they'd married. What she hadn't known was that she hadn't loved him in that way either. Not then. She'd had no idea of the nature of love between a man and a woman. No idea of how consuming it was, how uncontrollable, how exciting and poignant and painful it was.

She knew now. Perhaps Drew still didn't know, but he cared enough to make the effort to sort out their marriage. He cared enough to want to stay with her. And he seemed to care more about that than he did about what was waiting for him at Singletrees.

Again panic struck her from behind. She should have told him, should have insisted he go to his old home and read his father's papers. But she'd been too afraid that he would somehow know that she had read them, that she had known the truth and hadn't yet told him. But she couldn't. Not yet. Not when they were making the beginning she'd thought never to have. Not until they were more at ease with one another and had learned how to deal with the anger that seemed to come so readily to the surface. Anger as they'd both experienced two days before. Anger that she suspected still simmered in Drew over her interference in his affairs. That he hadn't mentioned it at all while speaking of partnership worried her even as it relieved her. What was there to say unless one or the other of them backed down? She couldn't. She'd explained her motives to him and presented reasonable arguments against his anger. She couldn't apologize when she knew she would do the same thing all over again.

Perhaps she was terribly selfish and spoiled to want to avoid the subject. But she and Drew were all that was left. They had only each other. It was said that for all things there was a season, and the season of the past was gone. Perhaps Drew felt the same way, unwilling to linger in memories of rights and wrongs already done. She hoped so.

She rose and strolled back to her dressing room, praying with all her might that they could be happy with one another. That nothing would come along to spoil it.

Chapter 15

Priscilla sat atop the mail coach and fervently prayed that this journey would soon end. She wished she had not dressed like a servant. Perhaps then the driver would have given her a seat inside. But then if she had dressed in her fine clothing and allowed her hair and face to be fully seen, she surely would have been set upon by some miscreant with an eye for a pretty face. Willie and Drew had taught her a few tricks with which to defend herself, but it would not do at all to draw attention to herself. Besides, struggling with some boor looking for the use of a woman's body might bruise her. And what if her struggles were in vain?

She shuddered at the thought of any man but Drew having her.

What a fool she'd been not to ask directions before taking the coach. If she hadn't caught the wrong one, she would be at Singletrees by now, implementing the first part of her plan.

It had been ridiculously easy to escape the school. She'd left a note for the headmistress, forged in Willie's hand, informing her that he was taking his sister home. No one at school knew that Willie was, in fact, heading in the opposite direction, off to explore antiquities and sleep outside like some aborigine. Staying out of sight until everyone was asleep had been simple as well. She giggled at how she'd sauntered out the front door, bold as brass.

No doubt Drew would be quite happy to have such a clever girl for his wife.

Of course, Lady Saxon was clever, too, but she was not right for Drew. How could she have written such angry letters to him when he'd been struggling for his very life in the wilderness? She hadn't even thought to go after Drew when she'd learned he was missing. Priscilla would have been the first thing he saw when he'd regained consciousness if she could have found a ship's captain to take her to America.

Smoothing her cloak, she smiled smugly. Actually, this was much better. She'd learned so much about Lady Saxon and other things that she could easily manipulate circumstances to hurry the annulment along. Drew would have been furious with her for venturing into the wilderness. Instead, he would be grateful that she would be here to show him how a proper wife behaved.

And every night for the rest of their lives, she and Drew would share a bed and make noises of pleasure all night long.

The bed seemed so large and so empty to Harriet as she stood in the threshold between her dressing room and bedchamber. A few minutes

ago, she could not wait to finish her bath and
crawl between the bed linens, exhausted after a
sleepless night and a day of jumping every time
she heard a sound, thinking it might be Drew.

She'd felt unaccountably shy and awkward in
those moments and then torn between relief and
disappointment when he didn't appear. He'd been
closeted with Briggs in the library all morning,
studying his ledgers, she supposed. Then he'd
spent an inordinate amount of time conferring
with Mr. Fellowes in her office. She should have
joined him then and there, but she'd been reluctant to test the integrity of their agreement so
soon. They'd parted this morning with hope between them. She wanted to give it time to grow
and bloom into conviction. Late in the afternoon,
she'd watched him stroll toward the stables and
exchange words with the stable master while looking over Drew's horse. From the stable master's
gestures, he was quite taken with the beast and its
unusual markings.

Drew seemed so natural in his role as master of
all he surveyed. The servants accepted him immediately. Her secretary appeared to enjoy
Drew's company, if his animated gestures were
any indication. Cook suggested that perhaps they
should change the menu to include some of
Drew's favorite dishes.

Harriet wondered when she'd lost control of her
domain, and had to struggle against resentment
that she could so easily be unseated. This was the
natural order of things, she told herself. As Drew
had said, and Mr. Beale had proven, no one would
deal with a woman when a man was present. She

had to choose her battles very carefully, undertake the ones that were important. Drew would do nothing to harm Saxon Hill or the people dependent upon it. He would listen to her opinions and honor her wishes regarding her people. *Partners*, she recited under her breath. The concept hadn't been nearly so difficult to embrace, or to implement, when she and Drew had been an ocean away from one another.

She'd wanted for so long to have time to do needlework, or sneak into the kitchens to bake, or wander through the gardens in search of a peaceful place to read. If only she'd been able to curb her restlessness, she might have enjoyed having a quiet day all to herself.

Instead, she entered her office to catch up on matters she'd ignored for the past few days, only to find them already done. She'd sneaked into the warehouse to see to having the last few items crated up and sent to various merchants, only to find Drew had already taken care of that, too. In frustration, she'd found a patch of weeds in the garden and yanked each one out by the roots, then sobbed because she knew how they must feel.

It was just as well she and Drew had not crossed paths. She would have likely snarled at him for not thinking to include her in his activities. Tomorrow, she vowed, that would change. If he did not invite her, then she would bloody well invite herself.

But worst of all had been entering the master suite to find the second bedroom changed—a pieced quilt in vibrant colors on the bed, the hangings stripped from the testers, dark blue hangings on the window, a large chair upholstered in blue damask in the corner, and a shaving stand in the dressing room.

She'd snooped without shame at Drew's things—his straight razor and soap, his brushes and collection of leather thongs for his hair, his meager but very fine wardrobe fashioned by one of the best tailors in London, and the single trousers and shirt of buckskin that had definitely seen better days. She couldn't imagine Drew wearing such a crude garment.

None of this was familiar to her, as Drew was not familiar to her.

Sighing, she stared at her bedchamber, feeling as if it, too, had changed, though nothing was different, not a single thing was out of place. It was she who had changed. It had taken only two days and nights for her life to be turned topsy-turvy, two days and nights for her to become unrecognizable to herself.

Two days and nights to become a wife in reality rather than fantasy.

She climbed onto her bed and slipped beneath the covers, turning to her side facing the open doorway. Wrapping the sheet and blanket around her in her usual cocoon, she stared at the moon outside her window.

She started as the door of the sitting room opened and closed with barely a click. Then she lay very still listening to Drew's footsteps crossing the room, heard the French doors to the balcony being closed, saw his shadowed form crossing in front of her doorway.

Holding her breath, she drank her fill of his silhouette in the darkness, then blinked as he struck a flint and lit the candle he held in his hand. The light threw the planes and angles of his face into eerie relief as he stared at the flame without expression.

His head snapped up, as if he'd sensed that she watched him. His gaze locked onto hers as something flickered, for just the barest of moments, in his eyes. Loneliness. Longing. Need.

Her breath quivered in her throat. Her heart reached out to him in her own need. Her body responded to the magnificence of him with moisture and heat and the memory of exquisite sensation.

Only her arm moved as she folded back the covers on the bare side of her bed, continuing to stare at him, saying with silence what she had not the courage to say with words.

He set the candle down on the table by the door and advanced on her, crossing the room slowly, his hands releasing his neckcloth . . . removing his shirt . . . his breeches. . . .

He halted and met her gaze. "Once I share your bed, I will expect to remain," he warned.

She squeezed her eyes shut, waiting for second thoughts to overwhelm impulse, but none came. It was as right as their agreement to try to make things work. Partnership. Marriage. The words sounded so right together, yet few couples she knew would countenance such sharing. "It is a good place to begin," she whispered.

The mattress dipped as he slid beneath the covers and lay still, staring up at the ceiling.

Propped up on one elbow, she leaned over him to tuck the blanket under his chin—

He caught her wrist and held her, watching her in the moonlight pouring through the window. And then he tugged her down to rest her head on his shoulder, holding her close to his side, saying nothing, doing nothing.

She waited until she could wait no more, then tentatively spread her hand over his chest, her fingers ruffling through the mat of hair, following it down. . . .

He grasped her wrist and removed it from his midsection, enfolding it in his. "Harry," he whispered hoarsely, "this, too, is a good place to begin—holding one another, being close, learning to be together."

"Learning not to be alone," she said on a sigh. "It is a shock, isn't it? In many ways I feel as if we have been frozen in the past, unable to finish growing until we settle things between us."

"I've dreamed of it every night for the past twelve years," he confessed. "I did not know what I had left behind until it was too late. I never felt alone with you, Harry. That has not changed."

"Don't, please don't." Tears that seemed always close to the surface in the past two days spilled onto her cheeks, onto his chest. "I am so very afraid, Drew." The words spilled as quickly as her tears, revealing everything to him, stripping her of pride and restraint. "I don't know if I can live up to what you expect of me. I don't know how to be a wife. I don't know how to stand back and allow someone else to manage my life. I'm not at all certain I wish to know."

Again the bed shifted as he scooted up to sit against the headboard, taking her with him, yet not speaking as he stroked her hair and held her so closely she did not know where his heartbeat began and hers ended.

"After the wretched way I've behaved, I wonder if I have grown up at all. I don't know myself. How could you know me?" she said.

"I didn't, remember?"

"That isn't what I mean."

"I'll always know you, Harry—your smile and your laughter, your bright spirit and your warm heart. I was so busy searching for a scrawny girl with spots on her face that I didn't make the connection. But I immediately compared your kindness to what I remembered. No one else had even noticed I was there, much less offered to help."

"Every woman present knew you were there," she said thickly, then peered up at his face. "Why is this so difficult now, after all those years of friendship?"

"We've changed, Harry," he said simply. "Our relationship has changed, become more complex. We want more from life than we did as children. We take less for granted."

She gave a watery giggle. "Yet we still share secrets as we did when we crawled beneath the bushes for privacy."

"It's easier in the dark," he murmured, "to share secrets."

"I still get a spot or two occasionally," she confided.

"I still have a liking for work over leisure."

"I used to stuff tissue paper and handkerchiefs in my bodice."

"I know."

"Oh."

"I still have too much pride."

"I know," she said with a smile against his chest. "Drew?"

"Hmm?"

"I don't want the success of our marriage to be just another goal you've set."

His chest heaved beneath her cheek as his hand began to stroke her arm. "Everything is a goal, Harry. Getting through each day is a goal."

"Sometimes a goal can become a trap, and pride can be the jailer," she said softly. "I think that perhaps sometimes it is better to escape than to wait for it to release you. That is what you meant last night about it being a waste, isn't it? You wanted to escape your ambition, but your pride wouldn't allow it."

He continued to stroke her arm in silence, his thumb brushing her breast, bringing desire slowly to life within her. "No, my pride wouldn't allow it," he said harshly. "You convinced me that my background didn't matter, yet I could not go on as I was. I could not face being dependent on others for the whole of my life. Make no mistake, Harry, I would make the same decisions today, though I would go about it differently."

"Drew, what happened in Ireland? What did you find?" Of course she knew from what she'd read in Lord Sinclair's papers, but she didn't dare tell him that. In any case, she wanted to know how Drew had felt and she could hear that only from Drew. It was important to her that *he* tell her. That he share it all with her.

"It's over, Harry. Let it be."

"But it isn't over, Drew," she said, as she sat up. "You haven't read the letter your father left for you. You don't know what it might reveal."

"Not now, Harry." He pressed her down on her back and rose above her, his hands on either side of her. "This is not the time." Lowering his head, he covered her mouth with his in a slow, thorough exploration. "Not when the present . . . is . . . so . . . much . . . more . . . enticing," he murmured between small nibbles around her lips.

"I thought you wanted just to hold," she gasped, as he kissed her breast through the light muslin of her nightgown, took her nipple into his mouth, wedged his knee between her thighs. "There is holding . . . and there is holding," he said against her, his breath hot on the fabric he had dampened. "And there is tasting."

He released the buttons of her nightgown and slipped it from her shoulders, caressing each bit of flesh bared with lips and tongue.

She tried to do the same with him, but he would not allow it, holding her still as his mouth trailed down her body, baring her one agonizingly slow inch at a time. The nightgown slipped to her hips and farther until he pulled it free and tossed it on the floor. His lips followed to her waist, her stomach, and down, shocking her with the intimacy, stunning her with sensation as he opened her, tasted her. . . .

She melted beneath him, flowed around him, arched her hips to give more, receive more.

He gripped her hips, raised her, drank of her deeply, rendering her mindless, a form with nothing but feeling and heart. Feeling, bursting inside her, radiated beyond her as she trembled inside over and over, her heart bursting with the beauty of it, the sheer giving of it.

She gasped as his hands held her closer, cried out as he took her completion and multiplied it with mouth and hands and breath. Arching, she begged for more even as she thought she could not survive more. He lifted his head to look at her in the waning moonlight, watching her as she sobbed her release, staring at him, letting him see that he had tasted more than her flesh, that he had kissed her soul.

She hadn't known such sharing existed between man and woman—an act of love, surely. An act of cherishing beyond words or description. Shame had no part of it. Doubt did not belong.

His. She was his, had always been his. She could no longer deny it or fight it. Her gaze lowered, saw his arousal hard and demanding between them, ached for him to become a part of her.

She lay beneath his gaze, her legs parted, her lips parted, every bit of her open for his taking. For her taking. He would be hers, for one moment and then another and another.

He loomed over her and lowered his mouth to hers, beginning the magic again. His hands spread enchantment over her breasts as his legs nestled between her thighs, weaving his spell of passion between them, weaving them together.

Pinning her legs to the mattress with his, he

held her still as he slowly—so slowly—entered her, driving her mad, swallowing her urgent cries with his kiss. He withdrew and entered her again, deeper. Over and over again, he tormented her, his mouth tight, the cords of muscle in his neck standing out, his eyes shut against the strain, never filling her completely. And then he left her again, remaining above her, apart from her, staring down at her with bleakness in his eyes, as if doubt held him back . . . or perhaps fear.

She raised her hands to frame his face. "I shouted my love to you once, Drew," she said softly, her voice trembling with need for him, for his understanding, for his acceptance of what she offered. "I don't know how to stop loving you. That, too, is something I don't want to know."

He inhaled sharply and plunged into her, filling her with every thrust, driving her over the edge of forever . . . following her . . . never once letting her go.

The moon dipped beyond the horizon, leaving darkness sprinkled with a thousand stars as she lay beneath him, knowing that no matter what, they belonged to one another. Knowing that forever lasted only one moment at a time.

And one moment was all it took to make a beginning.

Chapter 16

"There, it's finished," Priscilla said, as she watched the blank paper turn to ash. Now Drew and Lady Saxon would think that his letter was gone. Drew would be safe. No one would know the truth.

She still doubted her wisdom in keeping the letter rather than actually destroying it, but she couldn't bring herself to do it. Not something so personal as a letter. It was one thing to read it, but quite another to destroy it. The ashes would be enough to convince Drew that it was burned and that his wife was the culprit.

Priscilla would have to find a safe hiding place for the letter; she might need it in the future, though she couldn't imagine why. Still, it was better not to burn any more bridges than necessary.

She unfolded the will and the letter and marveled over the revelations. According to the will, Drew was heir to a barony in Ireland as well as Singletrees. It was all he needed to know. The rest was not important. The disgrace attached to the truth would serve nothing.

It was right for her to keep it from him—at least, the part that would hurt him and perhaps keep him from taking what he deserved. Drew was too honorable by half. Heaven knew how he might react or what he might do if he knew the whole of it. She sighed at the complexity of it all— layers upon layers of truth, allowing her to strip away the ones Drew needn't know and keep the ones that would benefit him.

She glanced out the window and calculated the hour. The moon had disappeared and all was silent. She had plenty of time to put everything to rights, change her clothing, and make her way to Saxon Hill.

To Drew.

Sighing, she surveyed the library at Singletrees, appreciating the luxury, and the vastness. Beyond, a park land gave way to forest—all part of the estate. She would be so happy here. She could make Drew so happy here. There would be no need to go anywhere else except to London for the Season. Drew would have no trouble finding someone to manage his other holdings.

She chewed her lip as she carefully spilled the ashes from the bowl she'd used back into the box inlaid with ivory and jade, and replaced the copy of Lord Sinclair's will, just where she'd found it beneath the other papers. A nice touch, that. Drew would have to brush away the ashes of the past to find his future.

Their future.

Guilt pricked her at the thought of Lady Saxon, but she quickly shooed it away. If Drew's wife had cared about him, she would have been the one to protect him. She would have been the one to make certain Drew got all that he deserved without exposing him to unnecessary hurt.

It pleased Priscilla to think that her efforts would give Lady Saxon freedom as well. Everyone would be happy, thanks to her.

Sighing with pure bliss, Priscilla tossed her servant's clothing into her valise and donned a lovely gown. She really ought to be wearing a traveling costume, but the morning gown was ever so much prettier. As she struggled with the fastenings she wished that Nanny was here to help her. But Nanny would never understand what she was doing or why. It was best that she'd left a note for Nanny, telling her to take a coach and meet her at Saxon Hill.

Priscilla smoothed down her skirts and ran to the library window, gauging the distance between here and the dark outline of Saxon Hill barely discernible in the distance. How perfectly lovely that there was a road between the two estates. She would collect a bit of dust but would avoid having to tramp through the grass and stain the hem with dew.

Everything had gone in her favor—a sure sign that it was meant to be.

How simple it would be to drift along with life as it was this very moment, Harriet thought, as she watched the sunrise shimmer in the eastern sky through the window opposite her bed. Drew was beside her, perhaps not loving her, but caring enough to remain with her, to want her, to want to build a future with her. To care enough to do what he had last night.

Languor stole through her at the memory of his mouth taking her in such an intimate way. She had discovered the depth of her trust in him to allow it . . . to find such pleasure in it, to be willing to give herself over to him without a single thought of protest or fear.

She'd been convinced then as never before that she hadn't been wrong all those years ago, that she and Drew made a perfect match.

He seemed content to carry her name and live at Saxon Hill. He certainly was in no hurry to go to Singletrees and see what his father had left him. She should let it be, take what she had and hold it tightly.

But what she had was Drew's trust. She could not betray that trust, even with silence. Yet she couldn't help but recall his reaction twelve years ago to her last revelation regarding his origins. She couldn't help but imagine how devastating it had been to him to hear the tales told him in Ireland. He'd never spoken of it with her, but she'd discovered enough by reading Lord Sinclair's papers. Surely the real truth would ease his mind. Surely, it would be easier to bear than what he now believed.

Surely. . . .

Doubt ate away at her resolve to insist he go to Singletrees and discover the truth about himself. Would it hurt him to know? She didn't want him hurt. She'd do anything to prevent it. Yet Drew was more than capable of taking care of himself. More capable than she was, given her behavior since he'd returned. It had been Drew who had ended the nonsense into which her emotions had led her. Drew who had focused on what was important and demanded she do the same.

Beside her, Drew muttered in his sleep and pulled a pillow over his head as someone scratched at the door.

She barely had time to jerk the sheet over her chest before her abigail pushed the door open and entered sideways to accommodate the large tray she carried, then halted abruptly at the sight of a man in her mistress's bed, at the sight of Harriet obviously naked beneath the sheet.

Dear heaven—she had slept the night through without a stitch on. Until now, Harriet hadn't given it any thought. Now, she thought she should blush or something.

"I thought the master had already gone out," Jane stammered. "I was going to return his coffee to the kitchens—"

"Shh, Jane. Please do not wake him." Harriet smiled as she sat up and crossed her legs to make room for the tray.

Jane recovered quickly and carried the tray to the bed, her gaze darting to the magnificent breadth of male back exposed above the covers, then skittering away. She could not leave the room fast enough.

Chuckling at how easy it was to become utterly shameless, Harriet watched Drew clinging to sleep and felt the side of the small pot holding coffee. It was still hot; she could allow Drew to sleep a little while longer.

He lifted one corner of the pillow covering his

head, sniffed, and opened one eye to peer at her.
"Coffee?"

"Yes. Shall I pour?"

"Mmph." He closed his eye again as a smile
crept across his face. "So warm here," he muttered. "Nice."

Warm, though he was barely covered—a far cry
from the way he'd shrouded himself with blankets
in the sitting room. One would almost think that
she was the reason for his warmth.

Feeling unabashedly smug, she prepared his
coffee and held it under his nose, then whisked it
away and grabbed the tray to steady it as he rolled
over and sat up in one fluid movement, resting
his back against the headboard. Silently she
handed him his cup and turned to pour chocolate
for herself.

"Perfect," he said, almost a purr. "Exactly as I
like it."

Holding the pot halfway to her cup, she glanced
at him, bemused by his smile, captured by it, suddenly breathless at the thought that they acted as
if they had done this every morning for the past
twelve years. She had absently noticed how much
sugar and cream he took in his coffee and instinctively remembered, as if it were of great importance.

Draining his cup, Drew leaned over and
plucked a slice of toast off a plate, quartered it,
spread a thin film of honey over a section until
every crumb was covered—exactly as she liked
it—then held it up to her mouth. He, too, had noticed and remembered.

She closed her eyes, bit into it, and savored the

burst of sweetness in her mouth . . . savoring in her heart the exquisite sweetness sharing brought.

Her eyes flew open as he hooked his arm around her and dragged her to his side settling her firmly against him.

"So warm," he murmured in her ear, as he held another bite of toast up to her mouth, then licked the honey from her lips, brushed crumbs away from her breasts, brushing away her covering as well.

How easy it was to be utterly shameless when one was being regarded with such approval . . . and lust. If this continued, they would have neither the time nor the energy to squabble, or disagree, or succumb to boredom.

What a lovely thought. She breathed deeply and caught his hand, holding it against her, then raising it to kiss each of his fingers in turn.

With a low growl, he grasped the tray with one hand and hefted it to the table beside him, setting it down with a plunk and clatter. Before she knew what he was about, he swept her up and over to sit facing him on his lap and bent his head to her breasts, drawing on one nipple, then the other.

Pleasure streaked to her belly and lower. So quickly, she was ready for him, hot and moist and needing. She rose on her knees, slowly lowered herself over his arousal, taking him in slowly, until she was filled with him.

Flattening her hands on his shoulders, she held him back, traced her tongue along his mouth, his jaw, his neck, his chest. He groaned and framed her face, urged her lips up to meet his, took them in a hot, wild kiss that kept rhythm with the rise and fall of their hips, with friction, creating an urgency that would not be denied—

Someone tapped at the door.

Lost to the frenzy of need, Harriet didn't care. The world was here, in this room, in this bed, in this single body they had formed from two, swaying and rocking to a primitive song of hearts pounding, of small cries of pleasure, and flesh joining.

"My lady?" Simmons called and tapped on the wood a bit harder. "We have a problem."

Drew groaned and cursed and stilled, his body becoming limp, no longer filling her so completely.

She sagged against him, suddenly cold. A problem. Simmons would never be so insistent, never say such a thing unless it were absolutely true.

Her breath shuddering with unfulfilled need, she left Drew and reached for her nightgown, wanting to cry out at the emptiness inside her.

Drew rose and jerked on his trousers. "You will not go to the door in that," he muttered, as he set her aside and strode to the door.

Her face burned as she glanced down, realized that the thin embroidered muslin did little to conceal her nakedness.

Drew opened the door only enough to see the butler and exchange a few words with him. He raked his hand through his hair, which hung loose down his back.

Harriet clenched her hands against the urge to smooth it for him, to thread her fingers through the thickness that shone with health and smelled of fine soap. It suited him as it would not suit most men. On Drew, everything looked masculine . . . seductive.

"I will be down as soon as I dress. Do not allow her to leave the salon," he said, and shut the door firmly in Simmons's face.

Her? Harriet shook off her lethargy. "Her?" she asked. "Who?" Belatedly, she wondered why Drew would go down to greet whomever was here.

"When is the school term over?" he asked.

"Priscilla," she said flatly. "How could I have forgotten Miss Priss?" She swept Drew's form, shirtless, his trousers only halfway fastened. "Never mind, I know exactly how." She turned toward her dressing room. "But Priss is never one to be overlooked for long," she said as she yanked a morning gown from a peg. "And to answer your question: the school term is not yet over, so she has no business being here."

"I'll see to her," Drew said.

"We will see to her," Harriet shot back.

"She's just a child, Harry."

"A child, my foot." Stifling an unladylike snort, Harriet rounded on him. "She has been a woman since the day she was born."

"Priss? She's a harmless little bit of a girl."

"Harmless? Watch the footmen around her and tell me how harmless she is with her pouty mouth and seductive form. She is a tart in training if ever I've seen one."

"You must be exaggerating," he said, in a patronizing tone she could not like.

"Priss is the exaggeration," Harriet said, as she swept into her dressing room, unaccountably hurt that Drew did not believe her, that he defended Priscilla to her, when she had put up with the girl to honor his friendship with Priss's family and what she'd thought were Drew's wishes. "With her corsets fashioned to push her breasts so high they almost touch her chin, and her wide-eyed look that disguises a calculating mind"—she raised her voice as she veered into the bathing chamber and paused as she cleaned her teeth— "and her pouty mouth that prompts unacceptable responses in every man who crosses her path. And how she prattles on and on about you, as if you alone had mounted every star in the sky."

"*Priss?*"

Dragging the spring green morning gown over her head, she peered around the doorway. "Really, Drew, you cannot possibly be that naive. Why, one day she was speaking to poor Whitson and touching his chest and he had to turn his back to keep me from seeing his—"

"Really, Harry, that is not a proper thing for a lady to observe, much less mention," he said mockingly.

She glared at him. "I have hardly been a proper lady since you arrived and see no reason for pretense with you," she snapped, wanting to wipe the smirk from his face. "And do not divert this conversation to my behavior. Priscilla is a problem which must be dealt with."

Dressed, she presented her back to him in a silent request for him to button her gown. "And it is perfectly obvious to me that you are not up to it. A child, indeed."

Drew turned her back around to face him. "I

cannot imagine that Priss has changed so much since I last saw her."

"As you and I have not changed since we last saw one another?" Shaking her head, she snatched up her brush and dragged it through her tangled hair. "For your information, I looked as I do now only two years after you left. How long did you say it has been since you last saw Priss?"

He frowned and swiped his hand over the back of his neck, then glowered as his gaze fell on the bracelet lying on her dressing table. "Why did you take it off, Harry?"

She stared helplessly at the band of gold, caught off guard that it should disturb him and not knowing how to explain. "It didn't feel right to wear it just now, Drew. Not until we're both certain. . . ."

"You aren't certain?" he asked in a low, dangerous tone.

"I told you I loved you. I am certain of that. But I wonder if it will be enough. We have so many things to work out, like Priss, and we can never seem to agree . . ." Her voice trailed off as she groped for words and found none to explain how special the bracelet was to her, how it seemed a symbol to her of all her dreams. Dreams that might not come true. Love wasn't always enough, as she'd so recently learned from reading Lord Sinclair's letter to Drew. And passion could not bind them tightly enough to keep their differences from wedging between them.

"I think I should change clothes now," he said without inflection. "I will meet you in the sitting room."

Harriet glared at his back as he left her room, crossed the sitting room, and entered his bedchamber. She'd heard other wives speak of how their husbands escaped being proven wrong by simply finding some other place to be. But she'd smugly thought that *her* Drew would never be so craven or so thick-skulled. Her Drew wouldn't, but apparently Priss's Drew was an entirely different matter.

Chastising herself for blaming Priss, Harriet picked up the bracelet and contemplated putting it back on, but she couldn't. Somehow, that would symbolize capitulation to only one opinion, one way of doing things, rather than a commitment to blending their opposing views into a way that would please them both. She set the bracelet down, confident that she would know when it was right to wear it again.

"Drew!" Priscilla squealed, as she ran across the entry hall, lunged into his arms, and draped herself over him like a weed.

"Priss?" Drew said, staring down at her as if he'd never seen a woman before. He pried her from his chest and held her at arm's length. *"Priss?"*

"And who did you think it would be?" Harriet asked.

"Oh! Lady Saxon. I did not see you standing behind Drew." Stepping back with an apologetic smile, Priss dipped a curtsy, never once removing her adoring gaze from Drew. "It is so good to see you, ma'am."

"Why *are* we seeing you, Priss?" Harriet asked. "The term is not quite over, is it?"

Drew scowled at her over his shoulder.

"No, ma'am, but I'm quite the quickest study at Chatsworth, and when Willie came to see me, I persuaded him to let me leave early. Truly, ma'am, I learned ever so much more from you than at that silly school."

"Where is William?" Drew asked.

"Oh, he left me off in the front and went on," she said vaguely. "You know how anxious he was to get to Hadrian's Wall, and he said something about ancient burial mounds in Ireland and stone circles . . . wherever." She fluttered her arms engagingly. "I'm quite resigned to not seeing him again for months."

The footmen flanking the door held their collective breath, their gazes fastened on the mounds of flesh quivering above Priss's bodice.

Taking pity on the hapless servants, Harriet swept her shawl from her shoulders and wrapped it over Priss's. "Really, Priss, it is too drafty this early in the morning. Shall we go into the sun room?" Leading Priss down the hall, Harriet steered her into a cheery blue and yellow room with windows on three sides.

She looked up as Drew followed them inside, consternation evident in his furrowed brow and thoughtful stare at Priss. Perhaps he saw through Priss's explanation. She heartily hoped so. William dropping her off at the front, indeed. More likely, Priss had come on her own. An enterprising young woman, was Priss.

But it would do no good to comment on it at

this point what with Drew being as gullible as every other man in Priss's path. There was something to be said for wide and pleading blue eyes and oversweetened gushing to raise a man's protective instincts to full mast.

Sighing, she sat at the small breakfast table and thought that even extraordinary men like Drew could be appallingly common when it came to a pretty face and buxom form.

Though she thought Drew was more shocked at the transformation of his "little bit of a girl" than fascinated with her buxom form, Harriet was torn between being peeved and being hurt at how he had disbelieved her earlier.

Being peeved won out.

Chapter 17

"**O**h Drew, please do not be cross with me for leaving school early," Priss said, as she sat on one of the cushioned seats built into the bay windows. I simply could not wait to see you . . . and Lady Saxon, of course. It must be wonderful to be reunited after so many years . . . I know what great friends you were."

Dumbfounded by the physical change in her, Drew stared at Priss as he took the chair across from Harry at the small breakfast table. Changes notwithstanding, he couldn't see what was so objectionable about her. She still prattled endlessly and punctuated every word with a flourish of hands and deliberate flashes of dimples, and she was still blond and a bit too flamboyant in her clothing for his taste. The girl had always been shallow and too full of herself by half, but she was harmless.

A niggle of unease slithered up his spine. Mr. Briggs had never liked Priss and had usually muttered about "trouble brewing" whenever he'd delivered letters at the plantation, and Drew had come to both trust and respect the man who had searched for him and literally hauled him out of the grip of death. Briggs had cared for Drew during his illness with such finesse that it had seemed logical to employ the man as his valet-cum-assistant. At a loss as to what he would do with a valet after so many years of taking care of himself, Drew had told Briggs yesterday to take a month for himself before assuming his duties—thank God. He would have no peace with both him and Harry badgering him about Priss.

Priss—poor girl. He couldn't help but feel sorry for her with Harry tossing questions at her and favoring her with a narrow-eyed stare that plainly stated she thought Priss's replies were suspect—

"And where is Clara?" Harry asked.

Priss's brow knitted in confusion, then cleared. "Oh! You mean Nanny. She is coming along, ma'am. I did so want to ride with Willie—it has been absolutely forever since I've ridden, and Nanny would never get on the back of a horse, so I left her a note instructing her to take a mail coach and meet me here. It was late when Willie and I left, and I didn't want to wake her, you see."

Harry gave an aggrieved sigh and yanked the bell pull. Whitson appeared immediately. "Whitson, please send the coach to Chatsworth to collect Clara Hawkins."

"But I'm certain Clara would have left by now," Priss said. "Willie and I rather dawdled along the way." She smiled sheepishly and shrugged.

Harriet snorted and stared at the ceiling. "Then Whitson will tell the driver to keep watch for the mail coach and if Clara is on it, he will take her off and bring her straight to Saxon Hill."

Priss clasped both of Harry's hands in hers. "Oh, ma'am, you are so kind to my dear Nanny . . . and to me." She beamed an earnest smile at Drew. "You were so naughty, Drew, not writing to your wife about me as you'd promised. She was quite overset at finding me on her doorstep and frightened me half to death. I thought she would surely dispatch me and poor sick Nanny onto the very next ship back to the Indies. Instead, she took me quite firmly in hand and arranged for my schooling straightaway. I absolutely adore shopping with Lady Saxon. She has such a wonderful eye and was quite insistent upon choosing my wardrobe for me."

Drew arched a brow at the plunge in Priss's neckline and glanced at Harry.

His wife rolled her eyes in response. "Apparently my 'eye' was off a bit, since you've obviously altered this gown," she said dryly.

"Oh, but I haven't," Priss said with genuine distress. Her face colored prettily. "I have grown, you see." She lowered her head in apparent chagrin.

"Yes, I do see," Harry replied skeptically as she rose from her chair. "Well, in a few days we shall go to London and see what the modiste can do to make your gowns . . . less constricting. Now, if you will excuse me, I have quite a lot to accomplish today. I'll have Mrs. Simmons show you to your room."

"Please do not trouble her," Priss said as she

stood. "I can find my way—it is the same room, is it not?"

"It is."

Priss skipped daintily to Drew and stood on tip-toe to kiss his cheek. "I am so happy you are well and all in one piece, Drew." She stood back and slid her gaze over him. "You belong in such fine surroundings. You will be such a wonderful master at Singletrees."

Harry paled and stilled, her frown frozen as she stared at Priss. "How did you—"

"Singletrees is not mine, Priss," Drew said at the same time.

"—Know?" Harry finished.

Drew's gaze snapped to Harry.

Priss looked frantically from one to the other. "I just assumed . . . I'm so sorry if I spoke out of turn. Please, Lady Saxon, I do so hate it when I have annoyed you."

Annoyed himself at the behavior of both females in the room, Drew took Priss's arm and steered her into the hall. He knew firsthand how formidable Harry was when irritated and thought it best to get Priss out of range as soon as possible. "You didn't, Priss. Now, be a good girl and go to your room. I'm sure you're weary after riding all the way from school."

He gently pushed Priss out into the hall and firmly shut the door, then turned to his wife as he mentally sorted through several issues at once. Singletrees first and then Priss.

"Judging from your sudden pallor, I assume you have something to tell me."

"I did tell you, Drew. I told you that your father

left papers for you. I suggested only yesterday in my office that you go to Singletrees, and again this morning—''

"You know what is in those papers?"

"I know what is in Lord Sinclair's will, naturally, but the letter is addressed to you." She whirled toward the windows and crossed her arms. "I really think you should read it for yourself."

Was it his imagination, or had Harry hesitated over her reply as if she were choosing her words carefully? Ridiculous. Harry wasn't the devious sort; that was Priss's forte. "Give over, Harry."

"Why don't you want to go to Singletrees?" she asked, without turning. "The will and letter are in Lord Sinclair's inlaid box—you know the one. There are things you should see."

Because he didn't want to go to his childhood home and the emptiness that would greet him without his father's presence. Because guilt still ran high for his not being there when his father died and for all the things he'd meant to say and hadn't. The reasons ran through his mind and remained like so many pieces of lead.

"Is it urgent?"

"I would not presume to specify what might or might not be urgent to you, Drew. But Lord Sinclair was quite adamant that you read the letter. He said it would answer all your questions."

"I have no questions," he said harshly. "But you must have a few to be so insistent."

"On the contrary," she said quickly. "I would as soon discard all questions concerning the past and address the present."

"All right. But since you know what is in the will, I would like you to tell me about it."

She sagged onto the window seat set in the center bay window and clasped her hands together. "Singletrees is not entailed, Drew, and therefore is not included in your cousin's inheritance. That is why Lord Sinclair moved there from his family seat. He wanted to raise you in the place that would always be your home. I still cannot fathom why he didn't tell you long ago."

Drew sank back onto the other window seat and rested his back against the sash. "He would not discuss anything that might lead to the past or raise questions. I was far too inquisitive for his comfort as it was. In light of what I learned in Ireland, I cannot imagine what would have caused him such fear when I spoke of the past. The truth was not pretty, and it hurt to discover it, but he should have known I would survive. I certainly would never have blamed him." He ran his hand down his face. "He never understood that I just wanted to *know*. I didn't need to be taken into the bosom of my long-lost family or any such melodramatic nonsense."

"You truly mean that, don't you?"

"I do."

"Thank heaven," she said, so softly he barely made out the words.

He smiled at the tears shimmering in Harry's eyes. Sweet Harry. She had such a compassionate soul. For that he loved her most of all. "In any event, by the time I discovered the truth, I was thoroughly distracted by the need to build a future for myself and my new bride. I grieved and

I was angry. I even felt sorry for myself. But it didn't last long after I discovered how much time it would take me to realize my objective. All I could think of was returning home and getting on with my life before I was too old to enjoy it."

"So you really have reconciled with the past?" she asked with a tentative quality unlike her. It was also unlike her to seek reassurances already given, though in light of his original reason for leaving her, he supposed she had a right to fear he might do it again. On the other hand, she seemed *too* fearful. If she had been one to keep secrets, he would suspect that she was hiding something from him. But Harry had never been able to dissemble for more than a heartbeat.

"As you once said, Harry: all I need do is look in the mirror to find myself. I am me—stubborn pride and all."

"You are also the owner of Singletrees," she said with a gentle smile. "And it is more profitable than the family seat in Cumbria, which, I might add, should be yours as well as the title. I think it horribly unjust that you cannot inherit."

"Have you become greedy, Harry? Is being a countess not enough for you?"

"I will not dignify that with an answer," she said. "I am incensed that you should dignify it with a question."

He wondered when she had become so sensitive that she could not quickly pick up on a tease? But then, he had been obsessed enough with having his own place in the world that she might be reacting to that.

On the other hand, she had always believed that

the place he had here at Saxon Hill should be enough for any man. As a woman, she had no concept of what a man must do in order to comfortably live with himself.

She rose abruptly and smoothed her skirts. "I really must see to a few things—"

"Not yet," he said, annoyed that she was suddenly so anxious to quit his company. "We still have the matter of Priss to settle." He reached out to hold her back and cursed as someone scratched on the door. "Can nothing be done around here without your attention?"

"I should hope not," she said tartly. "If my attention were not in such demand I should have gone mad long before this."

"Come in," Drew called, resigned to sharing his wife with the whole bloody world . . . for now.

Mr. Briggs entered, hat in hand. A very fine hat, as were his clothes.

"Why, Mr. Briggs," Harry said with delight, as she ran to him and gave him a hug. "I am so happy to see you. I have wanted very badly to thank you for looking after Drew so well and bringing him home safely." She stood back and surveyed his somber suit of good cut. "Please do not tell me you have found employment elsewhere. I won't have it. You cannot leave us."

"No, ma'am. I'm working for Mr. Sinclair-Saxon . . . if it meets with your approval."

She favored Drew with an arch look, then met Briggs's gravity with her own. "My husband's approval is all that is required, Mr. Briggs, though I am pleased."

"Thank you, my lady," he said with a short

bow, then looked up at Drew, his frown enough to curdle milk. "I heard that Miss P—, I mean, Miss Whitmore is here."

Drew nodded. Apparently Briggs's feelings for Priss hadn't improved over time.

"Then, if you don't mind, sir, I'll be starting my new position immediately."

"You're entitled to some time for yourself, Briggs," Drew said, knowing he was fighting a losing battle.

"Well, sir, I'd rather spend my time working than sitting about whittling sticks."

"All right then, report to Mr. Fellowes and ask him to acquaint you with my ledgers so that you may keep them in order for me and put your talent for numbers to work. You will also assist Mr. Fellowes whenever necessary."

"Yes, sir. And I'll keep an eye out, I will," he said to Harry. "Trouble won't be getting by me, it won't. I'll be looking after you both right and proper." With that, he bowed again, turned smartly on his heel, and left the room.

"Drew, I cannot be pleased that you hired an assistant for *my* secretary."

"I hired an assistant for me, Harry. Mr. Fellowes has enough to do with your affairs without seeing to mine as well. Briggs will also act as my valet when I need one."

"Oh. You didn't hire him to take care of my estate business?"

"I wouldn't dare."

"I'm quite happy to hear that you realize that. Now, may we discuss Priss and what we are to do with her?" She said it as if she already had a few ideas as to what to "do" with Priss, none of them pleasant.

"You've sent someone to find William. Until then, we can do nothing but treat her as a guest and perhaps temper her enthusiasm a bit."

"Her *enthusiasm?*"

His mouth tightened as he held on to his patience. "Harry, do you think I do not know what Priss is like? I'm neither blind nor deaf."

"What about: 'I was wrong, Harry,'" she said to the ceiling, as she paced the small room. 'She is not a child. She is not harmless—'"

"No, she is not a child, but I fail to comprehend your belief that she can do harm to anyone but herself. She is spoiled and selfish and a bit too fond of herself, but she is also young and naive and has no choice of where she is sent or to whom her welfare is entrusted."

"She is in love with you," Harry said flatly.

"No," he corrected, "she is infatuated. And you can't possibly be jealous."

"Jealous? Priss is nothing I care to be and has nothing I care to have."

"It isn't like you to overreact in such a way."

"It is exactly like me, Drew. I believe the girl not only is trouble, but means to cause a great deal of it for us. I do not find her amusing, as you seem to. How on earth you cannot see the calculation in her eyes is beyond me."

"You never used to be so uncharitable, Harry." Again unease squirmed up his spine. Harry was neither uncharitable nor judgmental, which raised some questions—most notably why now? Why Priss?

"I prefer to think of it as being cautiously suspicious," she said tightly. "I have discovered that not everything is what it seems." Again she looked uncomfortable, as if there were layers to the conversation to which he was not privy.

"Then why take her in to begin with?"

"Why?" She rounded on him and placed her hands on her hips. "Really, Drew, I do not suffer fools gladly and am beginning to wonder if I must learn in order to live with you. Are all men so ready to jump to the defense of anything in skirts, even if it is a snake?" Holding up her hands, she folded a finger down with every sentence she uttered. "First of all, I took her in to honor a promise I was led to believe you made. Second, I could not turn a young girl and her very ill companion out. Third, I thought having female companionship would be rather nice. Of course, that was complete madness on my part. At the time she seemed a rather shallow young lady whom I might be able to help. It wasn't long before I discovered that she knew far more than I ever want to learn."

He rose and swiped his hand over his face. "Since Hadrian's Wall extends from coast to coast, it will likely take some time to locate William. I would not like to send Priss home with sea battles being fought between Britain and America and privateers operating all along the shipping routes, so either way, she must stay and we must find a way to make the best of it."

"I have just gotten my husband back, Drew. The last thing we need is Priss wedged between us. She does not belong here."

"Blast it, Harry, we are the adults here. And

frankly, I do not understand your speaking of her as if she were a potential criminal. She is obnoxious and selfish and must be kept in check. Surely we can manage that." He winced and struggled to contain the temper obvious in his voice. "She is to be pitied for her lack of proper direction, rather than condemned, and I would like to think that she has a better chance here with you as an example than with complete strangers." He knew he sounded censuring, but Harry's attitude disturbed him far more than Priss's presence. "Harry, you've always seen the best in people and drawn it out of them whether they liked it or not. You've always understood that some things are beyond a person's control. To my knowledge, you've never judged anyone harshly before. It is bad enough to know one doesn't belong without having it pointed out by uncharitable attitudes."

As he spoke, Harry's back stiffened by degrees as she gave him an expressionless stare. "I do not think it is Priss that hasn't a chance here, Drew. It is becoming increasingly clear that I have little chance as well. There are far too many things upon which we cannot agree." With slow, deliberate motions, she twisted her arm from his grip and walked with regal grace from the room.

Drew stared after her and wondered what in bloody hell had happened here. And, more important: why?

Harriet sat curled up on the chaise in her office, doing nothing as she absently listened to Mr. Fellowes and Mr. Briggs discussing this account and that shipment. Everything was slipping away from her—her ability to deal with tricky situations, her sense of accomplishment, her composure.

She felt like a recalcitrant child sent to her room for bad behavior. Except that she didn't think she'd behaved all that badly. Not this time. She had a right to be unhappy that Priss had been thrust on her without anyone considering how she might feel about it. To have Priss defended while she was criticized entitled her to be hurt. And the way Priss had twisted things to make her sound churlish and petty hadn't helped. It seemed to her that Drew had been all too ready to believe she had treated Priss badly. But she hadn't. She had tried to befriend Priss from the beginning. She'd taken her shopping, and Priss had enthusiastically embraced every one of her suggestions for her new wardrobe. She'd even bought Priss a few things that the funds Mrs. Whitmore had sent didn't cover. And when Priss had admired the second bedchamber in the master suite that Lorelei had decorated and wistfully stated that she missed her pretty room at home, Harry had allowed Priss to do what she wished to make the bedchamber assigned to her to her liking.

She hadn't disliked Priss so much as she'd been exasperated by her. What did she know of raising overly stimulated young ladies who thought rules of proper behavior were not for pretty girls? Pretty girls could get away with so much more, Priss had informed her. Sadly, Harriet knew that to be true. Society was so much more indulgent of those with comely faces and feminine curves. It had been amazing how quickly society took to indulging *her* once she'd grown up and filled out a bit.

Drew had always indulged her, even though she had been the homeliest of ducklings. And now he censured her while indulging Priss. It hurt.

It hurt dreadfully.

She wasn't jealous, as Drew had accused her of being; she was frustrated. And she was exceedingly annoyed by how easily Priss could command Drew's tolerance.

She was overreacting. It had to stop.

A great many things had to stop, like her too-sensitive reactions to virtually everything, and her newly formed habit of being wary of Drew just because he had become so much more than the boy she'd loved for so long. Like not facing problems as they arose rather than taking her usual optimistic approach. In that Drew had been right. She really was not herself and it had to stop.

She sat up and began to rise, arrested by the discussion in the small office adjacent to hers. Tilting her head, she listened more carefully.

"Mr. Sinclair-Saxon's accounts are in good order," Mr. Briggs said. "I wonder what he thinks I will do to occupy my time until shipments begin arriving from America again."

"You will be occupied quite nicely," Mr. Fellowes said. "There will be regular shipments from the Indies as well as several European suppliers, and once the war is over, from America as well. Mr. Sinclair-Saxon has excellent agents who regularly purchase goods for import to England." Papers rustled and a chair scraped across a floor. "I admit to some relief that he has freed me to attend solely to my lady's business. I am not overly fond of dealing with merchants.''

Harriet stared down at her lap and shook her head. Drew *had* employed Mr. Briggs to see to his accounts only. He'd *not* taken over her affairs at all. She'd completely misinterpreted his actions.

Again.

She sprang up from the chaise and swept through the inner office on her way to find Drew. Having put her mistakes in proper perspective, she knew what to do to correct them. "Good morning, gentlemen," she said brightly. "Mr. Fellowes, I will be out the rest of the afternoon. Please set any appointments with tenants for next week."

"Mr. Sinclair-Saxon is at the stables with the beast he brought back from America," Mr. Briggs offered, without looking up.

Wonderful. A ride with Drew would be just the thing. They could talk without servants to interrupt them . . . and without a bed to distract them.

Harriet waved her thanks and crossed her office to the outside door, which conveniently faced the courtyard and stables.

A cloud of dust billowed as Drew's magnificent and oddly marked horse emerged through the stable doors carrying the most magnificent and beautifully made man she had ever seen. The stallion was bay with a blanket of white spots on his rump, at least sixteen hands and as aristocratic and restless as his rider.

Drew sat him as if he were an extension of the animal, his shoulders broad in his superfine riding coat and his legs long and sleek in doeskin breeches and tall boots. His dark, thick hair was pulled back, as sleek as the stallion's tail, emphasizing Drew's high cheekbones and beautiful, expressive eyes.

She could only stand and stare as Drew's horse danced skittishly in place, then sideways toward her.

"Enough, Spot," Drew commanded, as the stallion tried to raise its forelegs.

Spot? Harriet looked up at Drew. "Spot?"

He propped his forearm over the pommel and stroked the horse's neck with the other hand. "It seems appropriate."

"I have never seen such an animal."

"He is called an Appaloosa—not a common breed, especially with the bay coloration," he said. "I got him from a Nez Perce Indian in the northwest wilderness of America on our way back east."

"He must have cost the earth," she said, and immediately knew it had been a naive remark by the way his mouth tightened.

"Yes, the price was high. I was attacked by his owner and had to kill him."

"Oh, I'm so sorry." She glanced down at the ground, unable to imagine Drew killing anyone.

"As am I," he said on a heavy sigh. "It was the single most shameful moment of my life. We become animals when we are fighting for survival."

"You defended yourself. If he attacked you, then you had no choice," she said, shuddering at the alternative. "I would have been quite cross with you if you had accepted the alternative."

"I would not have been too pleased, either," he

said, then stared into the distance beyond the gates of Saxon Hill.

"Couldn't you find a crop in the tack room?" she asked, not knowing what else to say.

"It isn't required. Spot responds to knee pressure and voice commands quite nicely. Actually, he's a perfect gentleman when he isn't holding a grudge against me for the long sea voyage. He becomes quite peevish from long bouts of inactivity."

She smiled up at him then, thinking the same could be said for Spot's master.

Drew smiled back as he leaned over and reached out to tuck a stray tendril of hair back into her chignon.

She turned her cheek into his hand, then blinked as one of her graceful Arabians emerged from the stables. . . .

With a very smartly rigged Priss in the saddle.

"Lady Saxon, we were searching for you earlier. We are going on a picnic."

Belatedly, Harriet noticed the bag secured behind Drew's saddle.

"I was in my office," she said, not quite able to look beyond Drew and the way he remained leaned over, smiling at her. "Mr. Briggs seems capable of handling your accounts," she said softly to Drew. "I am sorry I misunderstood your intentions earlier."

"I should have explained more thoroughly." His smile became lazy, contemplative, seductive. "Get into your riding togs, Harry. We will wait for you."

"Oh," Priscilla said in dismay, destroying the

moment. "Cook packed only enough food for two, since we couldn't find you. I suppose I should return to the kitchens and interrupt her preparations for dinner."

"No, do not disturb Cook." Feeling suddenly cold and quite the odd man out, Harriet stepped back. "It would take too long to change and I'm quite done in. Perhaps another time." With a smile that felt pasted on, she turned and walked back to the main house, refusing to look back.

Illogical she might be, but she could not like having to share her husband with anyone only a few days after he had returned to her.

At the sound of hoofbeats on the cobbles, she glanced over her shoulder, not in the least comforted by the sight of the groom following Drew and Priss at a respectful distance.

Uncharitable she might be, but she thought that Priss within sight and hearing was far too close.

Chapter 18

The table was small by most standards, but the distance between them seemed as long to Harriet as Hadrian's Wall with Drew at one end, herself at the other, and Priss sitting halfway between. It struck her as being ironic in a grim sort of way.

"It was glorious," Priss said. "The meadow was ablaze with flowers and the sky was so clear except for some lovely white clouds. I wanted to look for shapes in the clouds, but Drew was rather stuffy about that."

Drew leaned to the side to slant a smile at Harriet, full of memories. How many times had she and Drew lain on their backs in a meadow or in the garden and translated the clouds into images?

She smiled back, clinging to his gaze, sharing the memory, happy beyond reason that he had not created a similar one with Priss—

"Drew's horse is extraordinary," Priss continued. "I can't imagine why he would want to name such a regal beast 'Spot.'"

"It seems appropriate," Harriet said, still smiling at Drew, still caught up in memories meant for two.

"Why is it that I must always look at you around a centerpiece?" he asked. "It's dashed hard on the neck."

Harriet chuckled as she realized he was indeed craning his neck to see her around the urn filled with tall stalks of Iris. "I shall see to it that our centerpieces are not more than twelve inches high from now on," she said, as she motioned to a footman to move the arrangement.

Holding up his hand to stop the footman, Drew rose and picked up his plate. "I have a better idea." He walked to the foot of the table and sat to her right.

Priss stared at them, chewing her lip.

"Come along, Priss," Harriet said, taking pity on her. She started as Drew squeezed her hand under the table.

Whitson stepped forward and took Priss's plate, carrying it to the place at Harriet's left.

Harriet's nose suddenly burned and itched. She raised her forefinger but she was too late, having just enough time to turn her head before she sneezed.

Drew laughed out loud, a hearty sound that filled the dining hall to the rafters. "Your sneezes always did sound like a mouse bark."

Harriet sneezed again, and again, her eyes watering as she gave Drew a look of realization.

"The meadow," they said in unison.

"I don't understand," Priss said with a pout.

"Harry is afflicted every spring and fall with fits of sneezing. It becomes worse when she goes out of doors to the meadow or gardens," Drew explained. "I'm afraid we carried a bit of the meadow back on our clothes. We should have taken the time to change for dinner." With a flourish, he produced a handkerchief from his pocket and leaned forward to dab Harriet's cheeks.

"Of course you understand, Priss," Harriet said with a sniff. "You were here last autumn when I had a similar problem."

"Of course. How could I have forgotten?"

"How, indeed," Harriet said dryly.

"But how ghastly that you cannot share the outdoors with Drew, Lady Saxon. He does so enjoy the fresh air."

"Harry is quite intrepid, Priss. I've yet to see her allow a sneeze or two to stop her."

Harriet felt ghastly. Her eyes were likely red and puffy and any moment now, her nose would embarrass her by dripping, but she could not avert her gaze from Drew, much less excuse herself. She *should* be horrified that he dabbed at her nose next, but she wasn't. Drew had seen her at her worst and at her best and at every state in between.

"You know one another very well, don't you?" Priss asked.

"We have been the best of friends all our lives," Drew replied absently.

A strand of hair fell over Harriet's eye as she sneezed again. Drew smoothed it back into place.

"I should not like marriage to someone with whom I was so familiar," Priss stated. "It would be quite annoying to have my husband know so much about me. I cannot imagine allowing him to see me when I am not at my best."

"Really?" Drew murmured. "I should think that would be even more boring. It is the different layers of a woman that makes her so fascinating, Priss. Too much perfection can be a strain to live up to."

"I shall remember that, Drew, for I intend to be the perfect—I mean the *ideal*—wife. I have concentrated all my efforts on the feminine arts so that my husband will always know where I am and what I am doing and that it is all for him."

"A noble endeavor, I'm sure," Harriet said.

Priss beamed.

"For the right man," Drew added.

Priss frowned and lowered her gaze to her plate, then turned to Harriet. "What a pity the waltz is not permitted in England. Drew is quite good at it. A lovely Viennese gentleman visited us in the islands and taught me how. I taught Drew. He knows exactly how to guide a lady about the floor. It really is a scandalous dance, which makes it all the more delicious."

Harriet sighed, sneezed, and closed her eyes in resignation. She could tolerate only so much of Priss's innuendo before afflicted with the urge to slap her.

"Oh, you poor thing. You look positively wretched," Priss said with a click of her tongue. "Please do not feel you must remain here on my account. In fact, Drew has promised me a game of backgammon. He learned it in Greece and taught me ages ago."

Harriet sneezed again and pushed away from

the table. Enough was enough and she had a great need for Cook's special steam filled with herbs. "Then I will leave you to it. No, do not get up, Drew. I really must see Cook."

"What a terrible pity that she is so afflicted, but then, I suppose such things worsen as one gets older. I do so admire Lady Saxon greatly for bearing up with such dignity. I'm sure I would not want anyone seeing me with reddened eyes and watery nose. . . ."

Older indeed, Harriet thought sourly as she took the shortest route to the kitchens and gave Cook a pleading look, punctuated by a very loud and very unladylike "mouse bark." Within minutes her head was covered with a length of linen as she bent over a pot of steaming water filled with soothing herbs, wishing she could drown Miss Priss in the stuff.

"I must beg off our game, Priss," Drew said, as he finished his meal and rose from the table. "I am quite weary, and—"

"Oh, but you can't!" Priss cried. "You promised."

"I am aware of that, and will be more careful of making such promises in the future."

"It is so early, Drew, and I have not seen you in such a long time."

"Exactly. I am four years older and therefore more susceptible to exhaustion," he said, tongue-in-cheek. "You must remember to allow for age."

"You are not old," she scoffed.

"But I am the same age as my wife and therefore must be considered as feeble as she is," he countered, throwing her own words back into her lap. "I suggest that you retire early also after such a full day. I understand that lack of sleep can age a woman before her time." With a small bow, he strode from the dining room, understanding now why Harry had so much difficulty being polite to Priss. Perhaps another school would teach her the fine art of subtlety. He would have to look into that.

Pausing at the entrance to the kitchen, he leaned against the door frame and grinned at his wife sitting at the table, her towel-covered head bent over a large bowl. "Soaking your head, I see," he said, using the same words he'd used so many times in their childhood. Cook had a talent for herbs and healing and had been taking care of the household illnesses for as long as he could remember.

"Go away," she replied, as she always had. "May I please have more hot water, Cook?"

"You've had quite enough, my lady. I've made you a cup of my medicinal tea to help you sleep."

The tall, gaunt woman picked up a bowl of sliced onions and held it out to Drew. "My lady will need this by her bed to help her breathe, sir. She's already sipped some onion water."

Harriet groaned. "They are offensive. No one will be able to stand being near me."

"Offensive or not, they will help you breathe," Cook said. "You will leave them by your bed, and you will drink my tea."

"Still a tyrant, I see," Drew said, as he pushed away from the door and took the bowl.

"And who else has there been to look after our

poppet with her Papa dying and you jaunting all over the world?"

Drew bussed the woman's cheek. "And what would you have done without your poppet to care for?" Drew countered. The household staff had always been protective of Harry, who had always treated them like favorite aunts and uncles. He'd loved the democratic way Saxon Hill had always been managed and was gratified to know that some things never changed.

"Get on with you, sir. 'Tain't proper."

He chuckled at that and bussed Cook's other cheek before pulling the towel from Harry's head and cupping her elbow to help her up. "Come along, Harry. I'll tuck you up with your onions and spoon-feed you Cook's special tea."

She straightened her back and squared her shoulders. "I am much better and do not require the onions," she said firmly.

"Ain't proper to argue with you my lady," Cook said, "so I'll just sneak them to your bedside after you're asleep. Now leave my kitchen so we can clean it, if you please."

"She will be a good girl, Cook, if I have to hold the onions under her nose all night."

"Who is countess here?" Harriet asked plaintively. "When did I lose control of my own household?"

"The day you were born, my lady," Cook said over her shoulder.

Drew chuckled all the way upstairs to the master suite. He'd heard variations on the same argument most of his life. Harry had never had the patience to take proper care of herself and so her father had given permission to the staff to care for her. Cook had proven to be the bossiest and most knowledgeable of the lot with Simmons, the butler, a close second.

"For an orphan, I seem to have a great many parents," she grumbled.

"It has occurred to me that parents are determined by the room they have in their hearts for us," he admonished. "You and I have benefited greatly from the people whose hearts are ever expanding."

She halted outside the door to their sitting room and peered up at him. "I know. And I am so grateful that you have benefited as well over the years. But really, Drew, they are too presumptuous," she said testily.

"Because you and your father encouraged it." He cupped her chin and tilted her face up to his. "Now you must live with it. Besides, who else would employ them? They are quite as spoiled as you are."

"I couldn't bear to part with a single one of them," she admitted. "And they know it."

"Nor could I. If you dismissed them, I daresay I would exercise my husbandly rights and hire them back again." He turned the latch and pushed open the door. "Jane will have your tea here by the time you are in your nightclothes." Ushering her into her bedchamber, he set the bowl of onions on the table by her bed, then marched her into the dressing room, turned her, and unfastened the back of her gown.

"I can manage from here," she said quickly, her gaze averted, a bright flush staining her cheeks.

Again he cupped her chin and raised her face, examining her closely. She looked a fright, with swollen eyes and red nose and hair damp and limp from the steam. She looked like the Harry he remembered.

Wrapping his arms around her, he hugged her tightly, wishing he never had to let her out of his reach. "Ah, Harry, I have missed you so." His body made it clear that it, too, missed her, though only twelve or so hours had passed since it had enjoyed intimate contact with her. Being in the dressing room didn't help at all as memories of that first night brought him to full alertness in a shockingly short period of time.

"Drew, I can't. I just can't," she said into his shoulder. "I feel so wretched and I smell of onions and I haven't the energy to bathe, much less . . . well, you know."

"I know, Harry," he said, resigned to being noble and sensitive to her plight. "Get into your nightgown. I will be right outside."

"Drew?" she called softly, halting him before he could shut the door. "I want to, but—"

"But you can't, and I won't, Harry," he said, and pulled the door closed before she saw the evidence of how easily he could make a liar of himself.

She emerged within minutes, covered from neck to toe in soft, well-worn cotton, if possible, looking worse than she had moments ago.

"Have you ever been this bad?" he asked, trying to remember all the other times she had suffered the malady.

"A few times," she said, as she rubbed her eyes.

"Please do not worry, Drew. I always get better."

He'd been reminding himself of that very fact since going into the kitchen and hearing how stuffy her voice sounded and how puffy her eyes had become. The physicians had never found anything seriously wrong with her beyond the obvious discomfort. They'd spoken of other such cases, none of them fatal, all of them inexplicable, and approved Cook's concoctions as being as good as any remedy.

He cleared his throat of the fear that had attacked him so suddenly and settled her into bed. Sitting on the edge of the mattress, he picked up the cup of tea Jane had brought in, sniffed it, and grinned. If he was not mistaken, Cook had added brandy to the honey and herb mixture to ensure a good rest. True to his word, he spooned the tea into her, one swallow at a time.

Harry batted weakly at his hands. "I can do it, Drew. I am not an invalid."

"Indulge me. Taking care of you makes me feel as if I am in control, for once."

She sneezed and groaned and looked thoroughly miserable.

He set the cup aside and kissed the dimple in her chin. "Go to sleep, love. I will be in the sitting room if you need me."

"I need you, Drew; I just can't do anything about it."

"Shameless," he said.

"I know, but it is too late to convince you otherwise," she murmured.

"Far too late," he agreed. "Thank God."

She gave him a weak smile. "Please don't sleep

out there," she said, as her eyes drifted shut. "I can still keep you warm. . . ." Her voice trailed off, as she became lost to sleep.

Sighing, he pulled the covers up to her neck and walked softly into the sitting room, thinking he should have a bed put in front of the fire. Better yet, he *could* sleep with Harry as she'd suggested. But being close to Harry and not touching her was a feat he doubted he could manage.

She'd done it again. She'd kept her eyes and ears open and found another way to manipulate circumstance to her own ends.

Priscilla slipped outside and followed the path to the edge of the garden, thankful for the full moon to light her way. How simple, and how convenient. Lady Saxon had an intolerance to nature. It caused no harm, yet rendered her ill and quite pathetic looking.

Perfect.

As Lady Saxon had sneezed through dinner, Priscilla had recalled how she had been similarly afflicted last autumn. It had been worse near the low garden wall, where weeds grew on the other side. Weeds and flowers, of all things! All she had to do was collect a supply, crush them, and sprinkle them where they would do the most good.

What a pity that Lady Saxon was so frail in her health. Priscilla felt quite sorry for her, though she felt sorrier for Drew. He needed someone like her, who rarely took ill and continued to look pretty. He needed someone who could travel with him without needing care every time they admired a patch of flowers.

How noble of Drew to leave to take care of his wife. How loyal. Priscilla could not imagine how Lady Saxon could tell such a wonderful man to go away, as she'd overheard her doing when she'd followed Drew to the kitchens. And whoever heard of giving servants liberty to speak to their masters in such a way? It never failed to shock Priscilla how different it was to have servants rather than slaves.

Still, she wasn't certain she cared for owning people and treating them like cattle. She wouldn't like it at all if she were in that position. Willie hated it and had convinced her long ago that it was wrong. Daddy didn't like it, either, but it was the only way to manage a plantation in the West Indies.

On the other hand, she would be quite happy to be Drew's slave, to a point.

Kneeling on the ground, she plucked weeds from the base of the garden wall, stuffing them into the reticule she'd brought for that purpose. It would take her a while to crush them finely enough not to be noticed, but the effort would be worthwhile.

A pity that Lady Saxon would be so miserable. Priscilla really didn't like to make her suffer, but as she was assured that the malady would not have lasting effects, it was the best way to keep her from intruding while Priscilla proved to Drew how much more suitable she was to be his wife than "Harry."

Why, even the name by which he addressed his wife proved that he had no passion for her. It was a boy's name, for heaven's sake! Certainly not one by which a man would address the woman he loved.

In fact, she would think of Lady Saxon by that name to remind herself that though the lady was kind and admirable in many ways, she was not meant to be married to a passionate man like Drew.

At least, she thought he must be passionate. He had to be. The dreams she had every night of being in his arms seemed too real to be simply a product of her imagination.

Her reticule full, she hooked it over her wrist and silently made her way back into the house and up to her bedchamber. She would stay up all night crushing the weeds with a rock on the hearth and tomorrow an opportunity would surely come for her to put them where they would do the most good.

Sometimes, Priss wondered if fate were an angel sent to guide her.

Chapter 19

〜◦◦〜

The sound reached him as Drew dozed off in the chair by the fire—a dry cough that went on and on and on.

Throwing off his blanket, he grabbed the candle and rushed into Harry's bedchamber to find her propped on her elbow, her body shaking with every cough.

She glanced up and waved him away. "It's nothing—just that blasted tickle in my throat," she croaked. "Really, Drew, I can breathe easily. This cough always plagues me when I sleep."

He yanked on the bell pull, then narrowed his eyes as he examined her face. Her eyes were streaming tears, but they seemed to be less puffy and he hadn't heard her sneeze in quite some time. The cough *was* dry rather than congested. . . . "You have the cough when you are asleep," he said, his mind working ahead. "When you lie down." Striding to her bedside, he gathered all the pillows and plumped each one, layering them behind her. "So you shall sleep sitting up after you have more of Cook's tea."

"Such fuss over nothing, Drew. You know this happens every year and that it is harmless."

"I know. It is an intolerance of some sort," he said, repeating the physician's best guess, hoping to convince himself as he poured water for her, eased her back against the pillows, and tipped the glass up to her lips. He hated it when Harry was rendered so helpless. It was an affront against her vibrant nature.

"A very annoying intolerance," she said with an arched brow, "that I always manage to survive without a lot of fuss and bother."

"I asked you to indulge me. A man likes to feel needed even if he isn't."

She grasped his hand and tugged him down to sit beside her, then caressed his cheek. "I could very easily become accustomed to such fuss and bother from you." She wrinkled her nose. "Those wretched onions. How can you stand to be near me?"

"I like onions. And if you will recall, I became accustomed to their scent a long time ago."

"Next, Cook will be hanging them about my neck on a chain."

"Stop grousing, Harry."

The door to the sitting room opened and Cook barged in, carrying a tray. "Thought this would happen," she said, as she glanced at the bowl on the table and nodded in approval. "Drink this and you'll sleep the rest of the night." Setting the tray down, she favored Drew with a smile. "She's not coughing now. Sitting up: that's the way. Common sense is all it takes. Seen others like her. Always, they recover as if naught happened. Make certain she takes every drop." Without another word, Cook barged out again.

Harry couldn't drink the tea fast enough. "Oh, heavens, this is good." She handed the empty cup back to him. "You didn't play backgammon with Priss after dinner."

"No. I could not ignore the opportunity to bully you."

"Enjoy it while you can," she said, with some of her old pluck. "I have no intention of giving you any more such opportunities. Though it is rather nice being pampered by you, I refuse to go to such lengths to have you to myself."

Sadness descended on Drew and seemed to surround him, darkened by regret.

"Do not, Drew." She combed her fingers through his hair. "Do not for one moment allow guilt for the past years to haunt you. We made our choices. Right or wrong, they cannot be undone. We can only hope to make better ones in future."

"Behave, Harry. It is I who am supposed to comfort you."

"Then hurry up and do so before I recover." She patted the bed beside her and sneezed.

"Much as I would like to join you, I have not yet bathed, and I daresay the meadow lingers in my hair."

"Then by all means, go bathe and then return to me." Already her eyelids were falling as the tea did its work. She smiled drowsily. "If I must reek of onions, then so should you. . . ."

Tucking the blankets around her, he rose and kissed his fingertip, then pressed it to her lips.

"Sweet dreams, Harry," he whispered, and left the room, taking the candle with him.

His hair damp from a bath, Drew shrugged into a robe and snatched the counterpane from his bed on his way to the fire blazing in the sitting room. He was so tired, even the chair looked inviting. He'd briefly considered sleeping in his own bed, but he would not hear Harry from there and the room was cold. Everything without Harry was cold. It was daunting to realize that after spending only one night with her, it had become a way of life to him.

The thought of being dependent upon another person had always been a concept he didn't care to apply to himself.

Yet depending on Harry for companionship and love brought him the first true happiness he'd ever experienced. With Harry, he knew exactly where he belonged and had no desire to be anywhere else. A pity he had not realized it twelve years ago.

Drew awakened at the sound of an intruder approaching and instinctively groped on the floor for his musket. . . .

He breathed deeply and remained still, orienting himself. It was carpet under his hand, not bare wood or grass. He didn't need to keep a loaded firearm within easy reach.

Yet he remained still, surveying all within his sight through eyes open only a slit. . . .

Delicate feet beneath a pink flounced hem.

Harry, in pink ruffles? He lifted his gaze and stared.

Priss . . . *carrying a tray?*

He snapped open his eyes and stared up at her. "What is it? Is something wrong?"

"Of course not," she said with a bright smile. "Jane was on her way up and looked frightfully weary, so I told her I would bring your breakfast. Poor thing. She must have been tending to Lady Saxon all night." She set the tray on the round table and opened the French doors and bustled about arranging plates and cups and saucers. "I took the liberty of dismissing her for the day. I'll be more than happy to look after Lady Saxon."

"You must be joking," he almost said, but bit it back just in time. Priss volunteering to help another was surely a miracle. Perhaps she was maturing, after all.

It wouldn't do to discourage her. It might even impress Harry with tangible proof that her influence on Priss was beneficial.

"I'll look in on her, shall I?" Priss asked.

Drew checked the mantel clock and nodded. Harry had slept the rest of the night through and was likely famished. And while Priss was in Harry's room, he could rush into his dressing room and put on proper clothing.

He would have to speak to Priss about knocking before entering private quarters.

Harriet swam up lazily from a deep sleep, aware that Jane had come in and was fussing about in the dressing room. "Just a dressing gown for now, Jane," she called drowsily. She'd slept so

well and felt so much improved that she wanted
to embrace the world, the sunshine, the flowers in
the garden. Well, perhaps not the garden just yet.

"Of course, my lady," Priss answered as she
swept out of the dressing room and dipped a
curtsy, Harriet's dressing gown over her arm.

"Priss?" Harriet said. 'What on earth?"

"I have fetched up your breakfast and set the
table just as you taught me. I have also told Jane
that I will take care of you today. She looked quite
frazzled from sitting with you all night."

"Jane told you that?" Harriet asked, completely
undone by Priss's uncharacteristic act of sponta-
neous kindness.

"Oh, no, but from her fatigue it was quite obvious that she must have sat up with you. You
once said that the best way to understand what
was reasonable to expect from a servant was to
observe that servant going about his duties for a
week. I thought it would be even more effective
to perform Jane's duties for a day."

Priss looked so pleased with herself that Harriet
could not tell her that Jane's fatigue was from
spending her free day helping her sister, who was
expecting her seventh child. "That is very indus-
trious of you, I'm sure," Harriet murmured, as she
slipped into her robe and buttoned the fitted bodice. "But you needn't go so far. I've done without
Jane before and can manage nicely on my own. I
have no doubt I can extend my self-sufficiency to
serving breakfast for Drew and myself."

"Oh!" Distress widened Priss's eyes just before
she stared down at her feet. "I suppose I have
committed a terrible gaffe. I assumed you would

want to remain abed and I brought up my own breakfast so I could keep Drew company. The dining room is so huge I just couldn't bear to sit in there alone. But of course, you don't want me intruding. I'll go and remove my meal and take it to my room. . . .''

"Don't be silly, Priss," Harriet interrupted, before Priss found a few more ways to evoke sympathy. "You will be welcome to share breakfast with us . . . *this morning.* It wouldn't do as a rule, since Drew and I rise early and employ that time to go over our plans for the day," she added for good measure . . . just in case. Priss like this was quite pleasant, but the girl was not someone Harriet wished to wake up to on a daily basis.

Heaven forbid Priss would walk in on her and Drew as they had been yesterday morning.

"Really? Oh, thank you, Lady Saxon." She frowned. "I don't suppose there is something else I can call you? Lady Saxon is so very formal, and you seem like family to me."

Harriet had immediate visions of Priss calling her "Auntie Harriet" and almost choked. "Harriet will do, Priss."

Priss beamed, appearing so happy that Harriet thought there might be hope for her yet. "Now, shall we join Drew?"

"You go on ma—Harriet. I want to straighten your bed linens first."

Dumbfounded by Priss's behavior, Harriet decided to leave well enough alone and nodded to Priss on her way into the sitting room. Perhaps performing these small duties would instill a little humility in her.

Drew emerged from the opposite bedchamber at the same time, pausing in shrugging on his coat to examine her with his gaze. "You're better," he stated.

"Much." She stared at him—so handsome with his strong, chiseled features and body that was wide and narrow in all the right places.

Why, oh why, had she given Priss permission to remain?

Drew stepped toward her with seduction in his eyes. "Always wear your hair down, Harry. And wear nothing else."

She trembled with desire and locked her knees to keep from burrowing in his arms. "We have a guest for breakfast," she said softly, regretfully. "Priss is straightening my bed linens."

"She is what?" He shook his head and chuckled. "The mind boggles."

"Hush. You might jinx it," she whispered conspiratorially. "Thank heaven I am well and will not require her attentions today. I don't know which is more nerve wracking—Priss being obnoxious, which is natural and expected, or Priss being solicitous, which is almost frightening."

Drew stifled a laugh as Priss entered the sitting room and stood with her hands behind her back, her head bent.

"I could not help but overhear. I'm terribly sorry I have been such a trial to you. I don't mean to be."

Drew walked over to her and took her arm, leading her to the table and seating her. "I seem to recall another young lady, once upon a time, who was rather spoiled," he said with a wink at

Harriet, easing her own sudden guilt. She might not care much for Priss's behavior at times, but she didn't wish to hurt her, either.

Waiting her turn to be seated, Harriet tried to take umbrage at his remark, but laughed instead. "Yes, I was rather a horror, wasn't I?" A sudden itch struck her on her back.

"Not a horror, just young and cocky, as we all were at Priss's age," Drew said. "I was so certain I could go off and conquer the world, and you were positive that you knew what was best for everyone. In fact, you still—"

"That is quite enough, Drew," she said with good nature, as she shifted, rubbing her back against the chair in an effort to relieve the itch.

"I know I am terribly spoiled," Priss said, staring down at her plate. "But it wasn't something I asked for, was it? And now that I am grown, I am trying to improve." Raising her head, she defiantly met each of their gazes in turn. "But I really think you should give me some credit. I am not useless, nor am I lazy. Mummy insisted I do chores, like making beds and caring for my own clothing, and learning to cook. She said there might come a day when I would thank her for teaching me to be self-sufficient. She said that one could never predict what course one's life might take and comfort and luxury should never be taken for granted. She and Daddy were once very poor, you know."

"I didn't know, Priss," Drew said softly.

Harriet leaned forward and covered Priss's hand with her own. "You're quite right, Priss. We should give you more credit." Removing her hand from Priss's, she scraped her forearm along the edge of the table to relieve another sudden itch. "I suppose that adults are as prone to thinking they know everything as adolescents. Please forgive me." She deliberately brushed her napkin to the floor, bent to pick it up, and scratched her instep, then her calf and a spot on her waist on the way back up.

"Well, of course I will," Priss said with a timid smile. "I just hope that you will continue to be patient with me and forgive me for anything I might do wrong."

Harriet frowned and glanced at Drew, wondering if there wasn't something odd about Priss's wording. And then she sneezed. Her eyes watered and her arms began to itch in earnest. Lowering her hands to her lap, she began to furiously scratch both arms at once.

Drew scowled as she again sneezed. "The effects of the tea must be wearing off. Where are your onions?"

"I refuse to have those ghastly things at the breakfast table. I'm fine, Drew. Stop fussing." She sneezed twice in rapid succession and tried to disguise scratching her neck by appearing to push her hair back.

Drew shot up from his chair and shut the French doors, then circled the table to lean over her and pull her hands away from her neck. "Good God, Harry," he said, as he pushed up her sleeves and stared at her arms.

Priss, too, shot up and stared in horror at the red raised welts spreading over Harriet's arms and chest and neck and even her face.

"Not again," Harriet moaned, as she lifted her hem and stared at her calves. The welts were itching so badly they burned.

"What is it?" Priss asked, looking genuinely afraid. It's happened before?"

"The spring I was thirteen and the flowers had run riot. Everything bloomed at once . . . oh, heaven help me," she cried, as the itching became unbearable and the sneezes more frequent.

"Priss, run down and tell Cook what has happened. She will know what to do."

"Does it hurt?" Priss asked.

"Yes," Harriet said through gritted teeth.

"You haven't by any chance fallen into the brambles while chasing a rainbow, have you?" Drew asked, every line of his face tight.

Harriet gave him a pained smile and rubbed her back against the chair, then wiggled her backside on the seat for relief. "I have been waiting for you to chase them with me," she said softly, in spite of her misery. Did he remember everything?

"Damnit, Priss, find Cook . . . now!" he roared.

Priss started and reached out for Harriet. "Yes, I will . . . please forgive me . . . I am so very sorry." Whirling, she ran out into the hall.

Drew cupped her elbow gently and helped her to rise, then guided her into her bedroom. She looked at the carpet longingly, wanting nothing so much as to strip and roll about on the wool like a cat scratching her back. She knew that until she bathed in Cook's herbs and had Cook's special paste slathered all over her, she would not even be able to bear lying down.

*   *   *

"Why bloody now?" Harriet groaned as she lay on her stomach while Cook applied her concoction to the rash. "It will be at least a week of being shut up in the room while the rest of the bloody world passes by."

"Mind your mouth, my lady," Cook admonished.

"Why should I? There's none here to hear me but you, and I learned most of these words by listening to you curse when your dough failed."

"Do you want your husband to hear you cursing?"

"He isn't here and I don't want him here. I look grotesque. Why should he want to be here?"

"He's seen you with your hair straight and stringy and pulled tight in braids and your body looking like naught so much as a door and spots blooming all over your face. Seems to me he wouldn't mind seeing you now."

"Thank you so much for reminding me," Harriet said. "For three days Drew has seen me looking as I always wanted to look for him, and now this."

The pressure of the hands at her back changed.

"You were beautiful to me even then, Harry," a deep voice said, as the hands stroked magic over her. "Spots and all."

She twisted to frown up at him. "You are unkind, Drew."

He smiled and flattened his hand between her shoulder blades to press her back down and hold her still. "You were beautiful to me when I returned, even though I was disappointed that you had changed," he continued, as if she had not spoken, "with your body so sleek and feminine and expressive, your hair like soft ash clouds burnished by sunlight, your complexion clear and soft as a pearl. And you are beautiful to me now, with your hair caught up to expose your neck and your body vibrant beneath my hands and the rash on your flesh that reminds me that you are like the rest of us—vulnerable and needing approval. That you are strong from within and sometimes are weary of being strong." His hands applied the soothing paste to her calves and her hips and over her waist, the sides of her breasts and over her shoulders, her neck. "I have never seen you as anything but beautiful." She felt his breath on her ear, felt his words more than heard them. "I will never see you as anything but beautiful because I see you with something other than my eyes."

Harriet lay still and quiet, captivated by the spell he cast over her with his words. Words she'd wanted so badly to hear for so many years—from Drew. Only from Drew. One would almost think he was in love with her. If she were not so miserably ill, and he so sympathetic, she might have allowed herself to believe it.

His teeth gently nipped her ear—the only place not covered with rash. "Red quite becomes you," he whispered with a grin in his voice. "Though I would not recommend that you wear a red gown, for we would surely not be able to tell where your clothing ended and you began."

She knew he left the room, felt his absence, felt Cook's hands once again dabbing the last of her concoction on the bottom of her feet. She heard a sniff and raised her head to peer up at Cook, see-ing moisture gathering in her eyes.

"Don't you do it, poppet. Don't you spoil the sweetest thing this old crow ever saw or ever heard."

Harriet lowered her head back down to the pil-low and closed her eyes as tears caressed her cheek as sweetly as Drew's whispered words that still lingered in the air.

Chapter 20

Five days of agony, being shut away, unable to venture out for fear something else would further stimulate her illness. Five days of finding momentary relief from Cook's herbs and then feeling them wear off, leaving her vulnerable again to the rash that was driving her mad. Drew might very well like her vulnerability, but she much preferred meeting life head-on rather than pacing a stuffy, closed-up room that reeked of onions.

Oddly enough, she felt better pacing. Every time she lay in bed, her condition worsened. Every time she put on clothes it was the same. Of course, she had to lock her door, and, for good measure, prop a chair against it to keep anyone from walking in on her wearing nothing but red welts and frustration. Aside from that, she needed respite from Priss, who hovered about her with a constant look of anxiety, as if she feared Harriet was about to die and kept murmuring apologies with tears in her eyes. Could the girl do nothing in moderation?

Priss's apologies and hovering concern struck

her as exceedingly odd. Yet the concern did not keep Priss from hanging about Drew at every opportunity. Every time Harriet looked out the window, she saw Drew and his voluptuous shadow riding or walking toward the office or warehouse.

She couldn't complain about Drew. Other than his extreme tolerance for their charge, he had been the model of an attentive husband, visiting her whenever she would allow it, reading to her or regaling her with some of the more entertaining accounts of his travels. He'd insisted upon calling in the physician, merely to hear the same explanations she had heard all her life. People so afflicted always recovered. It appeared to be seasonal. There was nothing to do but wait it out. In spite of her discomfort, her worst complaint was that Drew could not share her bed, for even if he brushed against her in sleep, it irritated the rash.

Harriet was tired of waiting, tired of sleeping alone while the crick in Drew's neck became worse from his sleeping in the chair. She'd suggested bringing a bed into the sitting room for him but he refused, insisting that she would be recovered soon.

She stood to the side of the window, where she could see without being seen, to study the garden again, searching for clues. But this spring was no different from any other ordinary spring. The flora bloomed on schedule and shed on schedule—nothing extraordinary like the year she was thirteen, when winter had moved on unusually early and warm rains had encouraged the flowers and the weeds to run riot.

Contrarily, it made no sense that nature itself would cause her affliction, yet it was the only explanation that did make sense.

She leaned forward as someone entered the garden and walked along the path, casting furtive looks over her shoulder. Priss. No one else led with her chest as Priss did. Why on earth was she carrying a reticule? Why was she darting from bush to bush?

Harriet watched as Priss seemed to slink to the garden wall, glance about again, and open her reticule, holding it upside down to empty its contents. What appeared to be a fine powder streamed out and drifted to the ground on the other side of the stone wall.

Harriet stared at her bed, at the linens that had been changed daily, a practice that had helped for precious minutes, but then the plaguey itching would return along with everything else.

Again, she glanced at the bed and then her dressing room as an idea squirmed impatiently in her mind.

Suspicion led her to the bed, to strip the linens and run her hands over the mattress tick. She sneezed, wiped her eyes and leaned closer. There, all over the mattress, were minute spots and a slightly gritty texture. What on earth? She buried her nose in the mattress and sneezed over and over again.

She ran to the small desk set against the far wall and searched for a lorgnette she kept for difficult-to-read letters, then back to the bed to examine the spots more closely. They looked like crushed bits of something.

Stronger suspicion prompted her to spread a sheet out on the floor, then carried her into her dressing room to pull out all visible clothing and shake out each piece of fabric. Small bits of green and brown and fuzzy bits of what appeared to be dandelion fuzz drifted to the sheet and through the air. The stuff was everywhere.

Stalking to the bell pull, she yanked hard and kept yanking until Jane and Cook pounded on her door, demanding to be let in.

Rummaging through her closet, Harriet opened a package that had arrived from the modiste and shook out a velvet dressing gown she had ordered for fall and pulled it on, then pushed the chair aside and jerked open the door.

Cook stormed in, followed by Jane, and gave her a startled glance as Harriet slammed the door shut and locked it again.

"Listen to me carefully. And don't you dare think me demented for what I am about to suggest. I am positive I know what is wrong and what must be done. And you are not to breathe a word." She fixed each woman with a warning look. "I will handle the rest of it in my own way."

But neither Cook nor her abigail thought her demented as they listened and nodded thoughtfully and took over in short order.

By nightfall her mattress had been replaced with another and all her clothing taken below stairs to be shaken, cleaned, and thoroughly brushed. Linens were washed and boiled. Everything was dried on lines hung in the ballroom.

By morning, Harriet felt some relief. By the next day, the rash began to fade.

Her anger did not.

Four days after her room and belongings had been dusted, cleaned, brushed—even the carpet had been beaten—Harriet looked close enough to normal to make an appearance. It had been a testament to Cook's and Jane's loyalty that they had managed most of the cleaning with a minimum of fuss. The beating of the rug was explained as a precaution against the master tracking in grass during his frequent visits to his wife.

Priss arrived at the same time she did every morning, with Harriet's chocolate and toast, and a ridiculously dramatic amount of solicitude. Ridiculous, that is, if one was not guilty of anything.

Priss halted abruptly at the sight of Harriet fully dressed and considerably improved. "Oh! You're so much better," she exclaimed, with a relief that was obvious.

At least the girl seemed to have a conscience, though what paths of logic it took, Harriet didn't care to guess.

"I am all but fully recovered," Harriet said, as she took the tray from Priss and set it on the bed. "Come sit with me."

Priss fairly bounced to the bed and sat down, spreading her skirts as if every bachelor in England were there to observe and admire. "How wonderful! I am so pleased to see you well! I never dreamed anyone could suffer so from a harmless malady."

"I pray that you never have to experience it firsthand, Priss," Harriet said, unsure of her own sincerity.

"I truly did wish it was me instead of you, ma'am. Truly I did. I felt so horrid about it all."

"Well, as you can see, I am none the worse for it and learned a valuable lesson as well."

"I can't imagine what one could learn from such a wretched experience," Priss said, as she accepted a cup of chocolate from Harriet.

Harriet took her time pouring her own chocolate and taking a sip. "I learned to examine my bed linens and clothing and have them all thoroughly cleaned of particles that found their way even onto my mattress under the sheets."

Priss's face paled and her hands shook.

"I also learned that I must be more careful about whom I allow to straighten my bed and venture into my dressing room."

Priss's cup clattered in her hand and tipped over, spilling chocolate all over her pretty yellow frock.

Harriet ignored it as Priss stared dumbly down at the brown stain spreading over the muslin. "From now on, I shall beware of mischief makers."

Priss's mouth trembled as she opened and shut it.

"So you see, Priss, even unpleasant things can turn out to be beneficial in one way or another."

"I'm so sorry," Priss choked out. "I didn't know how ill you would become. If I had, I would never have—"

"I do believe that, Priss." Harriet struggled against pity for the girl. "But you should consider that if you must resort to such tactics to gain attention, then you might receive the wrong sort of attention."

Priss lowered her head into her hands and sobbed, the cup and saucer still toppled on her skirt. "I didn't mean to cause you pain. I like you and admire you so immensely. I just—"

"Priss," Harry said gently, "can you not trust in what you are and who you are rather than in your schemes?"

"I'm horrid for what I did to you. Horrid! How can I trust that?"

"There is goodness in you, Priss. Your remorse and your guilt prove it. You simply must learn that you cannot always have what you want and that if you have to take it, you will not have the pleasure in it that would come if it was given to you."

Priss wiped her eyes with the backs of her hands and gave Harriet a watery smile. "I will try to remember that, ma'am. And I will never, ever again do anything that will physically hurt another. I couldn't bear it if I hurt another again."

Harriet didn't like the sound of that and had a bad feeling that Priss would turn her imagination to what she considered less harmless forms of manipulation. "You're a very bright young lady, Priss. I hope you realize that people will conduct their lives as they see fit rather than how you wish them to, and learn to use your talents in better, kinder ways."

"I will. I promise I will." She chewed the corner of her lip. "I want nothing but for you and Drew to be happy and for you both to have all that you deserve."

On the surface, it sounded quite lovely, yet again Harriet suspected her interpretation and Priss's meaning were two entirely different things. Unfortunately, she'd had time to think over the past few days of her recovery and realized that the very qualities in Priss that annoyed her were uncomfortably close to qualities she had misused in her own youth. With that discovery had come a certain sympathy and fellow feeling for Priss that was as unwelcome as it was unexpected. In some ways, she saw herself in Priss—beneath the pretty face and blond curls and voluptuous figure, of course.

"Then we shall speak no more about it," she said on a sigh.

"Has . . . does Drew know how—why—you have recovered?" Priss asked, as she carefully removed the cup and saucer from her lap as if she would spare her already ruined gown another drop of chocolate.

"I see no reason to bore him with the details. I daresay he is too relieved knowing that I will soon be fit enough to help with the tenants to ask. I've seen a steady stream coming and going from my office over the past week."

"Oh! But he has been quite wonderful with them. As you did last year, he allowed me to observe. He is so wise and strong and they respect him and seem relieved to have a man to deal with—" She frowned and dipped her head. "I suppose I should not have said that. It was unkind."

"Unfortunately, our society sees wisdom from a woman as idiocy while seeing idiocy from a man as wisdom. Fortunately, Drew is wise and kind and I'm certain our tenants appreciate having a fair man looking out for them." Harriet waited for resentment at so easily being replaced to bare its fangs and bite her, but nothing happened. She waited for the urgency to take up the reins of control to grip and shake her, but that didn't happen, either.

Instead, she knew she was smiling, pleased that Drew had immediately been accepted. That he fit in without trying. He'd never felt as if he'd fit in anywhere. Perhaps now he would realize he belonged here. That this was truly home and here was his real family, regardless of blood and names and the lack of marriage vows between the people who sired him. Here were the homes—Singletrees and Saxon Hill—and the people who had nurtured him and loved him and encouraged him to be the extraordinary man he was—

"I should go now," Priss said tentatively, "and change my gown."

She nodded absently as Priss slipped from the room, holding her sodden skirts away from her legs.

"Priss," she called out, stopping her halfway across the sitting room, "I think we should go into London next week to order some new gowns for you."

"Really?" Priss squealed, and ran back to hug Harriet and kiss her cheek. "Oh, thank you ma'am. Thank you for everything!"

Harriet shook her head in exasperation and shuddered with the thought of how easily one could become trapped by one's own manipulations. How easily one could begin to believe in one's own illusions.

How kind and understanding of Harriet to forgive Priscilla for her mistake. If she had known what suffering her actions would cause Harriet, she never would have done it. If she could have managed it, she would have rid Harriet's room and clothing of the powder herself. She'd tried to think of a way to undo the damage she'd caused, but cleverness had failed her.

Never in her life had she been so frightened. She'd been convinced that she had surely consigned Harriet to a slow death, despite Drew's and Cook's assurances that this had happened before and was essentially harmless. It hadn't looked harmless at all.

She had cried every night for causing Harriet such misery.

Harriet was really quite amazing, Priscilla thought, as she removed her stained gown and chose another. She hadn't been wrong to like her so much. She could understand why Drew liked her so much.

But liking wasn't loving, she reminded herself. Of course Harriet and Drew were friends. They had grown up together, which proved her point. People who knew so much about one another could not possibly be excited by each other. Mummy and Daddy were a perfect example. They, too, had grown up as friends. And ever since Priscilla could remember, they'd drifted through their days without surprises or excitement and seemed quite bored with it all. Daddy kissed Mummy with a peck and Mummy often didn't even react. Sometimes Mummy hugged Daddy and he was too distracted to notice. Of course there were the sounds from their bedchamber at night, but from what Priscilla had heard from the more common girls at school, anyone could do that—no love required. She'd also heard that when love was present, the experience was quite incredible. Quite special.

It would be special between her and Drew; she just knew it.

But if she soon didn't find a way to prove it to him, she might lose her chance. Drew was settling in much more easily than she'd anticipated. He seemed in no hurry to return to Singletrees or to read the papers his father had left for him. Of course, after his harrowing experiences in the American wilderness, she supposed he would welcome a peaceful respite.

But it wouldn't last, she was certain. Drew had ever been restless and impatient. He would be again. He wouldn't be content to live on Harriet's estate and handle Harriet's tenants for long. Priscilla knew that all she had to do was encourage him to go to Singletrees and read the papers. Once he knew the truth she had contrived for him by making it appear Harriet had burned the letter, he would be restless again, impatient to assume his proper place in the world.

Harriet would be happier, too, once this business of the annulment was taken care of. How ridiculous of her and Drew to cling to their marriage when neither of them wanted it. Yet

Priscilla couldn't help but admire their loyalty to one another.

Loyalty did not count for much in a marriage without love. The kind of love she and Drew would share, among other things, for which Harriet was plainly not suited. Like travel. And having children. Why, Harriet was almost thirty—too old to be bearing children. Priscilla couldn't even imagine a strong independent woman like Harriet making love.

Priscilla sank onto the delicate chair at her dressing table and arranged her hair in a more sophisticated coif. A hair ribbon tied in a bow at her nape was not the proper look for the wife of a baron.

All she had to do was get Drew to discover that he was a baron.

She wished she knew how to do it without implicating Harriet, but she didn't. In any case, it shouldn't matter overmuch. This was not the sort of thing that would cause Harriet pain or suffering or ill health. It might annoy her, but in the end she would probably thank Priscilla for making it easy for her to secure her freedom from a marriage that couldn't possibly make either her or Drew happy.

Both Drew and Harriet would soon discover just how much Priscilla loved them both.

Chapter 21

Drew rubbed his eyes and contemplated a short nap as he pored over invoices and old manifests in the library. Since Harry's illness began, he'd spent more time reading to her or making idle conversation than he'd spent working or sleeping. Not that he minded. On the contrary, he'd enjoyed those moments of simple companionship, removed from the world, feeling as if he and Harry were creating one of their own simply by being together.

Thank God, she was finally on the mend. He'd thought he'd go mad with worry over her condition, regardless of what the physician had said. He hated seeing Harry so weak and vulnerable. Hated that he could do nothing to ease her suffering.

He wondered if she was awake yet. His day never began properly until he'd shared breakfast with Harry, teasing her about her "morning grouch" and kissing every trace of honey from her lips to reach the real sweetness beneath.

Briggs entered the room that had become

Drew's office, slammed a ledger down on the large library table they shared as a desk, and opened it to a marked page. Pausing to read a sheet of foolscap tucked between the pages, he sputtered and grinned. "Sir, there's something here that you should see." He turned the ledger, slid it across the table, and reached over to point out an entry.

Curious as to what had caused the somber Briggs to almost laugh, Drew glanced down, read, and then read again, the notation of a disbursement issued a fortnight ago. He frowned at the amount hefty enough to make him choke and read the entry showing the recipient, not understanding what he was seeing.

Briggs handed him the sheet of foolscap. "I had the same reaction until I read this."

Drew leaned back in his chair as he recognized the handwriting and began to read.

Mr. Sinclair Saxon,

On this date I tender my resignation as your agent. As my last act, I have authorized a draft for the sum noted in the ledger to be placed in my account for services rendered these past twelve years. Given the quality of said services, the good intentions with which I undertook them, and the amount of profits they brought to you, I have calculated the amount of payment upon fees set by the highest paid agents in England. I trust that this transaction will place your opinions of my activities in proper perspective.

Harry Saxon

His frown lifted into a smile. Harry Saxon, indeed. He chuckled as he realized the date on the letter was the same as the day he'd discovered that Harry had been managing his interests in England. That discovery had been smarting ever since. He'd been trying to set his anger aside, to focus on the present. He'd failed as reminders of what Harry had done behind his back jumped out at him every time he opened a ledger or arranged for dispersal of merchandise in the warehouse.

Now, all he could do was laugh and find a surprising pleasure in her temerity. Only Harry would do such a thing. Only Harry had the ability to reduce what might have hung over them both like a headman's ax to a butterfly flitting away on a refreshing breeze. Only Harry could find a way to present the subject of his ire in such a way that he couldn't help but see the absurdity of his grudge against her. Perspective, indeed. One would think his intrepid wife had invented the word.

Briggs watched him with raised brows and twitching mouth. "I'm glad to see that you find the humor in it . . . sir."

"I find a great deal more than that, Briggs," he said as he rose from his chair and headed for the double doors leading into the main hall. "I find that life with my lady will never be dull or tranquil."

"No, sir." Briggs cleared his throat, as if to banish his own amusement over the situation. "What shall I do about this?" He pointed at the ledger entry.

"Let it stand, Briggs," Drew said with a grin, as he opened the door and strode toward the stairs. "God knows she earned it."

He burst into the master suite and halted abruptly in the threshold to Harry's bedchamber. The bed was made and the window hangings were open to sunshine. No sounds came from the dressing room. Harry wasn't there.

Drawn by a gleam of gold, he strolled to the dressing table and picked up the bracelet. She hadn't given it to him as she'd said she would do the night he returned to her. Neither had she moved it since she had taken it off, leaving it in plain sight . . . like a promise.

As if she had not yet taken the promise completely to heart.

But she wanted to; that much he knew. If he had his way, she would believe it and accept it. He would see to it. He didn't blame her for being wary. He'd spent his adult life up to this point refining wariness to a fine art. But, the moment she'd given him her body, he'd known that she had taken his heart in return, not because they'd made love, but because she had accepted him so completely in those moments of wild passion. Because she had trusted him in those moments. More than anything he'd ever wanted in his life, he wanted that trust to become a part of every moment with Harry.

An eerie frisson rippled up his spine as he studied the engraving inside the band. Was it his imagination, or did the writing seem a bit clearer, as if the inscriptions were taking their original form, the signs of wear that had blurred them reversing itself?

Surely it was his imagination. Surely, he was seeing what he wanted to see—a sign that all would be well. That a future with Harry would banish every doubt he'd ever had about himself, every phantom that still visited him in his dreams.

He set the bracelet back down on the dressing table and turned away, determined that she would wear it again. That she would know that it was meant for her.

It felt wonderful, Harriet thought, as she pushed a stray strand of hair away from her face with her forearm and continued to knead dough. It had been so long since she had sneaked down to the kitchens in the early morning hours to help cook make bread and pastries. "Jenny, would you mind . . . ?" she asked a scullery maid, as she nodded toward her cup of chocolate.

Following the ritual established during Harriet's childhood, the maid picked up the cup and held it to Harriet's mouth.

"Thank you. I should have finished my breakfast before I became elbow deep in dough," she said with a smile.

"Humph," Cook snorted. "This is supposed to be a chore and my lady acts as if she were making mud pies."

"My lady is a peasant at heart," a soft, masculine voice said from the entrance to the kitchens.

Harriet paused, her hands still in the dough as her head jerked up. Drew walked into the chaos of the kitchens, a slow stride toward her that almost seemed like stalking, an unfamiliar gleam in his eyes and a quirk to his mouth that stalled her breath in her throat. She quickly bent her head to stare at the shiny, smooth mass of dough and began to knead again. "Perhaps I am," she murmured, feeling unaccountably shy at Drew's presence, at the reminders it conjured of other times they'd shared in the kitchens.

He halted beside her and cupped her chin, raising it to examine her face. "You're well," he stated. "Amazing, how quickly you've recovered."

"Humph!" Cook mumbled.

Harriet could only stare at Drew, at his bemused smile, and feel the subtle caress of his thumb on her jaw.

"I would like an audience with my lady."

"And leave me with more dough than these two old hands can manage?" Cook said.

Drew released Harriet's chin, shrugged out of his coat and rolled up his shirtsleeves. "Take a rest, Cook. Harry and I can finish up."

"Oh!" Jenny exclaimed. "But it ain't proper, sir. I can—"

"You'll do no such thing," Cook interrupted. "I'll not be deprived of time to put my feet up and have a dish of tea." Batting her hands, she shooed everyone out of the kitchens. "Just don't eat too much of the dough or we'll not have bread for my lady's morning toast."

Drew immediately snatched a bit of the dough and popped it in his mouth. Snatching another, he tossed it at Cook's back as she left the kitchen.

Caught in the memory of past mischief, Harriet did the same.

"I swear, you two hooligans will never grow up," Cook admonished over her shoulder, and brushed at the back of her skirt.

Silence fell in the large room as Harriet continued to knead, trying to ignore Drew's probing stare. "I'll get you some coffee," she said, for want of anything else to say.

"I've been doing for myself for a long time, Harry."

She had the odd feeling that he wasn't talking about coffee and bit her lip at the gravity of his tone. The sound of Drew looking in on her right after dawn had awakened her, though she'd feigned sleep, not wanting to speak with him until she was fully dressed and alert. She'd had quite enough of looking a horror and wanted him to see her at her best for a change. After he'd left the suite to conduct whatever business he had planned, she'd jumped out of bed, feeling as if her illness had been nothing more than a bad dream and all was right with the world.

She spotted the paper he'd set on the massive wood work table and knew that the world was in for a surprise. Perhaps a nasty one. She'd forgotten about the ledger entry and letter she'd written him out of pique.

Forming the dough into a round loaf, she set it aside to rise and rolled another lump of dough onto the table and began kneading with a vengeance.

"Harry," Drew said softly.

She continued folding and pressing and folding again. "Let it go, Drew, please."

He sighed heavily and rubbed the back of his neck as he rounded the table and sat on a high stool facing her. "Not yet. We must clear it away, Harry. It is important that we both understand."

"All right. I did that in anger," she admitted, with a nod toward the letter.

"You did it in wisdom," he said. "You made me laugh with it, and when one can laugh over a source of agitation or hurt, one realizes that it is not as shattering a thing as one thought."

"You laughed? I didn't think it was funny at all . . . at the time."

"And now?"

She shrugged. "I'd forgotten about it." Breathing deeply, she plunged on. "I'd hoped that you had also, but of course, that was silly. How could you forget? I did go against your expressed wishes. I did interfere. I think . . ." Pausing, she struggled to control the tremor in her voice. "I think I must have robbed you of something that was important to you."

He reached across the table and tugged her hand from the mess she was making, held it with both of his, and plucked bits of dough from her fingers. "It was important to me that I succeed on my own, Harry. It was the dream I clung to throughout my youth, and the dream that drove me when I was so weary and lonely I thought of giving up. Call it male pride, if you wish, but the dream and the ambition were all that I was."

"Was?" she asked, realizing that he wasn't here to confront her or blame her or give vent to any lingering anger. Realizing that something important was being said.

"All that I allowed myself to be," he corrected himself. "I had to be something and someone and I thought that material accomplishment was the way to be both. Until I spent a winter with death

as my shadow, I didn't realize that we are defined
by those who love us. By *why* they love us." He
met her gaze, his expression sad, wistful. "I did a
lot of dreaming that winter, of things I had no idea
of how to accomplish. Things which could not be
planned out and sought by reason. For all my
travels, there are some rather alarming gaps in my
experience. I know nothing of relationships with
women and learning from you can be quite hair-
raising."

She swallowed tightly and forbade herself to cry
at the sweetness of his voice, his words. "I fail to
see what I can teach you. My gaps in experience
are as wide as yours."

"You can teach me how to live for the sheer joy
of it, Harry. You can continue to teach me to see
things from more than one side." He set her hand
down on the planks very gently and looked up at
her, a wealth of emotion in his expression. More
emotion than he had ever shown her beyond humor and anger. "You can teach me who I am."

Moved beyond the tears that had threatened
only moments before, she leaned across the table
and framed his face with her hands, her elbows
sinking in the dough she'd all but destroyed in her
agitation. "You are *you*, Drew . . . too full of pride
and restraint and quite remarkable for all that. If
you weren't, I certainly could not have put up
with you and waited for you and loved you since
forever."

"We have so far to go yet, Harry. You are more
patient than I. After so many years of pursuing
the wrong objectives, I now want everything all at
once."

"I have patience only when it is worthwhile, Drew. Otherwise I dispatch the problem as quickly as possible and move on."

He turned his face into her hand, kissing her palm, nibbling at the dough clinging to her fingers. "I still wonder that I deserve you."

She jerked away from him, broke off a piece of dough, tossed it at him, then planted her hands on her hips at his startled glance. "We deserve each other, Drew. No one else would have us. Please do not ever say that again or I shall begin to believe you."

"Heaven forbid," he said with a broad smile that brought rainbows into the room. "To prevent it, I shall proceed to nurture your illusions day and night."

Feeling as shaken as if he'd proclaimed his love for her from the rooftops, she fed him a piece of dough and smiled. "It's a beginning, Drew, and that is all we need to go on."

Chapter 22

⁓◦◯◦⁓

The afternoon sun had reached its zenith and began the downward slide toward the other side of the world as Jane slipped into the estate office, where Drew was meeting tenants, and handed him a note. Distracted by the problem of a unwanted tree stump in a field a farmer wanted to cultivate, he nodded at her, barely aware that she left as silently as she'd come.

"Thank you, sir," the farmer said. "With the help you promised, we'll get it out right enough."

Had he promised to help? Drew wondered, as he recognized the paper upon which the note was written. Harry's stationery. Unfolding it, he forgot the farmer and his tree stump entirely as he read.

Sir,

I and my illusions are in want of nurturing. We await you in my bedchamber.

Drew abruptly rose and left the office, brushing past Fellowes and Briggs, and hastily offered apologies to the tenants still waiting in the courtyard.

Pigs and crops and damaged cottages were nothing compared to Harry and her illusions.

He'd seen her every chance he'd had over the past—had it been almost a fortnight since Harry had been stricken?—but it hadn't been the same. He hadn't been able to share conversation with her or touch her or hold her. And Harry struggled so to hide herself from him that he'd felt uncomfortable in her presence. She still didn't understand how beautiful she was.

Halting in the corridor, he veered toward the door leading out to the garden, then muttered a curse under his breath as he returned to his original direction. This was a bloody backward way of courting a woman. He couldn't even give her a bloody handful of flowers before ravishing her.

He snagged a picture off the wall as he strode into their apartment, crossed the sitting room, and halted abruptly in the doorway to her bedchamber, his body already rising to her call.

He stopped short one step into the room and stared at her lying in nothing but her chemise, her hand curled under cheek and one bare leg hooked over the linens.

Damn. She was asleep.

He walked softly across the carpet and leaned over her, planning to kiss her awake.

She turned slightly and sighed. She might be recovered but shadows still lurked beneath her eyes and her complexion was still pale.

Enfolding her hand in his, he raised it to his lips, then returned it to rest beneath her cheek.

She smiled and turned back to her original position.

Damn. If he didn't leave now, he would wake her with kisses on her shoulder, her lips, the breast that spilled from the neck of her undergarment. He wouldn't be able to stop until he buried himself inside her and slept joined with her until morning.

He reminded himself that tenants still waited as he scribbled a message on the back of her note and propped it against the picture he left on the bedside table.

Resigned to another night of sleeping alone before the fire, he returned to the office, where Briggs and Fellowes gave him a wide berth for the rest of the afternoon.

Oddly enough, Priscilla didn't make an appearance that day. Just as well. He likely would have bitten her head off. Priss was best taken in small doses, as far apart as possible.

What he needed—desperately—was a continuous dose of Harry's smile and sparkle and warmth. Especially her warmth.

Cool air brushed Harriet's flesh as she stirred and moved her hand over the mattress, searching. . . .

Her eyes snapped open. She'd fallen asleep while waiting for Drew. Frantically, she glanced around the room, hoping to see him standing above her or sitting in the chair by the window, or lying beside her.

No one was there. Nothing stirred but the lace curtains dancing in the evening breeze.

Evening. She'd slept until evening.

Rolling to her side to rise, she squinted at the

small painting on the table. A still life of flowers that usually hung in the hallway. Propped against the frame was what appeared to be a note.

She reached for the single candle burning in a brass chamber stick on the table, opened the note and smiled.

Flowers for my lady. Later, we will nurture one another. Rest well, my love.

                                                              Drew

Her breath caught on a sob as she sank back down into the feather mattress, hugging the painting and note to her chest. He'd come to her and left her to sleep. He'd brought her flowers that would not cause her any discomfort.

He'd called her his "love."

"It's grateful I am that I never got me a fondness for a woman. Downright pathetic, what a woman does to a man," Briggs grumbled that night, as he put away the clothes Drew removed and set out his dressing gown.

"Do not speak of what you do not know," Drew said, as he dried his hair with a length of linen. "Better men than you and I have been rendered 'pathetic' by a woman."

"Well, pathetic wouldn't be so bad if it weren't accompanied by bad temper. I always thought you the most congenial of men except when those natives attacked us on the way home. Decided then I wouldn't be around you when you were in a temper, but I can't avoid it now." He took the towel Drew unwrapped from his waist and held up the dressing gown. "Mayhap I should look elsewhere for work. Don't know that I want to tolerate another of your fits."

"As you wish," Drew said shortly. "And if you ever do develop a fondness for a woman, I will be there to laugh and remind you of your superior attitude. Now, get the hell out of here before I give you no choice but to find other employment."

"My lady doesn't snap at her folk, no matter how out of sorts she is." Briggs sidestepped Drew on the way to the door.

Relieved to be free of Briggs's constant reminders of his foul mood, Drew carried his pillow and blankets to the chair in the sitting room and sank into the cushions, immediately stretching his legs toward the fire. Harry had continued to sleep through the afternoon and evening even when Jane had eased her into a nightgown. Little wonder. She'd not had more than an hour's sleep at a stretch for over a week. He'd planned to join her in her bed, but decided against it, knowing that all his efforts to protect her rest would be for naught if he came within kissing distance of her. And he didn't know if his pride could withstand the indignity if she should sleep right through his amorous attentions.

Before he'd completely pulled the blankets up to his chin, he fell into an exhausted sleep.

It had been one bloody hell of a week. . . .

A muffled groan reached Harriet from the sitting room, dragging her up from a deep sleep. A painting fell onto her lap as she sat bolt upright at a second sound of distress.

Drew. She'd fallen asleep again, holding the painting of flowers he'd brought her. She'd dreamed of his voice telling her that he loved her—

Another groan came from the sitting room, chasing the last traces of fog from her mind.

Drew.

She rolled from her bed and ran into the sitting room, found him swaddled in blankets in the chair by the fire, his hair damp, his body shivering as his head shook from side to side.

His nightmare.

His mouth was a thin tight grimace as his arms flailed. "No. Grandmother, don't send me away . . . be a good boy . . . forget all this . . . I don't want to go . . . I don't want to swallow it . . . don't want to sleep."

She wanted to cry at the fear of a small child she heard in his voice, at the way it mercilessly haunted him.

Harriet gripped his forearms and pushed them down as she spoke softly. "Drew, it's all right. You're here with me. Drew, it's over and done. . . ."

He opened his eyes and stared at her as his breathing slowed and the wildness left his expression, relaxing his features. "Damn," he muttered as he sat straighter in the chair. "I woke you."

"No," she lied. "I was reading. You had a nightmare."

"Go back to bed, Harry. You need rest," he said, his voice so flat and bleak she could almost feel his loneliness.

Her loneliness.

She sank to her knees before him and rested her cheek on his thigh. "I need you, Drew, far more than rest."

He shuddered as he placed his hand on her hair, his fingers, freeing it from the loose braid down her back, sifting through it. "I'm afraid to touch you, Harry, afraid I'll hurt you."

She raised her head and smiled at him as she pulled the blankets down and parted his robe and flattened her hands on his chest. "You're cold."

"Not now," he said around a groan, as she caressed his chest, ruffling through the sprinkle of hair that wedged downward into a narrow path. Still the bleakness was in his eyes, the frustration, the stark loneliness she'd seen in him so many times before.

"I will always be here to keep you warm at night, Drew. Always." She pressed her lips to one nipple then the other, trailing her mouth up to his strong neck, corded with strain, his hard jaw, clenched against passion, his mouth that softened the moment she kissed it. "You will never be rid of me," she whispered against his lips.

She felt his smile against her cheek. "It was just a nightmare, Harry."

"No, not just a nightmare. It's a cruelty that will never let you forget the thoughtless secrets of others."

He gripped her arms and pulled her up to lie along his length. "What do you know of it?"

His grip did hurt her still sensitive flesh, but she let it pass without mention. "I know what everyone else knows—that you were sent away without knowing why. I know that a memory like that

could not possibly leave you, no matter how old
you become or how much logic you try to apply
to it. I know that some demons follow us, refusing
to allow us to forget or to understand and that
sometimes those we love most help them without
meaning to. Not knowing is a terrible thing, Drew.
They told me you were dead and I did not, could
not, believe them. But still, the not knowing was
a torture I will never forget." She buried her face
in the crook between neck and shoulder. "Every
night that you have slept out here, I awakened
with the fear that you were gone and that I would
not know where you were or if you would ever
return."

"It seems a weakness I cannot overcome," he
admitted softly, and turned his head away from
her. I cannot control my sleep. I try, but I cannot."

Framing his face with her hands, she forced him
to look at her. "It is not weakness. You have never
been weak, Drew. No one else I know would live
with voices you cannot silence and go on building
and trying. No one else I know would accept what
you have accepted and not allow it to fester into
a wound that killed a part of yourself. You are
whole, Drew, as few men are whole."

He cupped the back of her head and turned her
head into his kiss, consuming her slowly and with
infinite tenderness. On and on it went, the kiss,
the simple holding, the eloquence of need.

He ended the kiss—minutes or hours?—later,
then began over again, his tongue mingling with
hers in a sweet marriage of breath and taste and
emotion. She thought she tasted the salt of tears
yet let that, too, pass without mention, allowing

her kisses on his cheeks and eyes to take the tears from him, to take them into herself and share them.

She had somehow touched him with her words and he had not turned away in pride or shame at such a show of vulnerability. That alone made this one of the most precious moments of her life. That alone convinced her that she and Drew could overcome any doubt, any fear, any discord. Their marriage was meant to be.

They were meant to be.

She slid down his body, taking the blankets with her, parting his robe along the way and settling on her knees between his thighs and taking his arousal between her hands.

"Harry, no. Not out of—"

"Yes, Drew . . . out of love."

Instinct guided her as she took him in another way, accepting him completely, loving him without a single doubt or fear, every lingering trace of anger for twelve years of loneliness and uncertainty falling away to die of neglect.

She gave him no mercy as he groaned in pleasure and stiffened and clutched the arms of the chair, giving her complete power over him. She took it as she took him—as only a woman in love could take a man.

"Harry, stop . . . now. You don't have to—"

She raised her head for a moment, only a moment. "I must, Drew. I must make you believe that you are mine. That you have always been mine as I have always been yours. You must understand that you have always belonged to me and I will not let you go so long as we both shall live."

His protests ended in another groan as she lowered her head over him, taking possession of him, taking him to a place where nightmares did not exist, taking him to a place where only love flourished.

Shaken to his soul, Drew shuddered and fought for air, and then succumbed to the death of lovers. The death of pride and self shared by perfect mates.

Harry, too, cried out and placed her hands over his on the arms of the chair, digging her nails into his flesh, sharing the experience as if his pleasure was all she needed for completion. And then she lay her head on his thigh as her hands soothed him, bringing him gently down from the clouds.

He reached down and lifted her to his lap, tucked her into his side and pressed her head down on his shoulder, finding an even more profound satisfaction in holding her as she shuddered and calmed and clung to him.

"Soon, Harry," he murmured in her ear as he smoothed her hair and kissed her brow, "soon I will tell you how much I love you. But not now. Not when so many utter the words in the madness of passion and then quickly forget their meaning. Soon, when you will know without doubt that I mean them. . . ."

"Hush, Drew. Hush . . ."

Something dark inside him seemed to lighten and drift away, demon memories banished and fading as the past faded leaving only the present and dreams for the future.

He closed his eyes and fell easily into sleep, holding Harry, knowing he would never let her go.

Priscilla quietly opened the door to the sitting room, not wanting to wake Drew if he still slept and froze at the sight of him and Harriet sleeping together in the chair.

Panic drove her from the sight of them, drove her down the hall and out into the garden, her mind racing ahead of her.

They were becoming too close. If she did not do something now, they would become even closer, perhaps make love. She couldn't let that happen. Couldn't let them make a mistake that would make them both miserable for the rest of their lives.

But desperation scrambled her thoughts. She couldn't sort through it all. It didn't matter. She would allow instinct to guide her. After all, what had careful planning got her except a horrible guilt for making Harriet so ill? Logic had obviously failed her.

She would do what she must to have Drew. To save him from his own pride and sense of honor.

Doubt wormed its way into her thoughts. Maybe he did care for Harriet. Maybe Harriet really loved him. Maybe she was wrong about them.

But no. Harriet had not done anything to protect Drew from the truth. Harriet had not taken steps to ensure that Drew would have what had been denied him. Priscilla had done all that. Priscilla loved him as he deserved to be loved.

She sat in the garden and waited, her mind seeing nothing but the door through which Drew would emerge. She didn't need to think. She needed only to act.

Chapter 23

Drew awakened to the scent of strong coffee and sweetly perfumed woman. He opened his eyes to Harry, fully dressed and standing before him, holding a cup of steaming brew under his nose.

"There is much to do today, Drew, and it is already eight o'clock."

Eight o'clock? He'd always been up with the sun, anxious to end the night, yet this morning he could have slept until noon or beyond.

She pulled the cup away as he sat up and rose from the chair, held it out to her side as he leaned over to kiss her, then smiled and handed him the cup. But her smile was strained and her gaze not quite fully on him as she gave him his coffee and pushed him in the direction of his bedchamber.

"I will wait breakfast until you are dressed." Her expression became even tighter.

"We will breakfast now, Harry, so that you may tell me what disturbs you." He strode to the table, set down his cup, and held out her chair, waiting with lifted brow for her to join him.

"Very well." She crossed the sitting room and took her seat, making no move to pour chocolate or smear honey over her toast.

"Tell me," he ordered softly as he sat down, ignoring his coffee.

"Drew, you must go to Singletrees," she blurted. "There are things that have gone on far too long and cannot be resolved in pieces. We must face the whole of it I think."

"And what has Singletrees got to do with any problems we have yet to solve?" he asked, becoming increasingly alarmed as she appeared to struggle for words, as if she were afraid to utter them.

"For one thing, Singletrees is yours. You must see to your tenants and the staff and make certain all is in order."

"I have visited the tenants this past fortnight and Briggs has met with the staff. All is in order, Harry. Singletrees runs as well without its master as do most of the estates in England."

She closed her eyes briefly, as if gathering herself, then met his gaze head on for the first time that morning. "I have great hope and ambition for our future together. But I cannot trust in it completely until I know how you respond to what you find in the box your father left for you."

"Are you afraid that it will drive me away?" he asked.

"Perhaps. I don't know, do I, Drew?" She pressed the bridge of her nose with thumb and forefinger as if she were developing a headache. "It is a fear I cannot banish. It doesn't matter if it makes sense or not, if it is justified or not. It exists on a level I cannot reach with hope, or with your

assurances, or anything but your going to Singletrees and then returning to tell me how you feel
about it . . . and if you wish to do anything about
it." She spoke more and more quickly, yet her
gaze clung to his, as if she were pleading for
something other than what she asked. "Please do
this, Drew. I need the past to be put where it belongs. I need to know that *you* have put it where
it belongs." She rose without ever touching her
breakfast. "I've sent Jane to inform Priss that I am
taking her into London today to order her some
new gowns. We will go as soon as she is ready."

He caught her as she turned toward her bedchamber and pulled her close to stand chest to
chest and toe to toe with him. "I will go to Singletrees, today, Harry. And when I return, I will
keep the promise I made to you last night."

She closed her eyes and swayed against him. "I
pray so, Drew. I pray for it with every breath I
take."

Disturbed by the tremble of fear in her voice, he
tipped up her chin. "Look at me, Harry."

She obeyed, revealing the fear he'd heard.

"Nothing can change what we have begun together," he said harshly. "Believe it." He covered
her mouth with his, taking it in a hot, demanding
kiss that conveyed both his confidence that all
would be well and his anger that she did not completely trust in that.

She held onto him, communicating her fear and
a desperation he did not understand, then tore her
mouth from his. "I hid the box in the old priest's
closet," she said hoarsely, then ran into her bedchamber without looking back.

*   *   *

"Drew!" Priscilla called from the garden, as he stepped outside and headed for the stables.

He paused and frowned at the anxiety in her expression, in the way she wrung her hands together. Was it something in the air that rendered all the females in his life irrational today?

Aside from that, he was not ready to see Priss after what Cook had told him when he'd stopped off in the kitchen for a cup of fresh coffee. He'd been ready to throttle Priss for what she had done to precipitate Harry's illness, but Cook had threatened his life and limbs if he said a word. Harry had taken care of the problem, she'd assured him, and gone on to tell him how frightened Priss had been that she had "almost killed Harry." Priss was still a child. She did have a conscience. The scare was sufficient punishment. If Harry could forgive Priss, he could do no less. And since Harry had suffered most, she had the right to dictate terms.

He'd agreed with Cook, though he didn't like it.

Settling matters with Harry was far more important than any problem Priss might have, but as he saw the anxiety in Priss's face and how small and alone she looked, he remembered how frightening it was at any age to have one's moorings cut. Priss had been sent far from home with only a sick old woman to link her to all that was familiar to her and then even Clara Hawkins had defected, sending a letter informing them that she was too old to be chasing after a capricious adolescent and would retire immediately. Clara had not had the strength to control Priss. The Whitmores had raised their children with benign neglect, loving them but never having or taking the time to attend to them. Priss was alone but for him and Harry.

Muttering a curse, he veered toward the gardens while warning himself to keep silent about the crushed weeds, to let well enough alone as Harry wished. "What is it, Priss?"

"I had hoped we could ride today."

"Not today. I am going to Singletrees. And Harry has planned for you to go into London with her to order a new wardrobe."

Her eyes brightened as her gaze skittered away from him. "Oh. Are you going to Singletrees to read the papers in the box?"

"How do you know of that?"

She caught the corner of her lower lip between her teeth, seemingly reluctant to answer. "Before I went to school, Harriet once took me with her when she went there to look after things. I saw her with the box." She again glanced away then clutched his arm. "Drew, you must understand how it was for her. She had just recently received Mummy's letter that you were dead, and I was thrust upon her without warning. And then Lord Sinclair died and she had so much to do. Of course she was angry; wouldn't you be? She didn't believe you were dead. She thought you had just decided to go on without her and devil take everything here."

"What are you talking about?" Drew asked, impatient to get on with it so he and Harry could get on with the rest of their lives.

"We all do things when we're angry, Drew,"

she said frantically. "Things we don't mean to do and regret later, when it's too late to change it back."

He pulled his arm from her hold. "If this is a confession, save it for another time, Priss."

"It really isn't my confession to make, but someone must prepare you for what you might find," she said softly, with a look of pity in her eyes. "I don't know exactly," she added in a rush, "but I did see smoke and Harriet putting what appeared to be ashes into the box. I hope she didn't burn the papers. I do so hope I am wrong . . . but if I am not, please don't think badly of her for it. She was so distraught and lost and so very angry."

"You've said quite enough, Priss." Drew tightened his mouth against any further response and turned toward the stables, every curse he'd ever learned in several languages running through his mind.

"I hope I am wrong, truly I do," she said breathlessly, as she followed him and again clutched his arm. "I hope you return with reason to lecture me for jumping to conclusions—"

He shook her off and entered the stables and saddled Spot himself, too impatient to wait for the stable boy to do it. Leaping into the saddle, he gave Spot his head and rode out of the courtyard in a cloud of dust.

Now, whether he liked it or not, he had to do as Harry requested. Not because he gave a damn about what light the papers might shed on his past, but because he needed to know why Harry was so anxious about them, why they had been given such importance to their marriage, and why

Priss thought Harry might have burned them.

For a single moment of pure agony, he wondered if Priss were telling the truth.

But then sanity prevailed. It would be entirely out of character for Harry to do such a thing. He could imagine Harry being unable to resist reading the letter his father had left for him, but she would never, for any reason other than life and death, destroy something that did not belong to her. He couldn't imagine that the answers Father had left for him would be a matter of life and death.

After what Priss had done to cause Harry's illness, it was easier to believe that she was lying.

Whatever the case, Harry was right. One way or another, no matter what he might find, it was time to lay the past to rest.

Drew strolled through the familiar rooms and corridors of Singletrees, taking his time, revisiting memories of love and acceptance, saying goodbye to what had passed on, never to return. What a fool he had been, to leave all that he'd had in search of what he had forgotten!

He paused in the grand salon to stare up at the portrait of his father and himself, painted so long ago. Not a formal portrait stiffly posed, but one of Edward, Viscount Sinclair, in his shirtsleeves, holding a six-year-old boy on his shoulders, both of them smiling in front of the ancient tree that had stood alone on a corner of the property.

Grief thickened in his throat and spilled down his face, unchecked by pride or manly sensibilities. "Ah damn, father, but I miss you," he whispered, and then turned away, knowing all he could do for his father now was honor his wishes.

He climbed the stairs to the nursery, where a distant Sinclair ancestor had built a hidden room in which to hide priests during the English Civil Wars. How many times had he and Harry played in the nursery and hidden in the closet to torment their nursemaids?

He found the secret latch, which would open the concealed door, knowing instinctively what he would find in the box Harry had so carefully hidden. It didn't matter. Harry's presence in his life was all the answer he needed. Yet though he kept telling himself that, the closer he came to the box, the more difficult it was to believe it.

All the demons Harry had spoken about the night before seemed to be lurking in the shadows as he located the box secreted away in a small bench, used to hide religious papers and books, and carried it to the child-sized table nicked and stained with paint. Demons rubbing their hands with glee at having yet another opportunity to rise up and torment him. Sitting on one of the small chairs, Drew held his breath as it creaked in protest, then steadied under his weight. The box opened easily and new demons began to pluck and poke at him and feed off his shock.

He hadn't believed Priss. He hadn't expected to find ashes piled on top of a single document. He hadn't been able to believe that anyone could do such a thing.

It shocked him into mute paralysis. For the second time in his life, he'd found ashes where truth should lie. Truth that had been so easily and thoughtlessly erased, without regard to anyone save the person who'd destroyed it. In spite of his belief that the past no longer mattered, its destruction infuriated him. It was his past to dwell upon or to ignore. No one else's. The answers had been his to destroy. Fury burned out of control into flames of the same helpless rage he'd felt in Ireland when he'd found speculation and opinion shaping the truth, and a burned-out shell too far gone to evoke any lingering recollections of his life before the age of four. Hadn't enough people already played with his life, determining its course without consulting him and leaving carnage where his memories should be?

And now this—a violation of the man who had given him so much. A violation of the peace his father had sought in leaving the truth behind.

He poked his finger in the ashes, trying to discern when it had happened. Last year? Or a fortnight ago?

Calling upon the discipline that he'd depended upon all his life, he contained his fury and carefully lifted out the document, spilling the ashes to the bottom of the box and unfolded the last will and testament of Edward, Viscount Sinclair. A good man who had lived simply and for each moment rather than for what had gone before or what might come later. A gentle man who had loved his adopted son so much he had moved from his ancestral home to raise Drew in a place he could always call home. Regardless of what was or was not important to Drew, the contents of the box had held importance for his foster father. He could at least read the will and make it official.

A sheet of paper fell out from between the second and third pages of the will and lay on the table in front of him. Maneuvering around his knees in the short chair, he picked it up and read the faded script.

A marriage document between Baron Cassidy and Mary Margaret Collins dated well before his birth.

His hand shook as he returned to the will reading quickly to see what it revealed.

. . . if my son, Drew Sinclair-Saxon, so chooses after reading the sealed letter I have left for him in the care of his wife, Harriet, Countess Saxon, he may legally claim the estate in Ireland known as Cassidy Tower, along with all lands and tenants and the title of Baron Cassidy. Cassidy Tower and all lands and tenants belonging to same came to me upon the death of my half-brother, Baron Cassidy, to hold in trust for his legal heir, the child of Mary Margaret Cassidy, whom he took to wife in secret, according to her wishes. I have not been able to return to the scene of so much loss and grief since finding Drew, but I have sent funds and instructions to ensure that what is left is preserved for him. I ask that Drew respect the sacrifices made for him and the love that prompted them and that he honor the memories of Baron Cassidy and Mary Margaret, whose actions were inspired solely out of love for an innocent child, by continuing to preserve the lands and the people of the county those extraordinary people loved so much. God rest my brother's soul and reward him for his generosity and loyalty. Even in death he placed our

welfare above his own. And God bless Mary Margaret's soul, which I pray has found peace in the arms of her Maker.

Drew stared at the clause, too stunned to do more than note the curious wording, as if something were intentionally being left out. Of course something had been left out of a document that could be read by any number of people. Something so private that it was set down in a private letter as a deathbed confession and given over to Harry—the only person who could be trusted.

A sound rumbled up from his chest and erupted before he could stop it. A bitter, hollow laugh. He was not a bastard, but legal heir to Cassidy Tower and all lands and tenants belonging to same. Baron Cassidy had married Mary Margaret Collins before he was born. He had a legal name. His foster father was in fact his uncle. According to the will, he'd had a father who had not tossed him away. His mother had cared enough to wed and give him a future.

They'd even given him a title.

This was the secret from which he'd been protected? This was what had caused such fear in his foster father? This was what had warped his young boy's perceptions and sent him on a fool's crusade?

Demons scattered and fled as he laughed and crumpled the will and the certificate in his hand. He laughed as he smoothed them out, folded them, and placed them back in the box, laughed until his gut ached as much as his heart.

Abruptly he sobered at the sight of the ashes, at

the cruel reminder they represented that there had to be more. He didn't want there to be more. He'd had enough of all of it. He'd been ruled by people long gone for too much of his life.

He might not care what truths had been left to find, but he bitterly resented having the choice of knowing, or not knowing, taken from him—a vicious irony he could not appreciate.

Who had done this, and why? The question came from the only demon who lingered to taunt him. Could Harry have been angry enough to commit such a violation? Could the letter have contained answers that she felt could hurt him? He could forgive her for either reason. Harry always acted out of love or compassion—never to achieve her own ends.

He couldn't believe that Harry would do something like this for any reason.

Which left only one other person . . . and the question of "why" growing ever larger in his mind. To discredit Harry in hopes that it would create a breach between him and his wife? Most likely. It made sense, in light of the lengths to which Priss had gone to keep Harry in her sickbed. So many things made sense now. Little things said and implied. Things he had not taken seriously.

Tucking the box under his arm, he left the nursery and sought out the steward and housekeeper to inform them he was returning to Saxon Hill. There was nothing left to do here.

And he had a lot of hell to raise at Saxon Hill.

Chapter 24

"**L**ondon will be hell tonight," John Coachman said, as Harriet handed parcels to him to pack in the coach. "You'd best be hurrying, my lady. I'm bound to get you home before the fog rolls in." He nodded toward the bank of dense gray mist creeping along the horizon and clinging to the ground. "Mr. Sinclair-Saxon will have me head if I don't."

Harriet studied the fog bank, judging from the experience all Londoners had of how long it would take to reach the city. Already the air was chilling and beginning to feel more liquid than usual. "You shall keep your head, John. I have no intention of being stranded in London tonight."

"Maybe more than one night," the driver said. "This pea-souper looks a bad one."

"All right, John, Miss Whitmore and I have only one more errand and then we will return posthaste."

"Begging your pardon, my lady, but I'll be driving you to your errand and waiting for you right outside."

"We are right outside," Harriet said, well used to the protectiveness of her staff that never failed to touch her. "I must collect a parcel from the jeweler. It will take only a few minutes, I promise. In the meantime, why don't you go into the Winged Lion for a mug of ale to keep you warm, and a meat pie, if you're hungry? Miss Whitmore and I will come straight into the coach when we're finished."

John Coachman cast a longing gaze at the tavern and regretfully shook his head.

"I order it, John," Harriet said. "You will get us home all the more quickly if you are fortified against the chill."

John needed no further urging. "I'll bring some hot tea for you and the young miss as well."

"No need, John. Mr. Branson always greets me with tea when I frequent his shop. Now go on with you or we will be at the coach before you and have to wait."

Not if she could help it, Priscilla thought, as she was seized by yet another inspiration. It always amazed her how even nature conspired in her favor. It couldn't be better if she'd planned it herself.

Following Harriet into the jeweler's shop, she glanced over her shoulder at the gray, shapeless monster lumbering ever closer to the city. Fog. How lovely. Harriet would be trapped in London and forced to remain all night, perhaps longer. The best part was that it wouldn't hurt a soul. Harriet would be able to take shelter in the townhouse of any one of her many friends.

And Priscilla would have Drew to herself. She

would have all night—perhaps longer—to prove to Drew how grown up she really was, and how passionate. He would see that he needed her, that she could give him everything a man could possibly want.

As predicted, Mr. Branson served them tea the moment they were inside his shop. Priscilla sipped as she wandered about the shop, absently studying the displays of the less expensive trinkets. The more valuable pieces, she knew, were kept in the back in a private salon, under lock and key—a lovely convenience, since Priscilla knew that was where Harriet would go to make her selections.

If only this had happened sooner, she thought with genuine regret. Then she wouldn't have crushed the weeds and scattered them throughout Harriet's bedchamber. Harriet would not have become so dreadfully ill. Priscilla wouldn't have had to suffer through the fear that she might at any moment become guilty of murder.

Of course, that wouldn't have happened, she realized now. But at the time, she had been certain Harriet was dying. How could anyone look so frightful and not be dying? She shuddered as she waved Harriet on and continued to browse, keeping one eye on the coach outside.

Harriet disappeared into the elegant little room reserved for special clients and sat down in a gilt chair that surely had been made in France during the reign of one Louis or another. There were so many she could never keep them straight.

Priscilla finished her tea in one gulp and motioned to a clerk. "Please inform Lady Saxon that

I will wait for her in the coach . . . but do not interrupt her now. Wait until she has finished her business, please."

"Of course, miss," the clerk said, as he took the cup from her.

Within minutes, she saw John Coachman emerge from the tavern across the street and anxiously study the fog as he climbed up to the driver's box on the elegant Saxon coach.

Smiling smugly, she knocked on the roof to signal her presence.

Immediately, the coach rolled forward into the rapidly diminishing traffic.

Priscilla breathed a sigh of relief as they left London behind and the driver urged the team to a faster pace.

"I'm sorry, my lady," the clerk said as he wrung his hands. "I tried to stop the coach, but the driver left in rather a hurry. I should have informed you immediately that the young miss was leaving."

"It isn't your fault," Harriet said. "How could you have known my driver would assume we were both in the coach? He was anxious to get us home." Harriet wished she could believe it, but she couldn't. Priss had intentionally left her behind, no doubt giving John the impression they were both inside and waiting for him. She was certain of it. "I must get home," she said to anyone who was listening.

"I have no means of transport to offer you, my lady," Mr. Branson said. "And there won't be a single hackney out with the fog moving in so quickly."

"I have a horse," the clerk said proudly. "If you don't mind riding while I lead, I will be honored to escort you to the home of a friend."

Harriet thought quickly of all her friends who occupied townhouses in the city during the Season, calculating which of them lived closest to the shops. "Mr. George Brummell lives at Number Thirteen Chapel Street. Would that be too far for you to escort me and still get back to your own quarters before we are completely blinded by the fog?"

"I'll run down to the livery and get my mount." He bowed as he backed toward the door. "It will be my most pleasant duty to see you safely sheltered, ma'am." With a final bow, he pivoted and ran outside. "I will be right back," he called over his shoulder, his young face rosy and eager.

"A very nice young man, Mr. Branson. I do hope you will advance him soon. He appears quite knowledgeable and is certainly accommodating beyond what is expected."

"Yes, my lady. I have been pleased with his performance though I am not happy that he allowed your coach to get away. He—"

"He could not have known," she interrupted. "And he did chase my coach until it turned out of sight. Surely there are few others so diligent."

"As you say, my lady," Mr. Branson said, with apparent relief that she blamed neither him nor his clerk for her predicament. "I will most certainly increase Mr. Dodd's salary immediately."

"By the way," Harriet said, as she thought of Beau and a gift he had recently presented to her. "I believe Mr. Brummell collected a music box for me and I neglected to send payment with him. Since I have not received an invoice from you, I wonder if you directed it to Mr. Brummell instead."

"Ah, I believe I did, my lady. I was under the impression that Mr. Brummell purchased it himself as a gift." To his credit, Mr. Branson kept a straight face, though this was not the first time Harriet had paid for her own gift. Beau was sadly deficient in both funds and in his ability to manage what he did happen to have either through his allowance or his winnings from gambling. She would not see her friend's resources strained by his frequent generosity, no matter how ill advised.

"Please redirect the invoice to me and I will arrange for payment to be sent to you immediately."

"As you wish, my lady."

"I do not see a need to inform Mr. Brummell of this, do you, Mr. Branson?"

"I doubt he would notice in any event, ma'am," he said dryly.

"Quite so, Mr. Branson. I'm pleased we understand one another."

Young Mr. Dodd appeared outside with a rather beaten down horse of questionable ancestry, yet he stroked the beast's neck as if he thought it the finest in the realm.

As she said good-bye to the jeweler and stepped outside, she thought the animal to be the grandest thing she had seen all day. Her feet hurt and the prospect of walking to Beau's was less than appealing. The fog was indeed lumbering in, so thick and heavy it smothered. Already, she could not see across the street.

Mr. Dodd settled her on an ancient sidesaddle he had surely borrowed from the livery and immediately led the horse in the direction of Chapel Street, squinting to see through the rapidly thickening fog.

Every sound was muffled and ominous as she thought of the stories she'd heard of foot pads lurking in the fog, waiting to take what they could from anyone foolish enough to be out and about in such weather. The horse's hoof beats sounded like an echoing heartbeat. The sound of her own breathing seemed to be swallowed by the wet, gray blanket of mist that snuffed out the afternoon light.

Scuffling seemed to be all around her, closing in. She thought she saw shadows to her left, scurrying like rats in a gutter.

It was definitely a scuffle somewhere to her left. "Mr. Dodd," she whispered. "I believe we are in a bit of a coil. Perhaps you should take us to the very next residence—"

"Please hush, my lady, and please forgive me," Mr. Dodd said, as he abruptly swung onto the horse's back behind her and took the reins. "Hold on, my lady. I am going to try to get far enough away that they will lose us."

The horse balked at being commanded to increase his gait in a blind world as Harriet grabbed his mane and held on for dear life. Mr. Dodd urged his mount forward. Harriet added her own pleas for the beast to move as the scuffling sounds increased and seemed to surround them.

Someone *was* out there, stalking them, waiting—

At her back, she felt Mr. Dodd slip his hand inside his coat. Turning her head, she saw a wicked-looking pistol in his hand.

"Don't be alarmed, my lady," he whispered. "It's a night made for miscreants and it's best to be prepared—"

"My laidy, is it?" a voice said, the body attached to it hidden in the mist. "Well, if today ain't bringin' old Jimmy good fortune." A bulky shape appeared dangerously close.

Mr. Dodd raised his pistol. Another shape emerged behind him, pulled him from the horse, and struck the back of his head with a club. He crumpled to the ground, barely a shadow in the fog.

An arm hooked around her waist and dragged her from the saddle so quickly, Harriet had no time to think. Panicked, she flailed her arms and legs, striking out wherever she could reach.

"Help me with the bluidy bitch," her attacker shouted, his foul breath gagging her. The second shape grabbed her legs. "I got 'em, Jimmy. Get 'er purse."

Think! Harriet commanded herself, struggling to regain calm. Poor Mr. Dodd was unconscious or worse on the ground, and she could be next. She went limp, throwing both men off balance. They each toppled forward, dropping her and falling in a heap on top of her, crushing the air from her lungs. She lay still and stunned, fighting for breath and nearly retching at the odor of the unwashed bodies scrambling to gain their feet and not caring what they gouged in the doing. Pain shot through her midsection as an elbow jammed into her. Her shoulder burned from the stomp of a foot. Another foot caught her on the side of her head. Lights flashed behind her eyes and pain enveloped her inside and out.

The larger man gained his balance and stood over her, his legs straddling her. She gasped for air and kicked upward. He screamed and staggered and fell to his knees, still straddling her.

"Blast it, Jimmy where are you?" his companion called. Can't see in this fog."

Jimmy made a choked sound as he cupped his privates and began to heave.

Raising up on her elbows, Harriet scrambled backward, sliding out from under him, just as he fell forward and retched in earnest.

"Goddamn bitch," the second man said from right behind her, and drove his fist against her head, catching her on her cheekbone.

" 'Elp me," Jimmy croaked. "Over 'ere."

A foot slammed against Harriet's eye as the second man rushed to aid Jimmy.

Pain exploded in her head, everywhere at once. She fought to remain conscious, to crawl away, out of sight, groping along the ground to find Mr. Dodd. Her hand connected with cold metal. The pistol! She wrapped her hand around the grip and held the weapon in front of her, pointing straight ahead. If either of the thieves came within sight, she would fire. She had to.

Consciousness threatened to desert her, leave her helpless, but she refused to give in. She had to get home to Drew. She'd promised him she would never let him sleep alone and cold again.

Footsteps sounded, startling her to alertness.

Her finger pulled back on the trigger. Someone yowled in pain. "Crikey, Jimmy, we got to get out of 'ere." Footsteps and a dragging, grunting sound faded rapidly into silence.

Sobbing with the effort to remain conscious, she crawled over the cobbles of the street. "Mr. Dodd, where are you? Oh, please, answer me." Her hand connected with something solid—a shoulder. She shook it and groped for his face. "Mr. Dodd, wake up. Please wake up."

He stirred and groaned and gripped her hand. "My lady? Oh, thank the good Lord. Are you hurt?"

"I'm all right. What of you?"

Silence.

"Mr. Dodd?"

He moaned in obvious pain. "If you please, my lady," he panted, "do not shake my arm again; I'm quite certain it is broken."

Struggling to her knees, Harriet leaned over him and gently felt along his arm. It was misshapen and swelling rapidly. "I fear you are correct," she said thickly, her tongue seeming too large for her mouth. She blinked, feeling as if the fog were creeping into her head, smothering her thoughts, overwhelming her will to fight the darkness. She heard a sound and realized Mr. Dodd was struggling to his feet.

"I cannot carry you, ma'am, but I can drag you to the side of the street, if you will permit."

She swallowed a hysterical laugh at the absurdity of it. "I won't tell, if you won't," she gasped. "Just . . . please hurry. I have not survived thieves to be run down by a carriage."

"No carriages tonight—dash it all," he said, then grunted as he wrapped his good arm around her waist and hauled her to her feet. Pain cut across her ribs and radiated through her shoulder. Her head felt as if it were about to explode as he half dragged, half carried her to the walkway and lowered her to sit against a wall.

"How badly are you injured, ma'am?" he asked.

"I am shaken, nothing more," she said.

"Begging your pardon, my lady, but you are not being truthful. Now, please tell me what I must know. I would not like to presume to see for myself."

"My midsection and my head," she admitted weakly, "are the worst, I think . . . but I must get home to my husband. I must—"

She heard him curse under his breath and then winced as he shouted for help at the top of his lungs.

The fog swirled around her and inside her. She tried to fight it, to keep a clear head but the shouting was like a hot blade inside her skull. "Drew," she recited to herself. "I'm coming. Drew. . . ."

The fog inside her became a solid darkness, shutting out sound and thought and the swirling patterns of gray mist overtaking the city. She was falling . . . falling into darkness until she heard Mr. Dodd's shouts no more.

"I'm sorry, Drew . . ." She heard the voice as if it were far away, then realized it was hers.

PART III

Truth

The truth shall make you free.

THE HOLY BIBLE, JOHN 8:32

We know the truth not only by the reason,
but also by the heart.

O. W. WRIGHT—PASCAL, *PENSÉES*

Chapter 25

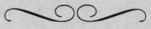

Where was Harry?

Drew kept one eye on the fog ominously rolling in outside his window as he pulled on his boots and reached for the coat Briggs had left out for him. Uneasiness had rolled in with the mist, and was quickly thickening into fear.

Soon, total darkness would rule—the kind of darkness he'd experienced in the dugout. The kind of darkness that soaked into a person. No star would twinkle; no moon would spill a silver glow over the landscape. Nothing in London would move except those too stupid or too greedy to heed the danger of a blind world.

He'd seen the beginnings of it on his return from Singletrees and had pushed Spot, needing to get home and assure himself that Harry was safe. But the coach had not returned.

Where was she?

He snapped his head up and stilled at the sound of a woman's skirts swishing over the carpet in the next room. "Where have you been?" he barked, as he strode from his bedchamber into the dark sitting room ready to chain her to the bed if she could not employ better sense.

She was a shadow approaching him, reaching him and pressing herself against him, her arms around his waist, her hands tentative on his back. "I'm here," she whispered. "I couldn't wait to be here. We can be alone together and plan our future."

He pulled away from her. The voice didn't sound right, even though it was barely audible. The words struck him as odd. The scent was wrong—too sweet, too heavy, rather than fresh and intoxicating, like Harry.

Priss.

He stepped past her in the direction of the mantel, finding flint and striking it, holding it to the wick of a candle. Pale yellow light cast a circle around him . . . and Priss.

Priss, standing in the center of the room, staring up at him with adoring eyes.

"What are you doing here, and where is Harry?" he asked.

"I didn't want to stay in London." She swayed toward him with unschooled movements. "I wanted to be with you, Drew. To show you how much I love you and how right we are for one another. To help you decide to get an annulment. I'm certain Harriet will be happy about it. It was what she wanted last year until Lord Sinclair died."

He clamped his mouth shut, afraid to say anything that she might misconstrue. Obviously she had misconstrued a great many things. He stared at her, at a complete loss, terrified by such blind innocence. What in the hell did she mean by saying she would wait for him? Wait for what?

He glanced over his shoulder, hoping Briggs would hear and rescue him. His gaze snagged on the clock. He frowned as he read the time—six o'clock in the evening.

"Where is Harry?" he asked again.

"She remained in the city," Priss replied with a timid smile. "She said she had more shopping to do and would rather not have to travel back in again," she hastened to explain in a breathless voice.

He shook his head in disbelief as he reached for the bell pull and jerked, wondering if he had gone mad and acquired another nightmare.

Cold seemed to pour into him, freezing him with dread. Harry would not willingly remain in the city. She didn't even have a townhouse there. Harry was a homebody, preferring her own things about her when she went to sleep for the night. *I will always be here to keep you warm at night, Drew,* Harry had said to him. A silly thing, some might say. A thing lovers say in the throes of passion. But Harry had known about the cold, how it froze every part of him. Harry had known what she was promising and why. Harry had meant it.

"I brought some cream cakes from the baker, Drew—not as good as Mummy's, but I know how you like them. We will dine and I will show you what an accomplished hostess I am—"

Impatient, Drew picked her up as if she were so much flotsam and plopped her onto the settee. "Tell me where Harry is," he said coldly. "The truth this time."

"She's quite all right, Drew. Truly. She sent me back and asked me to entertain you. Of course she must know—"

"She knows," Drew gritted, his anger on a quickly unraveling leash, "that you are a thoughtless, selfish, foolish little girl. Now tell me where she really is, before I shake it out of you." Again he yanked on the bell pull, and again.

Fear sparked in Priss's eyes, yet she didn't let it stop her. "But Drew, we have the whole night, maybe two. How can you want her when I am here?"

"She is my wife."

"But she isn't—not really. I heard all about the annulment when she was discussing it with her solicitor and the vicar. She hasn't given you what you need. I will be happy to give you what you need, if only you'll show me how."

"She is my wife, Priss. Never doubt it."

"No, you're just saying that!" Priss cried as she grasped his meaning, then collected herself. "You're worried because of my age. But girls get married when they are much younger than I." Her voice trembled now. Her eyes were wide and frightened. "Why are you making me beg?"

"I'm not doing a bloody thing," he said through clenched teeth, clenching his hands against the urge to throttle her. "Now, sit down and don't say a word except to tell me where Harry is."

Her mouth worked in fright as she sank like a stone into the chair.

"My wife!" he roared. "Where is she?"

"All right, Drew," she said, making a visible effort to become calm, and strangely enough, to mimic Harry when she was playing countess to the hilt. "I left her at Mr. Branson's. I'm certain she left right after I did and would have gone . . . somewhere. She has so many friends, and the Season is going on, and—"

The door flew open as Mr. Briggs stormed in, followed by the butler and the rest of the household staff.

"Simmons, get John Coachman up here! Briggs, Fellowes, Cook, Jane, Hinton—stay; the rest of you—out."

"John is gone, sir," Mr. Fellowes said. "The moment he realized that my lady was not in the coach, he found me and said he was going back to London."

"Fool," Briggs muttered. "He'll kill himself for sure."

"He thought he had a better chance in the fog than with my lady's husband," Mr. Fellowes said. "It's deadly outside, sir."

"Briggs, have Spot saddled. Hinton, take this piece of work somewhere, lock her up, and stand guard."

"Not likely," Cook said. "Me and Jane will handle this one. Our brains stay in our heads, where they belong."

"Fine," Drew said.

"You can't go out in this," Briggs said. "My lady would kill me if anything happened to you. I'll go."

"Damnit! She is *my* lady, and *I* will go after her." His throat convulsed. "Do you think my life is worth a damn without her?"

Priss sobbed. "You can't mean that, Drew."

"Shut up, Priss," Drew said thickly, then turned to Briggs, who stubbornly stood fast in the doorway. "Spot is Indian bred and Indian trained. He carried me through a spring blizzard that put this fog to shame and across the whole length of America . . . now, get him saddled!"

"If anyone will find her, it's you," Cook said. "But not if you don't compose yourself, sir." None too gently, she gripped Priss's arm, dragged her up from the chair, and frog-marched her to the door. "Come along, Jane. I know a nice cupboard where we can put this one. I haven't the time to watch her every move, and it's close to the kitchens."

"You should run into the coach along the way, sir," Mr. Fellowes said anxiously as he ran to keep up with Drew on his way out of the house and to the stables. "He'll be going at a snail's pace. May I suggest you take the coach on in for my—I mean, for Lady Saxon's comfort?"

Briggs waited with Spot and another horse, two pistols tucked into a wide belt. Tossing the reins to Drew, he mounted and reached for a lantern Hinton held up to him.

Drew paused in mounting Spot to regard Briggs. "Thank you, my friend," he said softly, then settled into the saddle and gathered the reins, controlling the horse that seemed to sniff his master's urgency.

"And who else would be guiding you through the city, sir?" Briggs asked, then spurred his horse forward.

Hinton gave Drew a lantern and the long rifle he'd brought from Kentucky, then made a show of handing him a brace of pistols, powder and balls. "Godspeed, sir."

"Godspeed and God help us all," Drew prayed, as he gave Spot his head, knowing the seasoned horse would do a better job than he of finding his way.

And with every inch they gained, he prayed for Harry's safety.

Spot lived up to his reputation, carrying Drew with a sure-footed slow trot that made better time than anticipated. The fog was like a whale's gullet, dark and sodden and making him feel as if he were inhaling liquid. His arm ached from holding the lantern high, searching for dim shadows barely discernible from the fog to indicate landmarks.

He heard a slow creak ahead.

Spot halted abruptly and stomped his hoof. Briggs ventured ahead slowly and called out. John Coachman answered.

Giving Spot the command to move on, he barely halted abreast of the coach. "Follow only to the boundary of the city. We will meet you there," he ordered, then again gave Spot his head, leaving the squeak of the lumbering coach far behind.

He heard the reassuring sounds of Briggs's presence behind him. "We're past the woods now, sir, and the road is straight."

Drew prodded Spot to pick up speed, keeping his seat with his knees as he held the lantern high.

At the outskirts of London, Briggs caught up with him and leaned over to catch Spot's reins.

"We won't be doing any more of that, sir. You won't do *your lady* any good if you lose your way or run into a building, now will you?" Without waiting for a reply, Briggs handed Drew his lantern and took the lead, still holding Spot's reins.

Drew allowed it, hating it, yet knowing Briggs was right. He would waste valuable time stumbling around the city.

Dawn made a poor appearance with a dim smudge of light in the East. Outlines appeared only as Drew and Briggs came within feet of one structure or another.

"There's the jeweler's shop," he called back. We'll take the route to Chapel Street, as it's closest. The countess would go to the nearest shelter."

"Who lives at Chapel Street?"

"Mr. Brummell, sir. And lucky his house is close. She might have made it there, and Mr. Brummell ain't no fool. He'd of kept her there 'til it was safe."

Oddly enough, Drew was reassured by the thought that Harry might be with Brummell. He'd only had two conversations with him, but he'd been impressed enough to confide in him. Whatever else "the Beau" might be, Drew had no doubt that he was a loyal friend to Harry. That Brummell was no fool added to his hope.

He dismounted and began to walk the streets, feeling his way, feeling for human forms, praying he would find none crumpled on the walk. He knew that the only souls idiot enough to prowl the London streets in a fog were criminals, looking for an easy mark.

The cold dampness eating into his bones, he be-

gan to call Harry's name as they slowly and me-
thodically searched every inch of the way to
Chapel street.

Silence. Nothing but empty, chilling silence in a
blind world.

The voice called her, a faint sound burrowing
through the darkness of her mind, insistent, desperate, even angry.

She didn't want to open her eyes, didn't want
to face a world without light to guide her to Drew.
But another voice called to her, hoarse and
strained and pain arrowed through her shoulder
as a hand shook her.

"My lady?" the hoarse voice croaked weakly.

"Go away," she said, and batted at the hand.

"My lady, you must attend. Please. Does anyone call you Harry?"

"Harry . . . Drew's Harry. I must get to Drew. I
promised I would keep him warm . . . promised to
be there."

"Harry, where are you? Damnit, answer me!"

"Here," the voice beside her called weakly.
"She is here."

She heard footsteps and cowered, afraid that
Jimmy had found her again. Her eyes opened,
found only a gray wall . . . and then shapes leaning toward her. "No!" She batted at them, the pistol still clutched in her hand, connecting with
something hard. She heard a grunt and kicked
out, tried to scream her rage that they would still
be here, still wanting to keep her from Drew. "I'll
kill you," she snarled, "if you touch me again."

She raised her foot, aimed it at the groin of one of the shapes.

"Be still, Harry. Be still," a familiar voice crooned. "It's all right. I'm going to take you home."

Arms wrapped around her, held her tightly. Warm arms. Strong arms. Drew's arms.

"Home," she said, "must get home . . . keep you warm . . . I promised." She cried out as pain seemed to surround her. "Hurt. Too tight."

His arms released her and then his hands moved over her, slowly, finding bruises and cuts and pain. So much pain, she was drowning in it.

"Her ribs, sir, and her head," the hoarse voice said. "She fought them. Kicked one in the ballocks, sir. They hit her. She fired the gun and scared them off. Saved us both."

"Quiet, now, lad," another familiar voice said. "We'll get you cared for right and proper."

Wheels creaked, approaching closer and closer. The sudden silence startled her when they stopped.

"I couldn't wait, sir," another voice said. "It's my fault. I couldn't wait in case you needed help.

Harriet whimpered as she was lifted and held against a solid chest. She calmed at the beat of a familiar heart in her ear. "Drew?"

"Yes, love, it's me. I was so cold without you."

He sounded odd—frightened and happy at the same time as movement stopped and she was snug in his arms, a blanket over her, that strong and familiar heart beating against her ear and a harsh, wrenching sob filling the space. Her coach, she realized. And Drew seemed to be weeping, for wetness ran down her cheek and she tasted salt in the gentle kiss he placed at the corner of her mouth. "Don't cry, Drew. I'm quite all right, you know. I think I broke Jimmy's ballocks. . . ."

Her voice deserted her as his breath wafted over her face. But the fog was inside the coach and she couldn't see him. "Drew? I can't hear you any more," she said in panic.

"Hush, Harry. Let me give thanks to God for saving you. Let me pray that you are all right."

Sighing, she closed her eyes, knowing that the darkness would not swallow her now. Drew would never allow it.

Chapter 26

"**O**h, please let me out," Priscilla wailed. "I didn't mean to hurt anyone. I didn't mean it. I can help search. I can ride. I've been in hurricanes. I can help!"

She huddled in a corner of the butler's pantry, sobbing until her chest hurt and her tears had long since dried, more frightened than she'd ever been in her life. She'd done something wrong; she could see that now. She'd heard of the dangers of London fog, but hadn't believed it could be that horrible.

How could she make such mistakes? How could everything she'd done cause so much trouble? "I don't want Harriet to be hurt. Oh, please let me help. Please let me make it up to everyone!"

Fresh tears spilled down her face. She didn't care. Drew was angry with her. She'd never seen him angry before. That, more than anything had convinced her that she'd done something horribly wrong. That once again, she'd hurt Harriet and put her in danger.

She pushed to her feet and pounded on the

door. "Let me out. Please don't leave me here in the dark."

"Aye, and I'll wager, my lady is none too fond of it about now, either," Cook said through the door. "Now, be a good girl and shut your mouth. None here is interested in your carrying on."

Priss gulped and stared, dumbfounded, at the door. Never had a servant dared to speak to her in such a way. She crumpled to the floor and sagged against a cupboard, reaching for a tablecloth to hug to her. They weren't going to let her out. She would be here all night.

She didn't dare ask them for the rag doll Mummy had made for her. "It doesn't matter," she said with a loud sniff. She deserved this. She knew she did.

Please, God, let Harriet be all right.

She curled into herself on the floor with the tablecloth rolled into a ball in her arms and tried not to think of what might go wrong with her other plan. It was too late to worry over it. All she could do was pretend ignorance. She would do anything if Harriet would be found safe and dry and warm. Anything to keep Drew from being angry with her again.

"She's only sleeping, Mr. Sinclair-Saxon," the physician said, as he straightened from Harriet's bed. "Your wife has a hard head. I see no signs of her being concussed—a miracle to be sure. I detect no indication of broken ribs, though they are badly bruised as are her shoulder and her face. All will heal in time."

"Then why does she appear unconscious?"

Drew asked, not convinced that Harriet's injuries could be reduced to mere bruising. She looked as if she had been run down by a team of at least four horses.

"I have observed that people who are in such situations experience abnormal surges of strength and energy. It is only logical that extreme exhaustion would follow. My best guess is that the pain and fear was great enough to cause her mind to retreat rather than deal with it . . . mind you, now, this is conjecture on my part. How the human body works with the mind is still a great mystery." Dr. Phillips sorted through his bag. "I am often accused of being a bit unorthodox in my beliefs, though the Saxon family seems to appreciate them."

Drew rubbed the back of his neck, paced to the door and back, then stood at the bedside, his hands on his hips, his gaze fixed on Harry. "You're certain she is just sleeping?"

"I am certain. You can shake her or speak with her and she will wake and respond, though I suggest you allow her to rest for the night. Knowing my lady, she will be driving everyone in the house to distraction within a day or so. Cook knows what your wife should have, and you may give her this, if need be." He handed Drew a bottle of laudanum. "I doubt she will stand for it, but she will rest better if she has a dose when the pain is plaguing her."

"I'm not sleeping," Harry said, proving Dr. Phillips correct. "How could I, with all of you standing about? And I won't take that vile stuff."

The physician raised a brow. "As I said: she has

a hard head in more ways than one. As to the young man—Mr. Dodd, is it?—the break in his arm is quite bad. I've set it and can only hope for the best. He tells me he is learning to be a gold-smith. I pray he has not been robbed of his abil-ity." He shook his head. "Only time will tell. A brave young man, remaining with my lady and shouting himself hoarse all night."

"Whatever it takes, Dr. Phillips, do it," Drew ordered. "Make certain he does not lose his ability to realize his ambition."

"Of course, of course," Dr. Phillips said as he picked up his bag and left the bedchamber. "Now, I'm told you also have a hysterical young lady about?"

Drew scowled at the mention of Priss. He didn't want to look at her, think about her, or be any-where near her.

"Please take care of her, Drew," Harry said, her eyes closed. "She is not a bad person, just a short-sighted and foolish one."

Drew surrendered. He would give Harry any-thing she wished—the moon, the stars, the uni-verse. But to take care of Priss was a wish beyond his ability to grant.

"I suggest you dose her with some laudanum and allow her to sleep it off," Dr. Phillips said over his shoulder, "so that the rest of you can sleep. I hear her sobbing below stairs all the way in here."

As the doctor left, Drew turned to Cook. "You didn't really lock her in the cupboard, did you?"

"That I did. I couldn't be watching her every move to make sure she didn't run away, could I?

She's none the worse for it. I gave her a pillow and a blanket and let her wail. To her credit, she wasn't hollering out of spite. She was wanting to know about *your* lady. Real worried, she is."

"A bloody lot of good it does now," Drew said harshly.

"Will everyone please go away so I may sleep?" Harry said.

Drew ushered Cook and Jane out and firmly closed the door. Turning back to Harriet, he stared at her, not knowing what to do next.

"Here, Drew." She patted the unoccupied half of the bed.

He shook his head. "Harry, you are a mess. I could brush you with a hair and hurt you."

"I need you close, Drew. All day I feared that I would lose you. I didn't know why, but the fear was there. And then I feared I would die and never see you again. Put pillows between us, but please sleep with me. I need to know you're within reach."

Relieved that at least one of them had the mental acuity to solve a problem, Drew left her long enough to collect pillows from his own bed and place them in a wall down the middle of her mattress. Carefully easing down, he lay on his side on top of the covers, facing her. "I need to know that you are within reach, too, Harry. I may very well shackle you to my side for the rest of our days."

She turned her head toward him. "Are you quite certain?"

"I fail to see why you should doubt it."

"The box, Drew. Will you tell me about the papers in the box?"

Rage again reared up to strike him, rendering him mute as he battled against it. It didn't belong here—not in Harry's bed. Not between them.

He sighed as the demon retreated, recognizing the truth of Drew's thoughts. "Later, Harry, we will speak of it. We have plenty of time."

Time seemed to crawl on its belly for the next week as Harriet's bruises faded from black and blue to yellow, purple, and green. She was going mad with inactivity. Even a visit from Priss would be welcome. Actually, Harriet did want to speak with Priss, but Drew kept her confined to the guest wing of the house and allowed her out of doors only when it was convenient for Jane and Mr. Briggs to accompany her. The poor girl must be going as mad as she, since it had rained off and on for five days and was often quite chilly.

"We should put you in your office," Beau quipped, as he followed Drew into the sitting room, where she was allowed to languish in a chair with wheels, of all things. "You will fade right into the decor."

"Beau! I am so happy to see you." She held out her arms. "Can you abandon propriety long enough to give me a hug?"

"Certainly not. I do not 'hug,' " her old friend said in mock affront, as he sketched an elegant bow and kissed the air above the back of her hand. His only concession was to squeeze her fingers gently before releasing her hand and closely examining her face. "You frightened the very starch from my neckcloth, my lady. Do not do it again."

Delighted by his rare show of concern, she

framed his face and kissed his cheek before he could straighten away from her.

"Really, Drew, you must take this hoyden in hand," he said gruffly. "This excess of affection is quite maudlin . . . makes one think that one is dying unawares." He smoothed the intricate knot of his pristine neckcloth and fussed with the drape of his coat. "Now, what mischief have you been up to now that you have mobility?"

"I've asked Mr. Briggs and Mr. Fellowes to refurbish the office," she replied. "It is *our* office now, and Drew looks rather silly among the fripperies. In fact, since you're here, I do wish you would advise them. Mr. Briggs tends toward the primitive, and Mr. Fellowes has a fondness for the flamboyant. I believe he is colorblind, Beau." She glanced at Drew from the corner of her eye, wondering why he remained propped against the mantel looking for all the world like a disapproving chaperon.

Beau groaned. "An office, Harry? How tedious. What do I know of places where people work?" He said the word as if it were the most distasteful of all curses.

"All right, Beau. It was just a thought. You will just have to tolerate clashing colors and gilt chairs and foolish whatnots when you visit us. And I shall tell everyone who sees it that you are responsible."

"Were you aware that your wife is an accomplished blackmailer, Drew?" Beau asked.

Drew's mouth twitched. "I am still learning the extent of my wife's accomplishments, George," Drew said affably as he pushed away from the mantel. "I have just received a bottle of French brandy. Why don't you join me in a drink and tell me all you know of my wife? It will no doubt save me from a good many surprises." He strolled over to her where she sat by the French doors and gave her a hard, fast kiss, then escorted "George" to the library, their discussion of French brandy as opposed to some spirits Drew had imbibed on his travels carrying through the halls.

Harriet stared openmouthed at the doorway long after they disappeared. George? Only Beau's close friends called him that. When had Drew developed an affinity for Beau? When had Beau decided that Drew was not a "thoughtless lout" as he'd claimed for so many years?

And why had Drew been avoiding being alone with her for the past few days? He was ever nearby, but he gave her no opportunity to engage in private conversation with him, and at night, he took her hand in his, slipped them both under the pillow, and promptly fell asleep.

A myriad of reasons paraded through her mind to be quickly discarded. He had tired of always seeing her, either covered with blemishes, or rashes or bruises. He'd determined that she was too independent for his taste. He missed his adventures. Each rang hollow and too unlike the Drew she had come to know so well in a few short weeks.

Only one reason riddled her with uncertainty. Drew had read the letter from his father. How that related to her she did not know, now that she was confident he had no intention of leaving again.

She smiled. She *was* confident. She *did* believe

he was here to stay, that he *wanted* to stay. She knew without question that he loved her, though he had yet to say it outright. It didn't matter. Until the past few days, Drew had been amazingly generous in displaying his emotions to her. And being shown was so much more satisfying than being told.

So what was wrong? Did he not wish to discuss the letter with her? A probability. Drew had never discussed any details pertaining to his origins, his lack of memory, or his nightmare with her.

A circumstance she was determined to change, once and for all.

He could show her his emotions and his passion all he wished and she would not require a single word to verify them. But this was different. This, her woman's instinct told her, was something that had been kept a secret for far too long.

"Jane," she said softly, with a touch of breathlessness, "I don't feel well all of a sudden." She pressed her hand to her forehead and wondered if it was too much. How she wished she had Priss's talent of summoning a pretty flush or paling complexion with a thought. It would be quite useful in some situations.

Jane peered down at her. "You look a bit peaked, at that. I'll take you to bed and then get you some tea."

"No, not bed, Jane. I vow I am developing a sore spot from lying down so much, but tea would be nice . . . oh, and would you please ask Hinton to come in here for a moment?"

Harriet grinned in satisfaction as her abigail bustled from the room and Hinton rushed inside.

"Hinton," she said conspiratorially, "I have a very great favor to ask of you."

"Anything, my lady," the footman answered eagerly.

A moment later, Hinton resumed his post outside her door, stationed there by Drew to keep Priss away.

Now all she had to do was wait. Within minutes, Jane would have told Drew all about his wife's sudden relapse and Drew would be haring up the stairs and storming into the apartment, protective instincts blazing, and she would have him neatly trapped.

Drew stormed into the sitting room, his gaze fixed on Harry, searching for signs of illness. He turned as the door slammed shut behind him and the lock clicked into place.

Harry sat calmly in her wheelchair with a stubborn set to her bruised jaw and mutinous gleam in her blackened eyes.

"You look like a raccoon," he said, as he advanced on her, knowing he had been tricked and having a good idea why. He'd known it was only a matter of time until she cornered him. He'd been preparing for it and supposed now was as good a time as any. "Have I told you about raccoons, Harry? They have a black mask around their eyes, like bandits, which is exactly what they are. They would steal inside camp when we were asleep and take our food. They can be quite devious about it." He leaned over, his hands gripping the arms of her chair. "What is it you feel you must be devious to obtain?"

She sat calmly, her head tilted slightly, her chin as bruised as the rest of her except for the dimple in the center, startlingly fair against the riot of color on her face. "I want answers, Drew. You've avoided the issue of your father long enough."

Would he ever become accustomed to her directness? A better question was whether he would ever become accustomed to her depth of caring more about him than about herself. "All right," he said, as he swiveled a chair from the table on one leg and sat astride, his arms layered over its back.

"All right?" Her eyes narrowed. "Surely it cannot be that easy."

"A great deal easier than avoiding the subject until I am certain you are on the mend," he replied. "I don't know how you will react, but if it is anything like my reaction, then I felt you should regain some strength first."

"You are still avoiding the issue, Drew. Tell me. I really must know."

He contemplated the carving on the back of his chair, wondering how to begin.

Harry drummed her fingers on the arm of her chair.

"You want to know about my father," he said without preamble. "According to Lord Sinclair's will, he was in truth my uncle, and his half-brother was my legal father. But then, you knew that, since you read the will."

"I am not interested in what the will says, Drew."

"No? Well, it will have to do, Harry," he said, as the rage threatened to rise again. "Because all I found was the will, the marriage certificate that proves my legitimacy, and a pile of ashes."

Her face paled beneath the bruises throwing them into stark relief in the dreary light of a rainy day. "Ashes? You found ashes?"

Harriet's stomach knotted as he stood, pushed the chair aside, and paced the room, one way, then the other, his mouth tight with anger.

"How? Someone burned the letter, that is how. Before I went to Singletrees that day, Priss warned me of what I might find. She was quite earnest in her pleas that I understand and forgive you. You were so angry at me, she said. You were not yourself, having to cope with father's illness and death. To hear her tell it, you were unhinged enough to take out your unhappiness on me."

Suddenly, a red haze swirled before her eyes. Fury threatened to choke her. She started to rise from her infernal chair, but quickly realized that she was too angry even to walk. Angry at Priss for her machinations, and angry at Drew for giving them credence. Gripping the wheels of her chair, she steered toward the door, nearly collided with the wall, and tried again. A wheel connected with the door frame as she reached for the latch and remembered the door was locked. "Botheration! Hinton! Let me out!"

Hinton opened the door and stared at her in surprise. Little wonder. Never had she been so infuriated. "Take me to Priss's room, please," she said, her voice vibrating with temper. "And do not bother looking to my husband for permission . . . now, Hinton."

Hinton complied.

"Call Cook, Briggs, Jane, Mr. Simmons, and Mrs. Simmons and tell them to meet me in Miss Whitmore's chamber," she ordered an upstairs maid passing them in the corridor.

She knew that Drew followed and wondered why he did not try to stop her, or at least question her. She almost hoped he would so she could burn his ears with the curses piling up in her mind.

But by the time they reached Priss's room, some semblance of reason had returned. Unfortunately, anger made her ribs ache and she had never developed the knack of sustaining a good fit of temper.

That thought revived her anger enough to put more authority into her voice than she had ever used with the household staff arriving at a run. "Take this room apart, item by item," she said tightly. "And you, Priss—" She pointed her finger at the girl sitting stunned at the head of her bed. "—Stay right where you are. Do not move, and do not say a thing except to answer my questions."

Noting Priss's chalky face, wide, frightened eyes, and the way the girl hugged a pillow to her chest as if it were a shield, she nodded in satisfaction. "You're afraid of me, Priss? Good. Be very afraid as you watch us violate your privacy and treat your possessions with disrespect. And if we do not find the letter you took from Lord Sinclair's box, I will have Cook and Jane search your person."

"Damnit, Harry—" Drew said.

"You can't stop me, Drew," she said, her voice brittle with cold fury. "This time Miss Priss has gone too far."

Chapter 27

"**P**lease do not tell me I cannot share this with the *ton*," George said in a stage whisper, as he stood beside Drew, each of them propping up a corner of the mantel.

"This is private, George," Drew warned. "It's family business."

"I suppose I should be flattered to be included in the spectacle."

"Yes, you should," Drew replied, as he kept a watchful eye on Harry. It was indeed a spectacle as his wife sat in her wheelchair as if it were a throne, directing the search of Priss's room while she coldly explained to the tearful and panic-stricken young lady that it would be far better if she simply told the truth. But Priss was mute with fear and cowering at the head of her bed as the staff went through every possession she owned.

"Should we stop this? Or perhaps take over?" Beau examined his nails. "It seems the manly thing to do."

"I would, but I am too fascinated to do more than watch," Drew said.

"We will find it, Priss," Harry said, with utter conviction.

"I don't know what you mean," Priss wailed. "Truly I don't."

"Truly?" Harry said, with regally arched brow and a flush of anger, adding yet another hue to the palette that was her face. "*Truly*, Priss, you might want Drew to believe the letter is burned. *Truly*, you might even have come close to burning it. But *truly*, you would not be able to bring yourself to do it."

Drew and George exchanged puzzled glances.

"I wouldn't?" Priss gulped on a sob. "Why not?"

Harry imperiously motioned for Jane to wheel her over to Priss. Nose to nose with her, Harry took Priss's chin in a none too gentle hold. "Because somewhere beneath all your guile and self-absorption, you have a nagging conscience."

"How would you know?" Priss asked sullenly.

"I know because I see myself in you, Priss," Harry said with a sigh, as if her anger had suddenly left her. "Because if I had been raised just a bit differently by my papa and all the people in this room, I would not have recognized the line dividing acceptable behavior from irresponsible actions. And even so, I engaged in certain manipulations to get what I wanted. The problem was that I promptly lost it because I did not think beyond my own wishes." She released Priss as if she were tossing away questionable food. "One day, *if* you prove me right and give me the letter, and when I am not so furious with you, I would like to tell you about it. And then I would like to see you learn from it before you do harm to yourself."

"Why should you care?"

"Other than the fact that I actually like you, Priss, I have no idea why I care." She rolled her chair back and rubbed her temple. Each person in the room seemed to be keeping one eye on their task and the other on Harry.

"Do you suppose we could unleash Harriet on the French?" Beau asked from the side of his mouth.

"It's a thought," Drew said. "She would crush Boney with a look."

"And perhaps a word or two," Beau added. "Upon my word, but she is good."

"Very good," Drew agreed.

Harry threw them both a glare cold enough to freeze hell.

"A look would do it," Beau commented.

Lowering her hand, Harry pinned her glare back on Priss. "I can assure you that there is a limit to my caring, Priss." She drummed her fingers on the arm of her chair as if to emphasize her diminishing patience. "If I have to find the letter myself, I will lose all respect for you, and I will not give a hangnail what happens to you." Wheeling around, Harry presented her back to Priss—a countess's back, proud and arrogant and formidable.

Priss stared at her with confusion, then sought Drew's gaze.

He arched a brow and crossed his arms over his chest.

She glanced at Brummell and received a bored shrug.

The servants continued to examine every piece of her clothing. Cook found a bundle of letters and began to unfold them one by one, scanning the contents.

"You cannot win, Priss." Harry sighed again as she fixed her gaze on Drew, a hard, determined gaze that he'd never seen before. "I have always believed that Drew and I belong together. I love him. He is mine. I will not let him go."

"You bought him," Priss cried.

"No, Priss, I did not, though in fairness, I should admit that it is a matter of interpretation. But I did not buy his presence here now. I did not buy his passion. You can rightly assume he gave both to me of his own volition."

Brummell gave a small, almost soundless whistle at Harry's mention of the unmentionable in mixed company.

"You . . . he . . ." Priss sputtered. "You made love?"

Cook gave a toothy grin. Hinton flushed. Briggs didn't flinch. The butler coughed and his wife, the housekeeper, dropped the petticoat she was searching.

Brummell seemed to straighten a bit as if he were listening for the answer.

Harry said nothing. Drew could do nothing but hold her gaze and give her a small, private smile.

Harry turned her head, without further response.

"You love Drew," Priss stated. "I didn't know. I heard you talking to your solicitor about an annulment and thought you wanted to be free. And Drew always seemed so lonely and frustrated. I wanted to make him happy. I thought I would be the perfect wife. I didn't *ever* mean to hurt you. I wanted to help you both be happy. . . .''

She ran to Drew and stared up at him, a small trace of defiance lingering in her expression. "Tell me that you don't resent having to take her name. Tell me that you wouldn't like to be a baron and have your own lands. That is why I did it, you know—to protect your birthright. It was never, ever, to hurt you or Harriet. I love you both so much that I don't know what I should do anymore. Mummy and Daddy love me, but they were always too busy to pay attention to me. Daddy just patted my head and Mummy didn't listen when I asked her questions. Even when I annoyed you, you listened to me and answered my questions.''

"Priss," Drew said, as he met the gaze of each person in the room, ending with Harry, remaining with Harry. "All of you, listen carefully. I am proud to carry the Saxon name, which was given to me out of love. I have no desire to be a baron or a duke or even the Regent. I am Drew Sinclair-Saxon. I have earned my place in the world and I am satisfied. Are there any questions?''

"But how can you say that?" Priss asked in genuine confusion. "You are a man. How can you be content with a name that is not your own?''

Shrugging, Drew held Harry's gaze. "I am a man who has given up his pride for a rewarding life with an extraordinary woman.''

With a wrenching sob, Priss whirled and came face to face with Harry.

Harry stared at her without expression in her bruised and battered face.

"I'm sorry," Priss whispered. "It's my fault—all of it." She lifted her hem to reveal a pocket sewn into her petticoat. Releasing the button, she pulled out what looked to be several sheets of foolscap folded into quarters. She pressed it to her chest as she approached Harry.

Petticoats and ribbons and trinkets fell to the floor as each person in the room immediately dropped whatever he was searching and turned as one to watch Harry and Priss. Drew would swear that no one breathed. Even Brummell was rendered speechless.

He started as Cook slapped Priss's letters onto the small desk and Simmons ushered the servants from the room.

"Hurry along, now," he heard her whisper to them in the hall, "we know they will be all right now, don't we? We needn't know more than that . . . and we needn't speak of this. It's family business," she said, repeating Drew's earlier words to Brummell.

Drew knew without doubt that they would heed Cook's warning, as extraordinary as it might seem. Servants were notorious for their grapevine, but these people were more than hirelings. They'd certainly never been treated like hirelings—

"Let it go, Priss," Harry said gently, with a weariness that made Drew ache inside. But he couldn't stop her, not now. She would never forgive him if he interfered—

"When I was a child, I liked to chase rainbows," Harry continued, "I caught one in Drew's first smile at me. He never smiled before that, you see. I knew then that the rainbow was more important than the pot of gold. You are searching for the gold, Priss, and it is easily spent, as is love for the sake of love. But if you become the woman I believe you can be, then you will learn the difference and recognize the rainbow that is meant for you."

Harry sat in her chair and waited.

Her head hung low enough to trip over, Priss handed Harry the letter.

Harry kept her hands folded in her lap.

Priss frowned and then approached Drew warily, as if she were terrified of him.

Though he still had a strong desire to throttle her, Drew also felt sorry for her. She might be loved by her parents, but she was female—to be indulged because girls were to be indulged, and neglected because females were ornaments and goods for barter. A misconception society perpetuated for its convenience. A belief structured to uphold male pride. But then not everyone had grown up with Harry to show them the error of such nonsense.

He accepted the letter and held it, wondering why a few sheets of paper had held such power over them. He glanced at the embers in the grate—

"Don't you dare," Harry said without looking at him. "You may burn it only after you have read it."

He tucked it into his coat pocket and left the room without another word.

*   *   *

Harriet watched Drew disappear into the hall with a sadness borne of futility. Drew would read his letter and know the truth. Too late. He'd so desperately needed it as a child. But no longer. He had formed himself in the last twelve years, without knowing to whom he was really connected or to what he really belonged. He had looked into the mirror of his soul and found himself. Perhaps that was a good thing rather than a sad one. So many of her acquaintances were bound to and ruled by tradition and names rather than to their own humanity.

"Priss, you may set your room to rights now, and then I suggest you sleep. We will speak again in a day or two. By then I should have forgiven you for what you have done."

"How can you forgive me?" Priss cried. "I have been so horrid."

"It is easier to forgive than it is to stop caring, Priss," Harriet said, fighting exhaustion.

Beau stepped forward and silently took the handles of her chair, turning her and wheeling her from the room.

"We will leave you now, Miss Whitmore, to put your house in order, so to speak," he said, ever the guardian of good manners.

As if he knew Harriet wanted to leave Drew alone to read his father's letter, he motioned for two footmen to carry her chair down the stairs.

"No," she said. "Drew will have gone back to Singletrees. I wish to wait for him in our rooms. I can manage."

"You were put in this contraption to keep you from moving too much until your ribs heal and I can't imagine that handling the wheels is comfortable for you," he said. "And I would not like to experience your husband's wrath should he find you on your feet. He'd likely ruin my coat."

Harriet smiled as he steered her to the master suite. In this she would accede to Drew's wishes. He was, after all, the man of the house.

Drew rode Spot toward Singletrees, barely noticing the rain and the mud and the chill in the air, knowing only that he must read his father's letter at the place where the spirit of Edward Sinclair seemed to still linger. He had avoided reading the letter ever since his return but could do so no longer. Harry had been hurt and her life put at risk because of it. It was important to her that he read it.

It was important to him that he read it and get back to her. Something was not quite right with Harry. More than her anger and more than her outrage, she had seemed hurt . . . and afraid.

He'd known the moment she'd been in such a rush to get to Priss that he'd not made himself clear to her, that she was defending herself from his implied accusation as much as she was seeing justice done. But then, she had not given him much chance to correct her.

He'd asked Cook to make Harry some of her soothing tea with a dash of brandy, hoping that Harry would perhaps take a nap while he was gone. If she didn't, she would be in a fine stew by the time he returned.

They were going to have to work on communicating with one another. He would see to it the moment he returned to Saxon Hill.

Tossing Spot's reins to a startled butler, he took the front steps two at a time and headed straight for the salon.

He sat before the hearth, the portrait of him and his father looking down on him as he carefully unfolded the letter and forced himself to read . . .

My dear son,

Do not presume to contradict me. You are my son, a truth I should have given you long before this. In my defense I can only say that I did what I thought best for you at the time. For many years I have planned to tell you this truth and the events that brought it into being, but I did not want to do it in a letter. Now, I have no other choice. Though you have a right to know of my folly, I do not wish it to become public knowledge and I have ever mistrusted the post. Now that I have dawdled about trying to explain myself, I suppose I should get on with it.

I met Mary Margaret Collins during a visit to my half-brother, Baron Cassidy. The moment I saw her I knew I loved her, and it appeared to be the same for her. Still, it was an impossible situation. I had been married to Lady Sinclair only the year before—a marriage of convenience and no affection whatsoever. And Mary Margaret had a cause. I know what you heard in Ireland, so I must cast sensibilities aside and tell you that your mother was a virgin until I came along. What she did in the salon of the English officer, she did for Ireland—to gather information from both sides of the continuing dispute between Ireland and the Crown in an effort to neutralize potentially volatile situations. She had hoped so strongly that our differences could be settled in peace. We did try to keep apart, but could not. I did not know that she had conceived a child as she contrived to keep it from me in an attempt to protect me. Since I had to return to England to my wife (who was not with me on that first visit), I was none the wiser, though I should have realized the possibility. I was young and entirely too arrogant to think of consequences. My half-brother knew and persuaded Mary Margaret to marry him, to give you a name and a legacy. He had no wife or children, and being the good man he was, thought to ensure my son's future as well as my peace on the matter. Mary Margaret agreed with the provision that their marriage be kept secret for as long as possible. She did not want to cease her activities, and as long as the marriage was legal, there was no need for anyone to know until you were older.

I discovered the truth upon my next visit some four years after your birth. Mary Margaret had sent you to her mother so that I would not know of your existence, but events conspired against us all. My brother was dying; he had known for some time. He called Mary Margaret in and told us both what had to be done. I was stunned to know that the woman I loved had married my brother. And I was moved beyond description by the love and loyalty of the man with whom I shared a mother. My brother—God rest his soul—passed on quietly that same night.

Unbeknownst to my brother and myself, my wife overheard. In anger, she reported to the authorities that Mary Margaret was a spy and a traitor to the kingdom. Mary Margaret was still at Cassidy Tower when they came for her. Rebels also came, and you can guess the results. Mary Margaret was mortally wounded in the fight. Cassidy Tower caught fire with my wife trapped inside. We will never know how the fire started, and though the tower was stone, the window hangings and tapestries and furnishings burned hotly. I could not get inside to save my wife.

Mary Margaret died in my arms, but not before telling me where I might find you. She asked for my promise that I would not tell you the truth, that I honor my brother's actions by not allowing you to be known as anything but his son. I could do nothing but ease her passing and my own conscience with my promise. I put off telling you of my brother for your entire childhood, selfishly wanting to be your father in your eyes.

But your mother and my brother are gone from this world and I daresay are not troubled by anything but your own peace. I cannot allow you to continue believing that Mary Margaret Collins was anything but a good woman who loved the wrong man. I kept the secret as much out of fear as out of honor. Few men in our society can forgive a father who condemns them to the life of a bastard, particularly when steps have been taken to give them not only legitimacy, but an inheritance as well.

I must also admit that it was the bracelet Harriet took from one of your shipments that convinced me that I must tell you the truth. If you look carefully, you will see names inscribed on the inside. Names of ten men and ten women who loved throughout the history of my family. There is a mate to the one your wife wears day and night—both symbols of love, both holding the memories of those who loved so well and so completely. I know not why the bracelets have disappeared from time to time over the centuries, or why certain men and women have found them again, but the tradition was upheld and each couple had their names etched into the gold. Mary Margaret and I wore those bracelets until they disappeared that horrible night. It is my hope that you and Harriet will be compelled to add your names to the others . . . I am weary, and having done the right thing after years of fearing it, I can now rest in peace. Please forgive me.

> With all my love,
> I am your devoted and proud father,
> Edward Sinclair

Drew folded the letter and tucked it into his pocket, seeing nothing but the love and tragedy of the past. The love of his parents for one another and for him. The love of one brother for the other. The love of a man and a woman.

He stepped out into the rain and walked slowly to the small family chapel where only one Sinclair rested. *His father.* The words were a chant in his mind as he entered the sanctuary of stone and stained glass, as he descended into the crypt and knelt before the stone holding the shell of the man who had lived with so much loss and torment.

"Father," he said. "I hope that you hear me say it. I hope that you know I say it with pride and love. As you once said to me: there is nothing to forgive."

He rose and touched the plaque engraved with his father's name and saw another just beside it.

He stared and swallowed and released a deep shuddering sigh as he squinted to read the name.

MARY MARGARET CASSIDY
BELOVED

He touched the bronze square, traced the letters one by one. "I know you now," he said. "It is enough."

He emerged to a cleansing wind and dark clouds scudding across the late afternoon sky and rode home to his home, his future, his wife.

Chapter 28

Drew saw her in the distance, her head down as she walked the intricate labyrinth set out in flat colored stones in the garden. Riding straight into the stables, he leapt off Spot's back and strode toward her, stopping for no one.

"What are you doing out here?" he asked, in a deceptively soft voice.

"I feel only an ache now," she replied, without looking up from her path along the design. "Aside from looking like a raccoon, I feel much better."

"Nevertheless, you are not healed yet. You should be resting."

"I cannot bear another minute in that room. When the sun appeared, I had to come outside."

"Chasing rainbows?" he asked.

"I haven't seen one."

Slapping his gloves against his thigh, he stared down at the labyrinth, tracing its pattern. "I remember when you saw a picture of this in a book and begged your Papa to make one."

"Yes. It took the gardeners two months to lay it out just right." Her mouth curved up in a small smile of remembrance. "You and I spent many hours walking around and around, so careful not to step over the lines of the path and concentrating so hard we would forget to speak." She raised her head suddenly and caught his gaze. "You read the letter?"

"I did."

"So did I," she said, as if she were commenting on tomorrow's menu. "I broke the seal and read the letter and then used Lord Sinclair's ring to seal it again."

"I know—"

"I didn't do it out of any noble purpose," she continued, the words tumbling over one another as they spilled from her tongue. "I did it out of curiosity—because you would never tell me anything but what was common knowledge and I was overset enough to convince myself that I deserved to know—" She gulped and halted. *"You know? How do you know? Did Priss tell you that, too?"*

"No, Priss didn't tell me. There were tear stains on the letter—the page about father and Mary Margaret, to be exact." He tipped up her bruised face with his forefinger under her chin.

"Tear stains?" An incredulous laugh escaped her, then she tightened her mouth in a straight seam to contain it.

He nodded. "I could not imagine Priss weeping over the tragic love affair of people she didn't know." He paused to swallow the emotion that lingered so close to the surface. "And who else but you would have brought Mary Margaret to rest beside my father?"

"I cannot imagine how you reached that conclusion. Perhaps your father brought her to Single-trees all those years ago."

He shook his head in reproach. "The set of the stone and the bronze plaque are recent. You did it, Harry, and I am flummoxed at how you managed it." He swallowed down the emotion that was so close to the surface. He lowered his mouth to take hers in a gentle, lingering kiss. "Thank you, Harry."

She said nothing as she stepped back from his touch and resumed her stroll around the labyrinth. "I am amazed that you are not angry. You should be angry. Reading your letter and then presuming to move Mary Margaret was as much a violation of your privacy as what Priss did."

"Perhaps as angry as you were that I had left you for twelve years? Or as angry as you surely were when I promised to return and was almost three years late?" He stepped onto the labyrinth at the beginning of the maze and began to walk it behind her. "And I am amazed that you feel guilt over it." He stared at her, at the fall of rich hair she'd left hanging down her back from a ribbon tied at her nape. Long, straight silky hair, like golden smoke. The workings of her mind awed him, as intricate as the design they walked, yet as easy to read as the pattern set in stone. "I have seen fear in your eyes and wondered at it. You pushed and pushed for me to read the letter because you couldn't stand knowing a secret and not being able to share it with me. And you admit such a heinous act without tears or hysteria or pleas for forgiveness."

Sniffing once, she surreptitiously swiped at her

eyes. "I was so afraid you would not understand that I had to know what had driven you all of your life, and what caused you such torment in your sleep. At the time I believed I did it out of love, but my dratted curiosity played a part. It has always been my downfall."

"Why else are you curious, but when it involves someone you love? Why do you ever do anything, but out of love?"

She sighed and said nothing, as if she felt awkward in his presence. As if she had things to say and didn't know where to begin.

He echoed her sigh, though his was one of exasperation. "We have had quite a day of truths and will continue to do so until there is nothing left to question." He had almost caught up to her and adjusted his pace accordingly, not wanting to touch her again. Not until everything had been said. "And here is a truth you should heed: You are my wife. A wife who has endured and tolerated a great deal more than you should have from me. A wife who has known every facet of my business dealings for twelve years. How many correspondences addressed to me have you read and answered on my behalf?"

"But that was business," she said, seeming completely scattered by his attitude.

"*Our* business," he said firmly. "As my father's letter was *our* business. It affects *our* marriage."

"All right, Drew. I am convinced that I should not writhe with guilt any longer. And of course you're right. The letter does affect our future. It does trouble me."

"You have never had difficulty speaking your mind, before, Harry. Why now?"

Abruptly, she veered off the labyrinth and walked to a bench beneath a latticed arbor. "I really can't appreciate your staring at me all the time, Drew. I look positively hideous."

He sat beside her in the place where they had sat as children, caught in the memories. "This is where you taught me how to be a child—how to explore and how to find delight, how to be silly, and how to get into mischief without fear of rejection. This is where I learned how to trust the love of a father—even a foster one, as I'd thought—without fear of losing that love."

He leaned back and spread his arms along the back of the bench, his hand brushing her shoulder, caressing it. "I have seen you with spots on your face and I have been with you when you reeked of onions. You have seen me fall in the fishing pond and come out with reeds on my head. You insisted on marrying me when I didn't even have a whisker on my chin, making me feel all the things a man needs to feel—needed, wanted . . . and strong. You made me feel strong enough to accomplish anything." Her continued silence unnerved him, annoyed him because he didn't know how to end it. "We consummated our marriage against the dressing room wall," he said in desperation, hoping to shock her, "so why are we having such difficulty conversing about our future?"

Rather than displaying shock, she smiled, a delicate, fragile bow of her lips. "Our future."

"I can't imagine a future with anyone else. Can you?"

"I never could," she said in a near whisper.

"Then let us dispense with this nonsense and get on with it. You seem to be bursting with subjects you are afraid to broach. When did you become so timid?"

"When I realized that I could not bear to part with you again, Drew. I feel quite desperate and I don't know how to manage it."

"Is that what frightens you, Harry? That the letter and my inheritance will change things between us? Pray, tell me how."

"I don't know, do I?" she said, in that small voice that disturbed him. "The past has taken you from me before and now that you have an estate in Ireland—"

"*We* have an estate in Ireland," he corrected. "And I am going to accept it, because as Baron Cassidy's nephew by blood and son by law, I am the only legal heir to Cassidy Tower. Someone must see to the people there."

She closed her eyes. "You will have to go—"

"*We* will." He couldn't resist leaning over, kissing her eyelids with a feather touch. "It was once a grand place, Harry. I would like you to help me restore it and only you can bring it to life."

"*We* will," she repeated, as her eyes snapped open. "Good. I could not—will not—again stand by, waiting for you to return to me, Drew."

"And I cannot—will not—leave you again, Harry. For any reason." He nibbled her ear and lowered his hand to her breast, stroking the center in slow, lazy circles.

She trembled beneath his touch, and caught his hand, holding it tightly in her lap, as if she would never let him go. "You also own Singletrees."

"Perfect, isn't it?" he said with a grin. "Saxon Hill for our firstborn—I insist upon a girl to be the next Countess Saxon. Cassidy Tower for our second—a boy, since only males can inherit that title. Singletrees will be a handy spare."

"Children? You want children?"

"I want our children, Harry. And if we have more than three, we will simply purchase more houses so that each will always have a place to call their own."

"Drew, stop," she cried, and buried her face in her hands. "Please stop."

"I think not," he said as he pried her hands away from her face. "Any other questions? Doubts? Mild concerns?"

"I don't need to hear more, Drew," she said frantically. "I really cannot bear to doubt you any further."

"Blast it, Harry!" he roared as he lunged to his feet and angrily prowled the small arbor. "We have always been forthright with one another. It is what makes us special." He halted to keep from plowing down a bush and softened his voice. "I do not want blind faith from you. I cannot live up to that."

"If I ever questioned why I love you so much, you have just provided the answer," she said, yet still did not meet his gaze.

"Then look at me, *my* lady, and tell me why I sense such sadness in you."

"It shouldn't matter, Drew, but it does," she

choked. "I should be able to overlook what was a perfectly natural assumption on your part, but it won't . . . stop . . . hurting." Her chest heaved with her effort not to cry as she covered her mouth with her hand to hold back a sob.

He knew immediately what it was—how he had hurt her. He'd thought of it before but it had been lost among all the revelations and emotions of the day. "Priss," he said harshly. "You think I believed her. That I believed you burned the letter."

"How could you not believe her? I think I *was* a bit unhinged then, insisting to anyone who would listen that you were not dead and then ranting at you in my letters."

"You never rant, Harry, though your anger is a frightening thing. Even Briggs was impressed with your display today." He swiped at the back of his neck, disgusted that he was avoiding the issue after insisting that it be aired. Turning, he closed the distance between them in three long strides, leaned over her, fenced her in with one hand on the arm of the bench and the other on the back of it beside her. "I believed her, Harry—"

A tortured sound came from her throat. "I know. And I understand. It's ridiculous that I allow it to upset me. But I always wanted you to know that you had me to trust and to believe in. I wanted so badly for you to know that, with me, you would be forever loved and forever wanted and forever needed—"

"Hush, and allow me to finish," he ordered, more brusquely than he intended. "I did believe Priss, for the space of a single thought. It was

more than enough to chastise me for my gullibil-
ity."

She stared up at him, as if she were an animal
caught in the light of a torch, her gaze searching,
and so unbearably sad.

"You don't ask what thought, Harry. Has your
opinion of me fallen so low that you do not think
it significant?"

"What thought, Drew?" she asked, her chin
quivering.

"That you would never do such a thing," he
said, as he crouched before her and took her
hands in his. "That you value people too much to
violate them in such a way." He kissed each of
her fingers, then enfolded her hands between his
again. "And later that night, I realized a very profound and humbling truth. I realized that even *if*
you had done it, I wouldn't give a damn."

She sobbed and gulped it back and continued
to stare at him.

"I wouldn't give a damn," he continued, needing to say it, needing her to know, "because *if* you
had done it, it would have been for the best of
reasons, unselfish, loving reasons. Because I trust
you that much, and because I love you that
much."

She did cry then, copious, sweet tears that twinkled on her cheeks in the sunlight.

Fresh rain-washed air seemed to dance about
them as Drew eased her down to sit on his lap,
his back against the bench, holding her and shush-
ing her, adoring the depth of her caring whether
he loved her or not, worrying that she would hurt
her healing ribs if she continued to sob. The sun

peeked out from behind lingering clouds. Water glistened on the trees like dainty crystals radiating light.

Crooking his finger gently under her chin, he tilted her face up, taking each of her tears with a kiss, absorbing the heartache he'd caused her, wishing he could bear it instead of her.

She quieted and became limp in his arms. "I suppose I will be Harriet Cassidy now," she said, "if that is your choice. I've never paid much attention to details of names and lineage and inheritance, but I did look into it after reading the will. You are still the only living male of blood descent in the Cassidy line, regardless of whether your father was the baron or Lord Sinclair."

"You are Harriet Sinclair-Saxon and I am Drew Sinclair-Saxon," he said, as he smoothed her hair over her shoulder and stroked the length down her side, over her breast to her waist, and wound a strand around his finger, loving the feel of it, the fresh carnation scent of it.

"But—"

"I have no need of titles and I've had enough names in my life. I'm quite attached to yours. It is the only one I had any say in acquiring."

"It wasn't right of any of us to insist you add the Saxon name to yours."

"It's only a name, Harry—a means of identifying one person from another, and of connecting one person to another." He twined another strand around his finger.

"Sinclair is your family name," she argued. "As is Cassidy."

"So I am to become Drew Sinclair Cassidy? It

doesn't ring right, not like Sinclair-Saxon." He bent his head, nuzzled her neck, frustrated that there were only a few places he could safely kiss her without hurting her. "If we were to say that a single name must be attached to everyone in a family, each person in your household would have to change his name to Saxon." Lifting his head, he stared at the multihued tapestry of her face, seeing only the beauty that was Harriet. "If I have learned nothing else, it is that family is made up of hearts coming together in love, souls knowing they belong together. It has nothing to do with bloodlines and names."

She sighed and laid her head against his shoulder, her head tipped up to look at him. "I used to believe you were perfect, Drew. I was so very relieved to discover that you were not. It is a terrible burden trying to live up to perfection, yet now I wonder. . . ."

He swooped down, captured her mouth, demanding with his tongue that she part her lips and allow him entrance, then plundered slowly, completely, feeling as if they were melting into one another, becoming one with only a kiss.

A swath of color caught his eye as he raised his head, glimmering in the rain-washed sky. He smiled and pointed. "There's your rainbow, Harry. Look."

She touched his lips, traced his smile with her forefinger as she stared up at him and nowhere else. "Yes, I see my rainbow, Drew. A curve, a bit skewed, and holding every dream I ever had."

He breathed deeply, wanting to crush her against him, wanting to hold her as close as he could. "I wonder if I will ever get enough of you, Harry."

"Well, you have forever with me to try . . . oh, look."

His gaze followed the path of her finger, to the second rainbow appearing alongside the first, following its mate into forever.

Epilogue

❦

Sunlight poured through the diamond panes of the chapel windows at Singletrees—pure radiant golden light after another week of rain and fog. Harriet hadn't minded. She and Drew had spent the time in his bed in her bedchamber, with the luxury of wood fires in the hearth and their meals served wherever they happened to be in the suite.

She'd had Drew's larger bed moved into her room. Never again would he be cold in the night. Never again would she be lonely in the silence.

He waited for her at the altar, watched her as she walked down the aisle toward him on Beau's arm, stopping to embrace Lorelei, her friend in good times and bad, to kiss the cheek of Lorelei's husband, Viscount Dane, who had shown society how deeply love could run.

On the other side of the aisle stood Mr. and Mrs. Simmons, Cook, Mr. Briggs, Mr. Fellowes, Jane, Hinton, the footmen, gardeners, stableboys, grooms, scullery maids and chambermaids from both Singletrees and Saxon Hill. Their tenants waited outside.

Harriet stepped away from Beau and looped her arm through Drew's, standing with him as she had twelve years ago. She tugged on his arm, urging him to lean closer so she could whisper a secret in his ear. "You are marrying me just in time, sir. Another seven months or so and we would be found out."

"I know," he said blandly. "I am relieved that we will now know what to do with the second bedchamber in our suite. There will be no nursery on the third floor for our children. I want to be able to hear if they cry out in the night." And then he gave her the smile of joy she had wanted so badly the first time they had spoken their vows.

Disregarding the vicar and those who looked on, he gathered her in his arms and lifted her, then slid her down his body, took her mouth in a kiss that would have shocked less earthy souls than those gathered in the stone chapel.

"I am quite certain you are supposed to wait for that," the vicar said indulgently. "Shall we behave—I mean, begin?"

"By all means," Drew replied. "And perhaps you should hurry."

"Don't you dare," Harriet said with a reproachful glance at Drew. After all, repeating their vows had been Drew's idea—foolish to most, incredibly romantic and sentimental to Harriet. And she had once thought that romance left a great deal to be desired.

Apparently, Drew was determined to prove her wrong. For the past four weeks, he had taken her into London to enjoy what was left of the Season, courting her as if they were seventeen again and in love as only the very young can be. And every night, he made up to her—and perhaps to himself—all the nights she'd spent alone, making love to her with all the passion and giving of emotion that only those who have lived a while can understand and treasure.

The vicar intoned the vows, and this time Harriet listened intently and repeated them properly.

Drew took her hands in his. "I, Drew Matthew Sinclair most certainly do take Twinkle as my wife and all else that you said, sir."

Moved beyond bearing, she didn't hear the rest. She didn't need to. Not when he was smiling down at her, giving her rainbows with every moment that passed.

And then he gave her the unexpected—two gold bracelets fashioned in Celtic bands interwoven with two herons, the sign of the creator of life. He had not allowed her to wear hers again, and his had disappeared from his arm. Drew had refused to tell her why.

As if by arrangement, the vicar held a candelabra near as Drew turned the bracelets to the light.

She looked because she knew it was what he wanted, though try as she might she had never been able to read the ten sets of inscriptions. But the gold shimmered in the soft light and the engravings seemed to waver and deepen as if they were new again. She read the names of men and women and those they had loved.

Four more names had been added. Edward Sinclair and Mary Margaret Collins. Drew Sinclair and Harriet Saxon.

And then, as she blinked away tears and smiled, all the names faded into barely recognizable script . . . except for hers and Drew's, new and deep, signifying a beginning that would continue for many years to come.

The vicar removed the candelabra and said the words that would weave them together in an everlasting braid as the ones fashioned of precious gold they placed on one another's arms.

"Now you may kiss," the vicar said good-naturedly.

They obeyed willingly, each placing a hand over the bracelet worn by the other.

Lorelei wept openly, a rarity for her stalwart friend, who wiped her eyes with one hand and rubbed her growing belly with the other. Her husband, Lord Dane, beamed and threw her a wink.

Harriet paused at the last pew and took the hands of a young girl in hers. "One day, you will have this, Priscilla. Please do not be impatient. Love is well worth the wait."

They turned at the entrance to smile at their guests, at the people who, in one way or another, had shaped their lives and their perceptions, sharing experiences and truths and wisdom, caring for and comforting two children who had, each in his own way, lost more than any child should lose and known more loneliness that any person should know.

Hearts gathering together in love and souls recognizing that they belonged to one another. . . .

A family, sharing dreams and rejoicing together in their fulfillment.

Dear Reader,

I just love Julia Quinn! So I'm so excited that, next month, her latest Avon Romantic Treasure is coming our way. It's called *How to Marry a Marquis*, and it's one of the most perfectly charming, witty and romantic love stories you'll ever read. In it, a delightful heroine stumbles upon a Regency-style version of *The Rules*, and needless to say romance follows.

Contemporary romance fans are in for a tender, heartwarming, wonderful treat as Neesa Hart makes her Avon debut with *Halfway to Paradise*. Single mom Maggie Crandall has faced tragedy and vowed to never love again. But handsome Scott Bishop has some very different ideas. Sprinkle in a touch of magical intervention and you have a love story sure to make you laugh and cry.

Genell Dellin returns to Avon Romance with a fabulous new historical mini-series, *The Renegades*—these are tough men tamed by the women who love them, beginning with *Cole*. He may be a gunslinger with a dangerous past, but he's about to be changed by the love of one very special woman.

Suzanne Enoch returns with *Taming Rafe*, a delightfully sparkling Regency-set Avon Historical Romance from an author whose humor, lively dialogue and sparkling sensuality have made her a reader favorite. Here, a confirmed rake wins a tumbling down manor on a bet...but what he doesn't bet on is also winning the hand of the manor's very beautiful owner.

Until next time,
Enjoy!

Lucia Macro

Lucia Macro
Senior Editor

Avon Romances—
the best in exceptional authors
and unforgettable novels!

ENCHANTED BY YOU   **by Kathleen Harrington**
79894-8/ $5.99 US/ $7.99 Can

PROMISED TO A STRANGER   **by Linda O'Brien**
80206-6/ $5.99 US/ $7.99 Can

THE BELOVED ONE   **by Danelle Harmon**
79263-X/ $5.99 US/ $7.99 Can

THE MEN OF PRIDE COUTNY: **by Rosalyn West**
THE REBEL   80301-1/ $5.99 US/ $7.99 Can

THE MACKENZIES: PETER   **by Ana Leigh**
79338-5/ $5.99 US/ $7.99 Can

KISSING A STRANGER   **by Margaret Evans Porter**
79559-0/ $5.99 US/ $7.99 Can

THE DARKEST KNIGHT   **by Gayle Callen**
80493-X/ $5.99 US/ $7.99 Can

ONCE A MISTRESS   **by Debra Mullins**
80444-1/ $5.99 US/ $7.99 Can

THE FORBIDDEN LORD   **by Sabrina Jeffries**
79748-8/ $5.99 US/ $7.99 Can

UNTAMED HEART   **by Maureen McKade**
80284-8/ $5.99 US/ $7.99 Can